About the Authors

Helen Lacey grew up reading *Black Be*
Green Gables and *Little House on The F*
childhood classics inspired her to write
when she was seven years old, a story ab
her horse. She continued to write with the
day being a published author and writin
Boon is the realisation of that dream. She
stories about cowboys and horses and her
their happily ever after.

Margaret Way was born in the City of Brisbane. A Conservatorium trained pianist, teacher, accompanist and vocal coach, her musical career came to an unexpected end when she took up writing, initially as a fun thing to do. She currently lives in a harbourside apartment at beautiful Raby Bay, where she loves dining al fresco on her plant-filled balcony, that overlooks the marina. No one and nothing is in a rush so she finds the laid-back Village atmosphere very conducive to her writing.

Marion Lennox is a country girl, born on an Australian dairy farm. She moved on, because the cows just weren't interested in her stories! Married to a 'very special doctor', she has also written under the name Trisha David. She's now stepped back from her 'other' career teaching statistics. Finally, she's figured out what's important and discovered the joys of baths, romance and chocolate. Preferably all at the same time! Marion is an international award-winning author.

Australian Nights

December 2020
Longing for Summer

January 2021
Her Outback Fling

February 2021
Heat of the Night

March 2021
The Marriage Conquest

April 2021
Sun, Sea, Seduction

May 2021
Waves of Desire

Australian Nights: Her Outback Fling

HELEN LACEY

MARGARET WAY

MARION LENNOX

MILLS & BOON

First Published in Great Britain 2021
By Mills & Boon, an imprint of HarperCollins*Publishers*
1 London Bridge Street, London, SE1 9GF

ISBN: 978-0-263-29892-5

MIX
Paper from responsible sources
FSC™ C007454

This book is produced from independently certified FSC™ paper to ensure responsible forest management.

For more information visit: www.harpercollins.co.uk/green

Printed and bound in Spain
by CPI, Barcelona

ONCE UPON A BRIDE

HELEN LACEY

For Robert
Because you get me…

Chapter One

"You made a *what?*"

Lauren Jakowski shrugged her shoulders and bit down on her lower lip, musing whether she should repeat her words. But her two best friends' imploring looks won over.

"I made a vow," she said, and glanced at both Cassie and Mary-Jayne. "Of celibacy."

The other women snorted through the drinks they were sipping, sending liquid flying across the small poolside table. It was her brother's wedding, and once the bride and groom had cut the cake and shared their first dance, her bridesmaid's duties were officially over for the night. So she'd left the hotel ballroom and met her friends by the pool.

"Yeah, sure you did," Cassie said with a laugh, wiping her face.

"I did," Lauren insisted. "When my marriage ended."

"So you, like—" Mary-Jayne mused slowly as her dark hair swayed in the breeze "—made a commitment to never have sex again?"

"Exactly," she replied. "Not until I'm certain he's the right one."

"*He* being this dull and passionless individual you think you'll find so you can have your mediocre happily ever after?" Cassie asked, watching Lauren over the rim of her glass of soda.

She ignored how absurd it sounded. "Yes."

Cassie's brows came up. "And where are you going to find this Mr. Average?" she asked. "ReliableBores.com?"

"Maybe," Lauren said, and pretended to drink some champagne.

"So no sex?" Mary-Jayne asked again. "Even though you caught the bouquet, look sensational in that dress and there are at least half a dozen single men at this wedding who would happily throw you over their shoulder, carry you off and give you the night of your life?"

"I'm not interested in anything casual," she reiterated.

Mary-Jayne's eyes widened. "Not even with—"

"Not with *anyone,*" she said firmly.

"But he's—"

The original tall, dark and handsome...

"I know what he is. And he's not on my radar."

Which was a great big lie. However, she wasn't about to admit that to her friends. Lauren stared at the flowers sitting in the center of the small table. She *had* caught the bouquet. But she didn't want some meaningless romp at her brother's wedding.

And she certainly didn't want it with Gabe Vitali.

In the past six months, she'd been within touching distance of the ridiculously good-looking American several times. *And avoided him on every single occasion.* He was exactly what she didn't want. But since he was her brother's friend—and Crystal Point was a small town—Lauren accepted that she would be forced to see him every now and then.

"I like Gabe," Mary-Jayne said, and grinned. "He's kind of mysterious and…sexy."

Lauren wrinkled her nose. "Trouble."

"But still sexy?" Cassie laughed gently. "Come on, admit it."

Lauren let out an exasperated sigh. "Okay, he's sexy. He's weak-at-the-knees sexy…. He's handsome and hot and every time I see him I wonder what he looks like out of his clothes. I said I was celibate…not comatose."

The two women laughed, and Lauren pushed aside the idea of Gabe Vitali naked.

"Still, you haven't had sex in over two years," Mary-Jayne, the more candid of the two women, reminded her. "That's a long time. Just because you got divorced doesn't mean you can't have sex."

Lauren shrugged. "Isn't there an old saying about not missing what you don't have?"

Mary-Jayne shook her head. "Please tell me you've at least *kissed* a guy since then?"

"No," she replied. "Nor do I intend to until I know he's exactly what I've been looking for."

"You mean, *planning* for," Cassie said, ever gentle. "You know, there's no neat order to falling in love."

"Who said anything about love?" Lauren pushed back her blond bangs.

Cassie's calm expression was unwavering. "Is that really what you want? A loveless relationship without passion and heat?"

Lauren shrugged. "Marriage doesn't have to be about sexual attraction. Or love."

She saw her friends' expressions, knew that even though they were both fiercely loyal and supported her unconditionally, they still thought her thinking madness. But she wasn't swayed. How could they really appreciate her feelings? Or understand what she wanted?

They couldn't.

But she knew what she wanted. No lust, no crazy chemistry. No fairy-tale love.

No risk.

"That's just grief talking," Cassie said quietly. "When a marriage breaks down, it's natural to—"

"I'm not *mourning* my divorce," she insisted. No, definitely not. Because she knew exactly what mourning felt like. "I'm glad it's over. I shouldn't have married a man I hardly knew. I've tried being in love, I've tried being in lust…and neither worked out. Believe it or not, for the first time in a long time, I actually know what I want."

"Which is?" Mary-Jayne prompted, still grinning.

Lauren smiled at her friend. "Which is an honest, uncomplicated relationship with someone I can talk to…. Someone I can laugh with…have children with…grow old with. You know, the usual things. Someone who's a friend. A companion. And not with a man who looks as though he was made to pose for an underwear ad on one of those highway billboards."

"Like Gabe?" Mary-Jayne suggested playfully, and drank some champagne. "Okay, I get it. You want short, chubby and bald…not tall, dark and handsome. But in the meantime, how about we all get back to the ballroom and find some totally *complicated* man to dance with?"

"Not me," Cassie said, and touched her four-month-pregnant belly. Her boyfriend was a soldier currently on tour in the Middle East. "But I'll happily watch from the sidelines."

Lauren shook her head. "I think I'll stay out here for a while. You two go on ahead."

Her friends took another couple of minutes to leave, and when she was alone, Lauren snatched up the colorful bouquet, stood and walked the ten feet toward the edge of the pool. Solitude crept over her skin, and she sighed. Weddings always made her melancholy. Which was unfortunate, since she owned the most successful bridal store in Bellandale. Weddings were her life. Some days, though, she thought that to be the most absurd irony.

Of course, she was pleased for her brother. Cameron deserved every bit of happiness with his new bride, Grace Preston. And the ceremony had been beautiful and romantic. But she had a hollow spot in her chest that ached with a heavy kind of sadness. Many of the guests now inside the big hotel ballroom had witnessed her union to James Wallace in similar style three years earlier. And most knew how it had ended. Tonight, more than ever before, Lauren's sadness was amplified by her embarrassment at being on the receiving end of countless pitying looks and sympathetic greetings.

She took a deep breath and exhaled with a shudder. Somehow, her dreams for the future had been lost. But two years on, and with so many tears shed, she was stronger. And ready to start again. Only this time, Lauren would do it right. She wouldn't rush into marriage after a three-month whirlwind romance. And she definitely wouldn't be swept off her feet. This time, her feet were staying firmly on the ground.

Lauren swallowed hard, smoothed the mint-green chiffon gown over her hips and turned on her heels.

And was unexpectedly confronted with Gabe Vitali.

Stretched out on a sun lounger, tie askew and with his black hair ruffled as if he'd been running his hand through it, he looked so gorgeous, she literally gasped for breath. He was extraordinarily handsome, like one of those old-time movie stars. His glittering, blue-eyed gaze swept over her, and a tiny smile creased the corners of his mouth.

And she knew immediately…

He'd heard.

Everything.

Every humiliating word. Heat raced up and smacked her cheeks. *Great.*

Of course, she had no logical reason to dislike him… other than the fact he was good-looking and sexy and made her insides flip-flop. But it was enough to keep her from allowing her fantasies to take over. She gripped the bouquet tighter and planted her free hand on her hip in a faux impression of control, and spoke. "Whatever you might have thought you heard, I assure you I wasn't—"

"How are the knees?" he asked as he sprang up.

He was tall, around six-two, with broad shoulders and a long-legged frame. And he looked way too good in a suit. Resentment burned through her when she realized he was referring to her earlier confession.

"Fine," she replied, dying of embarrassment inside. "Rock solid."

He came around the lounger, hands thrust into his pockets. "You're sure about that?"

Lauren glared at him. "Positive," she snapped, mortified. She wanted to flee, but quickly realized she'd have to squeeze herself in between him and the sun lounger if she wanted to make a getaway. "I think I'll return to the ballroom now, if you don't mind."

His mouth curled at the edges. "You know, just because someone knows your vulnerabilities, it doesn't necessarily make him your enemy."

Lauren's skin heated. *"Vulnerabilities?"* She sucked in a sharp breath. "I don't quite know what you mean by that, but if you're insinuating that I'm *vulnerable* because I haven't… Because I… Well, because it's been a while since I was…you know…" Her words trailed off as mortification clung to every pore. Then she got annoyed as a quick cover-up. "Let's get this straight. I'm not the least bit vulnerable. Not to you or to anyone *like* you."

He grinned. "Whoa. Are you always so prickly?"

Prickly? She wasn't *prickly*. She was even tempered and friendly and downright *nice*.

She glared at him. "Do you always eavesdrop on private conversations?"

"I was simply relaxing on a pool lounger," he replied smoothly, his accent so delicious, it wound up her spine like liquid silk. "And I was here before you, remember? The fact you spoke about your sex life so openly is really no one's fault but your own." One brow rose. "And although it was entertaining, there's no need to take your frustration out on—"

"I am not *frustrated*," she snapped, figuring he was probably referring to her being sexually starved in some misguided, macho way. Broad shoulders, blue eyes and nice voice aside, he was a jerk. "I just don't want to talk about it anymore. What I'd like is to forget this conversation ever happened."

"I'm sure you would."

Lauren wanted a big hole to open up and suck her in. When one didn't appear, she took a deep breath. "So we have a deal. I'll ignore you, and you can ignore me. That way we never have to speak to each other again."

"Since this is the first time we have actually spoken," he said, his gaze deep enough to get lost in. "I don't think it will be a hardship."

He was right. They'd never spoken. She'd made sure of it. Whenever he was close, she'd always managed to make a quick getaway. Lauren sniffed her dislike, determined to ignore the fact that the most gorgeous man she'd ever met probably thought she was stark raving mad. And she would have done exactly that. Except she turned her heel too quickly, got caught between the tiles, and seconds later, she was tumbling in a cartwheel of arms and legs and landed into the pool, bouquet flying, humiliation complete.

The shock of hitting the water was quickly interrupted

when a pair of strong hands grasped one arm, then another. In seconds, she was lifted up and over the edge of the pool and set right on her feet.

He still held her, and had his hands intimately positioned on her shoulders.

She should have been cold through to her bones. But she wasn't. She was hot. All over. Her saturated dress clung to every dip and curve, her once carefully styled hair was now draping down her neck and her blood burned through her veins like a grass fire.

"Steady," he said softly, holding her so close she could see the tiny pulse in his jaw.

Lauren tried to speak, tried to move, tried to do something, *anything,* other than shake in his arms and stare up into his handsome face. But she failed. Spectacularly. It was he who eventually stepped back. When he finally released her, Lauren's knees wobbled and she sucked in a long breath to regain her composure. Of which she suddenly had none. He looked at her, *over her,* slowly and provocatively and with just enough male admiration to make her cheeks flame. She glanced down and shuddered. The sheer, wet fabric hugged her body like a second skin and left *nothing* to the imagination.

She moved her lips. "I should…I think I should…"

"Yes," he said quietly when her words trailed. "You probably should."

Lauren shifted her feet and managed one step backward, then another. Water dripped down her arms and legs, and she glanced around for a towel or something else to cover herself. When she couldn't find anything suitable, she looked back at him and noticed he still watched her. Something passed between them, a kind of heady, intense awareness that rang off warning bells in her head and should have galvanized her wobbly knees into action. But she couldn't move.

Seconds later, he shrugged out of his jacket and quickly draped it around her shoulders. The warmth from the coat and his nearness enveloped her like a protective cloak, and Lauren expelled a long sigh. She didn't want to feel that. Didn't want to *think* that. She only wanted to escape.

"Thank you," she whispered. "I appreciate—"

"Forget it," he said, cutting her off. "You should get out of those wet clothes before you catch a cold," he said, and then stepped back.

Lauren nodded, turned carefully and rushed from the pool area, water and humiliation snapping at her heels.

One week later Gabe pulled the for-sale peg from the ground, stuck the sign in the crook of his arm and headed across the front yard. The low-set, open-plan brick-and-tile home was big and required a much-needed renovation. But he'd bought the house for a reasonable price, and it seemed as good a place as any to settle down.

And he was happy in Crystal Point. The oceanfront town was small and friendly, and the beaches and surf reminded him of home. He missed California, but he enjoyed the peacefulness of the small Australian town he now called home instead. He'd rented a place in the nearby city of Bellandale for the past few months, but he liked the seaside town much better. Bellandale, with its sixty thousand residents, was not as populated as Huntington Beach, Orange County, where he'd lived most of his life. But it was busy enough to make him crave the solitude and quiet of Crystal Point. Plus, he was close to the beach and his new job.

He liked the job, too. Managing the Crystal Point Surf Club & Community Center kept him occupied, and on the weekends, he volunteered as a lifeguard. The beach was busy and well maintained, and so far he'd only had to administer first aid for dehydration and a couple of jellyfish stings. Nothing life threatening. Nothing he couldn't handle. Nothing that made him dwell on all he'd given up.

Gabe fished the keys from his pocket, dropped the sign into the overgrown garden bed and climbed the four steps to the porch. His household items had arrived that morning, and he'd spent most of the day emptying boxes and wishing he'd culled more crap when he'd put the stuff into storage six months ago. His cousin, Scott, had offered to come and give him a hand unpacking, but Gabe wasn't in the mood for a lecture about his career, his personal life or anything else.

All his energy would go into his job and renovating the house, which he figured would keep him busy for six months, at least. After that, he'd tackle the yard, get the place in shape and put the house on the market again. How hard could it be? His brother Aaron did the same thing regularly. True, he wasn't much of a carpenter, and Aaron was a successful builder in Los Angeles, but he'd give it a shot.

He headed inside and flicked on some lights. Some of the walls were painted black, no doubt a legacy from the previous tenants—a group of twenty-something heavy-metal enthusiasts who were evicted for cultivating some suspicious indoor plants—so painting was one of the first things on the agenda. The kitchen was neat and the bathrooms bearable. And although the furniture he'd bought a few months ago looked a little out of place in the shabby rooms, once the walls and floors were done, he was confident it would all look okay.

Gabe tossed the keys in a bowl on the kitchen table and pulled his cell from his pocket. He noticed there were a couple of missed calls. One from Aaron and another from his mother. It would be around midnight in California, and he made a mental note to call them back in the morning. Most days he was glad the time difference let him off the hook when it came to dealing with his family. At least his younger brother, Luca, and baby sister, Bianca, didn't stick their nose into his life or moan about his decision to move to Crystal Point. As the eldest, Aaron always thought he knew best, and his mom was just…Mom. He knew she worried, knew his mom and Aaron were waiting for him to relapse and go running back to California.

He'd come to Crystal Point to start over, and the house and job were a part of that new life. Gabe liked that his family wasn't constantly around to dish out advice. Bad enough he got lectures on tap from Scott. Hell, he understood their motives…he might even have done the same thing had the situation been reversed. But things had changed. *He'd* changed. And Gabe was determined to live his life, even if it wasn't the one he'd planned on.

The private cul-de-sac in Crystal Point was an ideal place to start. It was peaceful, quiet and uncomplicated. Just what he wanted. A native bird squawked from somewhere overhead and he stared out the kitchen window and across the hedge to the next house along just as his cell rang. He looked at the screen. It was an overseas number and not one he recognized.

Uncomplicated?

Gabe glanced briefly out the window again as he answered the call. It was Cameron Jakowski, and the conversation lasted a couple of minutes. *Sure, uncomplicated.* Except for his beautiful, blonde, brown-eyed neighbor.

The thing about being a *go-to,* agreeable kind of person…sometimes it turned around to bite you on the behind. And this, Lauren thought as she drove up the driveway and then pulled up under the carport, was probably going to turn out to be one of those occasions.

Of course, she *could* have refused. But that wasn't really her style. She knew her brother wouldn't have called if there was any other option. He'd asked for her help, and she would always rally her resolve when it came to her family.

What she didn't want to do—what she was *determined* to avoid doing—was start up any kind of conversation with her new next-door neighbor. Bad enough he'd bought the house and moved in just days after the never-to-be-spoken-about and humiliating event at the wedding. The last thing she wanted to do was knock on his door.

Ever.

Lauren had hoped to never see him again. But it seemed fate had other ideas.

She took a breath, grabbed her bag and jacket and stepped out of the car. She struggled to open the timber gate that she'd been meaning to get repaired for the past three months and winced when the jagged edge caught her palm. Once inside her house, she dumped her handbag and laptop in the hall and took a few well-needed breaths.

I don't want to do this....

But she'd promised Cameron.

And a promise is a promise....

Then she headed next door.

Once she'd rounded the tall hedge, Lauren walked up the gravel path toward the house. There was a brand-new Jeep Cherokee parked in the driveway. The small porch illuminated with a sensor light once she took the three steps. The light flickered and then faded. She tapped on the door and waited. She heard footsteps before the door swung back on its hinges, and she came face-to-face with him.

And then butterflies bombarded her stomach in spectacular fashion.

Faded jeans fitted lean hips, and the white T-shirt he wore accentuated a solid wall of bronzed and very fine-looking muscle. His short black hair, clean-shaven jaw and body to die for added up to a purely lethal combination.

He really is gorgeous.

Memories of what had happened by the pool came rushing back. His hands on her skin, his glittering gaze moving over her, his chest so close she could almost hear his heartbeat. Mesmerized, Lauren sucked in a breath. He knew all about her. He knew things she'd told only her closest friends. He knew she'd thought about him…and imagined things.

But if he dares say anything about my knees being weak, I'll...

She finally found her voice. "I'm here…"

One brow cocked. "So I see."

"Did Cameron—"

"He called," he said, and smiled as he interrupted her.

"Is he…"

"He is." He jerked his thumb over his shoulder and toward the door behind him. "Safe and sound and flaked out in front of the television."

She ignored the smile that tried to make its way to her lips and nodded. "Okay, thank you."

When she didn't move, he looked her over. "Are you coming inside or do you plan on camping on my doorstep all night?"

"All night?" she echoed, mortified that color was creeping up her neck. The idea of doing *anything* all night with Gabe Vitali took the temperature of her skin, her blood and pretty much every other part of her anatomy up a few notches. "Of course not."

He dropped his arms to his sides and stepped back.

Lauren crossed the threshold and walked into the hall. He was close, and everything about him affected her on a kind of sensory level. As much as she didn't want to admit anything, she was attracted to him. And worse luck, he knew it.

Her vow of celibacy suddenly seemed to be dissolving into thin air.

She walked down the short hallway and into the huge, open-plan living area. The furniture looked new and somehow out of place in the room. And sure enough, on the rug in front of the sofa, was her brother's one hundred and fifty pound French Mastiff, Jed. Fast asleep and snoring loudly.

"Thanks for picking him up from my brother's place," she said as politely as she could. "When Cameron called this morning, he said the house sitter had left quickly."

He nodded. "Her daughter is having a baby. She took a flight out from Bellandale after lunch and said she'd be back in a week."

Lauren bit down on her lip. "A week?"

"That's what she said."

A week of dog-sitting. Great. As much as she liked Jed, he was big, needy, had awful juicy jowls and a reputation for not obeying anyone other than Cameron. Too bad her parents had a cat that ruled the roost, or she would have dropped him off there. She had to admit the dog seemed comfortable draped across Gabe's rug.

She looked around some more. "So…you've moved in?"

"That was the general idea when I bought the house," he replied.

Lauren's teeth ground together. "Of course. I hope you'll be very happy here."

She watched his mouth twist with a grin. "You do? Really?"

"Really," she said, and raised a disinterested brow. "Be happy, or don't be happy. It's nothing to do with me."

His blue eyes looked her up and down with way too much leisure. The mood quickly shifted on a whisper of awareness that fluttered through the air and filled up the space between them. A change that was impossible to ignore, and there was rapidly enough heat in the room to combust a fire.

Warmth spread up her neck. He had a way of doing that to her. A way of heating her skin. "I need to…I need…"

"I think we both know what you need."

Sex...

That was what he was thinking. Suddenly, that was what *she* was thinking, even though turning up on his doorstep had nothing to do with her *lacking* love life or her vow to stay celibate. Lauren's cheeks burned, and her knees trembled. "I don't know what—"

"You don't like me much, do you?" he asked, cutting her off with such calm self-assurance, she wanted to slug him.

"I'm not—"

"Or is it because you *do* like me much?" he asked, cutting her off yet again. "And that's why you're so rattled at being in my living room."

Conceited jerk! Lauren sucked in some air, pushed back her shoulders and called Jed to heel. By the time the dog got up and ambled toward her, she was so worked up she could have screamed. She grasped Jed's collar and painted on a smile. "Thank you for collecting him from Cameron's."

"My pleasure."

Pleasure? Right. Not a word she wanted to hear from him. Not a word she wanted to think about in regard to him. And when she was safely back in her own home, Lauren kept reminding herself of one thing…Mr. Right was *not* Mr. Right-Next-Door.

Chapter Two

It was the dress.

That was why he'd had Lauren Jakowski on his mind for the past week.

When Gabe pulled her from the pool, the wet fabric had stuck to her curves so erotically, it had taken his breath away. She was as pretty as hell. A couple of years back he wouldn't have hesitated in coming on to her. He would have lingered by the pool, made small talk, flirted a little, asked her out and gotten her between the sheets by the third date. But he wasn't that man anymore.

Not so long ago, there had been no short supply of women in his life and in his bed. He'd mostly managed to keep things casual until he met Mona. She was the daughter of a colleague, and after dating for six months, they'd moved in together. At thirty years of age, he'd convinced himself it was time he got around to settling down. Gabe had a girlfriend, a career he loved, a nice apartment and good friends. Life was sweet. Until everything had blown up in his face.

Eighteen months later, he was in Crystal Point, working at the surf club and trying to live a normal life. A life that didn't include a woman like Lauren Jakowski.

Because she was too…wholesome.

Too…perfect.

A beautiful blonde with caramel eyes and porcelain skin.

Exactly my type.

But by the pool, she'd made it clear to her friends what she was looking for—stability, reliability, longevity. And since he couldn't offer her any of those things, she was everything he needed to avoid. He didn't want her turning up on his doorstep. He didn't want to inhale the scent of the flowery fragrance that clung to her skin. And he certainly didn't want to remember how it felt to have her lovely curves pressed against him.

The best thing would be to ignore her…just as she'd suggested.

Damned inconvenient, then, that he'd bought the house right next door. If he'd known that before he'd signed on the dotted line, he might have changed his mind. But it was too late to think about that now. All he had to do was get through the renovation and the resale without remembering that she was merely over the hedge.

Lauren was not one-night-stand material…and he couldn't offer anything more.

Gabe dropped into the sofa and flicked channels on the television for half an hour before he thought about eating something. He headed to the kitchen and stopped in his tracks when he spotted the pile of canine accessories by the back door. Damn. He'd forgotten about that. When Cameron had called and asked him to make an emergency stop at his home to collect the dog, the vacating house sitter had thrust the bed, bowls, food and lead into his arms along with a note listing feeding instructions. Things that Lauren would need.

Realizing there was little point in avoiding the inevitable, Gabe shoved his feet into sneakers, swung the bag of dog food over one shoulder, grabbed the rest of the gear and his house keys and headed next door.

Lauren's home and gardens were neat and tidy, and the only thing that seemed out of place was the rickety gate. He pushed it open and headed up the steps. The porch light was on and the front door open, so he tapped on the security screen. From somewhere in the house, he could hear her talking to the dog, and the obvious frustration in her voice made him smile. Maybe she was more a cat person? He tapped again and then waited until he heard her footsteps coming down the hall.

"Oh…hi," she said breathlessly when she reached the door.

Her hair was mussed and her shirt was pulled out from the front of her skirt, and Gabe bit back a grin. She looked as if she'd been crash tackled on the thirty-yard line. "Everything all right?"

She glanced over her shoulder. "Fine."

Gabe didn't quite believe her. "I forgot to give you this."

Her mouth set in a serious line. "Just leave it out there and I'll grab it later."

"It's heavy," he said, and jangled the bag of kibble resting on his shoulder. "I should probably set it down inside."

She looked at him for a second and then unlocked the screen. "Okay. Take it to the kitchen, at the end of the hall."

Gabe pushed the screen back and crossed the threshold. When he passed the living room doorway he immediately figured out the reason for her distress. Stretched out with legs in the air and jowls drooping, the dog was rolling around on her flowery chintz sofa.

"Jed looks as though he's made himself comfortable," he said, and kept walking.

"Yes, very comfortable."

When they reached the kitchen, Gabe swiveled on his heels and stared at her. She had her arms folded, her chin up and her lips pressed together, and even though she looked like she'd rather eat arsenic than spend a moment in his company, Gabe couldn't stop thinking about how beautiful she was.

I haven't gotten laid in a while...that's all it is.

He wasn't conceited, but he'd heard enough by the pool that night to know the attraction was mutual. He also knew she clearly thought it was as impossible as he did. Which suited him just fine. He didn't want to be stirred by her. He didn't want to spend restless nights thinking about having her in his bed.

"Where do you want it?" he asked.

"By the door will do."

He placed the gear on the floor and turned around to face her. "Would you like me to remove him from your sofa?"

"How did you know I couldn't...?"

"He's got about thirty pounds on you," Gabe said when her words trailed. "I just figured."

She shrugged. "I tried dragging him off, but he's as heavy as lead."

Gabe smiled and withdrew the note from his pocket. "Feeding instructions," he said, and dropped the paper onto the countertop. "If you want to get his food sorted, I'll get him off the sofa."

"Thank you," she said, then laid her hands on the back of a dining chair and grimaced. "Ouch."

He saw her shake her hand. "What's wrong?"

"Nothing," she replied and shook her hand again. "Just a splinter I got earlier from my gate."

"Let me see."

She curled her hand. "It's nothing."

Gabe moved around the kitchen counter. "It might become infected," he said, suddenly serious. "Do you have a first-aid kit?"

"It's nothing, really."

"It won't take a minute," he insisted. "So your first-aid kit?"

She shook her head. "I don't like needles."

"Don't be a baby."

Her eyes flashed, and she pushed her shoulders back as she marched into the kitchen and opened the pantry. "Here," she said, and tossed something through the air.

Gabe caught it one-handed and placed the kit on the table. "I'll be gentle. Sit," he said, and pulled out a chair.

She glared again, and he marveled that she still managed to look stunning with a scowl on her face. She sat down and waited while he dropped into a chair opposite.

"Hand?"

She pushed her hand into the center of the table and turned it over. "Gentle, remember?"

He smiled, opened the kit and took out an alcohol swab and an individually wrapped needle. When he took hold of her fingertips, his entire body crackled with a kind of heady electricity. Being so close wasn't helping his determination to steer clear of her.

"So what kind of work do you do?" he asked to try to get his mind off her soft skin and flowery perfume.

"I own a bridal shop in Bellandale."

He stretched out her palm. "That sounds interesting."

"Does it?"

Gabe looked up. She really did have the most amazing brown eyes. Warm and deep and intoxicating. She was remarkably beautiful, and he doubted she even knew it.

"Just making conversation," he said.

Her brows shot up. “To what end?”

“Are you always so suspicious?” he asked.

“Of what?”

“People,” he replied. “Men.”

She tensed, and Gabe held her hand a little firmer. “Not usually,” she said quietly.

So it was just him? “I don’t have any sinister intentions. So relax,” he said as he extracted the splinter without her noticing at first and then gently rolled her fingers into her palm. “I’m not making a pass.”

She swallowed hard. “I didn’t think—”

“I would,” he said quietly. “If you were looking for a no-strings, no-commitment kind of thing. But you’re not. You’re a commitment kind of girl, right? Abstaining from anything casual and with a clear plan for your future. Isn’t that why you made your vow of celibacy?”

It felt right to get it out in the open. Maybe it would help diffuse the heat between them. Maybe it would stop him from thinking about kissing her.

She jerked her hand back and stood. “I… What I said at the wedding… It was private and personal and not up for discussion.”

“I’m not mocking you,” he said, and rested his elbows on the table. “On the contrary, I think I admire you for knowing what you want. And knowing what you don’t.”

Lauren’s skin burned. He admired her? He’d pretty much admitted he wanted her, too. The awareness between them intensified, and she wished she could deny it. She wanted to dislike him. She wanted to resent him. She wanted to get away and never speak to him again.

“Thank you for the first aid,” she said, and managed a tight smile. “I didn’t feel a thing.”

"Then we should keep it that way."

There was no mistaking his meaning. He thought it was a bad idea, too. She was happy about that. Very happy.

"So...about the dog?"

He stood up and pushed the chair back. "Get his feed ready and I'll drag him off your sofa."

Once he'd left the kitchen and disappeared down the hall, Lauren got to her feet and quickly sorted the dog's bedding and food in the laundry. A couple of minutes later, Gabe returned with Jed at his side. The dog ambled across the kitchen and into the back room and began eating.

Relieved the hound was no longer taking up her couch, Lauren took a shallow breath. "Thank you...Gabe."

He looked a little amused by her sudden use of his name and the slight tremor in her voice. His mouth twisted fractionally, as if he was trying not to smile. "No problem... Lauren."

"Well...good night."

His glittering gaze was unwavering. "I'll see you tomorrow."

Her eyes widened. "Tomorrow?"

He grinned a little. "I told Cameron I'd take the dog to work tomorrow so he doesn't destroy your yard trying to escape...until you can make other arrangements, of course."

She hadn't spared a thought to how she would care for the dog during the day. "Oh, right," she said vaguely, thinking about how the darn dog had suddenly become a reason why she would be forced to interact with Gabe. She made a mental note to call her friend Mary-Jayne and ask her to help. Lauren knew one thing—she didn't want to turn up on Gabe's doorstep again. "I'll tie him in the back when I leave, and you can collect him from there. You don't start until ten tomorrow, right?"

Gabe frowned. "How do you know that?"

"Cameron left me the roster," she replied. "I said I'd work the Sunday shifts while he's away if I'm needed."

"You're the fill-in lifeguard?"

"Don't look so surprised."

"I'm just curious as to why your brother didn't mention you specifically."

She shrugged a little. "I may have told him that I thought you were an ass."

Gabe laughed. "Oh, really?"

"It was after the wedding, so who could blame me?"

He raised his hands. "Because I innocently overheard your deepest secret?"

"Well, that was before I…" Her words trailed. Before what? Before she realized he wasn't quite the ogre she'd pegged him for. Now wasn't the time to admit anything. "Anyhow…good night."

Once he left, Lauren forced herself to relax. She took a long shower and changed into her silliest short-legged giraffe pajamas and made a toasted cheese sandwich for dinner. She ate in the lounge room, watching television, legs crossed lotus-style, with plans to forget all about her neighbor.

And failed.

Because Gabe Vitali reminded her that she was a flesh-and-blood woman in every sense of the word. The way he looked, the way he walked with that kind of natural sexual confidence, the way his blue eyes glittered… It was all too easy to get swept away thinking about such things.

And too easy to forget why she'd vowed to avoid a man like him at all costs.

She'd made her decision to find someone steady and honest and ordinary. No powerful attraction. No blinding lust. No foolish dreams of romantic love. Just friendship and compatibility. It might sound boring and absurd to her friends, but Lauren knew what she wanted. She wanted something lasting.

Something safe.

Since she spent most of the night staring at the ceiling, Lauren wasn't surprised when she awoke later than usual and had to rush to get ready for work. She fed the dog and then tied him on a generous lead to the post on her back patio and headed to the store. Her mother was there already, changing mannequins and merchandising the stock that had arrived Friday afternoon. Irene Jakowski had first opened The Wedding House twenty-five years earlier. Lauren had grown up around the gowns and the brides, and it had made her fall in love with weddings. During her school years, she'd worked part-time in the store, learning from her mother. When school finished, she'd studied business and accounting for two years at college before returning to the store, taking over from her mother, who now worked part-time.

Lauren dropped her laptop and bag on the desk in the staff room and headed to the sales floor. The rows of wedding gowns, each one immaculately pressed and presented on hangers, filled her with a mix of approval and melancholy.

"How's the dog?" her mother queried when she moved around the sales counter.

Lauren grimaced. "Missing his owner and slobbering all over my furniture. You know, like in that old movie *Turner & Hooch?*"

Irene laughed. "It's not that bad, surely?"

"Time will tell," she replied, and managed a rueful grin. "I don't know why he can't go into a boarding kennel like other dogs."

"You're brother says he pines when he's away from home," Irene told her. "And it's only until the house sitter returns, isn't it?"

"Yeah," Lauren said, and sighed. "Gabe is taking him to the surf club today, so at least my patio furniture is safe while I'm here."

Her mother's eyes widened. "Gabe is? Really?"

Of course her mother knew Gabe Vitali. She'd mentioned him several times over the past six months. Irene Jakowski was always on the lookout for a new son-in-law, since the old one hadn't worked out. The fact he'd bought the house next door was like gold to a matchmaking parent.

"Matka," Lauren warned, using the Polish word for *mother* when she saw the familiar gleam in her mother's eyes. "Stop."

"I was only—"

"I know what you're doing," Lauren said, smiling. "Now, let's get the store open."

By the time Gabe returned home that afternoon, he was short on patience and more than happy to hand Jed over to his neighbor. Damned dog had chewed his car keys, his sneakers and escaped twice through the automatic doors at the clubhouse.

When he pulled into the driveway, he spotted the fencing contractor he'd called earlier that day parked across the lawn. He locked Jed in Lauren's front garden and headed back to his own yard. He was twenty minutes into his meeting with the contractor when she arrived home. Gabe was in the front yard with the tradesman, talking prices and time frames, as the older man began pushing at the low timber fence that separated the two allotments and then wrote in a notepad.

She walked around the hedge and met him by the letterbox, eyeing the contractor's battered truck suspiciously. "What's going on?" she asked, looking all business in her black skirt and white blouse.

"A new fence," Gabe supplied and watched her curiosity quickly turn into a frown.

"I wasn't aware *we* needed a new one."

"This one's falling down," he said, and introduced her to the contractor before the other man waved his notepad and said he'd get back to him tomorrow.

Once the battered truck was reversing from the yard, she clamped her hands to her hips. "Shouldn't we have discussed it first?"

"It's only an estimate," he told her. "Nothing's decided yet."

She didn't look convinced. "Really?"

"Really," he assured her. "Although the fence does need replacing."

Her eyes flashed. "I know it's my responsibility to pay for half of any fence that's built, but at the moment I'm—"

Gabe shook his head. "I intend to pay for the fence, should it come to that."

She glared at him, then the fence, then back to him. "You don't get to decide that for me," she snapped, still glaring.

He looked at her, bemused by her sudden annoyance. "I don't?"

"It's my fence, too."

"Of course," he replied. "I was only—"

"Taking over? And probably thinking I couldn't possibly afford it and then feeling sorry for me, right?"

He had a whole lot of feelings churning through his blood when it came to Lauren Jakowski…pity definitely wasn't one of them. "Just being neighborly," he said, and figured he shouldn't smile, even though he wanted to. "But hey, if you want to pay for half the fence, go ahead."

"I will," she replied through tight lips. "Just let me know how much and when."

"Of course," he said.

She huffed a little. “Good. And have you been messing around with my gate?”

Ah. So the real reason why she looked like she wanted to slug him. “Yes, I fixed your gate this morning.”

“Because?”

“Because it was broken,” he replied, watching her temper flare as the seconds ticked by. *And broken things should be fixed.* He’d spent most of his adult life fixing things. *Fixing people.* But she didn’t know that. And he wasn’t about to tell her. “No point risking more splinters.”

“I liked my gate how it was,” she said, hands still on hips.

Gabe raised a brow. “Really?”

She scowled. “Really.”

“You’re mad at me because I repaired your gate?”

“I’m mad at you because it wasn’t your gate to repair. I don’t need anyone to fix things. I don’t need a white knight, okay?”

A white knight? Yeah, right. But there was an edge of vulnerability in her voice that stopped him from smiling. Was she broken? Was that part of what drew him to her? Like meets like? He knew she was divorced, and at her brother’s wedding she’d admitted her marriage hadn’t been a happy one. But Gabe didn’t want to speculate. And he didn’t want to ask. The less he knew, the better.

“Okay,” he said simply.

For a moment, he thought she might argue some more. Instead, she dropped her gaze and asked an obvious question. “What happened to your shoe?”

He glanced down. The back of his left sneaker was torn and the lace was missing. “Jed.”

She looked up again, and he saw her mouth curve. “Was that the only damage?”

“Other than chewing my car keys and making a run for it whenever he got the chance.”

She moaned softly. “Sorry about that. I’ll get Cameron to replace them when he gets back.”

Gabe shrugged. “No need. It’s only a shoe.”

She nodded, turned and walked back around the hedge. Gabe shook his shoulders and made a concerted effort to forget all about her.

And failed.

I really need to stop reacting like that.

Lauren was still thinking it forty minutes later when she emerged from the shower and pulled on frayed gray sweats. Her reaction, or rather her *overreaction,* to Gabe’s news about the fence was amplified by his interference with her gate.

She didn’t want him fixing things.

Lauren didn’t want *any* man fixing things.

It was a road she’d traveled before. She knew what she wanted and white knights need not apply. Her ex-husband had tried to fix things—to fix her—and it had ended in disaster.

James Wallace had ridden into her life in his carpenter’s truck, all charm and good looks. He’d arrived at The Wedding House to make repairs to the changing rooms, and she’d been unexpectedly drawn to his blatant flirting. An hour later, she’d accepted his invitation to go out with him that night. They ended up at a local bistro for drinks and then dinner, and by midnight he’d kissed her in the car park, and she was halfway in lust with him.

Three months later, she had a fairy-tale wedding.

Even though it was the wedding she’d planned to have to someone else.

To Tim. Sweet, handsome Tim Mannering. Her first love. Her only love. He had been her college boyfriend and the man she’d intended to marry. They’d made plans for the future. They’d talked about everything from building their dream home, taking an African-safari vacation, to how many kids they would have. They'd loved one another deeply and promised each other the world.

Except Tim had died three weeks before their wedding.

And Lauren walked down the aisle with another man less than two years later.

She swallowed the tightness in her throat. Thinking about Tim still filled her with sadness. And she was sad about James, too. She should never have married him. She hadn't loved him. They'd shared a fleeting attraction that had faded just months into their marriage. They'd had little in common and very different dreams. Within a year, James was gone, tired of what he called her *cold, unfeeling heart.* And Lauren was alone once more.

But she still hoped to share her life with someone. And she wanted the children she'd planned for since the day she and Tim had become engaged. Only next time, Lauren was determined to go into it with her eyes wide-open and not glazed over by romantic illusions. What she'd had with James wasn't enough. And what she'd had with Tim had left her broken inside. Now all she wanted was the middle road. Just mutual respect, trust and compatibility. No fireworks. No deep feelings. Lust was unreliable. Love was painful when lost.

There was nothing wrong with settling. Nothing at all. Settling was safe. All she had to do was remember what she wanted and why. And forget all about Gabe Vitali and his glittering blue eyes and broad shoulders. Because he was pure heartbreak material. And her heart wasn't up for grabs.

Not now.

Not ever again.

Chapter Three

Gabe went to his cousin's for dinner Wednesday night and expected the usual lecture about his life. Scott Jones was family and his closest friend, and even though he knew the other man's intentions were born from a sincere interest in his well-being, Gabe generally pulled no punches when it came to telling his cousin to mind his own business.

Scott's wife, Evie, was pure earth mother. She was strikingly attractive and possessed a calm, generous spirit. Gabe knew his cousin was besotted with his wife and baby daughter, and he was genuinely happy for him.

"How's the house coming along?" Scott asked over a beer while Evie was upstairs putting little Rebecca down for the night.

Gabe pushed back in the kitchen chair. "Fine."

"Will you stay there permanently?"

"I doubt it," he replied.

"Still can't see you renovating the place yourself," Scott said, and grinned.

Gabe frowned. “I can fix things.”

Like Lauren’s gate, which hadn’t gone down so well. He should have left it alone. But she’d hurt herself on the thing and he didn’t want that happening again. There was no harm in being neighborly.

“Job still working out?”

Gabe shrugged one shoulder. “Sure.”

Scott grinned again. “And how’s it going with your next-door neighbor?”

He knew his cousin was fishing. He’d told him a little about the incident at the wedding, and Scott knew he’d bought the house next door. Clearly, he’d told him too much. “Fine.”

“I like Lauren,” Scott said, and smiled.

Gabe didn’t respond. He didn’t have to. His cousin spoke again.

“You do, too, judging by the look on your face.”

Gabe didn’t flinch. “You know my plans. They haven’t changed.”

“Your five-year plan?” Scott’s eyes widened. “Still think you can arrange life to order?” He looked to the ceiling, clearly thinking about his family upstairs. “No chance.”

“I know what I’m doing.”

It sounded good, at least. Pity he didn’t quite believe it.

“You know she’s divorced?” Scott asked.

“Yes.”

Scott nodded. “Evie knows more about it than I do. And, of course, about the other guy.”

His head came up. The other guy? “I don’t—”

“He died about five years ago,” his cousin said, and drank some beer. “They were engaged, that’s all I know.”

Gabe’s insides contracted. So she’d lost someone. And married someone else. The wrong someone else. It explained the haunted, vulnerable look shading her brown eyes. But he didn't want to know any more. Hadn't he already decided the less he knew, the better?

"Not my business."

Scott's eyebrows shot up. "So no interest at all?"

He shrugged again. "No."

Scott chuckled. "You're a lousy liar."

I'm a great liar. His whole life was a lie. Gabe stood and scraped the chair back. "Thanks for the beer."

He left shortly after, and by the time he pulled into his own driveway, it was past ten o'clock. There were lights on next door, and when he spotted a shadowy silhouette pass by the front window, Gabe fought the way his stomach churned thinking about her. He didn't want to be thinking, imagining or anything else. Lauren Jakowski was a distraction he didn't need.

And he certainly didn't expect to find her on his doorstep at seven the next morning.

But there she was. All perfection and professionalism in her silky blue shirt and knee-length black skirt. Once he got that image clear in his head, Gabe noticed she wasn't alone. Jed sat on his haunches at her side.

"Am I stretching the boundaries of friendship?" she asked, and held out the lead.

He nodded. Were they friends now? No. Definitely not. "Absolutely."

She chewed at her bottom lip. "I wouldn't ask if it wasn't important."

Gabe shrugged. "What's the big emergency?"

She exhaled heavily. "He chewed off a piece of my sofa and broke the table in the living room when I left him home on Tuesday. Then he terrorized my parents' cat when I left him there yesterday. Mary-Jayne said she'd take him tomorrow and Saturday. She's got a fully enclosed yard and a dog, which will keep him company. But today I'm all out of options. I can't take him to the store and…and…I don't know what else to do."

Her frustration was clear, and Gabe knew he'd give her exactly what she wanted. Because saying no to Lauren was becoming increasingly difficult. "Okay."

"O-okay?" she echoed hesitantly.

"Yeah. Okay."

Relief flooded her face. "Thanks. I…I owe you for this."

Gabe shrugged again. He didn't want her owing him anything. Owing could lead to collecting…and that was out of the question. "No problem," he said, and took the lead.

"So dinner?" she asked and took a step back. "Tonight. I'll cook. My way of saying thanks."

His back straightened. "You don't need to—"

"I insist," she said quickly, and then looked as though she was itching to get away. "Say, seven o'clock?"

She left, and Gabe didn't go back inside until she disappeared around the hedge.

Dinner. Great idea. *Not.*

What were you thinking?

Lauren spent the day chastising herself and making sure she didn't let on to her mother that she'd somehow invited Gabe into the inner sanctum of her house, her kitchen and her solitary life. But she'd made the offer and it was too late to back out now. Besides, he was doing her a favor looking after the dog. Dinner really was the least she could do in return. He'd helped her out, and it was her way of saying thank-you. It was nothing. Just a simple meal between neighbors.

Only, simple seemed at odds with the way her nerves rattled just thinking about it.

She stopped by the supermarket on the way home, and by the time she pulled into the driveway, it was nearly six. She jumped into the shower, dried off, applied a little makeup and changed into loose-fitting cargo pants and a red knit top. By six-thirty she was in the kitchen marinating steaks and prepping a salad. And ignoring the knot in the pit of her stomach as best she could.

The doorbell rang at exactly seven o'clock.

Jed rushed down the hallway the moment she opened the door, clearly eager to get to his food bowl in the laundry.

"Hi," she said, and stepped back.

"Hi, yourself," Gabe said as he crossed the threshold.

He closed the door, and she didn't linger. Instead, she pivoted on her heels and headed back to the kitchen. By the time she'd made her way back behind the countertop, he was by the door, watching her. She looked up and met his gaze. He looked so good in his jeans and navy T-shirt, her breath stuck in her throat. She noticed a tattoo braid that encircled one biceps peeking out from the edge of his sleeve. She'd never liked ink much, but it suited him. It was sexy. Everything about Gabe was sexy. His broad shoulders, black hair, dazzling blue eyes… The combination was devastating. And dangerous.

Be immune to sexy.

He moved and rested against the door frame, crossing his arms, and Lauren was instantly absorbed by the image it evoked.

"You know, you really shouldn't look at me like that," he said, and Lauren quickly realized she'd been caught staring. Or ogling. "I might start thinking you aren't serious about that vow of yours."

Her skin warmed. "Don't flatter yourself."

His lips curled at the edges. "I never do."

"I don't believe that for a second."

"Then what do you believe, Lauren?" he asked, and met her gaze.

"I don't know what you mean."

His stare was unwavering. "I think you do."

"You're talking about what you overheard at the wedding?" She shrugged as casually as she could manage. "I thought we'd agreed not to talk about that."

He half smiled. "Did we? You said you wanted a passionless relationship."

Her breath caught. She didn't want to talk about that with him. Not when her pulse was racing so erratically. She remembered how he knew her secrets. He knew what she wanted. "Yes," she replied and hated that it tasted like a lie. "Passion is overrated."

"Do you think?" he asked quietly, his intense gaze locked with hers. "And chemistry?"

"Even more overrated."

"That's a handy line when you're in denial."

She tried but couldn't drag her gaze away. "I'm not in denial," she insisted. "About...anything."

About you. That was what she meant. And he knew it, too.

"Good," he said, almost as though he was trying to convince himself. "Shall I open this?" he asked, and gestured to the wine bottle he carried.

Lauren nodded and grabbed two glasses and a corkscrew from the cupboard, laying them on the counter. "How do you like your steak?"

"Medium rare," he replied. "You?"

She shrugged. "Same. Did Jed behave himself today? No disasters? No sacrificial sneakers?"

He grinned and grabbed the corkscrew. "It was moderately better than the last time."

She laughed softly. "He's usually very civilized when Cameron is around."

"He's pining," Gabe said, and popped the cork. "Missing the people he loves most. It's natural he would."

Lauren nodded. "You're right. And it's only for a few more days. I heard from Cameron's house sitter this morning, and she's flying back into Bellandale on Sunday afternoon."

He passed her a glass of wine, and Lauren's fingers tingled when they briefly touched his. If he noticed, he didn't show it. "How long have you lived here?" he asked.

"Just over a year."

"It's…nice. My sister, Bianca, would love it," he said easily and rested against the countertop. "She's into decorating."

Lauren pulled a couple of plates from the cupboard. "Do you have one of those large Italian-American families?"

"There are four of us. Aaron is thirty five and the eldest. He's divorced and has twin four-year-old boys. And then there's me, three years younger." He grinned a little. "Then Luca, who's thirty and married to his IT job, and Bianca, who is twenty-six and the baby of the family."

She nodded. "And your parents?"

"There's only my mom," he explained, watching her with such blistering intensity, Lauren found it hard to concentrate on preparing their meal. "My dad died fifteen years ago."

Her expression softened. "I'm sorry. Were you close?"

"Very."

She nodded again. "What did he—"

"Lung cancer."

The awful words hung in the air between them, and an old pain jabbed between her ribs. She pushed the memory off as quickly as it came.

"I'm sorry," she said gently. "I feel very lucky to still have both my parents."

"And there's only you and Cameron?" he asked.

"Yes," she replied. "And he's actually my half brother. Our mother married my dad when he was three years old. I would have loved a sister, though. I mean, we're really close, but a big family would be wonderful."

His gaze absorbed hers. “You want children?”

She nodded. “I always thought I’d like to have three kids.”

He raised a brow. “With Mr. No-Passion?”

A smile tugged at his mouth, and Lauren couldn’t stop her lips from creasing into a tiny grin. “Maybe. Hopefully. One day.”

He looked at her oddly, as if he wanted to have an opinion about it but was holding his tongue. When he finally spoke, he surprised her. “You’ll make a good mom.”

“I… Thank you.” The air crackled, and she avoided eye contact by feigning a deep interest in the salad she’d prepared. When he spoke again, she looked up.

“Need any help?” he asked, and took both wineglasses to the table.

“No,” she replied and plated the food quickly. “I’m nearly done. Take a seat.”

A minute later, she placed the plates on the table and sat down. For one crazy second she thought…no, *imagined…* that the mood between them felt a little like a date. *A first date.*

Stupid. They were neighbors. Acquaintances. Nothing more. So what if he was the most attractive man she’d ever met? Attraction hadn’t done her any favors in the past. She’d been attracted to James, and that had ended badly for them both. This would be the same. And anything more than attraction was out of the question.

“So did you have a similar job in California?” she asked, determined to steer the conversation away from herself.

“Not really,” he replied vaguely and picked up the utensils. “I worked as a lifeguard part-time at Huntington Beach, near where I lived.”

“Cameron said the place has never run so smoothly. Do you enjoy the work?” she asked.

“Yeah…sure,” he replied casually. “I like the beach,” he

said, and when she raised a brow indicating she wanted him to elaborate, he continued. "And I get to teach a few classes, lifeguard on the weekends and juggle paperwork during the week." He shrugged. "It's not exactly rocket science."

She was itching to ask him more questions. Cameron had told her he was clearly overqualified for the role at the surf club. She knew he didn't talk about himself much, and that suited her fine. Most of the time. But tonight she was interested. As much as warning bells pealed, she wanted to know more about him. She wanted to know what made him tick. She wanted to know why he'd moved his life from California to Crystal Point.

"Don't you miss your old life? Your friends, your family?"

He looked up. "Of course."

"I could never leave my family like that," she said, and knew it sounded like a judgment. She shrugged and sighed a little. "I mean, I'd miss them too much to be away for too long."

If it was a dig, he ignored it. Because he was so mesmerized by her sheer loveliness, Gabe couldn't look away. He shouldn't have come around. He shouldn't have thought he could spend an evening with Lauren and not get caught up in the desire that thrummed through his blood. She was tempting. And he was…tempted.

"You really are quite beautiful."

The words were out before he could stop them. She fumbled with her cutlery, and the steak portion on the end of her fork fell back onto the plate. He watched as she pressed her fingertips against her mouth and discreetly wiped away a little sauce.

"Um…thank you. I guess."

Gabe rested back in his chair. "You don't sound convinced."

"That I'm beautiful?" She shrugged. "I've never really thought I was. Attractive, perhaps."

"No," he said quietly. "You're beautiful."

She grabbed her drink. "Are you coming on to me?" she asked bluntly.

Gabe chuckled. "No."

She met his gaze. "Because I'm not your type?"

"I'm not coming on to you because you're exactly my type."

Heat filled the space between them, and a sudden surge of blinding attraction clung to the air. But it was best to get it out in the open. He wanted her. And he was pretty sure the feeling was reciprocated.

"Is that because of what I said about you…you know… at the wedding?"

"You mean when you told your friends you've thought about me naked?"

Color quickly flamed her pale cheeks. "Is that what I said?"

"Yes."

She shrugged and smiled a little. "Well, since you were there and heard the whole conversation, there's no point denying it."

Gabe laughed. He liked that about her. She wasn't serious all the time. Even without her natural beauty, she had an energy and humor that fascinated him. For a moment, Gabe wished he could wind the clock forward, to a time in the future when he could guarantee any promises or commitment he might want to make. But he couldn't. And wishes were for fools.

He pushed some words out. "I guess not. Your friends don't seem to approve of your plans, though."

"They don't," she said, and sipped some wine. "But they support me, so that's all that matters. You know how family and friends can get sometimes…as if they know what's best, regardless of how a person might feel about it."

Gabe knew exactly. "You don't like weddings much?"

Her eyes widened. "Sure I do. Weddings are…my life."

"Really?"

She looked at him. "Well, maybe not my life. My job, at least."

He heard hesitation in her voice. "But?"

Her shoulders dropped. "Oh, you know, pretending the fairy tale exists on a day-in-and-day-out basis can be monotonous." She shook herself and picked up the cutlery again. "Sorry, I don't normally complain about it. But you're…" She stopped and looked at him. "Even though a week ago I was convinced you were simply another ridiculously handsome but conceited jerk, you're surprisingly…easy to talk to."

A good bedside manner is essential….

How many times had he heard that?

Gabe shook off the guilt between his shoulder blades. "Oh, I can be just as much of a jerk as the next guy."

She laughed, and the sound echoed around the room. "Well, thanks for the warning."

He placed his elbows on the table. "Don't thank me. I said I wouldn't make a pass. I didn't say it would be easy."

Her cheeks bloomed with color. "Oh, because I'm—"

"Because you're Commitment 101."

"And you're not?" she queried.

"Exactly."

"Have you ever been tempted? Or close?" she asked and pushed her barely eaten meal aside.

"Once," he replied and took a drink. "It didn't work out."

She stared at him, as if she was trying to figure out why. But she never would. He didn't talk about it. Ever. She took a second, swallowed hard and then spoke. "Did you love her?"

"It didn't work out," he said again, a whole lot quicker than he would have liked. "I guess there's your answer."

Her brows arched. "So you didn't love her? Not even a little bit?"

Gabe's mouth twisted. "I didn't realize there was such a thing as being a little bit in love. I cared for her, sure. But like I said, we didn't work out. There's no great mystery to it."

He wasn't about to tell Lauren that she was right—he hadn't really loved his ex-girlfriend. He'd done her a favor by letting her go. He was sure of it. And besides, Mona hadn't put up much resistance. Once she'd known she had an out clause, she'd left their relationship as quickly as she could.

Lauren bit her bottom lip, watching him. "So you got burned?"

He shrugged. "Not exactly."

"Then what, exactly?" she asked.

"We split up," he replied. "We went our separate ways. Neither of us was heartbroken."

"Which leaves you where?" Her eyes were full of questions. "Working at the surf club and having casual relationships and sex with women who are equally uninterested in commitment?"

"Ah…I suppose."

"Well, that sounds…like fun."

Not.

That was what she was thinking. Shallow and meaningless and hollow. Gabe thought so, too…even though he'd drilled himself to accept his present and future. But he suddenly lost his appetite.

"It is what it is," he said, and pushed back in his seat. "I'm not looking for…anything."

She watched him, her brown eyes darkening. "I've always believed that we're all looking for something…love or sex, belonging, companionship. Or maybe something more complicated, like peace of mind…or even isolation."

Which one are you looking for?

That was the question in her words. Gabe shrugged a shoulder casually. She was so close to the truth. "Is that why your marriage didn't work out?" he asked, shifting the focus back to her. "Because you wanted different things?"

She gripped her wineglass. "My marriage failed because my husband and I had nothing between us but fleeting physical attraction. Which isn't enough," she added.

It explained why she wanted a passionless relationship… sort of. "And now you're looking for more?" he asked. "Or maybe less?"

"Sometimes less *is* more," she replied. "Which is why I'm determined to think with my head next time…and not my—" she paused, smiling "—libido."

Gabe tensed. Thinking of *her* libido didn't do his any favors. "Or your heart?"

She smiled. "Precisely," she said.

He remembered what his cousin had said to him the night before. She'd lost someone. She'd lost love and settled for sex. The fact that she now wanted a middle road made perfect sense. "Someone did get it, though?"

Her gaze was unwavering. "You mean my heart? Yes. Someone did."

"Who was he?"

Silence stretched between them. He shouldn't have asked. He shouldn't want to know. The more he knew, the harder it would be to stay away from her.

"My first love. My only love, I guess."

She said the words so quietly and with such raw honesty, his insides contracted. He didn't want to hear any more. "You don't have to—"

"His name was Tim," she said, cutting him off. "We met

in college. I was nineteen and studying business. He was across the hall in engineering. We fell in love. A few years later we got engaged. And then…"

Gabe knew what was coming, but he asked anyway. "And then, what?"

She drew in a sharp breath. "And then he died."

"Was it an accident?"

She shook her head. "No. He was sick."

Sick...

Gabe's stomach churned uneasily, and he forced the next words out. "What kind of illness did he have?"

"Primary glioblastoma," she replied. "It's a—"

"I know what it is," he said quickly and pushed his chair back some more.

Brain tumor...

An aggressive, unforgiving kind of cancer that usually left a patient with months to live rather than years. It was all he needed to hear. It was time to go. He needed to finish eating and leave.

"I'm sorry," Gabe said, and spent the following few minutes pretending interest in his food. Even though he felt sick to his stomach. He pushed the meal around on the plate, finished his wine and declined the coffee she offered to make.

"I need to get going," he said as soon as he felt it was polite to do so, and stood.

"Oh…sure." She got to her feet. "Thanks again for looking after Jed."

"No problem. Thanks for dinner."

Once they reached the front door, he lingered for a moment. He liked her. A lot. She was sweet and warm and funny and so damned sexy, he could barely think of anything other than kissing her perfectly bowed mouth. He wanted Lauren in his bed more than he'd wanted anything for a long time.

But he wouldn't pursue it.

She'd lost the man she'd loved to cancer.

And he'd bet his boots it wasn't a road she'd ever want to travel again.

He needed to forget all about Lauren. And fast.

Chapter Four

Spending the evening with Gabe confirmed for Lauren that since her divorce, she'd gone into a kind of lazy hibernation. She'd quit volunteering at the surf club, rarely joined her mother for the tai chi classes she'd always loved and avoided socializing regularly with anyone other than her two closest friends. It hadn't been a deliberate pulling away, more like a reluctance to go out and put on her happy face.

That needed to change.

Lauren knew if she was going to find someone to share her life with, she actually needed to start having a real *life*.

But that real life didn't include her sexy neighbor.

On Friday night she went to the movies with Cassie and Mary-Jayne, stayed out afterward for coffee and cake and got home by ten.

There was a light on next door. Lauren ignored the fluttering in her stomach and headed inside. As soon as she'd crossed the threshold, she heard Jed's whining. Minutes later she discovered her great plan of leaving him locked in the laundry was not such a great plan. It was, in fact, a disaster. He'd somehow chewed a hole in the back door, and his big head was now stuck between the timbers. Lauren groaned, cursed her brother under her breath for a few seconds and then attempted to pull the dog free. But he was lodged. His neck was wedged around the cracked timber, and she didn't have the strength to pull him free.

Surprisingly, the dopey dog was in good spirits, and she patted him for a moment before she grabbed her phone. She could call her father? Or perhaps Mary-Jayne might be able to help?

Just get some backbone and go and ask Gabe.

She reassured the dog for a little while longer before she walked next door. The porch light flickered and she sucked in a breath and knocked.

Gabe looked surprised to see her on his doorstep.

"Lauren?" He rested against the door frame. "What's up?"

He wore faded jeans that were splattered with paint, and an old gray T-shirt. There was also paint in his hair and on his cheek. She wanted to smile, thinking how gorgeous he looked, but didn't. Instead, she put on a serious face.

"I need help."

He straightened. "What's wrong?"

"It might be better if you just see for yourself."

He was across the threshold in seconds. "Are you okay?"

"I'm fine. Jed, on the other hand…"

"What's he done now?" Gabe asked as they headed down the steps.

"Like I said, you need to see this for yourself."

A minute later they were in her house. They moved to the laundry and were facing Jed's bouncing rear end. And Gabe was laughing loudly. Really loudly. In fact, he was laughing so hard he doubled over and gripped the washing machine.

"It's really not that funny," she said crossly and planted her hands on her hips. "He could be hurt."

"He's not hurt," Gabe said, still chuckling as he moved across the small room and knelt down beside the dog. "The goofy mutt is just stuck."

"Exactly. He's wedged in and I can't pull him free."

He examined the door. "Do you have a hammer?"

"A hammer?"

"I need to knock a bit of this plywood out the way," he explained.

She nodded and grabbed the small toolbox under the sink. "I think there's something in here."

He opened the box, found the small hammer and got to work on the door. Jed whined a little, but Lauren placated him with pats and soothing words while Gabe made the hole large enough for the dog's head to fit back through. It took several minutes, but finally Jed was free and immediately started bounding around the small room, whipping Lauren's legs with his tail.

"Oh, that's good," she said on a relieved sigh. "Thank you."

"He looks okay," Gabe said, smiling. "But your door's not so lucky."

Lauren glanced at the door. The hole was bigger than she'd thought. "I'll need to call someone to fix it on Monday."

He nodded as he rose to his feet. "Sure. I'll board it up for you now so you'll be safe over the weekend."

Lauren's insides contracted. The way he spoke, the way he was so genuinely concerned about her, melted what was left of her resentment toward him.

Admit it...you like him.

A lot.

Too much.

"Ah—thanks," she said quietly and moved Jed out of the small room.

Gabe followed her. "Be back soon," he said as he strode down the hallway and headed out the front door.

He returned five minutes later with a large square piece of plywood, a cordless drill and a box of screws, and quickly repaired the hole. Lauren watched from her spot near the door, absorbed by the way he seemed to do everything with such effortless ease. Nothing fazed him. He was smart and resourceful and sexy and warmed the blood in her veins. Gabe made her think of everything she'd lost. And everything she was determined to avoid.

"Lauren?"

His voice jerked her back to earth. He was close. They were sharing the space in the narrow doorway, and Lauren's gaze got stuck on his chest and the way the paint-splattered T-shirt molded his chest. Her fingertips itched to reach up and touch him, to feel for herself if his body was as strong and solid as it looked. She remembered how he'd pulled her from the pool at the wedding and how his hands had felt upon her skin. It had been a long time since she'd felt a man's touch. Longer still since she'd wanted to.

Memories of Tim swirled around in her head. She'd loved him. Adored him. She'd imagined they would spend their lives together, loving one another, having children, creating memories through a long and happy marriage. But he'd never, not once, made her knees quiver and her skin burn with such blistering, scorching awareness. Even the fleeting desire she'd felt for James seemed lukewarm compared to the way Gabe made her feel. Her sex-starved body had turned traitor, taunting her…and she had to use her head to stay in control.

"I was…I was thinking…"

Her words trailed off when she looked up and met his blistering gaze. There was so much heat between them. Undeniable heat that combusted the air and made her stomach roll.

"Thinking?" he asked softly. "About what?"

Lauren willed some movement into her feet and managed to step back a little. "Your jacket," she muttered and turned on her heels and fled through the kitchen and toward the guest bedroom.

When she returned, Gabe was in the hallway, tools in hand.

"I forgot to return this," she explained and passed him the dinner jacket he'd given her the night of the wedding and which she'd since had dry-cleaned. "Thank you for lending it to me."

"No problem." He took the garment and smiled. "Well, good night."

"Ah—and thanks again for freeing Jed.... Your saving me from disaster is becoming something of a habit."

"No harm in being neighborly," he said casually.

Too casually. She knew he was as aware of her as she was of him. But they were skirting around it. Denying it.

"I guess not. Good night, Gabe."

He left, and Lauren closed the door, pressing her back against it as she let out a heavy sigh. Being around Gabe was wreaking havoc with her usual common sense. He wasn't what she wanted. Sure, she could invite him into her bed for the night. But that was all it would be. He'd called her Commitment 101, and he was right. He'd told her he didn't do serious. He didn't want a relationship. They were too different.

When she arrived at The Wedding House the following morning, her mother was there before her, as was their part-time worker, Dawn.

"You look terrible," her mother remarked, clearly taking in her paler-than-usual skin and dark smudges beneath her eyes. Lauren wasn't surprised she looked so haggard—she hadn't slept well. Instead, she'd spent the night fighting the bedsheets, dreaming old dreams, feeling an old, familiar pain that left her weary and exhausted.

"Gee—thanks," she said with a grin. "Just a little sleep deprived because of Jed, but I'll tell you about that later."

Irene smiled. "Are you heading to the surf club this afternoon? Or do you want me to go? We have to have the measurements for the stage and runway to the prop people by Monday, remember?"

She remembered. There was a fund-raiser at the surf club planned for two weeks away, and although Grace was the event organizer, Lauren volunteered to help in her sister-in-law's absence. Since she was organizing a fashion parade for the night anyway, it wasn't too much extra work liaising with the staging and entertainment people and the caterers.

"I'll go this afternoon," she said, and ignored the silly fluttering in her belly. All she had to do was measure the area for the stage and change rooms for the models. It was not as if she would be hanging around. It was not as if she had a reason to *want* to hang around.

"If you're sure," her mother said, her eyes twinkling.

Her übermatchmaking mother knew very well that Gabe might be there.

"I'm sure," she insisted. "And stop doing that."

Her mother raised both brows. "What? I just want to see my only daughter happy."

"I want to see me happy, too," Lauren said, and instructed Dawn to open the doors.

"I'm concerned about you," Irene said, more seriously.

"I'm fine, Matka," she promised. "Just tired, like I said."

The models for the parade had started coming into the store for their fittings, and that morning Carmen Collins crossed the threshold and held court like she owned the world. They'd gone to school together, and the self-proclaimed society princess made it her business to insult Lauren at every opportunity. But the other woman knew people with deep pockets, and since that was what the fund-raiser was about, Lauren bit her tongue and flattered Carmen about the tight-fitting, plum-colored satin gown she was wearing in the parade.

"I do adore this color," Carmen purred and ran her hands over her hips. "So are you modeling in the parade?"

"No," Lauren replied and saw her mother's raised brows from the corner of her eye. "I'll be too busy with the show."

"Pity," Carmen said with a sugary laugh. "You do look so sweet in a wedding dress."

Lauren plastered on a smile and pulled back the fitting room drapes. "Maybe next year," she said, clinging to her manners as though they were a life raft. "I'll have the dress pressed and ready for the show."

The other woman left by eleven, and her mother didn't bother to hide her dislike once Carmen was out the door.

"Can't bear that woman," Irene said, and frowned. "She was an obnoxious teenager and hasn't improved with age."

"But she married a rich man and knows plenty of people who'll donate at the fund-raiser," Lauren reminded her mother. "That's all that matters, right?"

Her mother huffed out a breath. "I suppose. Anyway, we've only got three more of the models to come in for a fitting and we're done. So off you go." She shooed Lauren and smiled. "I'll close up."

Lauren grinned, hugged her mother, quickly changed into gunmetal-gray cargo pants, a pink collared T-shirt and sneakers and then headed to the Crystal Point Surf Club & Community Center to measure the space she'd need for the catwalk.

The holiday park was filled with campers and mobile homes, and she drove down the bitumen road that led to the clubhouse. Almost a year earlier, the place had been gutted by fire, and the renovated building was bigger and better with much-improved facilities. She parked outside, grabbed her tape measure and notebook and headed through the automatic doors on the ground level.

And came to an abrupt halt.

Gabe was there.

Wet, laughing and clearly having a good time in the company of a lifeguard, a young woman who Lauren vaguely recalled was named Megan.

"Lauren?" he said as he straightened from his spot leaning against the reception desk. "What brings you here?"

She held up the tape. "Benefit stuff," she said, and tried to ignore the way the safety shirt he wore outlined every line and every muscle of his chest and shoulders at the same time as the little green-eyed monster was rearing its head.

Snap out of it.

"Do you know Megan?" he asked and came toward her.

She nodded. "Hello."

"It's Mimi," the girl corrected cheerfully, showing off perfectly white teeth and a million-dollar smile to go with her athletic, tanned body. "No one calls me Megan except my parents." She laughed and gazed at Gabe a little starry-eyed. "And you." Then she turned her attention back to Lauren. "So Gabe said you might be filling in for Cameron while he's away if we get too busy. The beaches have been crazy today.... Gabe just pulled an old man in from the rip."

Lauren smiled and looked at Gabe. That explained why his clothes were wet and why he had sand on his feet. "Is the man okay?"

"Shaken up, but fine," he replied and smiled. "But I wouldn't call him old. He was probably only forty."

Perfectly toned and tanned *Mimi* laughed loudly. "Ancient," she said, and grabbed Gabe's arm, lingering a lot longer than Lauren thought appropriate. "Well, I'd better get back on patrol. See you."

She breezed out of the room with a seductive sway that Lauren couldn't have managed even if she'd wanted to.

"Do you need help with that?" Gabe asked, looking at the tape in her hand.

Lauren shook her head. "No."

"So you're organizing the benefit with Grace?"

She looked at him. "The fashion parade. Why? Are you interested in modeling?"

He laughed. "Ah, no thanks. I did promise your brother I'd help out setting up, but that's all."

Lauren placed the retractable tape at one end of the room, and when it bounced back into her hand, he walked over and held it out straight for her. "Thanks," she said, and pulled the tape out across the room.

"If you need models, perhaps Megan can help?" he suggested and came across the room.

"Mimi," she corrected extrasweetly, and placed the notebook on the desk. "And I think I have all the models we need." Lauren remained by the desk and raised a brow. "She's a little young, don't you think?"

He frowned. "No. She's a strong swimmer and a good lifeguard."

Lauren flipped the notepad open without looking at him. "That's not what I meant."

The second he realized her meaning, he laughed loudly. "She's what, nineteen? Give me *some* credit."

Lauren glanced sideways. "She's perky."

"And a teenager." He moved closer. "Why all this sudden interest in my love life?"

"I'm not interested," she defended, and shrugged as she faked writing something on the notepad. "You can do what you like. Although, everyone knows that interoffice romances can be tricky and—"

Lauren was startled when he touched her arm gently. Mesmerized, she turned to face him. Side by side, hips against the desk, there was barely a foot between them. She tilted her head back and met his eyes. His gaze traveled over her face, inspecting every feature before settling on her mouth. It was intensely erotic, and her knees quivered. The hand on her arm moved upward a little, skimming over her skin, sending jolts of electricity through her blood.

Her lips parted…waiting…anticipating…

It had been so long since she'd been kissed. Too long. And she knew *he* knew that was what she was thinking.

"I'm not going to kiss you," he said softly, his gaze still on her mouth. "Even though I want to, and it would certainly stop you talking nonsense about Megan."

"All I—"

"Shh," he said, and placed two fingertips against her lips. "Keep talking, and I *will* kiss you."

Lauren knew she had to move. Because if she didn't, sanity would be lost, and she'd fling against him and forget every promise she'd made to herself. The fleeting attraction she'd experienced the first time they'd met six months ago had morphed into heady, hot desire that was slowly becoming all she could think about.

And it's not what I want….

Mindless passion was dangerous.

And if I'm not careful, I'm going to get swept up in it all over again….

"You promised," she reminded him on a whisper. "Remember? No making passes."

"I know what I promised," he said, and rubbed his thumb against her jaw. "I did warn you I could be a jerk, though."

Lauren took a deep breath. "You know what I want."

"And you seem to be of a mind to tell me what I want," he said, still touching her lips. "Which is not, I might add, a teenager with a silly crush."

"She's more woman than teenager, and—"

He groaned. "You really do talk too much."

If the automatic doors hadn't whooshed open, Lauren was certain he would have kissed her as if there was no tomorrow. And she would have kissed him back. Vow or not.

"Gabe," Mimi's squeaky voice called frantically from the doorway. "I need your help."

He dropped his hand and stepped back. "What's wrong?"

"There's a lady on the beach who's had a fall, and I think she might have broken her ankle."

Gabe moved away from her and grabbed the first-aid bag. "Okay…show me where."

He was out the door in a flash, and Lauren took a few seconds to get her feet to move and follow. By the time she reached the first crest of the sandbank, Gabe was already attending to the elderly woman. He was crouched at her side, one hand on her shoulder and asking her questions while Mimi unzipped the first-aid bag.

Lauren moved closer to assist. And took about ten seconds to realize that Gabe didn't need her help. He knew exactly what he was doing.

It wasn't broken, but his patient, Faye, had a severe sprain and probably tendon damage, and as he wrapped her ankle, he instructed Megan to call for the ambulance. The woman was well into her eighties, and her tender skin was bruising quickly. She needed X-rays and the type of painkillers he couldn't administer.

Gabe wrapped her in a thermal blanket to ensure she didn't go into shock and stayed with her and her equally elderly husband until the paramedics arrived. The beach was busy, and he sent Megan back onto patrol and remained with the couple…excruciatingly aware that Lauren was watching his every move.

Once the ambulance arrived, it was about a fifteen-minute process to get Faye from the beach and safely tucked inside the vehicle. Her husband chose to travel in the ambulance, and Gabe accepted the old man's car keys for safekeeping and was told their grandson would be along to collect the car within the hour.

His shift was over by three o'clock, but he lingered for a while to ensure the remaining bathers were staying between the boundary flags, as the water was choppy. Megan took off for home, and Gabe headed back to the clubhouse to lock up. He found Lauren in his office, sitting at the desk and writing in her notebook. He watched her for a moment, thinking that an hour earlier, he'd been on the brink of kissing her. It would have been a big mistake. Definitely.

"Did you get your work done?" he asked when he came into the room.

"Yes," she replied and collected her things together.

"I gather this benefit is important?"

She nodded. "It will raise money for the Big Brothers Big Sisters program. Cameron said you've been working with the program, too."

"A little," he replied, reluctant to tell her any more. Like the fact he volunteered his time to help coach an under-twelve's swimming and lifesaving team twice a week.

"You and Cameron put me to shame."

"How so?"

She shrugged and stood. "He's always been community focused. Not…self-focused. You're like that, too, otherwise you wouldn't be doing this job you're clearly overqualified for, or do things like volunteering with the kids from the Big Brothers program."

Discomfiture raced across his skin. So she knew. "It's nothing, really. Just a couple of hours twice a week."

"It's more than most people do," she qualified. "More than I do."

"You're helping with the benefit," he reminded her. "Raising money for the program is something important."

She shrugged again. "I guess. You know, you were

amazing with that elderly lady. Cameron was right about you…you have a talent for the first-aid side of things in this job."

Gabe's insides crunched. He could have told her the truth in that moment. He could have told her that she was right. But that it wasn't talent. It was experience. He could have told her that for ten years he'd worked as a doctor in the E.R. at the finest hospital in Huntington Beach. But if he did, she'd want to know why he left.

Why I quit...

And how did he tell her that? One truth would snowball into another.

And Gabe wasn't ready.

He wasn't ready to admit that an innocent woman and her baby had died on his watch.

Chapter Five

Lauren dropped Jed off at her brother's house on Sunday afternoon. The house sitter was back and would be in residence until Cameron and Grace returned from their honeymoon. It was past five by the time she got home, and by then she only had half an hour to shower, change and prepare an array of snacks for the girls' night she was having with Cassie and Mary-Jayne.

It was impossible to *not* notice the bright yellow car parked at the entrance of Gabe's driveway.

She'd spotted the same vehicle outside the surf club. Megan's car. Obviously.

So what? He can do what he likes.

But Lauren had to force back the swell of jealousy burning through her veins.

She'd never *done* jealous. Not even with Tim. And she certainly wasn't going to waste time thinking about her neighbor and the perky *Mimi* doing *whatever* over the hedge.

When her friends arrived, Lauren headed through the front door to greet them and immediately heard a woman laughing. She noticed that Megan and Gabe were now outside and standing by the yellow car, clearly enjoying one another's company. And her stupid, rotten and completely unjustified jealousy returned with a vengeance. She willed it away with all the strength she could muster. When Cassie and Mary-Jayne reached the porch steps, they must have noticed the scowl on her face, because they both had raised brows and wide smiles on their faces.

"Trouble in paradise?" Cassie asked and walked up the steps.

Her friends knew what had happened at the wedding. They'd called it fate. Kismet. *Providence.* The fact he'd moved in next door simply added fuel to their combined romantic foolishness.

Mary-Jayne blew out a low whistle. "That's some serious competition you have there."

Of course she meant Megan. Young, perky, chirpy… Everything she wasn't. Lauren's scowl deepened. Her friends were teasing, but she felt the sting right through to her bones. For Gabe's no-commitment, casual-sex-only lifestyle, the effervescent Megan was no doubt perfect. She was pretty and uncomplicated. She probably wasn't haunted by memories of a lost love. She almost certainly wasn't looking to settle down and raise a family. So, perfect.

"Glaring at her over the hedge won't make her turn to stone, you know," Mary-Jayne said, and grinned.

Worse luck.

She jabbed her friend playfully in the ribs. "I need a drink," Lauren said as she turned on her heels and followed the two other women back inside.

Ten minutes later they were settled in the living room, a tray of snacks on the coffee table and a glass of wine in hand. Except for Cassie, who made do with sparkling grape juice.

"Have you heard from Doug?" Lauren asked her pregnant friend as she settled back in the sofa. "Has he warmed to the idea of the baby?"

The fact that Cassie's much older soldier boyfriend hadn't taken the news of her pregnancy very well had become a regularly talked about subject between them. It had been a month since Cassie had told him the news about the baby, and Lauren was concerned for her friend.

"He said we needed to talk about it," Cassie explained, her eyes shadowy. "I know he'll come around and consider this baby a blessing. But I don't want to distract him while he's on a mission."

"He's a total jerk," M.J. said bluntly, and tossed her mass of dark curls. "You know that, right?"

Lauren quickly took the middle ground. Something she often had to do. Cassie was a calm, sweet-natured woman who avoided confrontation and drama, while effervescent M.J. attracted it like a bee to a flower. Lauren figured she was somewhere in between. As different as they were, she knew they shared one common trait—unfailing loyalty to one another and their friendship.

"Perhaps we shouldn't judge him too quickly," she said, and ignored M.J.'s scowl.

"He should be judged," M.J. said, and grunted. "Do you even know where he is at the moment?"

Cassie shook her head. "Not really."

Lauren tapped Cassie's arm. "His brother might know. Perhaps you should—"

"Tanner's in South Dakota," Cassie said quietly. "And he and Doug rarely talk. Besides, Doug will come around. You'll see."

Lauren hoped so, for her friend's sake. And if not, she'd

be there to support Cassie, just as her friends had rallied around her when she'd needed them.

Cassie smiled. "So let's talk about you, not me. What's been going on between you and Mr. Gorgeous from next door?"

"Nothing," Lauren replied, and drank some wine. She wasn't about to tell them about the near-miss kiss at the surf club the previous afternoon. They'd be all over that information in a second. It wasn't as though she really wanted to exclude them. She knew they worried about her. They'd been her rocks after Tim died. And then again when James had walked out. But they didn't really understand her determination to avoid those kinds of feelings…even though they supported her. But Gabe was a complication she didn't need to discuss with her friends. The more time she spent with him, the less she felt she knew.

And she had to get him out of her system once and for all.

Only, she had no idea how she was supposed to do that when he had a habit of invading her thoughts…and her dreams.

It was ironic how much Gabe had come to avoid hospitals. At one time, the four walls of Huntington Beach's largest health-care facility had been his life. But then everything changed. Funny how some lingering fatigue and a small lump in his armpit could so quickly alter his fate.

Biopsy...cancer...surgery...chemo...radiation therapy...

The disease had been caught early, and with a bit of luck he'd been assured of a long life, but that didn't mean he could avoid the necessary follow-up examinations every six months. The specialist asked the usual invasive questions on his visit—questions he'd never considered invasive until he'd been on the other end of the conversation. Being a cancer patient had certainly altered his perspective on having the right kind of bedside manner. If he did decide to practice medicine again, he would do it with a renewed respect for what the sick endured.

If...

Gabe missed his career more than he'd ever imagined he would. Becoming a doctor had been his dream since he was twelve years old, and getting into medical school had been the realization of years of study and hard work. But things changed. Life changed.

And then one arrogant decision had altered everything.

He'd gone back to work too soon. Everyone around him said so. His family. His colleagues. His oncologist. But after a bad reaction to the treatment and medication, and after six weeks in bed chucking his guts up, he'd had enough. He was determined to reclaim his life and return to the job he loved.

Two weeks later a young mother and her baby were dead.

Perhaps technically not his fault, but he knew in his heart that the blame lay at his feet. Nauseated and tired from that day's round of treatment, Gabe had left a second-year resident alone in the trauma room for a few minutes and headed for the bathroom. While he was gone, a patient had been brought into the E.R. and the young doctor didn't have the experience to handle the emergency. The young woman, who was seven months pregnant, had hemorrhaged, and both she and her unborn child died.

Plagued by guilt, after the inquiry, an undercurrent of uncertainty had shadowed him and he'd stuck it out for another month before he bailed on his career, his friends and his family.

His life as he knew it.

And Crystal Point was as far away from all that as he could get.

It was a place where he could wrap himself in anonymity. A place where he could forget the past and not feel defined by his illness or the tragedy of that terrible night in the E.R.

"Gabe?"

He stopped beneath the wide doorway of the specialist's rooms. Lauren stood a few feet away. Discomfort crawled along his skin. She was the last person he'd expected to see. And the last person he wanted to see outside the specialist's office.

"Hello," he said quietly, and wondered how to make his getaway.

She came to a stop in front of him. "What are you doing here?"

He took a second and considered all the things he wouldn't say. "What are *you* doing here?"

She frowned. "My friend Cassie works on reception in Radiology. I'm meeting her and Mary-Jayne for lunch."

She had a friend who worked at the hospital? One who might recognize him when he came in for testing? His discomfort turned into an all-out need to get away from her as quickly as possible before she asked more questions. Before she worked things out.

"I have to go," he said, and stepped sideways.

Her hand unexpectedly wrapped around his forearm and she said his name. Her touch was like a cattle brand against his skin, and Gabe fought the impulse to shake her off. Being this close didn't help his determination to stay away from her.

"Is everything okay?" she asked, and glanced up at the signage above his head. The word *oncology* stuck out like a beacon.

Any second now she's going to figure it out.

Dread licked along his spine. The thought of Lauren looking at him with sympathy or pity or something worse cut through to his bones. "Everything's fine."

She didn't look convinced. But Gabe wasn't about to

start spilling his guts. He wanted to get out of there as fast as he could.

She half smiled and then spoke. "I'm just surprised to see you here. Are you visiting someone or—"

"Last I looked I wasn't obligated to inform you of my movements."

His unkind words lingered in the space between them, and he wanted to snatch them back immediately. Even though he knew it was better this way. For them both. He knew she was struggling with the attraction between them, just like he was. He knew she wanted someone different… someone who could give her the picket-fence life she craved. And that wasn't him. She'd lost the man she'd loved to cancer. Of course she wouldn't want to risk that again.

"I'm…sorry," she said quietly. "I shouldn't have asked. I was only—"

"Forget it, Lauren," Gabe said sharply, and saw her wince as he pulled his arm away. "And I…I didn't mean to snap at you." The elevator nearby dinged and opened, and he wanted to dive inside. "I have to go. I'll see you later."

Gabe moved away and stepped through the doors. Away from her. And away from the questions in her eyes.

But by the end of the week, he was so wound up he felt as though he needed to run a marathon to get her out of his system. He needed to, though…because he liked being around her too much. He liked the soft sound of her voice and the sweet scent of her perfume. He liked the way she chewed her bottom lip when she was deep in thought. He liked how her eyes darkened to a deep caramel when she was annoyed, and wondered how they'd look if she was aroused. He wondered lots of things…but *nothing* could happen.

She'd lost her fiancé to cancer…making it the red flag of the century.

And Gabe had no intention of getting seriously involved

with anyone. Not until he was sure he could offer that someone a real future. He had a five-year plan. If he stayed cancer-free for five years, he'd consider a serious relationship. Maybe even marriage. Until then, Gabe knew what he had to do. He had to steer clear of commitment. He had to steer clear of Lauren.

Cameron returned from his honeymoon midweek and stopped by the surf club Saturday morning just as Gabe was finishing off first aid to a pair of siblings who'd become entangled with a jellyfish. He reassured their concerned mother her children would be fine, and then joined his friend at the clubhouse.

"Busy morning?" Cameron asked, looking tanned and relaxed from his weeks in the Mediterranean, as he flaked into a chair.

"The usual summer holiday nonsense," he replied. "Sunburn and dehydration mostly."

Cameron nodded. "Thanks for helping my sister out with Jed. She told me what happened to her door."

Gabe shrugged. "No problem," he said quickly, and tried to ignore the way his pulse sped up. He didn't want to talk to his friend about Lauren. He didn't want to *think* about Lauren. "Gotta get back to work."

Cameron stood and shook his head. "Thanks again. And don't forget to swing by my folks' house tonight, around six," he reminded him. "My beautiful wife is trying out her newly learned Greek cooking skills in my mother's kitchen, so it should be mighty interesting."

Gabe experienced an unexpected twinge of envy. His friend looked ridiculously happy. Cameron had the same dopey expression on his face that Scott permanently carried these days. He was pretty sure he'd never looked like that. Not even when he'd been with Mona.

"Sure," he said, thinking the last thing he wanted to do

was spend an evening at Lauren's parents' home, because he knew Lauren would be there, too. "See you then."

When he got home that afternoon, he changed into jeans and a T-shirt and started painting the main bedroom. It kept him busy until five-thirty. Then he showered, dressed and grabbed his car keys.

When he reversed out of the yard, he realized that Lauren was doing the same thing. Their vehicles pulled up alongside one another at the end of their driveways. He stopped, as did she. Their windows rolled down simultaneously.

"Hi," she said. "Are you going to my—"

"Yes," he said, cutting her off.

"My brother mentioned you were coming. Probably foolish to take both cars?"

She was right. He should have offered to drive her. But he hadn't seen her since their meeting at the hospital. He'd behaved badly. Rudely. Gabe nodded. "Probably."

"So…" Her voice trailed. "Yours or mine?"

Gabe sucked in some air. "I'll drive."

Her mouth twisted. "Be back in a minute."

He watched as she moved her car back up the driveway, got out and came around the passenger side of his Jeep. When she got in, the flowery scent of her perfume hit his senses. She buckled up and settled her gaze to the front.

"Ready?" he asked.

"Yes."

He backed the car onto the road and then came to a halt. He had something to say to her. "Lauren, I want to apologize again for being so dismissive the other day." He invented an excuse. "I was late for an appointment and—"

She waved a hand. "Like you said, not my business."

Gabe was tempted to apologize again. But he didn't. He nodded instead. "Okay."

She flashed him a brief look. “Just so you know, when we turn up together my mother is going to think it’s a date.”

“It’s not, though,” he said, and drove down the street. “Right?”

“Right,” she replied.

Gabe reconsidered going to the Jakowskis’. He didn’t want Lauren’s mother getting any ideas. Or Cameron. Whatever he was feeling for Lauren, he had to get it under control. And fast.

Lauren knew the moment she walked into her mother’s kitchen that she was going to get the third degree. Irene had greeted them at the door, explained that Cameron had been called into work and would be joining them later and quickly shuffled Gabe toward the games room to hang out with her father.

Her mother ushered Lauren directly into the kitchen. Grace was there, standing behind the wide granite counter, looking radiant. Her new sister-in-law was exceptionally beautiful. In the past, she’d always considered the other woman frosty and a little unfriendly, but Lauren had warmed toward Grace since it was clear her brother was crazy in love with her, and she with him.

Lauren stepped in beside Grace and began topping her mother’s signature baked lemon cheesecake, a task she’d done countless times. Her sister-in-law remained silent, but her mother wasn’t going to be held back.

“It’s nice that Gabe could join us this evening. He really is quite handsome,” Irene said as she busied herself pulling salad items from the refrigerator. “Don’t you think? And such a lovely accent.”

Lauren’s gaze flicked up briefly. *“Matka,”* she warned, and half smiled. “Don’t.”

But she knew her mother wouldn’t give up. “Just stating the obvious.”

"His ancestors are Roman gods," Lauren said, and grinned. "So of course he looks good."

Irene laughed softly. "That's the spirit…indulge my matchmaking efforts."

"Well, there's little point fighting it," Lauren said with a sigh. "Even though you're wasting your time in this case."

"Do you think?" her mother inquired, still grinning as she grabbed a tray of appetizers. "Don't be too quick to say no, darling. He might just be the best of both worlds," Irene said, and smiled. "When you're done decorating that cake, can you grab the big tureen from the cabinet in the front living room?"

Lauren smiled. "Sure," she replied, and waited until her mother left the room before speaking to her sister-in-law. "See what I have to put up with?"

"She just cares about you," Grace replied, and covered the potato dish she'd prepared. "And he seems…nice."

He is nice. That was the problem. He was also sexy and gorgeous and not the *settle-down* kind of man she was looking for. He'd said as much. And she'd had nice before. Tim had been the nicest, most sincere man she'd ever known. Even James had been nice in his own charming, flirtatious way. The kind of nice she wanted now didn't come with a handsome face and the ability to shoot her libido up like a rocket.

The best of both worlds...

What exactly did her mother mean? That Gabe was attractive, charming, funny and smart and just what any sensible woman would call the *perfect package?*

Too perfect. No one was without flaws. Secrets.

Lauren placed the cheesecake in the refrigerator and excused herself. The big living room at the front of the house was rarely used. It housed her mother's treasures, like the twin glass lamps that had been in their family for four generations, and the cabinet of exquisite crockery and dinnerware. Lauren stopped by the mantelpiece and stared at the family photographs lining the shelf. There were more pictures on the long cabinet at the other end of the room. Her mother loved taking pictures.

She fingered the edge of one frame and her insides crunched. It was a snapshot of herself and Tim. He looked so relaxed and cheerful in the photo. They were smiling, pressed close together, his blond hair flopping over his forehead. Had he lived, he would have been soon celebrating his thirtieth birthday. She looked at his face again. It was Lauren's favorite picture of him. Memories surged through her. Memories of love. And regret. And…anger. But she quickly pushed the feeling away. Anger had no place in her heart. Not when it came to Tim.

"You looked happy."

Lauren swiveled on her heels. Gabe stood behind her. Engrossed in her memories, she hadn't heard his approach. "Sorry?"

"In the picture," he said, and stepped closer. "You looked happy together."

"We were," she said, intensely conscious of his closeness. "That's…Tim," she explained softly and pointed to the photograph. "He was always happy. Even when he was facing the worst of it, somehow he never lost his sense of humor."

Gabe's eyes darkened. "Did he pass away quickly?"

She nodded. "In the end…yes. He died just a few weeks before we were due to be married."

"And then you married someone else?"

"Not quite two years later," she replied and immediately wondered why she was admitting such things to him. "It was a big mistake."

Gabe nodded a little. "Because you didn't love him?"

"Exactly," she said, and sucked in a short breath.

"There must have been something that made you marry him?"

Lauren's skin grew hotter. "Sex."

His blistering gaze was unwavering. "That's all?"

"I'd had love," she admitted, so aware of his closeness she could barely breathe. "And I'd lost it. When I met James, I thought attraction would be enough."

"But it wasn't?"

She sighed. "No."

"And now you don't want that, either?" he asked.

Lauren raised a shoulder. "I don't expect anyone to understand."

"Actually," he said quietly. "I do. You lost the love of your life, then settled for something that left you empty, and now you want to find that no-risk, no-hurt, middle road."

Middle road? Could he read her mind? "That's right. I married my ex-husband after only knowing him for three months. It was a foolish impulse and one I regret…for his sake and mine."

Gabe looked at the mantelpiece. "Which explains why there are no pictures of him."

"My mother was never a fan of James," she said, and felt his scrutiny through to her bones. "Once we divorced, the wedding pictures came down." Lauren looked down to her feet and then back up to his gaze. "Ah…what are you doing in here? I thought you were out on the back patio with my dad."

"I was," he replied, and grinned fractionally. "But your mother sent me on a mercy dash to help you carry some kind of heavy dish."

Lauren rolled her eyes and pointed to the tureen in the cabinet. "My mother is meddling."

He smiled, like he knew exactly what she meant. "To what end?"

Lauren raised a shoulder. “Can’t you guess? I told you she’d think this was a date.”

His gaze widened. “Should I be worried?”

She laughed a little. “That my mother has her sights set on you? Probably.”

Gabe laughed, too, and the sound warmed her right through to the blood in her veins. He was so…likable. So gorgeous. And it scared her. With James, she’d jumped in, libido first, uncaring of the consequences. Still grieving the loss of the man she’d loved, Lauren had found temporary solace in arms that had soon left her feeling empty and alone. Although she’d thought him good-looking and charming, she’d realized soon after they’d married that they had very little in common. But the attraction she had for Gabe was different. The more time she spent with him, the less superficial it felt. Which put her more at risk.

“I shall consider myself warned,” he said, and chuckled.

Lauren walked toward the cabinet and opened the door. “Thanks for being so understanding,” she said, still grinning.

“I, too, have a meddling, albeit well-meaning mother who wants to see me…shall we say, *settled.* So I understand your position.”

For a second, she wondered what else they had in common. He clearly came from a close family, as she did. “Doesn’t she know you’re not interested in commitment?”

His gaze locked with hers. “I don’t think she quite believes me.”

Lauren’s breath caught. “Have you…”

“Have I what?”

She shrugged, trying to be casual but churning inside. “Have you changed your mind about that?”

Lauren couldn’t believe she’d asked the question. And couldn’t believe she wanted to know. Her elbow touched his arm and the contact sent heat shooting across her skin.

She should have pulled away. But Lauren remained where she was, immobilized by the connection simmering between them.

"No," he said after a long stretch of silence. "I haven't."

Of course, it was what she needed to hear. Gabe wasn't what she wanted. Because he made her feel too much. He made her question the choice she'd made to remain celibate until she found someone to share her life with. He didn't want what she wanted.

He's all wrong for me....

Even though being beside him, alone and in the solitude of the big room, seemed so unbelievably normal, she was tempted to lean closer and invite him to kiss her. His gaze shifted from her eyes to her mouth, and Lauren sucked in a shallow breath. Her lips parted slightly and he watched with such searing intensity, her knees threatened to give way. There was heat between them, the kind that came before a kiss. The kind of heat that might lead to something more.

"Gabe..." She said his name on a sigh.

"We would be crazy to start something," he warned, unmoving and clearly reading her thoughts.

"I know," she agreed softly.

Crazy or not, she was strangely unsurprised when he took hold of her hand and gently rubbed his thumb along her palm. He was still watching her, still looking at her mouth.

"Do you have any idea how much I want to kiss you right now?"

She shivered at his question, despite the warmth racing across her skin. Lauren nodded, feeling the heat between them rise up a notch. "Do you have any idea how much I want you to kiss me right now?"

His hand wrapped around hers. She was staring up, waiting, thinking about how she hadn't been kissed for such a long time. And thinking how Gabe had somehow, in a matter of weeks, become the one man whose kiss she longed for.

Chapter Six

Gabe could have kissed her right then, right there. He could have lost himself in the softness of her lips and sweet taste of her mouth. He could have forgotten about his determination to keep away from her and give in to the desire he experienced whenever she was near. And he would have. But a loud crash followed by an equally loud shout pushed them apart immediately. The dish from the china cabinet was quickly forgotten as they both hurried from the room.

When they reached the kitchen, he saw there was glass and water on the floor and also a pile of tattered flowers. Lauren's father was sitting on the ground, knees half-curled to his chest.

"Dad!" Lauren gasped as she rushed to his side.

Irene and Grace came through the doorway and stood worriedly behind Gabe as he quickly moved between them to settle beside the older man. Franciszek Jakowski was holding up a seriously bleeding hand, and Gabe quickly snatched up a tea towel from the countertop and wrapped it around his palm.

"I knocked the darn vase off the counter," Franciszek explained as Gabe hauled him to his feet. "Cut myself when I fell."

"Can you walk?" Gabe asked, knowing he needed to look at the wound immediately.

Franciszek winced as he put weight on his left foot. "Not so good."

He looked at Lauren. "Hold your father's hand up to help with the bleeding, and I'll get him to a chair."

She did as he asked, and Gabe hooked an arm around the other man's shoulder and soon got him settled onto the kitchen chair. Blood streamed down his arm and splattered on Gabe's shirt. He undid the towel and examined Franciszek's hand. The cut was deep and would need stitches. Irene disappeared and quickly returned with a first-aid kit. Gabe cleaned and dressed the wound, conscious of the scrutiny of the three women hovering close by. Within minutes, he also had Franciszek's left ankle wrapped with an elastic bandage.

"The cut definitely needs stitches," he said, and wiped his hands on a cloth Lauren passed him. "And it looks like you've only sprained your ankle, but an X-ray wouldn't hurt just to be sure."

Irene extolled her gratitude and was on the telephone immediately, making an appointment to see their local doctor within the next half hour.

"I'll drive you," Lauren volunteered, but her mother quickly vetoed that idea.

"Grace can drive us," she said, and looked toward her daughter-in-law, who nodded instantly. "You can stay and clean up. And I need you to keep an eye on dinner. We won't be too long."

"That's for sure," Franciszek agreed cheerfully, although Gabe was pretty sure the older man was in considerable pain. He patted Gabe's shoulder. "Thanks for the doctoring, son. Much appreciated."

Gabe's stomach sank. Being reminded of who he was, even though no one but his family knew the truth, hit him like a fist of shame between the shoulder blades. He glanced at Lauren and then looked away. There were questions in her eyes. Questions he had no intention of answering.

It took several minutes to get Franciszek into the car, and when Gabe returned, Lauren was in the kitchen, picking up pieces of shattered glass from the floor. She was concentrating on her task, looking shaken and pale.

"Are you okay?"

She glanced up. "Just worried about my dad."

"He'll be fine."

Her small nose wrinkled. "Thanks to you," she said as she rose to her feet and walked around the countertop. "You might want to consider switching careers."

His gut sank. "What?"

"You'd make a good paramedic," she said, and grabbed a banister brush from the cupboard beneath the sink. "You clearly have a knack for it. You know, I have a friend who's an admin in emergency services. I could probably arrange for you to—"

"No...but thank you," he said, cutting her off before she said too much about it. "Need some help with this?"

She held his gaze for a moment, and then passed him the broom. "Sure. I'll get the mop and bucket." She propped her hands on her hips and looked at his blood-stained shirt. "I'll find you something to wear and you can pop that shirt in the machine before it permanently stains. I think Cameron has some clothes in one of the guest rooms. I'll go and check."

She disappeared, and Gabe stared after her. Guilt pressed

down on his shoulders. He wanted to tell her the truth about himself. But one would lead to another and then another. And what was the point? There were already too many questions in her lovely brown eyes.

When she returned with the mop and bucket, she placed a piece of clothing on the table. "I'll finish up here. You can go and change."

He met her gaze. "Okay."

Gabe left the room and headed for the laundry. Once there, he stripped off his soiled shirt and dumped it in the washing machine. He added liquid, cranked on the start switch and rested his behind on the edge of the sink. Then he expelled a long breath.

Damn.

He wanted to kiss her so much. He wanted to touch her. He wanted to feel her against him and stroke her soft skin. He wanted to forget every promise he'd made to himself about waiting to see if his illness returned before he'd consider being in a relationship. But it wouldn't be fair to any woman. More than that, it wouldn't be fair to Lauren. He couldn't ask her to risk herself. He *wouldn't.* He'd seen firsthand what it had done to his mom when his father had battled cancer for three years. He'd watched his mom lose the light in her eyes and the spirit in her heart. He'd watched her grieve and cry and bury the man she'd loved.

And Lauren had been there, too. He'd heard the pain in her voice when she'd spoken of her lost love. It should have been enough to send him running.

She thought he'd make a good paramedic? The irony wasn't hard to miss. There were questions in her eyes, and they were questions he didn't want to answer. But if he kept doing this, if he kept being close to her, he would be forced to tell her everything.

And admitting how he'd bailed on his life and career wasn't an option.

Pull yourself together and forget her.

He needed to leave. And he would have if Lauren hadn't chosen that moment to walk into the laundry room.

When Lauren crossed the threshold, she stopped dead in her tracks. Gabe stood by the sink in the small room with the fresh shirt in his hands. And naked from the waist up. He turned to face her.

It had been so long since she'd been this close to a man's bare skin. And because it was Gabe, he was thoroughly mesmerizing, as she'd known he would be. She'd known his skin would look like satin stretched over steel and that his broad shoulders and arms would be well defined and muscular. The smattering of dark hair on his chest tapered down in a line and disappeared into the low waistband of his jeans, and Lauren's breath caught in her throat.

His gaze instantly met hers, and she didn't miss the darkening blue eyes and faint pulse beating in his cheek. Somehow, she moved closer, and when Lauren finally found her voice, they were barely feet apart.

She dropped the bucket and mop. "I...I'm sorry...I didn't realize you were still in here."

Heat swirled between them, coiling around the small room, and she couldn't have moved even if she wanted to. She tried to avert her gaze. Tried and failed. He had such smooth skin, and her fingers itched with the sudden longing to reach out and touch him.

"You..." Her voice cracked, and she swallowed. "You were right with what you said before. We'd be...crazy...to start something...to start imagining we could..."

Her words trailed off, and still he stared at her, holding her gaze with a hypnotic power she'd never experienced before. Color spotted her cheeks, and she quickly turned and made for the doorway. Only she couldn't step forward because Gabe's hands came out and gently grasped her shoulders. She swallowed hard as he moved in close behind her and said her name in that soft, sexy way she was becoming so used to. The heat from his body seared through her thin shirt, and Lauren's temperature quickly spiked. His hands moved down her arms and linked with hers. She felt his soft breath near her nape, and his chest pressed intimately against her shoulders.

His arms came around her and Lauren pushed back. One hand rested on her hip, the other he placed on her rib cage. The heat between them ramped up and created a swirling energy in the small room. Her head dropped back, and she let out a heavy sigh as his fingertips trailed patterns across the shirt. It was an intensely erotic moment, and she wanted to turn in his arms and push against him. She wanted his kiss, his touch, his heat and everything else. She wanted him to plunder her mouth over and over and then more. Flesh against flesh, sweat against sweat. She wanted his body over her, around her, inside her. She wanted *him*... and not only his body. Lauren tilted her head, inviting him to touch the delicate skin at the base of her neck with his mouth. But he didn't. Instead, Gabe continued to touch her rib cage with skillful, seductive fingers, never going too high and barely teasing the underside of her breasts.

She could feel him hard against her. He was aroused and not hiding the fact. Lauren moved her arms back and planted her hands on his thighs. She dug her nails against the denim and urged him closer. His touch was so incredibly erotic, and she groaned low in her throat. Finally, he kissed her nape, softly, gently, and electricity shimmered across her skin.

"Lauren," he whispered against her ear as his mouth trailed upward. "I'm aching to make love to you."

Lauren managed a vague nod and was about to turn in his arms and beg him to kiss her and make love to her when she heard a door slam. The front door. Seconds later, she heard her brother's familiar voice calling out a greeting.

Gabe released her gently and she stepped forward, dragging air through her lungs. "I should go."

"Good idea," he said softly as he grabbed the shirt and pulled it quickly over his head. "I should probably stay here for a minute."

She nodded and willed some serious movement into her legs and was back in the main hallway seconds later. Cameron, dressed in his regulation police-officer uniform, greeted her with a brief hug and ruffled her hair.

"Hey, kid…what's happening?" he asked once they were in the kitchen and saw the pan of broken glass on the countertop.

She quickly filled him in about their father's mishap, and once she was done, he immediately called Grace. Her brother was still on the phone when Gabe walked into the room. Her body still hummed with memories of his touch, and their gaze connected instantly. If Cameron hadn't turned up, she was sure they'd be making love that very minute. And it would have been a big mistake. When the moment was over, there would be regret and recrimination, and she'd hate herself for being so weak.

When her brother ended his call, he explained that their father was being triaged, and that they'd be home as soon as he was released. In fact, they returned close to an hour and a half later. By then, Lauren had shuffled the men out of the kitchen and finished preparing dinner.

It turned out that Gabe was right. Her father had needed stitches for his hand, and his foot was only sprained. By the time they settled her dad at the head of the table, crutches to one side, it was nearly nine o'clock. Lauren was seated next to Gabe and felt his closeness as if it was a cloak draped across her shoulders.

Once dinner was over, she headed back to the kitchen

with Grace and began cleaning up. Gabe and her brother joined them soon after, and Grace tossed a tea towel to each of them.

"Idle hands," her sister-in-law said, and grinned when Cameron complained. "Get to work."

Lauren laughed and dunked her hands into a sink full of soapy water. Like with everything he did, Gabe ignored Cameron's whining and attended the task with an effortless charm that had both Lauren and Grace smiling. It would, she decided, be much better if he had the charisma of a rock. But no such luck. Aside from the insane chemistry that throbbed between them, Lauren liked him so much it was becoming impossible to imagine she could simply dismiss her growing feelings. Sexual attraction was one thing, emotional attraction another thing altogether. It was also hard to dismiss how her mother, Grace and even her brother watched their interaction with subtle, yet keen interest.

By the time they left, it was past eleven o'clock, and then a quarter past the hour when Gabe pulled his truck into his driveway. She got out, and he quickly came around the side of the vehicle.

"Well, thanks for the lift," she said, and tucked her tote under her arm.

He touched her elbow. "I'll see you to your door."

"There's no need," she said quickly.

"Come on," he said, and began walking down the driveway, ignoring her protest.

Lauren followed and stepped in beside him as they rounded the hedge that separated their front lawns. He opened the gate and stood aside to let her pass. By the time she'd walked up the path and onto the small porch, she was so acutely aware of him she could barely hold her keys steady.

Open the door. Say good-night. Get inside. Easy.

Lauren slid the key in the screen door and propped it

open with her elbow while she unlocked the front door. "Um...thanks again," she said, and turned on her heels. "And thanks for what you did for my dad. I'm glad you were there to—"

"Lauren?"

She stilled, clutching her tote, hoping he wouldn't come closer. Praying he wouldn't kiss her. "We...we need to forget what happened tonight," she said in a voice that rattled in her throat. "We agreed it would be crazy to—"

"Nothing really happened," he said, cutting her off. "Did it?"

Lauren took a breath. "Well, what *almost* happened. I've made a vow, a promise to myself...and it's a promise I intend to keep. And I'm never going to find what I want if I get drawn deeper into this...this attraction I have for you. We both know it won't go anywhere other than your bed, and I'm not prepared to settle for just sex. Not again."

He didn't move. But he stared at her. He stared so deeply, so intensely, she could barely breathe. The small porch and dim light overhead created extreme intimacy. If she took one tiny step she would be pressed against him.

"You're right," he said, and moved back a little. "You shouldn't settle for sex. You should find that middle road you want, Lauren, with someone who can give you the relationship you deserve."

Then he was gone. Down the steps and through the gate and quickly out of view. Lauren stayed where she was for several minutes. Her chest was pounding. Her stomach was churning. Her head was spinning.

And her heart was in serious danger.

Gabe knew he was right to leave Lauren alone. He hadn't seen her all week. Deliberately. He left for work earlier than she did and returned home before her small car pulled into the driveway each afternoon. Not seeing her helped. A lot. Or more like a little. Or not at all.

Unfortunately, not seeing her seemed to put him in a bad mood.

Something his cousin took pleasure in pointing out on Thursday afternoon when Gabe dropped by the B and B.

"You know, you'll never get laid if you don't ask her out," Scott said with a wide grin, and passed him a beer.

"Shut up," he said, and cranked the lid off.

His cousin laughed. "Hah. Sucker. Just admit your five-year plan is stupid and that you're crazy about Lauren."

Gabe gripped the bottle. "I know what I'm doing."

"Sure you do," Scott shot back. "You're hibernating like a bear because you don't want to admit you like her. That's why your mom has been calling my mom and my mom has been calling me. You haven't been taking any calls from your family for the past two weeks."

"They worry too much," he remarked, and shrugged. "They think I'm going to relapse and die a horrible death. And maybe I will. All I know is I don't want to put anyone in the middle of that. Not anyone. Not Lauren."

"Maybe you should let her decide that for herself."

"Will you just..." Gabe paused, ignored the curse teetering on the end of his tongue and drank some more beer. "Stop talking."

Scott shrugged. "Just trying to see my best friend happy."

"I'm happy enough," he shot back. "So lay off."

His cousin laughed, clearly unperturbed by his bad temper. "You know, not every woman is going to run for the hills if you get sick again."

"Mona didn't run," Gabe reminded the other man. "I broke it off with her."

Scott shrugged again. "Another example of you needing to control everything, right?"

Tired of the same old argument, Gabe finished his beer and stood. "I have to bail."

"Hot date?"

Gabe grabbed his keys off the table. "A wall that won't paint itself."

"Sounds riveting," Scott said drily. "Renovating that house won't keep you warm at night, old buddy."

His cousin was right, but he had no intention of admitting that. He took off and was home within a few minutes. Once he'd dropped his keys on the hall stand, he rounded out his shoulders. Pressure cramped his back, and he let out a long breath. He needed to burn off some of the tension clinging to his skin. There was easily over an hour of sunlight left, so he changed into his running gear and headed off down the street.

Gabe reached The Parade quickly. The long road stretched out in front of him. He crossed the wide grassy verge and headed for the pathway leading to the beach in one direction and to the north end of the small town to the other. He vetoed the beach and headed left, striding out at an even pace and covering the ground quickly. It was quiet at this end of town. Without the holiday park, surf club and kiosk there was only a scattering of new homes, and the waterfront was more rock than sand. He spotted a pair of snorkelers preparing to dive close to the bank and waved as another runner jogged past.

Up ahead, he spotted someone sitting alone on one of the many bench seats that were placed along the line of the pathway. It was Lauren. He'd recognize her blond hair anywhere. He slowed his pace and considered turning around. But he kept moving, slowing only when she was about twenty feet away. She was looking out toward the ocean, deep in thought, hands crossed in her lap. An odd feeling pressed into his chest. As though he suddenly couldn't get enough air in his lungs. God, she was beautiful. He stopped a few feet from the seat and said her name.

Her head turned immediately. “Oh, hi.”

She was paler than usual. Sadder. The tightness in his chest amplified tenfold.

He stopped closer. “Are you okay?”

“Sure,” she said quietly, unmoving.

Gabe wasn’t convinced. He moved around the bench and sat down beside her. “I’m not buying. What’s up?”

“Nothing,” she insisted.

“It’s four-thirty on a Thursday afternoon. You’re not at the store,” he said pointedly. “You’re sitting here alone staring out at the sea.”

She shrugged a little. “I’m just thinking.”

He knew that. “About what?”

She drew in a shallow breath. “Tim.”

Of course. Her lost love. “I’m sorry, I shouldn’t have—”

“It’s his birthday,” she said quietly, and turned her gaze back to the ocean. “I always come here on this day. It’s where he proposed to me.”

Gabe immediately felt like he was intruding on an intensely private moment. Big-time. He got up to leave, but her hand came out and touched his arm.

“It’s okay,” she said, her voice so quiet and strained it made his insides twinge. “I could probably use the company.”

“Do you usually?” he asked. “Have company, I mean?”

She shook her head and dropped her hand. “Not usually.”

Gabe crossed his arms to avoid the sudden urge to hold her. He looked out at the sea. “You still miss him?”

“Yes,” she said on a sigh. “He was one of the kindest people I’ve ever known. We never argued. Never had a cross word. Well, that is until he…”

Her words trailed, and Gabe glanced sideways. “Until he what?”

She shrugged again. "Until he was dying," she said, so softly he could barely hear. "It sounds strange to even say such a thing. But I didn't find out he was sick until a few weeks before the wedding."

"His illness progressed that quickly?"

She shook her head. "Not exactly. He knew for over six months. He just didn't tell me."

Gabe's stomach sank. But he understood the other man's motives. The unrelenting guilt. The unwanted pity. Gabe knew those feelings well. "He was trying to protect you."

"So he said. But all I felt was…angry."

The way she spoke, the way her voice cracked and echoed with such heavy pain made Gabe wonder if it was the first time she'd admitted it out loud. Her next words confirmed it.

"Sorry," she said quietly. "I don't ever whine about this stuff to anyone. And I don't mean to criticize Tim. He was a good man. The best. When we met we clicked straight-away. We were friends for a few months, and then we fell in love. Even though it wasn't fireworks and insane chemistry and all that kind of thing."

"But it was what you wanted?" Gabe asked quietly, his heart pounding.

"Yes," she replied. "But then he was gone…and I was alone."

Gabe uncrossed his arms and grasped her hand, holding it tightly within his own. She didn't pull away. She didn't move. Silence stretched between them, and Gabe quickly realized that despite every intention he'd had, his attraction for Lauren had morphed into something more. Something that compelled him to offer comfort, despite the fact he had to fight the sudden umbrage coursing through his blood when she spoke about the man she'd loved. He wasn't sure how to feel about it. He wasn't sure he should even acknowledge it.

Thankfully, a few seconds later, she slid her hand from his and rested it in her lap. Gabe sucked in some air and tried to avoid thinking about how rattled he'd become by simply sitting beside her.

"You don't like being alone?"

"No," she replied. "Not really. I guess that's why I married James. And exactly why I shouldn't have." She took a long breath. "I wanted the wedding I was denied when Tim passed away."

"And did you get it?"

She nodded. "Yes. I had the same venue, the same guests and the same themed invitations." Her voice lowered. "I even wore the same dress I'd planned on wearing two years earlier."

The regret and pain in her voice was unmistakable, and Gabe remained silent.

"When I was engaged to Tim, I was so wrapped up in the idea of being married," she admitted on a heavy sigh. "Up to that point my life, my world, had been about the store and weddings and marriage and getting that happily ever after. I was so absorbed by that ideal, I didn't realize that he was sick…that he was *dying.* When he was gone, I felt lost…and I turned that grief into a kind of self-centered resentment. Afterward, I was so angry at Tim for not telling me he was ill. And then James came along, and he was handsome and charming and…and *healthy.* Suddenly, I glimpsed an opportunity to have everything I'd ever wanted."

Gabe's chest constricted. Any subconscious consideration he'd ever given to pursuing Lauren instantly disappeared. She was looking for a healthy, perfect mate. Not a cancer survivor. "But you still want that, right? Even though your marriage didn't work out?"

"I want my happily ever after," she confessed. "I want someone to curl up to at night. I want someone to make me coffee in the morning. And I really want children. It doesn't have to be wrapped up in physical attraction or even some great love story. In fact, I'd prefer it if it wasn't. It just has to be real…honest."

Her words cut him to the quick. "I hope you find what you're looking for," he said, and got to his feet. "I'll walk you home."

"That's okay," she said, and twisted her hands together. "I think I'll stay here for a while longer."

"Sure."

"And, Gabe," she said as he moved to turn away. "Thanks for listening. I needed a friend today."

He nodded. "Okay."

On the run back home, Gabe could think of only one thing. Lauren had needed a friend. The thing was, he didn't want to be her friend. He wanted more. Much more. And he couldn't have it.

Not with his past illness shadowing him like an albatross.

He was broken physically. She was broken emotionally.

And he was stunned to realize how damned lonely that suddenly made him feel.

Chapter Seven

With the benefit at the community center only hours away, Lauren really didn't have time to dwell on how she'd literally poured her heart out to Gabe just days earlier. It was better she didn't. Better…but almost impossible. Her dreams had been plagued by memories of all she'd lost. Of Tim. And more. She dreamed about Gabe, too. Dreams that kept her tossing and turning for hours. Dreams that made her wake up feeling lethargic and uneasy.

But she had to forget Gabe for the moment. Tonight was about the benefit. Her sister-in-law had done an amazing job organizing everything. It was a black-tie event, catered by the best restaurant in Bellandale. On the lawn outside the building, a huge marquee had been set up to accommodate a silent auction of items ranging from art to fashion and jewelry and a variety of vacation destinations. Under a separate marquee, there were tables and chairs set out for dinner, and a dance floor. There was also a band in place to provide entertainment. Inside the building, the runway was decorated and ready for the models to begin the fashion parade. Lauren stayed behind the scenes, ensuring hair and makeup were on track before the models slipped into their gowns. She'd also changed into a gown—a stunning strapless silk chiffon dress in pale champagne. It was shorter at the front, exposing her legs to just above the knees and then molded tightly over her bust and waist, flaring off down her hips in countless ruffled tiers that swished as she walked. She'd ordered the gown months ago and had never had occasion to wear it. Other than Cameron's recent wedding, it had been too long since she'd dressed up. Too long since she'd felt like making an effort. But tonight was special. The money raised would help several children's charities, including the Big Brothers Big Sisters program that was so important to her brother.

She hadn't seen Gabe but knew he had been there earlier, helping out with the marquees and the staging setup. Avoiding him was her best option. Avoiding him made it possible to function normally. Avoiding him was what she needed to do.

"Lauren?"

She was alone in the foyer of the community center. She'd been checking the stage and working out the music cues with the DJ, who'd since disappeared. The models were upstairs; so were Mary-Jayne and Cassie, as they'd volunteered to help with the gown changes.

Lauren turned on her high heels. Gabe stood by the door. He wore a suit, probably the same one he'd worn to her brother's wedding, and he looked so gorgeous, she had to swallow hard to keep a gasp from leaving her throat.

"Need any help here?" he asked.

Her brows came up. "Changed your mind about strutting on the catwalk?"

He laughed. "Not a chance. But I hear you roped my cousin, Scott, into it."

"Not me," she said, and placed her iPad onto the stage. "He's Mary-Jayne's brother-in-law, so she did all the convincing."

Gabe's gaze rolled over her. "You should be modeling tonight…you look beautiful."

She shrugged. "What? This old thing," she said, and laughed softly. "Thanks. You know, you don't look so bad yourself."

He grinned in that sexy, lopsided way she'd become used to. "So, need any help?" he asked again.

Lauren shook her head. "I don't think so. Grace has everything under control. She's *very* organized."

He chuckled. "You mean the consummate control freak? Yeah, I kinda figured."

Lauren relaxed her shoulders. "Well, it's good to have someone like that at the helm for this kind of event. Actually, I…"

"You…?" he prompted when her words trailed.

"Oh…nothing…I was just thinking how I should apologize for the other day."

"No need," he said quietly.

"It's only that I don't usually talk about those things. It probably sounded like I was blaming Tim for dying. I wasn't," Lauren assured him, unsure why she needed to explain herself. But she did. "Sometimes…sometimes the grief gets in the way."

His eyes darkened and he nodded as if he understood. It struck her as odd how he could do that. It was as though he knew, somehow, the depth and breadth of the pain in her heart.

"I remember how my mom was after my dad died," he said quietly. "I don't think she ever really recovered."

"Sometimes I feel like that," she said. "I feel as if the pain will never ease, that I'll be grieving him forever. And then…and then there are times when I can't remember the sound of his voice or the touch of his hand." She stopped, immediately embarrassed that she'd said so much. "I don't know why I do that," she admitted. "I don't know why I say this stuff to you. It's not like we're…" She stopped again as color rose up her neck. "The truth is, I'm very confused with how I should feel about you."

"You shouldn't be," he said softly. "We're neighbors. Friends. That's all."

If she hadn't believed he was saying it to put her at ease, Lauren might have been offended. She drew in a long breath then slowly let it out. "After what happened at my parents' house the other night, I think we're both kidding ourselves if we believe that."

"What *almost* happened," he reminded her. "There's no point getting worked up over something that didn't happen, is there?"

Annoyance traveled up her spine. He thought she was overreacting? Imagining more between them than there actually was? She pressed her lips together for a second and gave her growing irritation a chance to pass. It didn't. "Sure. You're right. There's no point. Now, if you don't mind, I have to finish getting ready for the parade."

He didn't budge. "You're angry?"

"I'm busy," she said hotly.

As she went to move past him, one of his arms came up to bar the doorway. "Wait a minute."

Lauren pressed her back against the doorjamb. He was close. Too close. "No. I have to—"

"I'm trying to make this easy for you," he said, cutting her off.

Lauren's gaze narrowed. "I think you're trying to make this easy for yourself."

He moved, and his other arm came up and trapped her in the doorway. "Maybe I am," he admitted softly. "Maybe I'm just crazy scared of you."

Scared? She wouldn't have pegged Gabe to be a man scared of anything. Especially not her. "I don't understand what you—"

"Sure you do," he said, and moved closer. "You feel it, too. Don't you know I can barely keep my hands off you?"

Lauren had to tilt her head to meet his gaze. "So it's just about attraction?" she managed to say in a whisper. "Just…sex."

Their faces were close, and his eyes looked even bluer. Lauren sucked in a shaky breath, feeling the heat rise between them against her will. She wanted to run. She wanted to stay. She wanted to lock the door and strip off her dress and tear the clothes from his body and fall down onto the carpet and make love with him over and over. She wanted him like she'd never wanted any man before.

"I wish it was," he said, and inched closer until their mouths were almost touching. "I wish I didn't like spending time with you. I wish I didn't keep thinking about you every damned minute I'm awake, and could stop dreaming about you every time I go to sleep."

The frustration in his voice was both fascinating and insulting. He wanted her but resented that he did. Thinking of his struggle ramped up her temperature. And it made her mad, too.

"Sorry for the inconvenience," she said with way more bravado than she actually felt.

"Are you?"

She glared, defiant. "You're an ass, Gabe. Right now I wish I'd never met you."

He didn't believe it. Nor did she. He stared at her mouth. Lauren knew he was going to kiss her. And she knew *he knew* she wanted him, too. There was no denying it. No way to hide the desire churning between them.

"My vow…" Her words trailed as she struggled for her good sense. "I promised myself I'd wait until—"

"Forget your vow," he said, cutting off her protest. "Just for right now, stop being so sensible."

A soft sound rattled in her throat, and Gabe drew her closer, wrapping his arms around her as he claimed her lips in a soft, seductive and excruciatingly sweet kiss. She went willingly, pressing her hands to his chest, and she felt his heart thunder beneath her palm. His mouth slanted over hers, teasing, asking and then gently taking. Lauren parted her lips a little as the pressure altered and the kiss deepened. Everything about his kiss, his touch, was mesmerizing, and Lauren's fingertips traveled up his chest and clutched his shoulders. He was solid and strong and everything her yearning body had been longing for. When he touched her bare skin where the dress dipped at the back, she instinctively pressed against him, wanting more, needing more. He gently explored her mouth with his tongue, drawing her deeper into his own, making her forget every coherent thought she possessed.

"Hey, Lauren, have you seen the—" Cassie's voice cut through the moment like a bucket of cold water. Gabe dragged his mouth from hers and released her just as Cassie came into view, emerging through the open doorway on the other side of the room. "Oh, gosh! Sorry."

Gabe stepped back, his breathing a little uneven. He stared at her, through her, into a place she never imagined she'd ever let any man into again. "Good luck with the show," he finally said to Lauren, and slipped through the doorway.

She watched him disappear then took a deep breath and faced her friend. Cassie's eyes were wide and curious. "Did you need me for something?"

Cassie grinned. "Ah, the models are getting restless. Especially Carmen Collins. I said you'd come upstairs and give them a pep talk before the parade starts."

"Sure," Lauren said, and grabbed her iPad.

Cassie cleared her throat. "Sorry about that…I didn't mean to interrupt. But the door was open and—"

Lauren raised a hand. "Please, don't apologize. I shouldn't have let it happen."

"Why not?" her friend asked. "You're single. He's single. You're awesome. He's gorgeous. You like him. He *clearly* likes you. You're friends. Neighbors. Sounds perfect."

Lauren's brows shot up. "Have you been watching *When Harry Met Sally* or *Love Actually* again?"

"Don't disregard old-fashioned romance so easily," Cassie said, and grinned.

"I don't," Lauren said. "But you know that's not what I'm looking for." *Gabe's not what I'm looking for.* But her lips still tingled. Her skin still felt hot where he'd touched her. Lauren ignored the feelings and smiled toward her friend. "Come on, let's get the models ready."

The fashion parade was a success. And Lauren was so busy for the next four hours that she didn't have a chance to think about Gabe. Or talk to him. Or remember his kiss.

The models did a splendid job, and by the time the last gown had been paraded up and down the catwalk and the entire cast returned for one encore lap, Lauren was exhausted. Her mother was on hand passing out business cards, and made several bridal-fitting appointments for the following week.

The silent auction was also a hit, and Lauren put a modest bid on a vacation up north and was outdone by her brother. Dinner was served underneath the huge marquee, and thankfully, she wasn't seated at Gabe's table. He was with Scott and Evie and some of Evie's family, while she spent the evening at a table with her brother and parents. Grace was a fabulous emcee and the auction raised thousands of much-needed dollars.

By the time dessert was served, several couples had taken to the dance floor. Lauren turned to Cassie, who was seated beside her, and immediately took note of her friend's pale complexion.

"You know, you don't look the best."

Cassie shrugged one shoulder and drank some water. "It's nothing. I'm a little tired. It's just baby hormones."

Lauren frowned. "Are you sure?"

"Positive."

She was about to get started on her dessert when she noticed someone standing behind her. Lauren knew instinctively it was Gabe. He lightly touched her bare shoulder, and the sensation set her skin on fire.

"Dance with me, Lauren?"

She looked up and met his gaze, ignoring how Cassie bumped her leg under the table. "I really shouldn't leave Cassie alone."

"I'll be fine," her friend, the traitor, assured them. "Go ahead. I insist."

He held out his hand. She took it and got to her feet. He led her to the dance floor and drew her into his arms. The woodsy scent of his cologne immediately assailed her senses and she drew in a shuddering breath. His broad shoulders seemed like such a safe haven, and she was almost tempted to imagine for one foolish moment that they were *her* safe place. Hers alone. Where no one could intrude. The place she'd been searching for. But that was a silly fantasy. She knew the rules. She'd made them. She wanted commitment and he didn't.

Like with everything he did, he moved with an easygoing confidence, and Lauren followed his lead when the music suddenly slowed to a ballad.

"You can dance," she said, and relaxed a little.

"I'm half Italian," he replied against her ear, as though that was all the explanation he needed to offer.

She couldn't help smiling. "Are you one of those men who is good at everything?"

He pulled back a little and Lauren looked up. His mouth twisted. "I guess I'll let you judge that for yourself."

His words wound up her spine like a seductive caress. Suddenly, she sensed they weren't talking about dancing. With the beat of the music between them and the memory of their kiss still hovering on her lips, Lauren was drawn into the depths of his dazzling blue eyes. As a lover, she imagined, he'd be passionate and tender and probably a whole lot of fun. Of course, she'd never know. But still…a little fantasy never hurt anyone.

"I'm sorry about before," he said, and held her close.

He regretted their kiss? "Sure. Forget about it. I have."

His breath sharpened. "I meant that it was hardly the place to start something like that. I hadn't planned on kissing you for the first time while two hundred people were within watching distance."

"So you *planned* on kissing me at some point?"

"After what happened at your brother's wedding, and all the time we've spent together since, I really don't think we could have avoided it."

Her brother's wedding? Was he referring to what he'd overheard her say to her friends? How she'd thought about him naked? Conceited jerk. "You're not irresistible, you know."

"I'm not?" he queried, and rested a hand on her hip.

Lauren could feel him smile as her forehead shadowed his chin. "No."

He chuckled. "So I guess that means you won't want me to kiss you again?"

Her belly fluttered. "Exactly. You have to remember that we want different things."

"That's right. You're still looking for Mr. Reliable?"

"Yes. And not Mr. Roll-in-the-Hay."

"Too bad for me, then," he said, still smiling. "Incidentally, have I told you how beautiful you look tonight?"

"You mentioned it."

Lauren couldn't help smiling. Their banter was flirty and harmless. Nothing more would happen unless she wanted it to. Gabe was charming and sexy, but he also oozed integrity. And she might have been tempted to sleep with him. If she didn't like him. But she did like him. A lot. Too much. And with her heart well and truly on the line, a night in his bed wouldn't be worth the risk, despite how much she wanted it.

"You're easily the most beautiful woman here tonight."

It was a nice line, even if she did think he was being overly generous. The song ended and Lauren pulled back a little. "Thank you for the dance."

"My pleasure."

As he walked her back to her table, Lauren was very aware that her mother was watching them. She could almost see Irene's mind working in overdrive. Cassie wasn't at the table, and she immediately asked after her friend.

"I think she went inside to collect her bag," her mother explained, and then patted the vacant seat, inviting Gabe to sit down.

"Be back in a minute," Lauren said, and walked from the marquee.

She found Cassie in the clubhouse upstairs, sitting on the small couch in the corner of the same room the models had used earlier as a dressing room. There were rails filled with gowns along one wall and shoes were scattered across the floor. Her friend looked up when she came through the doorway.

"Everything all right?" Lauren asked.

Cassie had her arms wrapped around her abdomen and grimaced. "It's nothing. I'm sure it's nothing."

Lauren's gaze moved to Cassie's thickened middle, and she walked across the room. "Are you in pain?"

"I'm fine," Cassie replied, and then clutched at her abdomen with both hands.

Suddenly, her friend looked the furthest from fine that Lauren had ever seen.

"What is it?" she asked and dropped beside the sofa. "What can I do?"

Cassie shook her head. "I don't know…I don't know what's wrong. It might be the baby."

There were tears in her friend's eyes, and Lauren quickly galvanized herself into action. Falling apart wouldn't help Cassie. "You need to see a doctor. I'll get Cameron to carry you into my car, and then I'll take you to the hospital."

She turned on her heels and headed for the door. Evie, Grace and Mary-Jayne were at the top of the stairs talking. "What is it?" Evie, the original earth mother, asked, and stepped toward the room.

"Cassie's ill."

The three women were in the room in seconds, and Evie touched Cassie's forehead with the back of her hand. "She has a temperature."

Cassie doubled over and gripped her belly. "It hurts so much. I'm scared. I don't want to lose my baby."

"It's okay, Cassie, you'll be fine. I'll ask Cameron to—"

"Grace, M.J.," Evie said quickly, and cut her off. "You'd better go and find Gabe."

Gabe?

Both women nodded and backed out of the room. Lauren waited until they'd disappeared and turned her attention back to Evie.

"Evie, I'm sure Cassie would prefer my brother to get her to the hospital."

Evie shook her head. "She needs a doctor. Right now."

"I agree. But I can't see how—"

"Lauren, Gabe *is* a doctor."

When Gabe entered the room, he spotted Lauren standing by the narrow sofa, comforting her friend. She looked at him, and his chest instantly tightened.

She knows....

Damn. But he'd known it was bound to come out eventually.

He wavered for a second before quickly turning his attention to the woman on the sofa. He asked Cassie a series of questions, such as how severe was the pain, was it constant or intermittent, was she spotting. And as Cassie quietly answered, he felt Lauren's gaze scorching the skin on the back of his neck.

It was hard to stay focused. Memories of that terrible night in the E.R. flooded his thoughts, and panic settled in his chest. *Just do it.* That night another pregnant woman had needed his help, and he'd failed her. But he couldn't fail Cassie. Not when Lauren was watching his every move. This was Lauren's closest friend. She'd be inconsolable if anything happened to her.

It was all the motivation Gabe needed to pull himself together. Instinct and experience quickly kicked in, and he asked Cassie to lie back on the sofa. He gently tilted her to her left side and asked questions about the position and intensity of the pain. He then quickly checked her abdomen. After a minute he spoke. "Okay, Cassie, I need you to relax and take a few deep breaths."

Cassie's eyes were wide with fear. "Do you think it's the baby? I don't want to lose my baby. I can't…I just can't… Not when Doug is so far—"

"You'll be okay. Both of you," he assured her and patted her arm. "We'll get you to the hospital." He turned toward Evie. "Call an ambulance. Tell them we have a patient in her second trimester with probable appendicitis."

Cassie let out a sob. "Do I need an operation?"

He nodded and squeezed her hand. "It'll be all right. You and your baby will be fine."

By the time the ambulance arrived, Gabe had Cassie prepared, and they were ready to go. Lauren volunteered to collect some of her friend's things from her home and meet them at the hospital. Gabe spoke to the paramedics as they carefully loaded Cassie onto the stretcher, and then he followed in his truck.

By the time he reached the hospital, Cassie was already being transferred to the surgical ward and was being prepped for an emergency appendectomy.

He'd been in the waiting room for about forty minutes when Lauren walked through the doorway. She'd changed into jeans and a blue shirt and carried a small overnight bag in one hand. She came to a halt when she spotted him.

"Is she in surgery?" she asked quietly.

Gabe got to his feet. "Yes. Is there someone we should call?"

"Only Doug, her boyfriend," she replied and placed the bag on the floor. "He's a soldier on tour, and I don't know how to contact him. I guess I could check the numbers stored in her phone. She doesn't have any real family of her own other than her grandfather, and he's in an aged-care home and suffers dementia. Doug has a brother in South Dakota, so I could call him if anything…I mean, if something…" Her eyes shadowed over. "If something goes wrong with Cassie or the baby."

"She'll pull through this," he said, fighting the urge to take Lauren into his arms.

"Do you know what's happening to her?" she asked coolly.

"You mean the surgery?" He drew in a breath. "They'll probably give her an epidural or spinal anesthesia as it's safer than general anesthesia."

"And the baby?"

"The safest time for a pregnant woman to have surgery

is during the second trimester. Cassie is seventeen weeks along, so she and the baby should be fine."

"Should?" Lauren's brows shot up. "Is that your professional opinion?"

It was an easy dig. "Yes."

She dropped into one of the vinyl chairs and sighed heavily. "I feel like such a fool."

"Lauren, I wanted to—"

"It's so obvious now," she said, and cut him off dismissively. "That first night when I picked up Jed and I got the splinter. And the old lady on the beach. And then when my dad sprained his ankle." She made a self-derisive sound. "How stupid I would have sounded to you, prattling on about how you'd make a good paramedic. What a great laugh you must have had at my expense."

Guilt hit him squarely between the shoulders. She had a way of making him want to tell her everything. "I wasn't laughing at you."

She met his gaze. "No? Then why all the secrecy?"

Gabe shrugged one shoulder. "It's a little complicated."

"Handy cop-out," she said, clearly unimpressed. "I thought we were…friends."

I don't know what we are. But he didn't say it. Because he didn't want to be her friend. He wanted to be more. And less. He wanted to take her to bed and make love to her over and over. He also wanted to stop thinking about her 24/7.

"I lost a patient," he said, and heard how the hollow words echoed around the small room. "So I took some time off."

Her expression seemed to soften a little. "Oh…" He could see her mind ticking over, working out a way to ask the next question. "Was it because of something you did wrong?"

"Indirectly," he replied and sat down opposite her. "It was around midnight and I'd worked ten hours straight.

I left the E.R. for a while, and when I was gone, a young woman was brought in. She was pregnant and hemorrhaging, and a second-year resident treated her. Unfortunately, the patient and her baby died."

She stared at him. "How awful."

"Yes," he said, remembering the event like it was yesterday. "It was a terrible tragedy. And one I will always regret."

"You said you weren't there at the time," she said, and frowned. "Which means it wasn't actually your fault."

Guilt pressed down. "It was. Even though I wasn't the only doctor in the E.R. that night, I was the attending physician on duty, and I should have been there when I was needed the most. A less experienced resident was forced to handle the situation and because of that, a woman and her child died."

It wasn't an easy truth to admit. And it sank low in his gut like a lead weight. It didn't matter how many times he replayed it over in his mind. He should have been there. His arrogance and self-importance had been the reason he'd failed the patient. The blame lay at his feet. And his alone. If he'd followed his own doctor's advice, he wouldn't have returned to work so quickly. Instead, he'd ignored everything and everyone and done it his own way. With fatal consequences.

Her eyes widened. "Were you sued?" she asked. "Was there some kind of malpractice suit? Is that why you quit being a doctor?"

Gabe's stomach tightened. *Quitter.* He'd called himself that over and over. But it had been easier leaving medicine than swallowing the guilt and regret he'd experienced every time he walked through the hospital corridors.

"There was an inquiry," he said, and ignored how much he wanted to haul her into his arms and feel the comfort of her touch, her kiss, her very soul. "The hospital reached a settlement with the woman's family. I wasn't implicated."

"And the other doctor?"

"She was suspended and left the hospital soon after."

Lauren twisted her hands in her lap. "Would you have saved the patient if you were there?"

Gabe took a deep breath. "I believe so."

"But you don't know for sure?"

He shrugged lightly. "Who can know anything for certain?"

Her gaze was unwavering. "But as a physician, wouldn't you be trained to deal with absolutes? Life or death. Saving a patient or *not* saving a patient. There are no shades of gray. It's one or the other, right?"

Her words cut deep, and he wanted to deny the truth in them. "I can't—"

"So tell me the truth," she said, and raised her brows. "Why did you really quit being a doctor?"

Chapter Eight

Lauren pushed aside the nagging voice in her head telling her to mind her own business. She couldn't. He was a mystery. A fascinating and infuriating enigma. She wanted to know more. She wanted to know everything.

Because...because she liked him. As hard as she'd tried *not* to, she was frantically drawn toward Gabe. The kiss they'd shared earlier that evening confirmed it. She hadn't planned on having feelings for him. But now that she had them, Lauren was curious to see where it might lead. He was attracted to her.... Perhaps it might turn into more than that. Maybe he'd reconsider his no-commitment position. Just as she'd begun to rethink her own plans for wanting a relationship based on things other than desire or love.

Love?

Oh...heavens. *I'm in big trouble.* The biggest. *Desiring. Liking. Loving.* Her once broken and tightly wrapped-up heart had somehow opened up again. And she'd let him in. Even if he didn't know it.

"I told you why," he said, and got to his feet.

Lauren watched him pace around the room. The tension in his shoulders belied the dismissive tone in his voice. "You told me you felt responsible for losing a patient that wasn't directly *your* patient. How is that your fault? How is that a reason to throw away your career?"

He stilled and stared at her for the longest time. Lauren knew she was way out of line. He would have been well within his rights to tell her to go to hell. But she knew he wouldn't. There was something in his expression that struck her deeply, a kind of uneasy vulnerability she was certain he never revealed. Not to anyone.

"Walking away from that life was one of the hardest things I've ever done," he said quietly. "I don't expect you or anyone else to understand my reasons."

Lauren drew in a shaky breath. "I'm sorry. I don't mean to sound like I'm judging you. I'm not," she assured him. "It's just that I…I guess I…care."

He didn't budge. His blue-eyed gaze was unwavering. Only the pulse in his cheek indicated that he understood her meaning.

"Then, don't," he said, and crossed his arms. "We've been through this before, Lauren. You want something else, something and someone who won't give you grief or pain or disappointment. That's not me. If you waste your heart on me, I'll break it," he said, his voice the only sound in the small room. "I won't mean to…I won't want to…but I will. I'm not the middle road you're looking for, Lauren."

Humiliation and pain clutched at her throat. But she wouldn't let him see it. "Sure. Whatever." She stood and grabbed the bag at her heels. "I'm going to check on Cassie."

She left the room as quickly as she could without looking as if she was on the run. Once she was back in the corridor, Lauren took several long gulps of air. Her nerves were rattled. Her heart felt heavy in her chest. She made her way to the cafeteria and stayed there for the next hour. She was allowed to see Cassie when she came out of surgery, but her friend was groggy and not very talkative. By the time Lauren headed home, it was past midnight.

Gabe's truck was not in the driveway, but she heard him return about twenty minutes after she did. She didn't want to think about him.

If you waste your heart on me, I'll break it....

It was warning enough. She'd already had one broken heart when she'd lost Tim. Lauren wasn't in the market for another. He'd made his feelings, or lack thereof, abundantly clear.

After a restless night where she stared at the ceiling until 3:00 a.m., on Sunday morning, Lauren headed off to the hospital. Seeing Cassie lifted her spirits.

"You look so much better today."

"Thanks," Cassie replied, and sighed.

Lauren placed the flowers she brought on the small bedside table. "When are you getting out of here?"

"Tomorrow," her friend replied. "The surgery went well, and the baby is okay."

There was a huge look of relief on Cassie's face, and Lauren smiled. "I'm so glad to hear it. Did you manage to reach Doug?"

She shook her head. "But I left a message."

Lauren could see her friend's despair. "I could try to call him. Or perhaps you should contact Tanner, and he could try to get in touch with his brother."

Cassie sighed. "I haven't spoken with Tanner since the last time he came home, which was a couple of years ago. Last I heard, he was still horse whispering in South Dakota. Doug will call me," Cassie said assuredly. "He will. I know it. I left a message and said it was important. He'll call me," she said again.

Lauren hoped so. Doug's reaction to the baby had been lukewarm at best, and she knew Cassie hadn't heard from him since.

"So," Cassie said, and grinned. "About Gabe. I think—"

"Let's not," Lauren pleaded.

"Indulge me. I'm the patient, remember?" she said, and patted her IV. "I'm guessing you didn't know he was really a doctor?" she asked. "And a pretty good one, by the way he reacted yesterday."

"I didn't know," she admitted.

"I guess he had his reasons for keeping it a secret."

Sure he did. He was emotionally unreliable and therefore unattainable. She'd get over him soon enough. For the moment, he was just a distraction, and her fledging feelings would recover. Lauren was sure of it.

It didn't help that the object of her distraction chose that moment to enter the room.

With Mary-Jayne at his side.

Of course, she knew he was acquainted with her friend. He was Scott's cousin, and Evie was Mary-Jayne's sister. Still…a little burst of resentment flooded her veins.

She met his gaze. He looked so good in jeans and a black polo shirt, and walked with the easy swagger she'd come to recognize as uniquely his. Lauren tried to smile and failed.

"Look who I found outside," Mary-Jayne announced with a big grin.

"Ladies," he said easily, and stepped into the room. "Am I interrupting?"

"Not at all," Cassie was quick to say. "I'm so glad you're here. I wanted to say thank you for yesterday."

Gabe shrugged. "No thanks necessary. As long as you're feeling better."

"Much," Cassie said, and beamed a smile. "Are they for me?" she asked of the bunch of flowers in his hand. When he nodded, her friend's smile broadened. "Daffodils are my favorite. Thank you."

Lauren fought back a surge of jealousy and drew in a deep breath. So he met Mary-Jayne in the hallway, and Cassie was a little starstruck? *It means nothing to me.* One kiss didn't amount to anything. She had no hold on him and shouldn't care that her friend might have a harmless crush on the man who'd potentially saved her and her baby. Besides, Cassie was devoted to Doug.

She hopped up from her chair and took the flowers, careful not to touch him. He said hello, and she managed to reply and then disappeared from the room in search of a vase.

"What's up with you?"

Lauren came to a halt and waited for Mary-Jayne to catch up. "Nothing."

Her friend grabbed her arm. "We met in the hall, that's all."

"I don't know what you mean."

Mary-Jayne's slanted brows rose up dramatically. "Sure you do. Dr. Gorgeous in there only has eyes for you."

"That's...that's ridiculous," Lauren spluttered. "We're just neighbors."

"You can deny it all you want, but I know what I see."

If you waste your heart on me, I'll break it....

His words came back again and sat like lead in her stomach.

The nurses happily obliged her with a vase, and when they returned to the room, Gabe was sitting beside Cassie's bed, and her friend's hand rested against his forearm. The scene looked ridiculously intimate. Resentment bubbled, and Lauren pushed it away quickly.

"I was just telling Gabe how grateful I am," Cassie said, and patted his arm one more time before she placed her hands in her lap and grinned at him. "Again."

He shrugged in a loose-shouldered way, but Lauren wasn't fooled. "I'll get going. Good to see you all."

Once he was gone, Cassie blew out a low whistle. "Boy, could you two be any more into each other and less inclined to admit it?"

Lauren colored wildly. "That's ridiculous."

"Yeah, right," Cassie said, and grinned. "I'm not the most observant person in the world, but even I can see that you have some serious feelings for him."

"And I think right about now is the time for me to leave," Lauren said gently, and grabbed her bag. She loved Cassie. But now wasn't the time to have a discussion about her feelings for Gabe. Feelings he'd made perfectly clear he didn't want and couldn't return.

"You know, I'm sure he had his reasons for not telling you he was a doctor," Cassie said, ignoring her indication to leave. "If that's what's bugging you. Some people don't like talking about themselves."

I know...I'm one of those people.

"I'll see you tomorrow. Make sure you let me know when you're leaving so I can pick you up. My mother is insisting you stay with her and my dad for a couple of days."

She hugged both her friends goodbye, and by the time Lauren arrived home, it was past midday. She got stuck into some cleaning and sorted through a few cupboards in the kitchen. It was menial, mind-numbing work that stopped her dwelling on other things. Or at least gave the impression. Later she did some admin work for the store and spent an hour in the backyard, weeding and repotting some herbs. Gabe wasn't home, and that suited her fine.

When she was done, it was well past five, and Lauren headed inside to clean up. She took a long bath and dried herself off before cozying into candy-pink shorts and matching tank shirt. She called Cassie and arranged to pick her friend up the following morning. With that done and the store organized for next day, Lauren ignored the idea of dinner and mooched around the cupboards for something sugary. Being a usually health-conscious woman, the pantry was bare of anything she could call junk, and she made do with a bag of organic dried apples.

She was sitting on the sofa, watching television with her knees propped up and dipping in for a third mouthful of apple when the doorbell rang. Lauren dropped the bag and headed up the hallway. When she opened the door and found Gabe standing on her porch, Lauren took a deep breath. He looked tired. As though he hadn't slept for twenty-four hours.

Well, too bad for him.

"What do you want?"

He had an envelope in his hand. "I got the estimate for the new fence. You said you wanted to—"

"Sure," she snapped, and held out her palm.

He placed the note in her hand. "You're under no obligation to pay half. The fence is my idea and I'd rather—"

"I said I'd pay for it," she said, cutting him off.

He threaded his fingers through his hair, and she couldn't stop thinking how mussed and sexy he looked. "Okay. If you're sure. Check out the estimate and if you agree, I'll get the contractor to start work in the next week or so."

Wonderful. A great high fence between them was exactly what she needed.

"I'll let you know," she said through tight teeth.

He nodded, shrugged a little and managed a smile. "I'll talk to you later."

He turned and took a few steps. Lauren wasn't even sure she'd spoken his name until he turned back to face her.

"Yes, Lauren?"

She pushed herself out of the doorway, and the light above her head flickered. He was a few feet away, but she could still make out every angle of his handsome face. A question burned on the edge of her tongue. Once she had her answer, she'd forget all about him.

"Why did you kiss me last night?"

The words seemed to echo around the garden, and the sound of insects chorused the silence that was suddenly between them. He took a couple of steps until he stood at the bottom of the stairs.

"If you think this is such a bad idea," she went on, getting stronger with each word. "If you believe there's nothing going on here…why did you even bother?"

He let out a heavy breath. "Because I had to know."

She shivered, even though it was warm outside. "You had to know what?"

"I had to know what your lips tasted like just one time."

Her shiver turned into a burn so hot, so rampant, Lauren thought she might pass out. She grabbed the screen door to support her weakened knees. No man had ever spoken those kinds of words to her. Tim had been sweet and a little shy. James's flirtatious nature had been obvious and overt. But Gabe was somewhere in between. Not shy. Not obvious. He was a seductive mix of reserve and calm, masculine confidence.

"And that's all it was? Just…just a single kiss?"

"What do you want me to say to you?" he shot back. "Do you need to hear that I want to kiss you again? That I want to make love to you? Of course I do. I've told you that before. I've never denied that I'm attracted to you, Lauren. You're…lovely. You're smart and beautiful and the more time I spend with you, the more I want you. But I can't give you the kind of commitment you want. Not…not right now."

Not right now?

What did that mean? A possibility popped into her head.

"Are you married?" she asked. "Or separated? Is that why you—"

"Of course not," he cut her off tersely.

"I had to ask," she said, and sighed. "You're so hot and cold, Gabe. You say one thing to me and then do another. I'm confused, and it seemed plausible."

"Well, it's not. I've had three semiserious relationships and a few one-night hookups. But I've never been married. I thought about it when I was with my last girlfriend, but we never got around to making any firm plans. In between, I was busy with my career."

"A career you then gave up?"

His expression turned blank. And she'd never wanted to read him more. But couldn't.

"I have to go," he said. "Good night."

She watched him leave and waited until he rounded the hedge before she returned inside and closed the door.

On Tuesday morning, Gabe noticed five missed calls on his cell. Two from his mom. Three from Aaron. His brother had then reverted to text messaging.

What's going on with you?

He sent one back when he arrived at work.

Nothing.

Aaron responded immediately.

Mom's worried about you. Call her.

Sure.

Gabe knew his one-word replies would irritate his interfering older brother.

Ten minutes later, he received another message.

Just do it, Gabriel.

Gabe ignored the deliberate use of his full name in his brother's message and stuffed the phone in his pocket. Well-meaning relatives with advice he could do without.

Megan arrived, and he plastered on a smile. It would be best if he kept his lousy mood to himself. No one needed to know that he was so wound up, so frustrated, he could barely string a sentence together. She had her older sister with her, a remarkably attractive girl in her mid-twenties whose name he couldn't recall but who looked him over with barely concealed approval.

The teen dumped a few books on his desk. "Thanks for these," she said chirpily.

"They helped?" he asked, and pulled another medical textbook from the desk drawer.

"Yeah," she replied. "I sit the nursing entrance exam next week."

Megan had borrowed a few of his old medical texts to help with her studying and hadn't asked why he had them. Not like Lauren would have. She'd ask. She'd want to know everything. And the damnable thing was, he'd want to tell her.

"Well, good luck," he replied. "Just drop it back when you're done with it."

Megan grabbed the book and sashayed out of the room, but her sibling hovered in the doorway, brows raised suggestively. In another time, he might have been tempted to ask for her number, to take her out and get her into bed after a few dates. But he wasn't interested in the pretty brunette with the wide smile. Gabe cursed to himself. He was so wrapped up in Lauren that nothing and no one else could shift his distraction. Nothing could ease the unexpected ache in his chest and the unrelenting tension cramping his shoulders. Kissing her had been like nothing on earth. And he wanted to feel that again. He wanted to take her in his arms and make love to her over and over and somehow forget he couldn't offer her the future she deserved.

The cell in his pocket vibrated again. It was another message from his brother.

You said you'd call. Get to it.

Gabe ignored the message and got back to work.

But by two he'd had enough, and since no one was booked in to use the upstairs rooms that afternoon, he locked up and headed home. Back at the house, there was painting to be done, drywall to replace and plaster, and the lawn needing mowing. But he ignored every chore. Instead, Gabe started unpacking some of the boxes in the spare room. The box marked Personal Items got his full attention. Gabe rummaged through the papers and soon found what he was looking for. His diploma of medicine. Still in the frame his mother had insisted upon. He looked at it, and shame hit him squarely behind the ribs.

Quitter...

Like he'd rarely allowed himself to think in the past eighteen months, Gabe wondered what would have happened had he stuck it out. What would have ensued had he ignored the guilt and regret tailing him around the hospital corridors? Would time have healed his fractured spirit? Would it have lessened the remorse? Would he have been able to practice medicine with the self-belief it demanded? Right now, he felt healthy. His last round of tests had come back clear. He was cancer-free.

Perhaps it was time to take his life back?

A first step. A giant step. But one he had to do if he was ever going to be truly happy.

Gabe shoved the diploma back in the box and resealed the lid.

He needed a run to clear his thoughts and stretch out the muscles in his back and limbs. He changed his clothes and headed out. When he returned, he showered, pulled on jeans and a T-shirt and grabbed his keys. If he wanted to take his career back, there was no time like the present to start.

He had a patient to check on.

Lauren sat on the edge of the bed in the spare room at her parents' house and chatted to her friend. It had been her bedroom once. Back then, the walls had been pink, and posters of rock gods had covered the walls. Since she'd moved out, her mother had redecorated in the more subtle tones of beige and white.

"This isn't necessary, you know, for me to stay in bed," Cassie insisted, and patted the mattress. "I feel fine."

"Good," Lauren said, and smiled. "But humor us all anyway, and rest for a few more days. You had surgery, and you need to take it easy."

Her friend had resisted coming to stay at her parents' home to recuperate. But since Lauren's dad was now retired, it meant that someone would be able to watch Cassie around the clock. Cassie meant a great deal to her family. She was like another daughter to her parents and as close to Lauren as a sister could be. She wasn't about to allow her friend to be alone.

"Okay," Cassie said, and grinned. "I'll be a model patient. As long as I know Mary-Jayne is looking after my dog, I'll relax."

"She is," Lauren told her. "I'll go and make some tea and bring it up with dinner."

"What time are your folks getting back?" Cassie asked.

Lauren checked her watch. It was just after seven. "Matka is at mah-jongg and will be back by nine-thirty, and Dad's helping Cameron supervise a bowling expedition with a group of kids from the Big Brothers program tonight. So you'll have to put up with me until then." She grinned. "But I promise I won't smother you."

Cassie chuckled. "Good. Um…I think I heard the doorbell. You might want to get that."

Lauren had heard it, too. She left the room and headed downstairs and was stunned to find Gabe on the other side of the door when she swung it back on its hinges.

"Oh…hi."

"Hey," he said, looking gorgeous beneath the overhead light. "I just stopped in to check on Cassie. I called her earlier, and she said she was here."

She did? Lauren needed to have a talk with her friend. She'd bet her boots Cassie had deliberately arranged this meeting. Her friend wasn't averse to a little matchmaking. Too bad it was pointless. "I didn't realize you had her number."

His mouth twitched. "I got it from Cameron."

"Oh, right. Well, she's upstairs…third room on the right."

Lauren turned on her heels and headed back down the hall. He could close the door. He could make his own way upstairs. She didn't want to spend any more time with him than was necessary. It was the only way she'd succeed in getting him out of her system.

But damn it if she couldn't hear them talking and laughing from her spot in the kitchen. The sound traveled down the stairway and managed to spur on her mounting jealousy and resentment.

She was about fifteen minutes into preparing dinner when she felt Gabe's presence in the room. Lauren looked up and noticed him in the doorway, arms crossed and one shoulder resting against the doorjamb.

"How does she seem?" she asked stiffly, slicing cucumber as though it was the enemy.

"Good," he replied, and pushed himself off the door frame. "Recovering well."

"So nice of you to make a house call." She turned toward the sink. "You know the way out."

But he stepped closer. "Is every conversation we have going to be a battle from now on?"

She harrumphed. "Probably. I should have stuck to my guns that night at my brother's wedding and ignored you. My life was simpler then."

"We couldn't ignore one another if we tried," he said, and was suddenly behind the counter.

"Oh, I can try," she assured him. "And I will."

He turned and rested his behind on the countertop. "I don't know what it is about you, Lauren… You make me think about things. You have a way of getting under my skin."

"Like a burr?" She wasn't going to be nice to him. Lauren finished the salad and soup she'd prepared for Cassie and placed it on a tray. "I'm going to take this upstairs. When I come back down, I'd prefer it if you weren't here."

By the time she was upstairs, her knees were wobbling so much she had to quickly place the tray on the bed. She looked at her smiling friend.

"I figure this is your doing?"

Cassie shrugged innocently. "Maybe a little. I thought it was sweet that he wanted to make sure I was okay. He's very nice. You shouldn't give up so easily."

"I'm not giving up," she said, and propped another pillow behind her friend. "I'm just not going to waste time dreaming about something that will never happen."

She lingered in the room for a few more minutes, giving Gabe plenty of time to leave. But when she returned to the kitchen, he was still there, still standing by the counter.

She heard his phone buzz.

"I think you just missed a call."

"I didn't miss it," he said, and shrugged a shoulder. "I didn't answer it."

"Girl trouble?" she inquired, hurting all over just thinking about it.

He half smiled, as though he knew she hated imagining him with some faceless woman. "My mom," he explained. "Or my brother Aaron…checking up on me."

"Do you need to be checked on?"

"They seem to think so," he said, and pushed himself off the counter.

"Well, I guess it's natural for a mother to worry when one of her kids lives on the other side of the world. I don't imagine my mother would be any different. She likes that Cameron and I both live close by. It makes her feel as though everything is right in her world. I don't think it matters how old we get…she just needs to know we're safe and happy, because that makes *her* feel safe and happy."

His gaze darkened, and he looked at her oddly. "You know, I don't think I've ever thought about it quite like that before."

Lauren's knees wobbled again. She was trying hard to stay strong and ignore him. But staring into Gabe's brilliant blue eyes wasn't helping. Hearing the seductive tone of his voice wasn't helping, either.

She shrugged. "I don't think we ever fully understand how hard it is for parents to let us live our own lives. They want to protect us from being hurt and from enduring life's disappointments. Even though it can sometimes feel like being wrapped in cotton wool and then be overprotected."

"Is that what happened to you?" he asked quietly. "After Tim died?"

Lauren nodded. "And again when my marriage ended. With Tim… I think because it happened so quickly, I was in shock. One moment I was planning my wedding, the next I was dressed in black and standing beside his grave. There was no time to prepare…to say goodbye. I was so mad at him for shutting me out that I didn't spend time telling him the important things…like how much he meant to me and how much I would miss him."

"Maybe he didn't want to hear that," Gabe said, his voice soft and husky. "Maybe he couldn't have borne your sadness, and it was all he could do to control what was happening to him. Maybe he didn't want your pity and didn't want to witness your grief and your tears. And perhaps you being mad at him for shutting you out…well, maybe that made him feel *normal*…as though he wasn't defined by his illness. Like he was still the person you loved, still a healthy and strong man and not only a terminally ill cancer patient."

Lauren's throat burned. The raw truth in his words cut deep. Everything Gabe said made sense. Somehow, he knew how to reach into the depths of her soul.

She blinked to avoid the tears that threatened to spill. "Tim never got angry with me for reacting like I did. But *I* was angry with me. For a week I walked around in a daze. All I could think was how my wedding plans were ruined. I was so selfish."

"No," Gabe said gently. "Despair has many faces, Lauren. Focusing on your wedding plans was simply a coping mechanism. It's not so hard to understand."

She nodded, agreeing with him with her heart, even though her head told her to forget him and find someone who truly wanted her back. "I guess you would have seen grief like that before. I mean, dealing with patients and their families."

"I… Yes," he said quietly. "Of course."

His unwavering gaze was deeply intense and made Lauren's heart race. Heat and awareness coiled through the space between them, somehow drawing them closer, even though they were two feet apart. They weren't touching, but Lauren *felt* his presence like a lover's caress.

Suddenly, the middle road she'd been longing for seemed passionless and bland.

And the man in front of her was the one man she wanted for the rest of her life.

Chapter Nine

"Has Gabe gone home?"

Lauren picked up the tray from Cassie's bedside table and ignored the way her heart beat faster simply at the mention of his name. He'd left with the barest of goodbyes, and she'd breathed a sigh of immense relief once he'd walked out the door.

"Yes," she replied. "But he said he'd check on you in a couple of days."

"That's sweet of him," Cassie said, and grinned. "Although I'm not sure he's actually dropping by to see me."

Lauren frowned. "You're as obvious as my mother."

Her friend began ticking off his attributes on her fingers. "He's handsome, charming, single and a doctor…what more do you need?"

Commitment and love…

She wanted exactly what she'd been saying she didn't want. And neither she was likely to get from Gabe Vitali.

"He doesn't want a relationship. He's commitmentphobic." Lauren sighed heavily. "Looks, charm and medical degree aside, he's emotionally unavailable."

"I'm not so sure," Cassie said. "Maybe he's just been unlucky in love and is wary of getting close to someone again."

That's not it.

But there *was* something...some reason why he pulled back and made it clear he wanted to avoid commitment. And Lauren was sure it had nothing to do with a failed relationship. It was something else...something deeper. Something that was somehow wrapped up in the patient he lost, his decision to quit being a doctor and then choosing to move his life to Crystal Point.

"Perhaps," she said, and shrugged. "It doesn't matter anyway. He's not for me."

"Settling isn't the answer," Cassie said quietly. "I know you have this idea that you want an uncomplicated, painless relationship...but relationships *are* complicated. And they can be painful and messy. Just because things ended so tragically with Tim and then you married a man you didn't love, it doesn't mean you have to make do with ordinary."

But ordinary won't break my heart.

And Gabe would.

Hadn't he already told her as much?

"I don't believe in the fairy tale anymore," she said, and knew it was a lie. "You should rest. My folks will be home soon. I'll see you tomorrow."

She headed downstairs, and once the dishes had been done, Lauren made her way to the front living room. As always, the photographs on the mantel drew her closer. Dear Tim, she thought as she looked at his picture with a familiar sadness. Was Gabe right? Had Tim kept his illness a secret so she wouldn't pity him...so he wouldn't have to deal with her thinking of him as sick? As somehow less than a man? In the years since his death, she'd thought of his reasons countless times and always ended up believing he'd wanted to protect her from the inevitable grief and loss. But what if it was more than that? Had she been so blind? So self-centered, she hadn't considered that Tim was protecting himself, too?

When her mother arrived home, she was still sitting in the front room, still thinking about the man she'd loved and lost. And she thought about Gabe, too...and wondered how she'd managed to develop feelings for someone she hardly knew. It was different to the way she'd fallen for James. Her ex-husband hadn't made her think...want...need. He hadn't stirred her mind and body the way Gabe did. James had been an escape from the terrible anguish of losing Tim. Nothing more. She was ashamed to admit it to herself. He'd deserved better. And so had she.

By the time she returned to her house, showered and changed and rolled into bed, it was past ten. There were lights on next door, and she wondered if Gabe was up late working on the renovations in the house. Once the work was done, she was sure he'd sell the place. What then? Would they see one another as infrequently as they had before he'd moved next door?

Sleep eluded her, and after staring at the shadows bouncing off the ceiling for most of the night, Lauren snatched a few restless hours before she pulled herself out of bed at seven, dressed and drove into Bellandale. She swapped her car for the store's van and then headed back to Crystal Point Surf Club & Community Center to collect the gowns that had been left there after the benefit. She'd borrowed Cameron's key and hoped she could get the task done before Gabe arrived for work.

No such luck.

He turned up just as she was trekking the third armload of gowns down the stairs.

He stood at the bottom of the stairway. "Need some help?"

Lauren brushed past him and clutched the gowns. "No, thank you," she said as she stomped through the doorway and loaded the dresses neatly into the back of the van. When she returned inside, he was still by the stairs.

"How did you get in?" he asked.

"I borrowed my brother's keys. I didn't think it would be a big deal."

"It's not," he replied, and followed her up the stairs. "Stop being stubborn and let me help you."

Lauren glared at him. "I'm not stubborn."

He raised one dark brow. "Yeah, right," he said, and held out his arms. "Give me what needs to be taken downstairs."

Lauren's mouth tightened, but she did as he asked. It only took another twenty minutes to get everything in the van, including the three metal hanging rails he quickly pulled apart and loaded in the back of the vehicle.

"Thanks. I appreciate your help," she said as she closed the back door to the van.

"No problem. Do you want me to follow you and carry this stuff back into your store?"

"Ah, no," she said quickly. "My mother will be there to help. Thanks again."

"Do you like working with your mom?" he asked unexpectedly, and followed her around to the driver's door. "And running your own business?"

"It's what I've always done," she replied.

"Which isn't exactly an answer, is it?"

Lauren shrugged. "My mother opened the store twenty-five years ago. I took over when I graduated from business college. Do I like it?" She sighed deeply. "It's all I know. I like it well enough."

But his glittering gaze saw straight through her facade. "Sometimes it makes you unhappy."

"Some days," she admitted. "Other days it's not so bad. When I was younger, I guess I was wrapped up in the romance of it all. The gowns…the tradition… Back then it seemed to have a purpose. Now…not so much."

Because Tim died, and I discovered that not everyone gets their happy ending….

His phone beeped, and he ignored it like he had before. Lauren's eyes widened. "So did you end up calling your mother and brother?"

Gabe stared at her for a second and then grinned a little. "Not yet."

Lauren grunted under her breath. "I didn't peg you to be the inconsiderate type."

"Inconsiderate?" He repeated the word and frowned. "I'm not."

"You might want to remind your family of that the next time you speak with them," she said, and smiled ultra-sweetly. "If you ever get around to it."

Lauren watched as his resentment grew. To his credit, he kept a lid on his rising annoyance. She wasn't usually driven to lecture someone she hardly knew. He'd accused her of getting under his skin…. The problem was, he did exactly the same thing to her.

And no one had ever made her so reactive.

Gabe challenged her thoughts and ideals. He made her really *think* about things. And he had, in a matter of weeks, forced her out of the self-absorbed routine she'd disguised as her life. Even her plans to find someone to share her life with had been tainted with the memories of all she'd lost. But who was she kidding? Settling for a passionless, loveless relationship was no way to live. And in her heart, she knew she could never honor Tim by settling for less.

Looking at Gabe, it was easy to get lost in his blue eyes and handsome face…but there was so much more to him than that. And that was what she found so hard to resist. He was charming, certainly. And sexy. But he was also kind and generous, and despite her silly accusation, clearly considerate and helpful. Hadn't he come to her aid countless times? Like when she was forced to look after Jed. Or how he'd helped her dad after his fall. And he'd shown incredible concern for Cassie and her baby. There was something elementally *good* about Gabe. And that was what she was so attracted to. That was why her heart pounded whenever he was close.

That's why I've fallen in love with him....

She shivered, even though the breeze was warm.

Oh, God...it's true.

"Lauren?" His voice seemed to whisper on the wind. "Are you all right?"

She nodded, shell-shocked at the unexpected intensity of her feelings. How ironic that she'd done exactly the opposite of what she'd planned after her divorce. She'd derided attraction and desire and now found herself craving Gabe's touch more than she had ever wanted any man before. And love? She'd put it out of her head, too. Because it scared her so much to want love again.

"I'm…I'm fine," she stammered. "I have to go."

Another car pulled up just as she opened the door to the van. Two people emerged from the small yellow car. Megan and another equally pretty and sporty-looking woman in her mid-twenties. It took Lauren two seconds to notice how the other woman looked at Gabe as if she wanted to devour him.

"You could stay," he said with a grin as they approached. "For protection."

Lauren's mouth twisted. "I'm sure you're capable of protecting yourself."

"That's Megan's older sister," he explained.

"That's a woman with her eye on the prize," Lauren

said as she hopped into the van and drove off, drowning in jealousy.

And feeling like the biggest fool of all time.

It took Gabe twenty minutes to extract himself from the clutches of Megan's persistent sibling. She reminded him that her name was Cara and asked for his number. He avoided answering her, pleading a pile of urgent paperwork on his desk.

Once she left and Megan headed to the beach for her patrol shift, Gabe wrote a list of things he needed to do for the day.

Thing number one: stop thinking about Lauren.

Thing number two: stop dreaming about Lauren.

He snatched a glance at his cell phone on the desk. He really should call his mother. And Aaron. But he just wasn't in the mood to talk. Or to be talked *at.* His mom would know something was up. She'd dig and dig until he admitted that he'd met someone. That he *liked* someone. And that his beautiful next-door neighbor was driving him crazy.

Then Claire Vitali would want to know everything.

And he had nothing to say.

Lauren was broken emotionally. He was broken physically. It could never work. The more he knew her, the more it served to strengthen his resolve. Even though he could have easily talked himself into it. The way she looked at him, the way she'd responded to his kiss at the benefit, the way she argued and contradicted him at every opportunity… It was like pouring gasoline on a bonfire. Everything about Lauren drew him in. Her face, her body, the sweet floral scent of her skin…every part of her connected with every part of him.

Which was as inconvenient as hell.

Even more inconvenient was the sight of Megan's sister standing on his doorstep at seven o'clock that evening. He'd been home for several hours. He'd changed and gone for a run, then returned home to work on painting one of the guest rooms. He'd just emerged from showering and pulling on fresh jeans and a T-shirt when the tall brunette had arrived on his doorstep clutching the textbook he'd loaned to Megan. Returning the book had been her excuse for dropping by, and he made a mental note to query Megan about handing out his address.

His visitor managed to wheedle her way up the hall and into the front living room, and Gabe was just about all out of patience when he heard another knock on his front door. Gabe told Cara to stay put and headed up the hallway.

Lauren stood beneath the porch light. In a long floral skirt and pale blue T-shirt she almost stole his breath. Gabe quickly pulled himself together.

"Hey…what's up?" he asked.

She held out an envelope. "The estimate for the fence looks reasonable. There's a check in there with my half of the initial payment."

"Thanks for getting back to me," he said quietly and took the note. "I'll let the contractor know he can start as soon as possible."

She shrugged, and the T-shirt slipped off her shoulder a little. "Okay."

The sight of her bare skin heated his blood, and he swallowed hard. "If you like, I'll—"

"Gabe?"

Great.

His unwelcome guest chose that moment to come sauntering down the hall, hips swaying, calling his name. He saw Lauren's expression tighten. And as stupid as he knew it was, he didn't want her thinking he was entertaining some random woman in his home.

"Sorry," she said, breathing harder than usual. "I didn't realize you had company."

"I don't," he said, and her brows shot up instantly. It was stupid. They weren't together. They weren't dating. They weren't sleeping together.

One kiss…that was all it was…

And even though there was nothing going on with the unwanted woman in his hallway, Gabe still felt like an unfaithful jerk.

"You can do what you like," Lauren shot back, and swiveled on her heels.

She quickly disappeared down the garden, and Gabe let out an impatient sigh.

"You have to go," he said to the woman now at his side. "Good night."

Minutes later, after quickly packing Cara into her car and waving her off, Gabe walked around the hedge and tapped on Lauren's door. The screen was locked, but the door was open, and he could hear her banging pots in the kitchen.

He called her name. She responded with more banging. She was mad. And she was jealous. The notion made him grin stupidly.

"Lauren, come out here and talk to me."

"Go away."

"Not until you let me explain."

"I don't want to hear it," she said, and banged some more.

Gabe expelled a heavy breath and leaned against the door. "She was just returning a book I loaned to—"

"Yeah, I'm sure it's her reading skills that you like," she said loudly, cutting him off.

"I don't like anything about her," he said, and sighed. "I hardly know her. She was returning a book I loaned to her sister. Now, will you come to the door so we can stop yelling?"

Pots banged again. "I said, go away."

Exasperated, Gabe straightened his back. "I hardly know her, like I said. You've no reason to be jealous."

The banging stopped. Gabe waited, but she didn't come to the door. The sudden silence was almost eerie. After a few minutes, he gave up and headed down the steps. He'd been back in his own house for about ten minutes when he heard the sharp rap on his front door. Lauren stood on the other side of the screen, cheeks ablaze, chest heaving.

He pushed the screen back and watched, fascinated and suddenly wholly aroused as she glared at him, hands planted on her hips.

"I. Am. Not. Jealous."

Oh, yeah, she was.

Gabe raised a brow. "No?"

Lauren pulled the screen out of his grasp and held it back farther. "No."

"I think you are."

"And I think you're an egotistical jerk," she shot back. "I've no interest in anything you do."

Every feeling, every ounce of desire he had for her rose up, and in that moment, Gabe was powerless to do anything other than smile broadly. "Then why are you on my doorstep?"

Lauren's resolve crumbled a little. Damn him. She shouldn't have let her temper get the better of her. Coming to his door was crazy thinking. "Because…we're arguing and I—"

"No, we're not," he said, and reached out to take her hand. "I think…" He paused, looking deep into her eyes. "I think this is more like foreplay than an argument."

Lauren flushed and pulled back. "Of all the conceited—"

"Let's not have this discussion on the doorstep, okay?" he said as he turned and walked down the hall.

Lauren stayed where she was for a moment. *I should turn around and go home.*

I really should.

Instead, she crossed the threshold, closed the door and followed him into the living room. When she entered the room, she saw he was standing by the sofa. And he was smiling. Lauren wasn't sure if she wanted to slug him or kiss him.

"Come here," he said softly.

She took a deep breath and stepped toward him. "You are the most—"

"That woman who was here earlier is Megan's sister, Cara. She returned a book I loaned to Megan," he said, cutting her off again. "Megan is sitting a nurse's entrance exam next week," he said quietly, cutting her off again. "And that's all. She may have had another motive, but I'm *not* interested in her…okay?"

Her heart raced.

Oh, sweet heaven. She tried to ignore the heat that traveled across her skin as well as the seductive sound of his voice. But failed. Every sense she possessed was on high alert.

"I shouldn't care what you do…" When he grasped her hand, she crumbled some more. "Gabe…I…I just…"

He lightly shrugged his magnificent shoulders and gently urged her closer until there was barely a whisper of space between them. "I can't fight this anymore," he admitted hoarsely. "I want to. I know I need to, for your sake, because you deserve more than the empty words of a future I simply can't promise you. And I've really tried to stop wanting you…but I can't."

There was such raw passion in his words, and Lauren's breath was sucked from her lungs. She moved closer and they touched, chest against breast. Gabe wound his arms around her, urging her against him.

"I've tried, too," she said through a sigh.

Gabe touched her face and kept his gaze connected with hers as he rubbed his thumb gently across her chin. Lauren tilted her head back and smiled. In all her life, she'd never experienced anything like the sensation of being near Gabe, or his soft, mesmerizing touch.

Their mouths met, and Lauren's head spun. His kiss was like nothing on earth. His hands were warm against her back, his mouth gentle as he coaxed a response. Lauren gave it willingly. She would give him anything. Everything. And the revelation rocked her through to the core.

I am so in love with him. Completely, irrevocably, crazily.

She opened her mouth, tasted his tongue against her own, felt a rush of pleasure coil up her spine and across her skin. She whispered his name against his lips, and Gabe urged her closer. Lauren sighed deeply from that way-down place, which was fueled by need and longing and a powerful rush of desire.

"I want to make love to you," he whispered raggedly, moving his mouth from her lips to her cheek. "So much."

Lauren moaned, all resistance gone. *Just for tonight. I can have this. I can have him. I can pretend it will work out.* "I want that, too."

Gabe grasped her hand and led her down the hall and into his bedroom. He released her and flicked on the bedside lamp. The big bed was covered in a patterned blue quilt, and she swallowed hard as nerves spectacularly set in. His gaze never left her, and she felt the heat of his gaze through to her bones.

"So…here we are."

Lauren didn't move. "Here we are." She managed a tiny smile. "I'm a little nervous."

"You don't need to be."

There was desire and passion and tenderness in his eyes. He wouldn't rush her. He wouldn't coerce or manipulate her with empty words. He opened the bedside drawer, found a condom and dropped the packet on the mattress, and even that made her long for him all the more. He was sweet and considerate. He was everything she wanted.

"Lauren, come here."

She moved toward him and stopped about a foot away. Desire and heat swept through the room with seductive force. She wished she'd had a chance to change into something sexy and filmy. The skirt and T-shirt seemed way too ordinary.

She rested her hands against his chest and then trailed down to the hem of his shirt. "Take this off," she said boldly, and saw him smile.

Gabe pulled the shirt over his head and dropped it on the floor. "Better?"

Lauren nodded. "Much," she replied, and traced her fingertips down the middle of his bare chest and twirled her fingers through the dark hair. She noticed a faded crisscross of small scars near the curve of his armpit and instinctively reached up to outline a finger along the skin there.

He tensed instantly.

"What's this from?" she asked softly.

"It's…nothing," he replied, equally as quiet. "Forget about it."

"Gabe, I—"

"Shh," he said, and placed two fingers gently against her lips. "Later. Right now, let's forget about the past. Let's be in *this* moment."

Lauren's eyes widened as she slid out of her sandals. She liked the sound of that. She dropped her hands and deliberately took her time as she gripped the edge of the T-shirt and slowly lifted it up and over her shoulders. Then she tossed it onto the foot of the bed and inhaled deeply. The white lace bra she wore was modest, but beneath the smoldering brilliance of Gabe's blue eyes, she felt as though it was the sexiest piece of underwear on the entire planet.

Heat charged between them, and she pushed past any lingering insecurity. He wanted her. That kind of look couldn't be faked. He had no agenda. She sucked in a breath and spoke. "Your turn."

He quickly flipped off his shoes and grinned in such a sexy way, her legs trembled. "Back to you."

She sucked in more air, willed strength into her knees as she unzipped her skirt and hooked her thumbs into the waistband. She heard his breath catch, saw the hot desire in his eyes. And waited. Took a breath. Then met his gaze head-on and slowly stripped the garment over her hips. She pushed it aside with her foot and rounded out her shoulders. Her briefs were white cotton and lace high-cuts. Not nearly seductive enough. Not the kind that aroused desire. Except Gabe looked hotly aroused, and it made her want him all the more.

"So," Lauren said, way more steadily than she felt. "You?"

Gabe's hands stilled on his belt, and his smile was pure sexual heat. He released the buckle and slid the belt from the loops. "Done," he said, and dropped it on the carpet. "Next?"

At a distinct disadvantage, Lauren smiled and backed up toward the bed. She reached around and slowly unclipped her bra, then eased herself from the shoulder straps and pulled the garment free. The bra fell from her fingertips and landed at her feet.

He looked at her and let out a ragged groan. Her nipples peaked instantly. "Okay…enough."

Lauren wondered what he meant for a microsecond, wondered if he found her lacking. But then he was in front of her, reaching for her, wrapping his arms around her. His mouth hovered over her eager lips, waiting to claim, waiting for her surrender. She gave it, completely and wholly and pressed against his chest. He captured her mouth in a searing kiss and gently fisted a handful of her hair. There was no force, no reticence, only need and desire and the realization it was the perfect kiss. The perfect moment. And all other kisses were quickly forgotten.

They tumbled onto the bed, mouths still together, hands moving over skin. He cupped one breast, and Lauren moaned low in the throat. His fingers were firm yet gentle, his mouth hot against her as he trailed down her cheeks, to her neck and then lower still, to where she ached for his touch. There was magic in his hands and mouth, and Lauren experienced a surge of feeling so intense, so deep, that it warmed her through to her bones. For the first time in forever, she was exactly where she wanted to be, and she sighed heavily as she shook in his arms.

"What is it?" Gabe asked and looked up. "Are you okay?"

Lauren smiled and touched his face. "I'm fine. Don't stop," she pleaded, and grabbed his shoulders.

"I have no intention of stopping," he said, and kissed her hungrily.

It was what she wanted to hear. What she needed to hear. The kissing went on, soft and hard, slow and fast, mesmerizing and wholly arousing. Lauren pushed against him, felt the abrasive denim rub across her thighs. "You're still wearing too many clothes," she whispered, and placed a hand on the band of his jeans.

He smiled against her skin. "You, too," he said, and pushed her briefs over her hips in one smooth movement. The way Gabe looked at her was real and heady and made her spin.

Naked and without inhibitions, Lauren curved against

him and popped the top button on his jeans. She tugged at the zipper and laughed delightfully when he rolled her over and kissed her again.

"Please," she begged softly, and grabbed the waistband again.

"Relax, Lauren," he said, and curved a hand down her back and over her hip. "There's no need to hurry."

He was wrong. There was a need to hurry. She wanted him desperately. She wanted to feel his skin against her, taste his kiss over and over and have the weight of his strong body above her, inside her. It was a need unlike any Lauren had ever known. "I want you," she said against his mouth. "Now."

"Soon," he promised, and moved his hand between them, stroking her where she longed to be touched with skillful, gentle intimacy. Tremors fluttered across her skin, and Lauren responded instantly. The heat grew as her breath quickened, and she let herself go, up and up, shaken by a white-hot, incandescent pleasure so intense, she could barely draw breath. She'd forgotten that feeling—forgotten how good it felt to experience such powerful release. Gabe kissed her again and smothered her soft groans and whispered pleas.

She laid her hands on his jeans and felt him hard against the denim. "You really are wearing too many clothes."

He nodded and swung his legs off the mattress. As he watched her, the connection between them shimmered. Then he smiled that lovely smile she longed for more than any other. Seconds later, his remaining clothes were off, and once the condom was in place, he was beside her on the big bed. They kissed again, long, hot kisses, tongues dancing together, skin on skin. She touched him as she'd wanted to do for weeks—his thighs, his arms, his back. His smooth skin burned beneath her fingertips, and when his mouth found her breast and he gently toyed with the nipple, she arched her spine off the bed. He moved above her and Lauren lay back, urging him closer. She wrapped her arms around his strong shoulders, opened herself for him and waited for that moment. He rested on his elbows, hovered above her and looked into her face with scorching intimacy.

The moment was achingly sweet and unbelievably erotic at the same time.

He nudged against her until finally they were together. Lauren sighed deep in her throat. She loved the feel of him. Being with Gabe felt right. He didn't move for a moment, didn't do anything other than stare deeply into her eyes.

"You're so beautiful, you take my breath away," he said softly.

It was a lovely, romantic notion, and Lauren absorbed his words right though to her heart. No one had ever spoken to her with such quiet tenderness. She blinked back tears and shuddered, feeling every part of him against her in a way she'd never experienced before.

He moved, and she went with him, up and over into that place where only they existed.

Chapter Ten

Gabe stirred, stretched out and took a deep breath. The soft scent of flowers played around in his memory. Lauren. He snaked an arm across the sheets, expecting to find her asleep beside him. But he was alone.

The digital clock on the bedside table read 4:00 a.m. A thin sliver of streetlight shone through a gap in the curtains, and he heard a dog barking in the distance.

Gabe swung off the bed, grabbed his briefs and jeans from the floor and pulled them on. He left the bedroom, padded down the hall and found Lauren in the kitchen, sitting at the table with a mug between her hands. Her tousled hair and T-shirt was enough to stir his blood. He could easily make love to her again. And again. And every day for the rest of his life.

Whoa.

He couldn't promise that. What if he didn't have a rest of his life? Only now. This moment. If his illness returned, he wasn't about to drag Lauren into what that would mean.

She'd been through enough. She already buried the one man she'd loved. How could he do that to her again?

She looked up when he entered the room and smiled. "Hi. Tea?" she offered, and tapped the mug.

"Sure," Gabe said, even though he didn't really care for the stuff. He watched her get up, move around the counter and flick on the kettle. "Couldn't sleep?" he asked.

She shook her head and grabbed a mug from the cupboard. "Not really. Sorry if I woke you."

Gabe walked into the galley. "Everything all right?"

"Sure," she said quietly, and popped a tea bag into the mug. "I'm not a sound sleeper. Comes from living alone, I guess."

"You're not alone now, though."

The kettle dinged, and she poured the water. "For the moment…no."

An odd twitch caught him behind the ribs. He stepped closer and touched her arm. "Lauren, forget the tea."

She inhaled and turned toward him. "You mean you want to have *the* talk? Before you skedaddle me back home?"

There was a familiar spark in her eyes, and it was a look he knew. She was annoyed with him. "I mean, forget the tea and come back to bed."

She twisted back to the sink. "I thought we'd have—"

"A postmortem?" He reached across and touched her cheek. Unable to help himself, he smiled. "Let's not do that. You think too much."

"I don't," she insisted. "And it's insensitive of you to laugh at me."

Gabe gathered her in his arms, kissed her forehead and spoke gently. "You're being a little ridiculous, you know that?"

She sagged against his chest, and he tightened his grip. "I know. I'm just not used to feeling like this. I'm not used to *doing* this. We hardly know one another. I was looking for something else, and then you move in next door with your blue eyes and nice smile and I was…I was…"

He pulled back and softly grasped her chin. "You were what?"

She let out a long breath. "Done for."

Gabe's insides contracted. What was she saying? That it was more than a developing friendship and blinding physical attraction? That she loved him?

Sure, he had feelings for Lauren. A lot of feelings. And making love with her had been out of this world. But falling in love wasn't part of his plan. Hell, it was out of the question at the moment. Not when he didn't know if he actually *had* a future. He had a five-year plan and intended to stick to it. Lauren deserved more than empty promises. Or another casket to grieve over.

"Lauren, we're friends and I'd—"

"Friends with benefits?" she said, and cut him off as she pulled away. "I really hate that expression. It's a convenient line to avoid commitment."

Gabe bit back a frustrated sigh. "The only thing I'm trying to avoid is hurting you."

She blinked hard. "Well, you're not doing so great."

He knew that. There were tears in her eyes, and he'd put them there. "If I'd thought you wouldn't be—"

"Forget the condescending speech, Gabe," she said, cutting him off again. "I'm sorry I'm not able to take the emotion out of sex. Blame it on my traditional upbringing, but I've always thought that making love should mean exactly that."

She was right. It should. "I agree. And there was nothing casual about last night for me, Lauren. But I can't promise you more than this…." He paused and took a breath. "More than now. I can't say what the future will bring, and I don't know where I'll be."

She pulled herself from his embrace. “Are you leaving? Going somewhere? Are you going back to California? Is that why you—”

“No,” he said quickly, and urged her close again. “Of course not.”

“Then what do you mean?”

Guilt hit him between the shoulder blades. *Tell her the truth....*

But he couldn’t. “Forget it. Come back to bed, Lauren.”

Her eyes glistened, and she nodded.

Back in his bedroom they made love again. This time it was quicker, hotter, as though they had a need that had to be sated. Afterward, Lauren stretched and sighed and curved against him. And he was, Gabe realized as he drifted back to sleep, happier and more content than he could ever remember being before in his life.

At seven, Lauren rolled out of bed and met Gabe in the kitchen, wearing only a navy blue bathrobe he’d offered. He’d made pancakes, and she’d agreed to try them before she returned home to shower and change and head to the store. Despite her earlier display of emotion, there was an easy companionship between them, as if they’d done it before, as if they knew one another deeply and intimately.

Which they did, she figured, coloring a little when she remembered the way they’d made love just hours ago. Being with Gabe was like nothing she’d experienced before. He was an incredibly generous lover. He was thoughtful and attentive, and they were well matched in bed.

What about out of bed?

Was there enough between them to stand up to the test outside the bedroom? She hoped so. He’d made no promises, offered no suggestions that their relationship would go beyond one night together. But there was no doubt in her mind that what they’d shared was more than simply sex.

"Are you okay?" he asked, watching her as she mulled over her second mug of tea.

Lauren looked up and smiled. "Fine. Just thinking I should get moving. I have to open the store this morning, and if I'm late, my mother will ask a thousand questions."

He grinned. "Can I see you tonight?"

Lauren's insides jumped. "Are you asking me out on a date?"

"Yes."

Her brows arched. "That's quite a commitment. You sure you're ready for that?"

He came around the table and gently pulled her to her feet. "I guess we'll find out as we go."

He kissed her with a fierce intensity that had *possession* stamped all over it. And Lauren didn't mind one bit. They made out for a few minutes, and when he released her, Lauren was left breathless and wanting him all the more.

"I'll just grab the rest of my clothes," she said with a smile as she left the kitchen.

Back in his bedroom, she gathered up her clothes and quickly changed back into her underwear, skirt and T-shirt. She found her shoes at the foot of the bed and slipped into them before she walked into the en-suite bathroom to return the robe. She hung it on a hook and turned toward the mirror. Only to be faced with her pale complexion and mussed *bed* hair.

She moaned and finger combed her bangs. There were remnants of mascara clinging to her lashes, and she looked for a tissue to wipe beneath her eyes. When she found nothing on the counter, Lauren opened the overhead cabinet. And stilled immediately.

A long row of medication bottles caught her attention. Serious medication. Very serious. She'd seen similar medication bottles before. Along the same shelf, there were vitamins and several homeopathic tonics. Lauren's blood ran cold. Why would a strong, healthy man like Gabe need so much medicine? It didn't make sense. She suppressed the urge to examine one of the bottles, but her mind continued to race. A rush of possibilities scrambled in her head. He was a doctor…perhaps it was something to do with that?

It's none of my business.

But she still longed to know.

Immediately embarrassed that she'd even noticed the bottles, she was about to shut the cabinet when she heard a sound from the doorway.

"Lauren?"

Gabe's voice. Marred with concern and query. She turned to face him and found his expression was completely closed off. Unreadable. Guarded.

Her mouth turned dry. "I was…I was looking for a tissue." She stopped speaking and looked at him. "I'm sorry, I shouldn't have opened the—"

He stepped forward and closed the cabinet door. "You should leave if you're going to open your store on time," he said flatly.

Lauren's stomach lurched. He looked solemn. He looked annoyed; he looked as though she'd invaded his privacy in the worst possible way.

"What's going on, Gabe?" she asked, stepping out of the en suite and into the bedroom. "Why are you—"

"I'll see you out," he said, and swiveled on his heels.

Lauren followed him out of the room and was halfway down the hallway when she said his name. He stopped and turned.

"What?" he asked.

"Exactly," she said. *"What?"*

They were now both in the living room doorway, neither moving. He was tense, on edge, and Lauren resisted the urge to reach out and touch him. He looked as if he wanted her gone. And the notion hurt through to her bones.

"It's nothing," he said quietly. "We should both get ready for work."

Lauren shook her head. "Don't do that. Don't shut me out."

Silence stretched between them like a piece of worn, brittle elastic. Somehow, the incredible night making love with one another and the lovely relaxed morning sharing pancakes and kisses had morphed into a defining, uncomfortable moment in the hallway.

All because she'd seen medication in a bathroom cabinet.

An odd feeling silently wound its way through her blood and across her skin. And a tiny voice whispered in the back of her mind. As the seconds ticked, the whispering became louder, more insistent. Something was wrong. Had she missed signals? Had she been so wrapped up in herself she hadn't really seen him? And without knowing how or why, Lauren suspected the answer was within her grasp.

Just ask the question.... Ask him.... Ask him, and he'll tell you....

"Gabe..." Her voice trailed off for a few moments and she quickly regathered her thoughts. "Are you...sick?"

Shutters came down over his face. She'd seen the look before—that day at the hospital when they'd met near the elevator. He'd been coming from the direction of the specialist offices. *The oncology specialist.* Lauren scrambled her thoughts together. Suddenly, she wasn't sure she wanted to hear his reply.

"No," he said finally.

"But..."

"I was," he said when her query faded. "Eighteen months ago."

A sharp pain tightened her chest. A terrible, familiar pain that quickly took hold of her entire body. It was hard to breathe, and she didn't want to hear any more. But she pressed on.

"What did you—"

"Hodgkin's lymphoma," he said impassively, cutting her off.

Cancer...

Lauren's knees weakened. He'd had cancer.

Just like Tim.

She swallowed the thick emotion in her throat. Every memory, every fear, every feeling of despair and pain she'd experienced with Tim rose up and consumed her like a wave. Tears burned the backs of her eyes, and she struggled to keep them at bay as a dozen questions buzzed on her tongue.

And then, like a jigsaw in her mind, the scattered pieces of the puzzle came together.

Gabe seemed to understand the despair she'd experienced at losing Tim. And he also seemed to understand the other man's motives better than she ever had. Gabe didn't want commitment. He wasn't interested in a relationship.

If you waste your heart on me, I'll break it....

She put her hand to her mouth and shuddered. It was too much. Too hard. Too familiar. And then she ran. Out of his bedroom. Out of his house. Out of his life.

By midday, Gabe was silently thanking Lauren for doing what he couldn't. For walking away.

For racing away…

It was better than facing what he'd expected—the reflection, the realization. *The pity.*

Of course she'd taken off. What sane, sensible woman wouldn't? It certainly hadn't taken Mona long to find the door once he'd given his ex-girlfriend an opportunity to bail on their relationship. She hadn't wanted to waste her life on a man with a death sentence.

And neither would Lauren.

Which is what he wanted, right? No involvement, no feelings, no risk.

Now he just had to convince himself.

Last night had been incredible. The best sex he'd ever had. But it had been a mistake. And wholly unfair to Lauren. From the beginning, she'd been clear on what she wanted, and Gabe knew he'd somehow ambushed that goal by allowing himself to get involved with her. He had a five-year plan, and he still intended sticking to it.

He got a text message from Aaron around two o'clock.

You still haven't called Mom.

He replied after a few minutes and got back to work.

I'll get to it.

When?

Gabe snatched the phone up and responded.

When I do. Back off.

He turned the cell to mute, logged off the computer and sat deep in his chair. He was, he realized as he stared at the blank screen, out-of-his-mind bored with his job. Shuffling paperwork during the week and attending to jellyfish stings and sunstroke on the weekends simply didn't cut it. He wanted more. He needed more.

During the night, in between making love with Lauren and holding her in his arms, they'd talked about his career. For the first time since he'd left Huntington Beach, Gabe admitted how much he missed practicing medicine. As he sat at the desk that had never felt like his own, Gabe knew what he had to do.

It was after four, and he was just finishing a promising call with the human resources director at Bellandale's hospital when there was a tap on the door. It was Lauren.

She entered the room and closed the door.

"Hi," she said quietly. "Can we talk?"

Gabe's stomach tightened. She looked so lovely in her sensible black skirt and green blouse. She'd come to end it. Terrific. It was exactly what he expected. *And* what he wanted. They'd stay friends and neighbors and that was all. Perhaps *friends* was stretching it, too. A clean break—that was what they needed.

He nodded. "Sure."

Her hands were clasped tightly together. "I wanted to… I'd like to…"

Gabe stood and moved around the desk. "You'd like to what?"

She sighed and then took a long, unsteady breath. "To apologize. I shouldn't have left the way I did this morning. I think I was so…so…overwhelmed by it all, by what you told me…I just reacted. And badly. Forgive me?"

Gabe shrugged. "There's nothing to forgive. Your reaction was perfectly normal."

"Don't do that," she said, and frowned. "Don't make it okay. It's not okay."

"I can't tell you how to feel. Or how to respond to things." He perched his behind on the desk. "Considering what you've been through in the past, it makes sense that you'd react as you did."

"It's because of what I've been through in the past that I should *not* have reacted that way. I'm ashamed that I ran out this morning without asking you anything about it. But I'm here now. And I'd like to know." Her concerned expression spoke volumes. Gabe knew that look. He knew what was coming. He waited for it. "Would you tell me about your illness?"

And there it was.

Pity…

His illness. As though it suddenly defined him. As though that was all he was. The ultimate unequalizer. Healthy people to one side. Sick people to the other.

Gabe took a breath. Best he get it over with. "There's not much to tell. I was diagnosed with lymphoma. I had surgery and treatment. And I still take some medication. End of story."

She nodded, absorbing his words. "And you're okay now?"

"Maybe."

She frowned. "What does that mean?"

"It means there are no guarantees. It means that my last round of tests came back clear. It means that without a recurrence within five years, I should be fine."

Should be. Could be. Maybe.

If she had any sense, she'd turn around and run again.

"And that's why you don't want a serious relationship?" she asked, not running.

Gabe met her gaze. At that moment, he didn't know what the hell he wanted other than to drag her into his arms and kiss her as if there was no tomorrow. But he wouldn't. "Exactly."

"Because you might get sick again?" Her hands twisted self-consciously. "Isn't that a little…pessimistic?"

"Realistic," he corrected.

She stepped a little closer. "Then why did you make love to me last night?"

Because I'm crazy about you. Because when I'm near you, I can't think straight.

"I'm attracted to you," he said quietly.

"And that's all?"

"It's all I can offer," he said, and saw her eyes shadow. He didn't want to hurt her, but he wasn't about to make any grand statements, either. She'd be better off forgetting him and resuming her search for Mr. Middle-of-the-Road. "You know what you want and that's not…me. I care about you, Lauren, too much to lead you on."

Her eyes widened, and she laughed shrilly. "You're joking, right?"

"No."

"That's a convenient line for a man who's *afraid* of commitment."

Gabe squashed the annoyance snaking up his spine. "I'm not afraid of—"

"Sure you are," she shot back quickly, and waved her arms. "You work here instead of the job you're trained to do, even though you're clearly a skilled doctor. You won't even commit to a phone call to your family. And let's not forget the meaningless one-night stands."

"That's an interesting judgment from someone who can't bear to be alone."

As soon as he said the words, Gabe knew he'd pushed a button. But damn, couldn't she see that he wanted to make it easier for her, not harder?

Her eyes flashed molten fire. "I *can* be alone. But I'd prefer to not be. And maybe you think that makes me weak and needy." She cocked a brow. "And you know what—perhaps it does. But I'd rather be like that than be too scared to try."

Gabe's gut lurched. He didn't want to admit anything. She was right when she said he was scared. But he couldn't tell her that. Because she'd want to know why. "You don't know what you're asking."

She shook her head fractionally. "I'm not asking anything. I never have. I like you, Gabe. I…I more than *like* you. I wouldn't have spent last night with you if I didn't feel—"

"You want a future, Lauren," he said, and cut her off before she said something she'd inevitably regret. "A future that includes marriage and children and a lifetime together." He inhaled deeply. "It's a future we all take for granted. Until you're told you might not have it."

"But you said you were okay now."

"The cancer could still come back. I wasn't given a one hundred percent chance of making it past five years," he said, and ran a hand through his hair. "Not exactly dead man walking, but close enough that I knew I had to make a few decisions."

Her mouth thinned. "Decisions?"

"About my life," he explained. "About how I wanted to *live* my life. I left my home, my career and my family because I'd had enough of people treating me as though I was somehow changed…or that having cancer had changed me. Because despite how much I didn't want to admit it, I was changed. I am changed. And until I know for sure that I have a future, I'm not going to jump into a relationship." He stared at her. "Not with anyone."

"Jump?" She shook her head. "Most of the time I feel as though you've been dragged into this by your ankles. So, I guess *jumping* into bed with me doesn't count?"

"Of course it counts, and that's exactly my point," he replied. "But I can't give you what you want. I can't and won't make that kind of promise. It wouldn't be fair to you, Lauren. I've had eighteen months to think about this, and I didn't come to the decision lightly. I'm not going to get involved here, only to…"

"To what?"

He sucked in a breath. "To die."

Lauren stepped back and wrapped her arms tightly

around herself. He knew she heard fear in his voice, and he hated the sympathy in her eyes. But she kept on, relentless.

"I don't need that kind of promise, Gabe."

He shook his head. "You do. You would. If we got serious, you'd want it. Hell, you'd deserve it. And I couldn't give it to you."

"How do you know?" she asked. "You're imagining the worst when—"

He made a frustrated sound. "Because I just know. Because I've lived with it for eighteen months. I know what being sick did to the people around me. As a doctor, I saw sickness every day and didn't have one clue what my patients went through until I found myself on the other side of the hospital bed."

"I wasn't one of those people."

"No, you weren't. But you know how this could work out." He raised a hand dismissively. "You've been through it, you grieved...you're *still* grieving for Tim and that life you'd planned for."

"This isn't about Tim," she said quickly. "This is about you. Tim had a terminal illness. An inoperable brain tumor. He was dying...you're not."

"I might," he said flatly.

"So could I. No one can expect that kind of guarantee."

"Isn't that why you married a man you didn't love?" he asked. "Because he was healthy and could give you that kind of assurance?"

"I was—"

"You were looking for your happily ever after," he said, frustrated and annoyed and aching inside. "You were looking for a man who could give you the life you'd dreamed about. I can't do that. Damn it, I don't even know if I could give you the children you want so badly."

Her face crumbled. "Oh, I hadn't thought about—"

"About the possible side effects of chemotherapy and radiation." Gabe expelled a heavy breath. "Well, think about this…there are *no* guarantees. And as much as you say you don't want them, we both know you do. Go home, Lauren," he said coldly, knowing he was hurting her, and knowing he had to. "Go home and forget about this."

Forget about me.

Seconds later, she was gone.

Chapter Eleven

Lauren left the store early on Thursday afternoon and arrived home to find two battered trucks in Gabe's driveway and one in hers. The fence between the two properties, which had long since been hidden by the overgrown hedge, was now in piles of broken timber on both front lawns. She maneuvered her small vehicle around the truck and parked under the carport.

One of the workers came around to her car and apologized up front for the noise they were making and said they'd be finished for the day within a couple of hours.

"But that tree has got to go," he said, grinning toothlessly.

The tree was a tall pine that sat on the fence line and often dropped its branches on her roof. It wasn't much of a tree, and her brother had offered several times to remove it for her.

"Oh, really?"

"The root system will wreck the new fence. We'll get started on it this afternoon, if that's okay?"

Lauren shrugged. "No problem."

Once inside, she changed into jeans and white T-shirt and set her laptop up on the kitchen table. She had invoicing and wages to do and preferred to do it without the inevitable distractions at the store. She poured a glass of iced tea and sat down to work.

By four-thirty, the contractors were still at it. And they were noisy. They were digging new post holes along the fence line with a machine that made a loud *clunk* sound with every rotation. And the buzz of dueling chainsaws didn't help her concentration.

Not that she was in a concentrating mood. For two days, she'd been walking around on autopilot, working at the store, talking to her mother, pretending nothing was wrong when she was broken inside.

Gabe's words still haunted her. His admittance that he might not be able to father children played over and over in her mind. In her heart, she knew that didn't matter to her. Sure, she wanted children. She longed for them. But she wanted Gabe more. Even though he didn't want her back.

At the store that day, she'd arrived early and took inventory on a range of new arrivals. When that was done, she'd dressed two of the windows with new gowns and played around with matching accessories. When she was finished, she'd stood back and examined the results. Not bad, she'd thought. How long had it been since she'd enjoyed her work? *Years.* Too long. After Tim died, she'd lost interest in the fashions and could barely tolerate the enthusiasm of the clients looking for their perfect gown. Her own fairy tale was over, and Lauren took little pleasure in anything related to weddings or the store. It had stopped being fun and instead became a duty.

Perhaps it was time to sell the business and try something new?

She'd once had dreams of taking a break from the store when she was married and had a family of her own. But Tim's death had changed everything, and now that dream seemed as unreachable as the stars around some distant planet. Because despite how much she'd convinced herself it was what she wanted, her plans for a loveless, passionless relationship were stupid. If falling for Gabe had shown her nothing else, Lauren now knew what she wanted. Along with friendship and compatibility, love and passion were vital. In fact, she wanted it all. Everything. A full and complete relationship.

Maybe a vacation was in order. She hadn't been on a holiday for years. Perhaps that would quell her discontented spirit. In the meantime, she'd talk with her mother about putting on another part-time employee so she could take some time off. She thought she might even go back to college.

And she'd get over Gabe. She had to.

Lauren was just about to get herself a second glass of iced tea when she heard an almighty bang, followed by several loud shouts and then a crash and the booming sound of timber cracking. Another sound quickly followed—this one a hollow rumble that chilled her to the bone. The roof above creaked and groaned, and suddenly parts of the ceiling gave way as tiles and branches came cascading through the gaping hole now in her roof. She dived under the table as prickly branches and sharp barbs of shattered timber fell through the gap. Plaster from the ceiling showered across the room in a haze of dust and debris, and she coughed hard as it shot up her nose and into her lungs.

When it was over, she heard more shouts and the sound of heavy boot steps on the roof. She coughed again and wiped her watery eyes. Still crouching, she shuffled backward but quickly moved back when she felt a sharp sting on her left arm. A jagged branch had sliced her skin, and she clamped her right hand across the wound to stem the flow of blood. When that didn't help she noticed her T-shirt was ripped in several places, so Lauren quickly tore off a strip from the hem and made a makeshift bandage to wrap around her arm.

She moved forward and tried to make another exit point, but the branches were thick and too heavy for her to maneuver out of the way. Lauren swallowed the dust in her throat and coughed again. The kitchen table was completely covered in branches and debris from the ceiling support beams, shattered roof tiles and plaster. Her legs started to stiffen in their crouched position, and she stretched forward, looking for a way out from under the table. She tried to push a few of the smaller branches out of the way, but the sharp ends pinched her hands.

She could have been badly injured. Or worse. But she quickly put that thought from her mind and decided to wait for workers to come and help her. And finally, she heard a voice and heaved a relieved sigh.

"Lauren!"

Gabe. Her heart thundered in her chest when she heard footsteps down the hallway and then the sound of tiles crunching beneath his feet. She could see his jeans-clad legs through the twisted branches.

"Where are you?" he asked urgently, coming closer.

"I'm under here," she said, and rattled one of the branches. "Under the table."

"Are you hurt?"

"A few scratches," she replied, coughing again and ignoring the throbbing sting from the gash on her arm. "But I think I'm mostly okay. I have a cut on my arm."

"Stay still, and I'll be there as quickly as I can."

He immediately made his way through the room, easily hauling fallen plaster and timber out of his path. The branches around the table shook and swayed, and she heard him curse under his breath. Within seconds, he'd made a space large enough for her to crawl through. He crouched down, and relief coursed through her veins. She pushed back the swell of emotion rising up.

"Give me your hand," he said, and she reached out.

His fingers clasped around hers, warm and strong and lovely and safe. Lauren stifled a sob as he gently drew her out through the space and got her to her feet. And without a word, he folded her into his arms and held her close.

"I've got you," he whispered into her hair as he gently stroked her scalp. "You're okay now."

Relief pitched behind her ribs, and as Lauren glanced around, the enormity of the destruction struck her like a lash. The room was wrecked. Plaster and timber were strewn over the floor, and benches and dust from the shattered ceiling plaster covered every surface. The huge branch that had fallen through the roof covered the entire table, and there were broken branches and foliage everywhere.

"Oh…what a mess."

Gabe held her away from him. "Forget that for a minute. Let's check your injuries."

He quickly examined her and looked underneath her bandage. "I don't think it needs stitches, but you should probably see a doctor."

She smiled. "Isn't that what I'm doing right now?"

He stared at her for a moment, and then smiled back. "I guess so. I have a medical kit at home, so I can dress that for you. Now let's get out of here."

And then he lifted her up into his arms as though she were a feather.

"I can walk," she protested.

"Humor me, okay?"

Her legs did feel shaky, so she nodded. Seconds later, he

was striding down the hallway and out the front door. The contractors were all hovering by the bottom steps.

"I'm fine," she assured them when she saw their worried faces.

"Don't go inside," Gabe told the workers. "There could be structural damage. I'll be back soon, so wait here."

She smiled at his bossiness and then dropped her head to his shoulder. It felt nice being in his strong arms. When he rounded the hedge, she noticed how his front door was wide-open, as if he'd left the house in a hurry.

"I really can walk," she said once he'd carried her up the steps.

But he didn't put her down until they reached the kitchen. Then he gently set her to her feet and pulled out a chair. Once she was settled and he'd grabbed a first-aid kit, he undid the makeshift bandage and examined the wound.

"It's not deep," he said, and cleaned the area, applied a small bandage around her forearm and then circled it in plastic wrap. "That should keep it dry when you shower."

"Thanks," she said, and fought the urge to fall into his arms again. "I need to get back to my house and call my insurance company."

"Later," he said. "I'll go and check it out while you rest here."

"There's no need to—"

"There's every need," he said, and grabbed her hand. "You've just been through a frightening ordeal, and you're injured. Plus, there's a great gaping hole in the roof and there could be structural damage to the house."

Lauren ran her free hand down her torn T-shirt and jeans. "I need some fresh clothes, so I'll go home and change and then call the—"

"Stop being so damned obstinate," he said impatiently. "Let me check out the house, and I'll get your clothes while I'm there."

She pulled her hand free. "I'm not sure I want you rummaging through my underwear drawer. It's private and—"

"Lauren, I have seen you naked," he reminded her. "Remember? It's a little late for modesty. Go and take a shower, and I'll be back soon."

"A shower? I don't know why you—"

"Once you look in the mirror, you'll see why," he said, and smiled. "I'll be back soon."

He left the room, and Lauren tried not to be irritated by his high-handedness. She cradled her sore arm and headed for the en-suite bathroom. And worked out why he'd insisted she shower. She was covered in grime and plaster dust. Her face and hair were matted with the stuff, and her clothes were speckled with blood and dirty smudges.

Lauren stripped off the soiled clothes and stepped beneath the warm water, mindful of the plastic-covered bandage. She washed her hair as best she could, and by the time she emerged from the cubicle, wrapped her hair up in a towel and slipped into his bathrobe, she heard him striding down the hallway.

He paused in the doorway carrying a short stack of clothes. "Let me know if you need anything else," he said, and placed them on the bed.

She nodded. "Thank you. How does my house look?"

"Redeemable," he said, and half smiled. "I've told the contractor to tarp the roof so there's no more damage overnight. And I've arranged to have a certified builder assess the damage in the morning. Get dressed, and I'll make you a cup of that tea you like."

Lauren had to admit he'd done a fair job at choosing her clothes. Gray linen pants and a red collared T-shirt, a sensible black bra and brief set and slip-on sandals. As she stepped into the briefs, she didn't want to think about his lean fingers touching her underwear. Gabe's take-charge attitude should have made her as mad as ever, but she was actually grateful for his kindness. What had been a frightening experience was eased by him coming to her rescue. When she was finished dressing, she headed for the kitchen. He'd made tea, as promised, and was staring out the long window, mug in hand.

"I think I inhaled a bucket of plaster dust," she said when she entered the room.

He turned and met her gaze. "If the cough keeps up, let me know."

"I will. Thanks for the tea." She saw her handbag, dusty laptop and house keys on the counter. "Oh, that's good. I wasn't sure the computer survived the tree crashing on top of it."

"It seems okay," he said quietly. "I found your bag but couldn't find your cell phone."

She shrugged. "That's fine. I don't need it, anyhow."

"So how are you feeling now?" he asked.

"Pleased I dived underneath the table."

"Me, too," he said, and set the mug down. "I'd just gotten home when I saw the pulley snap and then saw the branch nosedive into your roof."

"Apparently, that tree was going to mess with the fence," she said, and grinned. "They didn't warn me about what it might do to my house, though."

He chuckled, and the sound warmed her blood. "I'm glad you're okay. I was worried about you."

He sounded uncomfortable saying it, and Lauren tensed. He might have been worried, but he clearly didn't want to be. She'd accused him of being hot and then cold, and that certainly seemed to sum up the way he acted around her.

"Thanks for coming to my rescue," she said as flippantly as she could manage.

His mouth flattened, and he passed her his phone. "You can call your parents if you like. Or your brother."

She shook her head and placed the phone on the table. "They'll only worry."

"Well, they'll know something's up when you stay with them tonight."

"I'm not going anywhere," she said, and pushed her shoulders back. "I'm sleeping in my own bed, in my own house."

"No," he said quietly. "You're not."

"Ah, yes I am."

"I'm not going to argue with you about this, Lauren. You stay with your parents or your brother, or if you like I'll drive you to Cassie's. But you're not spending the night in a potentially compromised building that has a huge hole in the roof."

She crossed her arms. "You don't get to tell me what to do."

"Right now, when you're being stubborn and disagreeable, I'll do whatever I have to do to keep you safe."

His words had *ownership* stamped all over them, and the fact he had the audacity to say such a thing when he'd made it clear they had no future only amplified her resentment. He really needed to stop interfering. Sure, she was grateful he'd gotten her out from under the table, but that didn't give him open season on deciding where she would sleep.

"I'll be perfectly safe."

The pulse in his cheek throbbed. "No, you won't…so you stay with your family, or you can stay here. Those are your only options."

Of all the bossy, arrogant, bullheaded...

"Fine," she said quickly, and saw the startled look on his face. "I'll stay here."

No way...

Gabe's stomach landed at his feet. She wasn't staying with him when she had a bunch of perfectly good relatives to rely on. She was simply being provocative. He was just about to say as much when the challenge in her eyes silenced any protests.

Instead, he called her bluff. "Okay…but you still have to call your parents and tell them what happened."

Her brows came up. "That's interesting coming from a man who won't pick up the telephone to call his own family."

"We're talking about you," he quipped, "not me."

She shrugged. "So where's my bedroom?"

"I'll sleep in the guest room. You can have my room. You'll be more comfortable there."

"Familiar surroundings, you mean?"

His body tensed. "I haven't finished painting in the guest room," he said, and grabbed his cell. "I can order pizza if you're hungry?"

She nodded. "Sure. No anchovies, please. And extra mushrooms."

He half smiled. "Why don't you rest in the living room, and I'll place the order."

She did as he suggested, and once the pizza had been ordered, Gabe grabbed a couple of ginger beers from the refrigerator and headed for the living room. He found her on the sofa, legs curled up, arms crossed, staring at the blank television.

"Everything all right?" he asked, and passed her a bottle.

"Just thinking about my wrecked house."

"It's a house, Lauren," he said quietly, and sat on the other end of the sofa. "Houses can be fixed."

"Not like people, right?" she shot back, and sighed. "Once broken, always broken."

The tremor in her voice made his insides contract. "Is that how you feel?"

"Sometimes," she admitted. "Lately more often than not. I think I just need to…make some changes."

"Changes?"

She raised her shoulders. "I was thinking of selling the store."

He didn't hide his surprise. "That's a bold move. Are you sure it's the right one?"

"Not really," she replied. "I'm not sure of anything. If I do decide to sell, I know my mother will be disappointed. But I don't know how much longer I can keep pretending that it makes me happy. I've been pretending since… since…"

"Since Tim died?"

She nodded slowly. "Yes. Some days I find it so stifling. And then other days I can't believe I'm having such ungrateful thoughts. I mean, what's not to like about being around people who are looking to create the perfect, most special day and then sharing in that joy? But all I feel is tired and weary of plastering on a wide smile every time a bride comes into the store looking for the gown of her dreams."

Her pain reached deep into his soul. "You've had a bad day…don't make a hasty decision when you might not be thinking clearly."

"Spoken from experience?" she asked softly.

"Yes," he replied.

She shrugged. "I won't."

The doorbell rang, and Gabe got to his feet. "Our dinner. Back in a minute."

They ate in the kitchen, and by eight-thirty were lingering over coffee.

"Are you okay?" he asked when he noticed her frowning.

"Tired," she replied. "And sore. I think I strained my back when I darted underneath the table. Which is a small price to pay considering what could have happened."

Gabe pushed his mug aside. "I don't want to remember what I thought when I saw that tree crash."

"I'm glad you were there to rescue me."

Was she? Was he? It seemed as though there was no escaping the pull that drew them together. It had a will of its own, dragging him back toward her at every opportunity.

"Nothing's changed," he said, and hated how cold his voice sounded.

"Everything's changed. I can't pretend and just switch off my emotions."

"Can't? Or won't?"

Her gaze was unwavering. "What are you so afraid of?"

Gabe sucked in a breath. "Hurting you."

"People get hurt all the time. You can't always control it."

"I can try," he said, and stood. "I won't mislead you, Lauren. I won't make promises I can't keep. I've told you how I feel about you and—"

"Actually," she said, cutting him off. "You haven't said how you feel about me at all…only how you feel about relationships and commitment."

Discomfiture snaked up his spine. "It's the same thing."

Her brows rose tellingly. "That's a man's logic," she said, and got to her feet. "And I'm a woman, Gabe. I think and feel deeply. And I know what I want. For the first time in a long time, I actually know what will make me happy. And who."

Guilt pressed onto his shoulders. "Don't pin your hopes on me, Lauren. I can't make you happy…because I can't promise you a future."

She stared at him, eyes glistening. "Is it because you think you might not be able to give me a baby?"

The burn in his stomach intensified. "You can't deny that's important to you."

"It was," she admitted. "It is. But there are other options, like IVF and adoption. I mean, no two people know if they'll be able to produce a child until they try. And you said it was a possibility, not an absolute."

Her relentless logic was butchering him.

"It's just one more complication, Lauren. One that you don't need."

"But I'm right?" she asked. "So now you're hiding behind this idea of potential infertility to keep me or any other woman at arm's length?"

"I'm not hiding. I'm laying out the facts."

"The facts?" she echoed. "You're like a vault when it comes to the facts. Right now, in this moment, you're well and strong and *here*...why isn't that enough?"

"Because it's not. Because it might not last," he replied, frustrated and angry.

"But you don't know what will happen…no one does."

"I know what the medical data says. I know what the odds are of it coming back. If I can stay healthy for five years and not relapse, then I'll consider my options. But until then—"

"Five years?" She cut him off and shook her head. "You can't organize feelings to order like that."

"I can. I will."

"So you plan to avoid getting close to anyone for the next few years just in case you aren't around to seal the deal? That's absurd. What made you so cynical?"

"Facing the prospect of death."

"I don't believe you," she said hauntingly. "There's more to it. You had a career where you saw death all the time, a career that obviously called out to you because you're mentally strong and compassionate and able to deal with grief and despair and hopelessness. I don't believe that all that strength disappeared because you were faced with the challenge of an illness you've now recovered from."

His chest tightened. "I can't talk about—"

"What happened to you?" she pleaded. "Tell me…what happened that made you so determined to be alone?"

Gabe's heart thundered, and he fought the words that

hovered on the end of his tongue. He didn't want to tell her; he didn't want to admit to anything. But the pained, imploring look on her face was suddenly harder to deny than his deep-seated determination to say nothing.

"My dad died when I was seventeen," he said flatly. "And I watched my mom become hollow inside. At first, I watched her become headstrong in her denial and refuse to admit the inevitable. I watched her use every ounce of strength she had to give him hope and keep him alive. I watched her argue with doctors and oncologists about his treatment and try every holistic and natural remedy she could to give him more time. And then when the treatment stopped working and he relapsed, I watched her care for him and feed him and bathe him, and then I watched her cry every day when she thought no one was looking. And when he died, part of her died, too. She was heartbroken. She was sad, and there was nothing anyone could do for her…there was nothing *I* could do for her."

He drew several gulps of air into his lungs. It was the first time he'd said the words. The first time he'd admitted how helpless he'd felt watching his mother fall apart.

"And I'm never going to put anyone through that…not ever."

She shuddered. "So instead you'll shut the world out?"

"Not the world," he said quickly. "Just…"

"Just me?" she asked, eyes glazed. "Or any woman who wants to be with you for more than a one-night stand?"

"Exactly," he said woodenly.

She shook her head. "It wasn't your job to fix your mother. No one can fix that kind of pain…only time can truly heal," she said quietly. "Believe me, I know. If your mother didn't recover, it's not your responsibility or job to question why. And it must be that your dad was the true love of her life."

"Like Tim was yours?"

Did he sound as jealous by that idea as he felt? He didn't want to feel it. Didn't want to think it. Didn't want to be so conflicted and confused that all he wanted to do was haul her into his arms and kiss her over and over and forget every other wretched thought or feeling.

Her mouth softened. "I did love Tim, very much. But I didn't honor that love when I married James. And when my marriage ended, I was determined to find someone who wouldn't make me feel anything that might dishonor those feelings again. And I tried," she said as tears filled her eyes. "And failed."

"And that's exactly why I won't do this, Lauren. That look you have when you talk about Tim… My mom had that same look. You've been through it, too. You know how it feels to lose someone you care about. Why the hell would you potentially put yourself through that again? It doesn't make sense. You need to walk away from this. And me."

"So you're doing this for me. Is that what you're saying?"

He shrugged. "I'm doing this for us both."

She inhaled resignedly. "I'm going to bed. Are you coming?"

Bed? He groaned inwardly. "No."

Her mouth twitched. "You're not going to make love to me tonight?"

Gabe's entire body tightened. She was pure provocation, and he wanted her so much, his blood felt as though it were on fire.

"No." It was close to the hardest thing he'd ever said.

Her eyes shadowed. "Would you just…hold me?"

Pain and longing sat in his gut like a lead weight. But she didn't know what she was asking. If he stayed with her tonight, there would be no turning back. He wanted her… he wanted her so much he ached inside thinking about denying that feeling. But Gabe wouldn't allow that wanting to turn into needing. Needing meant giving everything. Everything meant loving. And that was impossible.

"I can't." His voice sounded hollow and empty. "I can't give you what you want."

She looked at him, and he saw the disappointment and regret in her eyes. She was hurt.

"No, I guess you can't," she said, and left the room.

Chapter Twelve

"And that's it?"

Lauren dropped her gaze to the floor. If she kept looking at Cassie and Mary-Jayne, they'd see the tears in her eyes. And she wouldn't cry anymore. She'd cried enough over lost love throughout the years. She'd cried for Tim. She'd cried when he'd finally told her he was dying and wouldn't be able to give her the future he'd promised. She'd cried over his grave and in the years since. She'd even cried for James when he'd walked out the door. She'd cried for lost dreams and for the children she'd never borne.

And not once, during all those tears and anguish, did she ever think she'd love again. Nor did she want to. She'd planned on friendship and companionship and then marriage and children to help ease her aching heart. And instead had tumbled headlong into something that was all desire and heat and a longing so intense it physically pained her. She loved Gabe. And she knew, deep down to her soul, that it was the one love she would never recover from.

But she had to try.

And she would.

"That's it," she replied, and pretended to enjoy the glass of wine she'd been cradling for the best part of an hour. She managed a smile. "Looks like I'm back to trawling ReliableBores.com."

Mary-Jayne made a huffing sound. "Did he give you a reason?"

Sure he did. But Lauren would never betray Gabe's confidence and tell them about his illness. Now she had to concentrate on forgetting all about her fledging feelings and put Gabe Vitali out of her mind. And show a little more enthusiasm for her friends' company. But she wasn't in the mood for a Friday-evening movie and junk-food marathon. She simply wanted to lick her wounds in private.

"Don't forget it's my sister's birthday party tomorrow night," Mary-Jayne reminded them. "I'll pick you both up."

Lauren nodded and noticed that Cassie, who still hadn't heard from Doug, looked about as unenthused as she felt. An evening with Scott and Evie Jones was one thing… knowing Gabe would be there, too, was another thing altogether. However, she was determined to put on a brave face and go. Avoiding Gabe was pointless. They shared several of the same friends and were bound to run into one another occasionally. She might be able to steer clear of him over the hedge that separated their homes, but becoming a hermit to her friends wasn't an option.

"How's the house look?" Cassie asked.

"The repairs will take the best part of the weekend, but I should be back in by Tuesday."

"Well, you can stay here as long as you like," her friend offered.

And she was glad she had such loyal friends. She'd gone to bed the night before with a broken heart and awoke with more resolve than she knew she possessed. Gabe was gone by the time she pulled herself out of bed, and had left a cursory note telling her a builder would be at her house at seven-thirty to check for structural damage. By eight she was back inside her own house, cleaning up with the help of the fencing contractor and his crew, who'd arrived with sheepish faces and good intentions. And while the repairs to the roof were being done, she'd stay with Cassie and try to stop thinking about Gabe.

"Thanks, I appreciate it."

"That's what friends are for," Cassie assured her, then smiled. "You know, there's this man at work I think you might like."

Lauren groaned. "A blind date? Ah, no thanks."

"What's the harm? He's nice. He's in the pathology department. Want me to set you up?"

"No chance."

On Saturday morning, Lauren headed to the store early. She gave her mother an abridged version of what had happened with the house, leaving out how she'd stayed at Gabe's that night and only telling her she was bunking in with Cassie until the repairs were done. She didn't mention her thoughts about selling the store. She'd think about that later. When her heart wasn't breaking. When she was whole and was certain she'd finished crying wasted tears.

Late that afternoon, Lauren dressed in a pale lemon sundress in filmy rayon that tied at her nape. The garment fitted neatly over the bodice and flared from the waist. She matched it with a pair of silver heels and kept her hair loose around her shoulders. Mary-Jayne picked her up at six, and since Cassie had decided to give the party a miss, they drove straight to Dunn Inn. The big A-framed home was set back from the road, and the gardens always reminded

Lauren of something out of an old fairy story. There was a wishing well in the center of the yard, surrounded by cobbled paths and tall ferns, and it had been a bed and breakfast for over a decade.

Gabe's car wasn't out front, and she heaved a relieved sigh. She grabbed Evie's birthday gift from the backseat and followed Mary-Jayne inside. Evie was in the kitchen, as was Grace. Lauren had always envied the three sisters' relationship. They were as different as night and day and yet shared a formidable bond. Of course, she adored her brother, but sometimes wished she'd had a sister, too.

"Scott's running an errand," Evie explained, and Lauren wondered if she imagined how the other woman glanced in her direction just a little longer than expected. "He'll be back soon."

Mary-Jayne laughed. "Oh, with some big birthday surprise for you?"

Evie raised her steeply arched brows. "Well, it's certainly a surprise. Not for me, though. And since I'm not sure I really want to be celebrating the fact I'm only two years off turning forty, I'm more than happy about that."

"The gifts are all on the buffet in the front living room," Grace said as she cradled Evie's six-month-old daughter in her arms.

Her sister-in-law was glowing, and Lauren wondered if she was pregnant. It would certainly explain why her brother had sounded so chipper on the phone that morning when he'd called after hearing about her tree mishap from her mother. She was achingly happy for Cameron and knew he deserved every ounce of happiness that was in his life. But part of her envied him, too. He'd put his heart on the line when he'd pursued Grace, and it had paid off.

Not like me....

Her heart was well and truly smashed. Gabe was out of reach. As unattainable as some remote planet. He'd made it abundantly clear that he wasn't interested. He'd rejected her, wholly and completely. And she had to stop wasting her energy hoping he'd come around. There would be no fairy-tale ending.

Lauren offered to take the gifts into the living room and left the sisters alone to catch up. The big room was formal and furnished with a long leather chaise and twin heavy brocade sofas. A collection of Evie's artwork covered the walls, and a thick rug lay in front of the fireplace and hearth.

She'd just laid the gifts out when she heard the wide French doors rattle. A second later, Gabe was in the room. In black trousers and white shirt, he looked so handsome, it was impossible to arrest the breathless gasp that escaped her throat. But he looked a little tired, too, and she wondered if he'd had as much trouble sleeping as she'd had. She almost wished sleeplessness upon him. She wanted to share everything with him…including her misery.

He didn't say anything. He only looked at her, taking his time to rake his stare from her sandaled feet to her freshly washed hair. A gust of awareness swept into the room like a seductive wind, and she couldn't have moved even if she'd tried. Heat coursed up her limbs and hit her low in the belly. In a flash of a second she remembered every touch, every kiss, every moment of their lovemaking. And she knew, by the scorching intensity of his gaze, that he was remembering it, too.

It was hard to stop from rushing into his arms. Because they were the arms she loved. She wondered how it had happened…how she'd managed to fall in love with a man who didn't love her in return. Who wouldn't risk loving her in return. A man who was everything she'd sworn off and yet was everything she craved. A man who openly offered her nothing but heartache.

"Lauren," he said finally, breaking the thick silence. "You look lovely."

She swallowed hard and shrugged. "Thank you."

"How are you feeling? Is your arm getting better?"

"Yes," she said, and touched the narrow bandage. "Healing well."

"How's the house?"

"Good," she replied. "Actually, I wanted to thank you for getting the builder to come around and assess the place. He's been very accommodating and will have the repairs finished by next week."

"No problem. He's the father of one of the kids in the junior lifeguard program at the surf club. He was happy to help out."

"Well, I appreciate your concern. I didn't see your truck out front so I wasn't sure you would be here today."

"I'm parked out back," he explained. "If you'd rather I left, then I'll go."

"No," she said quickly. "It's fine," she lied, dying inside. "It's Evie's birthday, and Scott is your cousin. You should be here with your family."

He stepped closer. "I've been thinking about you."

She shrugged. "I can't imagine why."

His gaze was unrelenting. "We left things badly the other day and I—"

"It's fine," she assured him with way more bravado than she felt. "You said what you had to say. I'm over it."

I'm over you....

Liar.

He nodded slowly. "That's...good. You know, I never planned on hurting you."

Humiliation coursed through her blood, and she had to dig herself out of the hole she was in. "You didn't, so spare yourself the concern. I'm perfectly okay. We had one night together. The sex was great. The pancakes were not so great." She shrugged again and plastered on a tight smile as she counted off a few fingers. "And I'm back to day three of my new vow of celibacy."

"So…you're okay?"

Her smile broadened. "Never better. Don't worry on my account, Gabe. We had sex…it's not a big deal. People have sex all the time. We had an itch, we scratched it."

His mouth thinned. "An itch? Is that what it was?"

"Sure," she said, and shrugged. "What else? I mean, we really don't know one another very well, and we always seem to end up arguing. It's better we slept together early on rather than drag the whole thing out for an age. My plans haven't changed, and yours seem set in stone… so no harm done."

He stared at her, long and hard, and finally he crossed his arms and shook his head. "I don't believe you, Lauren. I think…I think you're saying what you imagine I want to hear."

She laughed loudly. "Maybe I just wanted to get laid… like you did."

"Is that what you think I wanted?" he asked quietly. "To get laid?"

"Sure," she replied, and shrugged. "You told me as much that night you came over for dinner, remember? You called me Commitment 101 and said you have casual and meaningless sex."

His brows came up. "I said that?"

"Words to that effect."

He smiled. "Well, I haven't had as much meaningless sex as you've clearly been imagining. And before you go accusing me of doing that with you, be assured there was nothing meaningless to me about the night we spent together. You told me you don't make love casually, and I believe that." He said the words with such arrogant confidence, she wanted to slug him. "But I think you're hurt and I think you're angry. And I also think—"

"And I think you're the most conceited jerk of all time," she said hotly, cutting him off. A door closed in the house, and she heard voices, but Lauren pressed on, battling with the humiliating fury she felt in her heart. He didn't want her. He didn't need her. Why couldn't he simply leave her alone? "I don't care how much I want to get laid in the future, I will steer well clear of your bed. One night in the sack with you isn't enough to—"

Lauren stopped ranting when she heard someone clearing their throat and noticed that three people were standing in the doorway. It was Scott and two others. A man, tall and handsome with fair hair and blue eyes just like Gabe's, and a woman whose eyes were equally as blue and who looked to be around sixty. She heard Gabe groan as he turned on his heels and faced the group.

When he spoke, Lauren almost fainted on the spot.

"Hi, Mom."

Seeing Claire Vitali in the doorway, with his brother Aaron hovering close by, was enough to quell any urge he had to kiss Lauren's amazing mouth. Since he'd walked into the room and spotted her by the buffet, it was all he'd wanted to do. With her temper flared and her cheeks ablaze with color, he'd never seen her look more beautiful or more desirable. But she was hurting, too, and even though she denied it, Gabe knew he was responsible for the unhappiness in her eyes. He hated that he'd done that…even though he felt certain it was for the best.

The group moved into the room, and before he had a chance to make introductions, his mother was clutching at him in a fierce and long embrace. Once she'd finished hugging, she kissed his cheek and stepped back.

"It's good to see you, Gabriel," she said, using his full name for deliberate effect, and smiled.

Despite his shock, he was genuinely pleased to see his parent. "You, too, Mom."

His mother noticed Lauren immediately and held out her hand. "Hello, I'm Claire Vitali."

Lauren took her hand and introduced herself. "It's nice to meet you."

Gabe saw the gleam in his mother's eyes. "And you."

"Well, I'll leave you all to catch up," Lauren said, and moved across the room as if her soles were on fire. He noticed she smiled at Aaron and Scott on her way out but didn't spare him a glance.

"I'll go, too," Scott said, and grinned.

"Yeah," Gabe said. "Thanks so much for the heads-up."

His cousin shrugged. "Our mothers swore me to secrecy. And don't be too long. It's my wife's birthday, and there's cake."

Once he was gone, Aaron stepped toward him. "That's one pretty girl," his brother said with a grin, and went for a bear hug. Gabe ignored the comment about Lauren and hugged him back.

When the hugging was over and they were settled on the two sofas, he asked the obvious question. "So what are you two doing here?"

"I'm here because she insisted I come," Aaron said, and grinned.

"I wanted to see my son," his mother replied. "And since you weren't returning my calls…"

Gabe glanced at his older brother, looking his usually cocky self on the opposite sofa, and scowled. "I did text and say I was busy."

"Mom didn't believe me," Aaron said, and grinned again. "She wanted to see for herself."

He looked to his mother. "See what?"

"I needed to make sure you were okay," she said, and gave him a look of concern.

"I'm fine," he said. "As you can see."

His mother's mouth thinned. "Are you really? You can tell me if you're not."

"You came all this way because you thought I'd had some kind of relapse?"

She sighed crossly. "I came all this way because you're my son, and you and your brothers and sister are the most important thing in my life. I won't apologize for caring."

Guilt pressed between his ribs. "I'm sorry I worried you. But I'm fine."

"You don't look fine," she said, and frowned. His mother never was one to pull punches. "You look tired and annoyed, and you're clearly not happy that we've turned up unannounced. So what's going on with you?"

Sometimes Gabe wished he came from one of those families where everyone didn't know everyone else's business. Was there such a thing as caring too much? When he'd been diagnosed with lymphoma, his mother and siblings had closed ranks around him, almost to the point of smothering him with concern. And it hadn't taken long for resentment to set in. Since then, they'd treated him differently, and it irritated the hell out of him. It was as though they'd wanted to wrap him in cotton wool and *fix* everything.

"Nothing," he assured her, feeling about sixteen years old. "Everything's fine. I'm healthy. I have a job I like, friends… You don't need to worry, Mom. I'm a grown man, and I can take care of myself."

"I'll always worry," she said, still looking grim. "It's a given that a mother worries about her children, regardless of how old they are." She sighed and patted his arm affectionately. "But if you say you're fine…then I believe you. You still look tired, though."

"I'm just not sleeping great at the moment. Otherwise, I'm in perfect health and have the results of my latest tests to prove it. Please, stop fretting."

"So," Aaron said, and stretched back in the sofa. "You're fine. Which doesn't explain why you've been avoiding our calls for the past month or so." His brows rose questioningly. "What's the story with the pretty blonde with the big brown eyes who you clearly got into bed but who now wants nothing to do with you?"

"Aaron," their mother chastised. "That's enough."

Gabe's mouth pressed tight. "My relationship with Lauren is no one's business and I don't—"

"Relationship?" His brother laughed and cut him off. "Ha...of course. Now I get it." Aaron propped forward on the seat and grinned broadly. He looked at their mother. "Mom, he's not sick...he's *lovesick*."

Gabe found the urge to crash tackle his big-mouthed brother. "Shut up."

"Aaron." Their mom said his brother's name again, this time quietly. "Go and eat some cake. I'd like to talk to your brother alone."

"I'm right," Aaron said with a grin as he stood. "I know I'm right."

Once Aaron left, Gabe faced his mother's stare. "Is that true?" she asked gently.

"Is what true?"

She made a face. "Lauren... Are you in love with her?"

Gabe got to his feet and paced around the sofa. "No."

"But you're involved with her?"

"Not exactly. It's complicated," he said, and shrugged. "And I don't want to talk about it."

"Well, that's always been your problem, really...not talking," his mom said, and sighed. "Just like your father. Not talking about your illness...not talking about what happened at the hospital when you went back to work…not talking about why you broke up with Mona…not talking about why you needed to put an ocean between your old life and your new one."

His shoulders tensed. "You know why I left."

"Because you blamed yourself for that woman and her baby dying," she said gently. "Even though it wasn't your fault. Even though you weren't there."

"I *should* have been there. I was on duty."

"You were sick," his mother reminded him.

"Yes," he said hollowly. "I was. And I went back too soon. I did everything I would have told a patient to *not* do. I ignored what was best and did exactly what I wanted, and because of that a young woman and her baby died. I am to blame, Mom. It doesn't matter how many times I try to get it clear in my head, or how often I'm told the inquiry didn't find me culpable." He pointed to his temple. "In here I feel the blame. In here I see her husband weeping over her body. Because I was arrogant and thought I could trick my broken body into being what it once was." He sighed heavily. "But it's not. And it might never be. I won't pretend anymore. And I certainly won't drag anyone else into that place if I do end up back where I was."

His mother's eyes glistened. "You mean Lauren?"

"I mean anyone," he said pointedly. "I saw what it did to you, Mom…watching Dad slowly fade away. It was hard to sit back and for a time watch you fade away, too."

"Gabe, I didn't—"

"We should get back to the party," he said, and held out his arm. "Before that lousy brother of mine eats all the birthday cake."

She blinked a couple of times. They weren't done. But his mother knew not to push too much. Gabe led her into the dining room and noticed that everyone was there, standing around the table as Evie prepared to blow out the birthday candles…everyone except Lauren.

Had she left?

He ducked out of the room and headed outside. She was in the front yard, standing on the cobbled pathway by the wishing well, partially hidden by large ferns, arms crossed and clearly deep in thought. Everything about her reached him deep down, into a place he'd never let anyone go.

Are you in love with her?

His mother's words came rushing back. He'd denied it. Because he didn't want to face what it would mean to truly love a woman like Lauren. Aaron had called him love-sick, and in a way that's exactly how he felt. He couldn't define it, couldn't put into words what he was feeling when he was around her. It was like a fever that wouldn't break. A pain that wouldn't abate. His chest hurt simply thinking about her. And his damned libido seemed to be on a kind of constant red alert.

Was that love?

He hoped not. He didn't want it to be. He was no good for Lauren.

"Are you making wishes?" he asked as he approached.

She shook her head. "I don't think I believe in them."

"You're going to miss out on cake," he said.

She turned her head sideways. "I'm going to skip the cake. And the party."

"Are you planning on walking home?" he asked, stepping a little closer.

"It's not far," she replied. "A few blocks."

"In those heels?" He stared at her feet for a moment. "I'll drive you home if that's what you want."

"No," she said quietly. "You should stay here with your family." She uncrossed her arms and turned toward him. "Your mother seems nice."

"She is nice."

"And clearly worried about you," she said, and smiled wryly. "I told you to call her."

Gabe shrugged. "I know you did. I should have listened. She was convinced I had…you know…relapsed."

"Well, she must be relieved to know you're fine. And I'm sorry if your mother and brother overheard our conversation before," she said, and Gabe noticed her cheeks were pinkish. "I shouldn't have lost my temper."

"My mom's cool. And don't worry about Aaron. He's a jerk, too," he said, and grinned a little. "You'd probably like him."

Lauren rolled her eyes. "I've decided to give up on handsome and charming men. Too much trouble."

"Maybe there's something safe in that middle road you were looking for."

"Maybe," she agreed. "Anyhow, I'm going home now."

Gabe reached for her instinctively. He took her hand and wrapped his fingers around hers. "I'm…I'm sorry, Lauren."

She didn't pull away. She didn't move. She only looked up at him, and in the fading afternoon light, he could see every feature. The morning after the night they'd made love, he'd watched her sleep, and in that time he'd memorized every line and curve of her face. He wanted to make love to her again. And again. He wanted to hold her in his arms and kiss her beautiful mouth. But she wasn't his to kiss.

"I know you are," she said so quietly, her voice whispered along the edge of the breeze. "I am, too. I'm sorry you think you're not worth the risk. And I'm sorry you think I'm not strong enough to handle whatever might happen. I guess after what happened with Tim, you have your reasons for believing that. But you're doing exactly what Tim did. He didn't trust me enough to try…. He didn't trust me enough to let me in and share the time he had…and you don't trust me, either."

Gabe's insides jerked. "It's not about trust."

"It is." She pulled her hand from his and reached up to gently touch his face, eyes glistening. "But do you want to know something, Gabe? I would have rather had five years, one year, one month with you…than a lifetime with someone else."

Chapter Thirteen

Lauren moved back into her house on Wednesday afternoon, and since the new fence was now complete, she had less chance of seeing Gabe. Which was exactly what she wanted.

She also made a few decisions. She talked with her mother about The Wedding House and agreed that they'd look to finding a buyer within the next twelve months if she was still keen to sell. In the meantime, Lauren had decided to cut back her hours at the store and return part-time to college to get her accounting degree.

And after much convincing from her meddling, albeit well-meaning friends, she agreed to go on a date with Cassie's pathologist on Friday night. She also made a commitment to walk Cassie's dog, Mouse, since her friend was still feeling the effects of her appendectomy, and at nearly five months pregnant, wasn't keen to be on the end of the leash of the huge Harlequin Great Dane. He was well mannered, though, and incredibly quiet and not unruly like Jed.

On Friday morning, she took him for a long walk, and was heading back along the pathway when she saw Megan jogging toward her. The teen's long limbs stretched out, and her tiny sports shorts molded her toned thighs. Lauren felt about as sporty as an old shoe in her baggy cotton shorts and sensible racer-back T-shirt when the girl came up to her.

"Hey, there," Megan said cheerfully. "Nice dog."

"Thanks," she said, and tried to be as equally cheerful.

"So," the other girl said, jogging on the spot. "Are you the reason why Gabe's in such a bad mood?"

Lauren's skin prickled. "I don't know what you mean."

She shrugged. "It was just something my sister said. But she can be pretty catty when she wants to be. She had this idea that you and Gabe were together."

"No, we're not."

Megan grinned. "Have you met his brother? He's hot. But then, I've always had a thing for blonds. Anyhow, if you're not the reason why he's in a bad mood, someone is, 'cause he's been unbearable all week." Megan laughed shrilly. "Gotta run. See ya!"

She watched the other girl jog away, and then turned Mouse back onto the path. She was about twenty feet from passing alongside the surf club when she spotted Gabe's brother outside the building, phone pressed to his ear. He was handsome, she thought, but not as classically good-looking as his younger brother. Lauren was hoping to pass by unnoticed, but he waved to her when he realized who she was.

Seconds later, he walked over. "Nice to see you again," he said, and smiled. "Although I don't think we were actually introduced. I'm Aaron. That's some dog you have there."

"He's on loan from a friend. So are you enjoying Crystal Point?"

"I like the scenery," he said, and grinned. "And nice weather. It's a lot like California."

She asked him about his twin sons, and was about to excuse herself when she saw Gabe standing on the second-story balcony, watching them. Or more to the point, glaring at them.

"Uh-oh," Aaron said, and waved to his brother. "He doesn't look happy. Can't figure why. Can you?" he asked with a devilish grin.

Heat seeped up her neck, and Lauren shrugged. "No idea."

"He can be a little uptight about some things."

She'd never considered Gabe to be uptight. Bossy and hardheaded, perhaps. And stubborn. And handsome and sexy, and she'd always thought him to be rather charming and easygoing. Stupidly, she didn't like that his brother was so openly criticizing him.

"I suppose we can all be like that," she said quietly. "Under certain circumstances."

He laughed loudly. "Ah, so you, too, huh?"

"Me, too, what?" she asked, puzzled.

He laughed again. "Nothing...just go easy on him, okay? He's been through a lot. And I don't think he quite knows what to do about you, Lauren."

Reject me...that's what.

She'd laid her heart on the line. She'd told him how she felt in the garden at Dunn Inn and he'd only turned around and walked away. No words. No comfort. No acknowledgment.

His silence had told her all she needed to know.

"Oh, I'm pretty sure he does. Nice talking with you. So long."

She walked off and felt Gabe's gaze follow her the entire way up the path until she disappeared from his view. He could stare all he wanted. She'd had nearly a week to pull herself together and had so far had done a good job. He was out of her thoughts.

Now all she had to do was get him out of her heart, as well.

Gabe missed Lauren like crazy. He missed talking to her. He missed how the scent of her perfume always seemed to linger on his clothes for ages after they'd spent time together. And he missed kissing her.

And he hated that he'd hurt her.

I would have rather have had five years, one year, one month with you...than a lifetime with someone else.

Her words haunted him. They were honest and heartfelt and much more than he was worthy of. And he'd been so tempted to take what she offered. More than tempted. He'd wanted it. Longed for it. *Ached* for it.

He'd wanted to wrap her in his arms and hold her there forever.

Except...he might not have forever to offer her. And she deserved that. She deserved more than an empty promise and his broken, defective body.

He headed back downstairs and started work. It was mind-numbing admin stuff, but at least it kept him busy. And gave him a chance to stop thinking about Lauren.

"That's one seriously gorgeous woman."

Gabe turned around. Aaron was hovering by the door. He knew his brother was talking about Lauren. "Aren't you supposed to be packing for your flight tomorrow?"

"Change of plans," he quipped. "Mom and I were just talking... We're staying another week."

Gabe groaned to himself. Another week? He wasn't sure he'd cope with another week of his well-meaning mother and annoying older sibling. "Why? Don't you have a life and two kids to get back to?"

Aaron smiled, walked into the office and plunked into a

chair. "You know very well that my ex-wife has the boys, and my business partner is running things while I'm away. And anyway, I wouldn't miss this chance to see you squirm for anything."

Gabe called him an unflattering name and pretended to work.

"You didn't answer my question," Aaron said.

He stared at the paperwork on his desk. "It wasn't a question," he reminded his brother. "It was a statement. And I'm not squirming."

Aaron laughed. "Oh, you sure as hell are. And I must say she's very pretty and kind of wholesome looking…but sexy underneath that whole girl-next-door thing, if you know what I mean."

Gabe knew exactly what he meant. He jerked his head up. "Haven't you got somewhere else to be? Someone else to irritate?"

Aaron linked his hands behind his head and stretched. "Nope…just you."

"I'm working."

"You're ignoring my question…got it bad, huh?"

Gabe scowled. "What I've got is work to do and no time to waste. I'll see you tonight, around six."

His family was staying at Dunn Inn for the duration of their trip, since Gabe had insisted his house wasn't ready for guests, and the B and B was more comfortable. But he'd put off having them around all week until they'd invited themselves over for dinner that night.

His brother left shortly afterward, and Gabe spent the day moving from bad mood to foul mood and in no particular order. Not even the news that he'd been successful in his interview with the hospital had lightened his spirits. There were licenses and insurances to renew, but he'd been offered a job in the E.R. and would start the following month. It meant he had time to hand in his resignation and help find a replacement.

By the time he returned home, it was well after five. He took a quick shower, dressed in jeans and T-shirt and was just marinating the steaks when he heard Scott's dual-cab truck pull up outside. He headed outside and walked down the steps. By the time he reached his brother and mother, another car had pulled up next door. He could see over the fence, and when he spotted Lauren walking down her driveway and then the male driver of the car get out, Gabe's body stilled. They were saying hello. She was smiling. The man opened the passenger door and she got into the car.

Aaron was now out of the truck and was also watching. He clamped Gabe on the shoulder and chuckled. "Looks as though you've got yourself some competition."

"Don't be an ass," Gabe said, and opened the door for their mother.

He greeted his mom and kept one eye on the car as it drove off down the cul-de-sac.

She's on a date....

It shouldn't have made him madder than hell. It shouldn't have made him feel anything. He'd made the rules. She'd opened her heart, and he'd refused to take it. But a date?

He was burning inside just thinking about it.

Over dinner, he stayed silent and let his brother and mom talk. Tension pressed down on his shoulders, and he couldn't quell the uneasy feeling in his gut. He'd told her to find someone else, and she'd done exactly as he'd suggested. It should have eased the guilt. But it didn't. It only amplified the confusion and discontent rumbling through his system and settling directly in the region of his heart.

When Aaron took a phone call and wandered off to the living room for some privacy, his mother cornered Gabe by the kitchen counter.

"So now that you've had a few days to calm down, would you like to tell me about Lauren?"

He shook his head. "No."

His mother sighed. "Do you know what I think? I think you're very much in love with her, and it scares you like you've never been scared before."

I'm not in love with her. I'm not in love with her. I'm not in love with her....

"Nonsense," he said, and started stacking plates in the dishwasher.

"Are you worried she'll leave like Mona did, should your health change?"

"Lauren is nothing like Mona," he replied, and continued stacking. "Actually, I'm concerned she'll do exactly the opposite."

His mother shook her head. "Gabe, isn't that her choice to make?"

"Not if I can help it." He straightened and placed his hands on the counter. "Please stay out of it, Mom. That means no interfering, no meddling… Promise me you'll just leave it alone."

"I can't do that," she said, and smiled. "When one of my kids is in trouble, I'll always interfere."

"I'm not in trouble," he insisted. "And I know what I'm doing. She's grieved for one man already. I won't be responsible for her having to do that over another."

"Another man? Who?"

He briefly explained about Tim. "Now, can we drop it?"

His mother nodded. "Yes, of course."

Gabe made coffee, and when Aaron returned, they sat around the table for a while, telling old tales about things they'd done as kids. Like the time Aaron got caught making out with the local minister's daughter, or when geeky, sixteen-year-old Luca got suspended from math club because he'd followed Gabe and Aaron and gotten a tattoo on his arm. The stories made him laugh and put him in a marginally better mood. He waved them off at nine-thirty but was back on the porch fifteen minutes later when he spotted a car return next door.

She got out and walked up the driveway as the car pulled away. So her date didn't see her to the door. *Schmuck.* Mounting dislike and rage festered in his gut for a few more minutes, and before he had a chance to stop himself, Gabe was striding around the fence, the hedge and then through the gate and up the steps.

He tapped on the door and waited. He heard her heels clicking on the timber floor, and when she pulled the door open, she looked genuinely surprised to see him.

"Oh…Gabe."

He shifted on his feet. She was so beautiful. Her hair was down, framing her perfectly lovely face, highlighting the deep caramel eyes that haunted him. She wore a little black dress that flipped over her hips and made every ounce of desire and longing he possessed surge to the surface in a wave.

"Who the hell was that?" he demanded once she'd opened the security door.

She moved back a little. "You mean my date?"

"Yeah," he shot back, so agitated he could barely get the word out. "Your *date.*"

She actually smiled. Like she thought him hilarious. Or the biggest fool of all time. Or both. "His name is Steve. Although I'm not quite sure how that's any of your business."

It wasn't. *She was on a date with someone named Steve.* Steve who? He hated the name, anyhow. *Forget about it… she can do whatever she likes. And with whomever she likes.* But be damned if the very idea of that didn't make every part of his flesh and bones ache.

"I was only…" He stopped, realizing nothing he could say would make him look like anything other than exactly what he was—a stupidly jealous idiot. It was a sobering realization. Had he ever been jealous before? Had he ever cared enough about anyone to garner such an emotional response?

No. Never.

I think you're very much in love with her, and it scares you like you've never been scared before....

His mother's words beat around in his head.

She made an impatient sound. "Goodbye, Gabe."

He didn't move. He stared at her. Long and deep. And the more he stared, the more he knew her impatience increased. And before he had a chance to question why, he reached out and pulled her close. She looked startled for a microsecond and then tilted her head and glared up at him. Body to body, breath to breath, Gabe experienced a connection with her that was so intense, so acute, it almost knocked him unconscious. Had her date kissed her? Had another man kissed those lips he'd somehow come to think of as his own? His arms tightened around her frame, drawing her against him so intimately, he could feel every lovely rise and curve.

She shook her head. "Don't you so much as think about—"

He claimed her lips, driving his own to hers with blatant passion and little finesse. He found her tongue and toyed with it, drawing it into an erotic dance as old as time. It took her seconds to respond, and she kissed him back, winding her tongue around his, and the sensation pitched an arrow of intense pleasure from his mouth to his chest and stomach and then directly to his groin. He urged her hips closer and groaned. She felt so good, and he wanted her so much. He wanted to strip her naked and feel every luscious curve and dip of her body. He wanted to lose himself in her sweet loving and forget he couldn't give her what she deserved.

Gabe was about to ease them both across the threshold

when she suddenly wrenched free. She pulled away from him and stumbled back on unsteady feet, dragging in big gulps of air.

She pressed the back of her fingers against her mouth. "Don't do that again."

"Lauren, I—"

"Leave me alone, Gabe. Don't kiss me. Don't touch me. Don't come over. Don't call. Don't so much as leave me a note in my letterbox. I'm done. You got that? *Done.*"

Then she closed the door in his face.

Lauren didn't sleep that night. She tossed in her bed and stared at the ceiling. How *dare* Gabe turn up on her doorstep and demand to know who she'd been out with. How *dare* he act all jealous and wounded. And how *dare* he kiss her like that! It was a kiss that had *possession* stamped all over it. And he didn't own her. Her broken heart had now turned into an angry one. He'd forfeited any rights she may have given him. She'd date whoever she wanted to. Even Steve, who had been the perfect gentleman over dinner and was polite and friendly and had done all the right things for a first date. And since he'd called her only ten minutes after dropping her off and asked if he could see her again, he was clearly emotionally available. Unlike Gabe, who obviously only wanted to kiss her and confuse her. So maybe Steve didn't make her pulse race.... He might, over time.

She finally dropped off to sleep after two and woke up with a headache. Saturday morning was busy at the store. Lauren had a gown fitting around ten and put on a smile when the exuberant client arrived with her wedding party. The dress was a beautiful concoction of ivory organza and lace, and it fitted the bride like a glove. By midday the last client had left, and Lauren closed the doors while her mother attended to the cashiering.

"Everything all right?"

Irene Jakowski was too smart to fool. Lauren had been on autopilot for most of the day, doing and saying the right thing, when inside she was confused and hurting and angry.

"Fine, Matka," she said when her mother repeated her question.

Her mother nodded and touched her arm. "There's someone special out there for you, I know it."

Lauren sighed. "I think I've already had my someone special."

"You mean Tim?" her mother asked. "Are you sure about that?"

She frowned just a little. "Of course. You know what he meant to me."

"I know," Irene said. "But you were young when you met, and teenage love can sometimes have you looking through rose-colored glasses."

"Are you saying Tim might not have been as perfect as I imagine he was?"

Irene nodded. "He was a nice young man, and I know you were compatible in many ways. And you might have been happy together. But sometimes easy isn't necessarily what will *keep* you happy. You married James on the rebound. All I'm saying is don't *settle* simply because you think you have to. And not when something wonderful might be within your reach."

She knew what her mother was suggesting. In her mother's romantic eyes, Steve was settling, and Gabe was Mr. Wonderful. "It was one date, Matka," she reminded her. "A nice date, but one date."

"That's how it starts."

No, it had started with heated looks, an argument and an unexpected fall into a swimming pool. Now she had to get him out of her system, her head and her heart.

"I'm not going to settle, I promise you. I've had enough of thinking I want the middle road. I told myself I would be happy with that because I felt so guilty about marrying James. I mean, the way I did it, the way I had everything the same as when I'd planned to marry Tim, only the groom was different. *That's* when I settled, when I married a man I didn't love because I was so wrapped up in having a big wedding. And it didn't make either of us happy. If my brief relationship with Gabe has shown me anything, it's that I want to be *in love.* Truly, madly and deeply. Because I know what it feels like now, and anything less simply won't be enough."

There were tears in her mother's eyes when she'd finished speaking. "I'm glad to hear you say that. I'm glad to hear you want to be happy. After Tim's death and then with James...I wondered if you'd ever risk your heart again. But you did. And I'm very proud of you."

Lauren shuddered out a long breath. "I did risk my heart, Matka. He just didn't want it."

On Saturday night, Gabe paced the rooms of his house like a caged bear. She'd gone out again. The same car had arrived to collect her at six o'clock. It was now close to ten, and she wasn't home. He tried painting the last of the bedrooms to take his mind off Lauren and her date and imagining her doing who knows what. When that didn't work, he poured bourbon he didn't drink, ordered pizza he didn't eat and ignored the two calls from Aaron on his cell.

He fell asleep on the sofa and woke up at midnight with a cramp in his neck. The lights were off next door and the realization that Lauren might have decided to stay out all night cut through him with the precision of a knife. By morning, Gabe was so wound up that he pulled on sweats and sneakers and ran for a solid hour, only caving when he got a stitch in his side. He jogged home, showered and changed into worn jeans and T-shirt and downed two cups of strong coffee.

When his mother arrived at ten, minus Aaron, he knew he was in for a sermon. He sat in the kitchen, cradling a mug of coffee and waited for it.

And got it in spades.

"I've been talking with Irene Jakowski," she said so matter-of-factly, she got his immediate attention. "And we've decided that we need to knock some sense into the pair of you."

Gabe actually laughed. "Mom, I think you and Mrs. Jakowski should stop colluding and accept the inevitable."

"And what's that? You're unhappy. Lauren's unhappy. The only thing that's inevitable is that it's going to stay that way unless you do something about it."

"She's moved on," he said, and pushed the mug aside. "Which is how it should be."

"Stubborn as a mule," his mother said, and tutted. "Just like your father."

"Realistic and sensible," he replied, and half smiled. "Just like you."

"Gabriel," she said with deliberate emphasis. "I'm going to say something I never thought I would ever have to say to you." She drew in a long breath. "Stop being such a coward."

"Mom, I—"

"All your life you've done the right thing. As a child, you never got into any serious trouble. You did well at school. You studied hard. You stayed away from the wrong crowds. You really were a pillar of strength when your dad died. Afterward, you pulled the family together. You were the glue, Gabe. I was so very proud when you got into medical school and then even more so when you became such a wonderful doctor. But I was so busy being proud, I failed to see that I'd relied on you too much."

His throat thickened. "You didn't, Mom."

"I did," she said. "And all that responsibility took a

heavy toll on you. While Aaron was acting wild and chasing girls and Luca was sticking his head into a computer to avoid thinking about what we'd all lost, you worked hard and got on with things. And I think a part of you closed down because of that responsibility. Aaron is charming and says whatever's on his mind, and Luca is all moody and mysterious and cross…but you don't let anything or anyone touch you."

She sighed and reached across the table to grasp his hand. "You got sick. And you should have shouted and complained and blamed something or someone…but you never did. You kept it inside and locked everyone else out. We were all falling apart at the idea of losing you, and you kept us at arm's length. Then you went back to work and something terrible happened." She squeezed his fingers. "You're not to blame, son. But the only way you're ever going to believe that is if you talk about it and share it and forgive yourself. And to do that, you need to let someone in."

Someone. *Lauren.*

"I can't," he said quietly. "I can't do that to her. Not after what she's been through. I can't promise her everything and potentially leave her with nothing. Not like Dad—"

"Nothing?" his mom said, and cut him off. "Do you think your father left me with nothing?" Her eyes glistened. "Gabe, your dad left me *everything.* He left me four incredible children and the memories of a wonderful life. Do you honestly think our marriage was defined by those last few years?"

Did he? Had he been so wrapped up in making sure they still worked as a family that he'd forgotten what it was like before his father became ill?

"I don't, not for one minute," his mother said earnestly, "resent a single moment of the time I spent caring for your dad when he was sick. He was my husband and the father of my children. He was my rock. My center." Tears welled in her eyes. "And I was honored that he trusted me when he was at his most vulnerable and let me care for him right up until the end."

Gabe swallowed the emotion in his throat. He remembered what Lauren had said to him about trust. She'd said Tim hadn't trusted her. She said he didn't trust her, either. And she was right. He didn't trust easily. Because he was afraid. Of being really seen. Of being considered less than strong and whole. Of being weak. And Lauren saw through that. She saw it all and had still wanted him. And like a fool, he'd pushed her away.

He looked at his mother. "You asked me a question a week ago, and I lied to you."

Her eyes widened. "What question?"

"You asked me if I was in love with her."

Claire Vitali smiled. "And are you?"

Gabe took a breath, felt the air fill his lungs and give him strength and nodded. "Yes, I'm completely and hopelessly in love with Lauren Jakowski."

Chapter Fourteen

Lauren was with a client on Monday afternoon and had finished lacing up the back panel on a beautiful beaded lace gown when a deliveryman arrived, carrying an extravagant floral arrangement. Her first thought was that they were from Steve, and although she considered it a bit too much after only two dates, flipped open the card and looked for his name.

Wrong.

No name. Just a message and an initial.

"Can we talk? G."

Not from Steve. He wasn't trying to change her mind about seeing him again. He'd texted her that morning to arrange another date. A text she'd put off replying to because she didn't want to lead him on. Then he'd called, and she'd declined his offer to go out that week. He was nice. But that was all. He'd taken her refusal easily and wished her well for the future.

She looked at the message again. Gabe. And he wanted to talk? As far as she was concerned, she'd said all she intended saying. They were done and dusted. She tossed the note in the trash and told Dawn, the salesclerk, to take the flowers home.

There was a note pinned to her door when she arrived home. "I would really like to talk with you." More talk? She scrunched the note in a ball and tossed it over the hedge and onto his front lawn.

Flowers arrived again the following day. Her mother and Dawn thought it was incredibly romantic. So did Cassie, when she relayed the story to her best friend. Mary-Jayne called her, too. And Grace. But she wasn't going to be swayed. She didn't want to talk to him. He'd had his chance, and he'd blown it.

On Wednesday, the flower deliveryman had a huge smile on his face when he entered the store. Lauren sent the young man away, flowers in hand, and felt an odd burst of triumph that she'd stuck by her guns. Of course, when she arrived home and found Gabe sitting on her porch steps, flanked by Jed, who wore a silly white bandana around his neck while Gabe held up a tiny white flag, her icy reserve thawed for a brief moment. Until she remembered he'd pushed her away time and time again.

"What's this?" she demanded, and flung her bag over her shoulder.

Gabe smiled and patted the dog on the head. "I borrowed him from your brother. I needed an ally."

She raised a brow and looked at the ridiculous flag. "You're looking for a truce?"

"I was thinking more along the lines of a complete surrender."

Her heart pounded. It was a romantic notion. But she wasn't falling for it. "I hear your family's still in town?"

"Yes," he replied, and got to his feet. The dog followed and rushed toward Lauren. "My mother would very much like to meet you properly."

"I can't imagine why." Lauren laughed loudly. "Since I intend to forget all about you, there's no point."

"You'll never forget me," he said, and stepped closer. "I'll bet that you'll remember me for the rest of your life."

Lauren laughed again. Egotistical jerk. "Have you been drinking?"

"I'm perfectly sober. Why did you send my flowers back today?" he asked.

"Because I don't want flowers or anything else from you."

He reached out and touched her hair, twirling the strands through his fingers. "The flowers are just a place to start."

"A place to start what?" she asked suspiciously as she pulled back from his touch.

"Our courtship."

"Courtship?" She laughed at the old-fashioned word and thrust her hands on her hips.

He *was* drunk. There was no other explanation. And he looked as if he was thinking of kissing her. Which was out of the question. She stepped back and frowned. "Why on earth would I want to do that?"

Gabe smiled that killer smile. "How about because you're in love with me?"

She laughed again, because she didn't know what else to do amidst the madness. "You're out of your mind. I'm going inside. Don't even think of following me."

"You didn't deny it."

"Because...because it's too ridiculous, and because I'm tired of this conversation."

She raced up the steps and fiddled with the door lock. She looked around, hoping he was gone. But no such luck. He stood at the bottom of the steps. Her body shook thinking about how handsome he looked, even holding the silly flag.

"I'll be here tomorrow," he said quietly. "Just in case you change your mind."

She frowned. "Don't you have to work?"

"I quit," he said softly. "I'm going back to medicine. I start in the E.R. at Bellandale Hospital next month."

"Good for you," she said extra sweetly.

"Don't you want to know why?"

She shrugged. "It's not my business."

He stared at her and didn't bother hiding the wounded expression. But she had no intention of backing down. He didn't have the right to simply snap his fingers and expect her to come running.

"I want to be the best man I can be…for you."

"What's the point?" she said flatly.

"Because I…I…"

"Good night, Gabe," she said exasperatedly. She unlocked the door. "And incidentally, I think courtship is meant to start before two people sleep together. We've had this back to front from the very beginning, and that's all the sign I need. And stop sending me flowers. I don't want them or anything else from you." Then she headed inside without looking back.

"Have you tried talking to her again?"

Romantic advice seemed to come out of the woodwork, Gabe discovered, when it became obvious to everyone he knew that Lauren wasn't about to forgive him anytime soon. This time it was his mother, who'd decided to hang around in Crystal Point for another week and dispense counsel about his failures to get Lauren's attention at every opportunity.

"Maybe it's time I had a talk with her," she suggested, and pushed her tea aside.

"You need another approach," a voice said from the doorway.

It was Cameron. *Great.* He was in for the big-brother talk. "Your point?"

Gabe figured he'd tried every approach he knew. He'd been on her doorstep each afternoon for the past four days, and she'd simply ignored him and gone into her house and locked the door. There were calls she wouldn't return, notes she wouldn't read and flowers she sent back. And he had a diamond ring in his pocket he wanted to give her, but was convinced she'd toss it in the trash. Total emasculation wasn't in his plans.

He'd wait. And hope she'd come around.

"No risk, no prize."

Cameron again. And this time, Scott and Aaron were behind him. Gabe looked up and scowled. "What?"

"Is she worth it?"

It was a stupid question, and with his patience frayed, Gabe dismissed the question with a barely audible grunt.

"Is she worth risking everything for?" Cameron asked again, relentless.

Gabe straightened in his seat. "Yes."

"Then tell her that."

In that moment, Gabe realized that he'd been so busy trying to woo Lauren with flowers and dinner invitations, he'd neglected to do the one thing he should have done an age ago.

Tell her the truth. Risking everything meant telling her everything. Like she'd told him time and time again. She'd trusted him. First with her past, then her body and then her heart. It was time he did the same. Because she knew what he'd been through and hadn't turned away. She accepted and wanted him. No questions. No prejudice. *No fear.* When, because of what she'd been through with Tim, she'd had every reason to run and not look back. But she hadn't. She'd put her heart on the line and he'd smashed it. Instead of applauding her courage and embracing that love, he'd brought up a whole load of excuses and reasons why they couldn't be together.

And one reason in particular.

Because he was scared of dying. Scared of living.

He let out a deep breath and looked at her brother. "So what's your big suggestion?"

Cameron grinned. "Well, asking her to forgive you for being a stupid ass hasn't worked, has it?"

Gabe thought about the flowers and the notes and the restrained effort he'd shown during the week. He talked about caring and wanting, and laughed at her attempts to ignore him. But he hadn't told her what she wanted to hear. "Not so far."

"Well, I reckon it's time for you to start begging and prove to her you'll do anything you have to do to win her heart."

And that, Gabe thought with a weary laugh, might just work.

Lauren was ever thankful that Saturday mornings were always busy at the store. It kept her mind away from thinking about anything else. Or anyone else. Or someone in particular.

A bridal party arrived at ten for their final fittings, and when the bride emerged from the changing room in her dress, Lauren set to work, fluffing the three layers of tulle and organza before she adjusted the straps and stepped away so the client's mother and attendants could admire her. When the fitting was complete and the bride was out of her gown, Lauren handed the client over to Dawn to process the sale and bag up the goods.

The bell above the door dinged and Lauren smiled when Cassie and Mary-Jayne entered the store.

"Hi, there," she said, and looked at her friends. "What are you both doing here?"

Cassie grinned. "Reinforcements."

"Huh?"

Her friend shrugged and kept smiling. "Trust me."

"You know I—" The door opened again. The bell dinged. And Gabe's mother walked into her store.

"Good morning, Lauren," she said before Lauren had a chance to move. "I'm not sure if you remember me from last week—I'm Claire Vitali." She grabbed her hand and squeezed it gently.

Lauren stared at the older woman. She had the same eyes as her son, the same smile. There was kindness in her expression and warmth in her hand. Her resolve to stay strong wavered. But she wasn't about to be easily swayed.

"It's nice to meet you," she said, and withdrew her hand. "I'd like to stay and talk but I have to—"

"It can wait," Mary-Jayne said with one of her famous grins.

The door opened again, and Grace and Evie entered.

Lauren frowned. "What's going on?"

"Reinforcements, like I said," Cassie explained.

Panic rushed through her blood. Something was wrong. "Has something happened? Is it my dad, or Cameron or—"

"You're father is fine," her mother said as she emerged from the stockroom.

"So is your brother," Grace added.

Lauren backed up. "I don't think—"

"That's just it, Lauren," Cassie said gently. "Stop thinking. At least, stop *overthinking.* We're all here because we care about you."

She stilled as realization dawned. "So this is, what, an intervention? That's why you're all here?"

"Actually, I think they're all here to stand point and make sure I do the right thing."

Gabe...

She hadn't heard him come through the door. He moved around Evie and Grace and stood near the counter. Lauren remained rooted where she was. Her legs turned to Jell-O. Her heart raced like a freight train. She looked at her family and friends. They were smiling, all hopeful, all clearly wondering what she would do next.

I wish I knew.

It was hard not to stare at Gabe. He looked so good, and she'd missed him. But he'd hurt her. And she didn't want to be hurt again.

"This isn't the right time or place to have this discussion," she said, and tried to politely ignore the bridal party hovering behind her.

"Since you won't talk to me, I reckon it's the only time," he said, and flashed her customers a breathtaking smile. "I'm sure everyone will understand."

The bride nodded, and before Lauren had a chance to protest, her mother had subtly ushered the bridal party from the store.

"What do you want?" she asked as stiffly as she could once the customers were gone.

He took a breath. "First, to apologize."

Lauren shuttled her gaze to her mother, Claire Vitali, Cassie and the other women and saw they were all smiling. Like they knew exactly what was going on. "Okay—apology accepted. You can *all* go now."

But they didn't move.

"I mean it," she said crossly. "Don't think just because you'd managed to swindle everyone into coming here today that I'm going to simply forget everything you've said and done and—"

"They volunteered," he said.

She looked at the sea of faces. "I don't believe it."

"You should. They care about you and only want to see you happy."

"Exactly," she said, and frowned. "Which has nothing to do with you."

"It has everything to do with me," he shot back. "I make you happy."

"You make me mad," she snapped.

"Well, I'd make you happy if you'd let me."

She forced her hands to her hips. "And how do you propose to do that?"

"I'll get to the proposing in a moment. Now, where were we? Oh, yes, I was—"

"What?" Her eyes bulged. "You're going to propose?"

"Well, of course I'm going to propose. But back to what I was saying. Oh, yes…and second," he said, and came a little closer, "I'd like to tell you a story."

"A story?" she echoed vaguely, certain she'd just imagined that he said he was about to propose. "I don't know what—"

"It's a story about a man who thought he was invincible." He spoke so softly she almost strained to hear, but she was quickly mesmerized by the seductive tone of his voice. "He thought nothing and no one could touch him. He went to medical school and became a doctor and spent his days trying to fix people who were broken. But underneath that facade of caring and compassion, he was arrogant and stubborn and always did what he wanted because he thought he knew best. And then one day he was told he was sick and everything changed. He wasn't strong. He wasn't healthy. Now he was broken but he couldn't fix himself. He had the surgery and the treatment, but because he was stubborn and arrogant, he went back to work before he should have."

Lauren's throat closed over. Her heart was breaking for him. His pain was palpable, and she longed to fall into his arms. She had been so attuned to him, she hadn't noticed that their mothers and friends had somehow left the store. Everyone was outside and they were alone. She could see them through the big front window. They were smiling. And suddenly, she almost felt like smiling, too. Right now, in front of her, lay her future. But she didn't smile. Because he was opening up, and she wanted to hear everything.

"Gabe, I—"

"I went back to work too early," he said, his voice thick. "I didn't listen. I didn't want to hear it. I just wanted to prove that I was the same. That I wasn't damaged and somehow less than the man I once was. Less than the doctor I once was. But while I was in the bathroom throwing up from the side effects of the medication I was on, the woman and her baby came into the E.R. I wasn't there. And she died, along with her baby. All because I wouldn't admit that I *was* changed. That I was suddenly not just a man. Not just a doctor. I was a cancer patient. And it felt as though those words defined me, made me, *owned* me."

Her entire body shuddered. The raw honesty in his words melted her. "That's why you quit being a doctor? Because you believed that patient died because you were sick? Because you were somehow less than who you used to be?"

"Yes."

Her expression softened. "But you're not."

"I know that now," he said, and smiled. "I know that because when you look at me, I know you don't see a patient. You don't see a man who was sick. You just see…me."

He stepped closer, and Lauren swayed toward him. "Of course I do."

"Doesn't anything scare you, Lauren?" he asked, and took her hand. "After what you went through with Tim, doesn't the very idea of being with me make you want to run?"

"I've only ever seen you, Gabe. Not the doctor, not the patient. The man…the man who has listened to me and comforted me and makes me feel more alive than anyone else ever has. A man who's kind and considerate and has never judged me. And I'm not scared."

He pulled her gently toward him.

"The only thing I'm scared of is waking up and finding that this is a dream."

"It's no dream," he said softly. "You must know that I'm in love with you."

Did Gabe just say he loved me?

She shook her head, not quite prepared to believe him. "No, you're not."

"I am," he said, and touched her cheek. "I love you. I love

that you make me laugh. I love that you tell me when I'm being an egotistical jerk. And I love that you had the courage to let me into your heart when you had every reason not to."

Lauren blinked back tears. "But…you said you had a plan and wouldn't—"

"A stupid plan," he said, and grasped her hand. "I was wrapped up in self-pity and afraid to get involved, and you knew it. You saw through me, Lauren, and still…still wanted me. Even when you knew there was a chance it might not be forever, or I could get sick again. Or I might not be able to give you the children you want." He linked their fingers. "You talk straight and make the complicated simple. You told me how you felt and it spooked me. I'm not proud of my behavior these past weeks, and I promise I'll always be honest about my feelings with you from this day. You have such incredible strength…a strength you don't even know you possess."

Lauren swayed, felt his arms beckoning her. He looked solemn, sincere and wholly lovable. "I don't know…I'm not sure I can."

He squeezed her fingers. "You can, Lauren. Trust me…I won't hurt you again."

"Trust you?" She looked at the sea of faces peering through the windows. "Even though you dragged my friends and family here today to give you an advantage?"

He smiled. "It was Cameron's idea. He thought if I made a big enough fool out of myself in front of our families, you just might just show mercy and forgive me for being an idiot." He came closer until they were almost touching. "I love you, Lauren. I think I've loved you from the moment I pulled you from that swimming pool. And I'm sorry I haven't said it sooner."

He really loves me? Her legs wobbled, and he took her in his arms. "You're not going to completely ruin my reputation and kiss me in front of all these people who are staring at us through the window, are you?"

"I certainly am."

She heard whoops and sighs from the people outside, and Lauren laughed. It felt good. She thawed a little more. Gabe's love was what she wanted. *All* she wanted. And suddenly having the whole world know it didn't bother Lauren in the slightest. He was right—she was strong. Strong enough to open her heart again. And strong enough to cope with whatever the future brought them. He'd pushed past his fears to claim her, and she loved him all the more for it.

"But first," he said, and stepped back a little, "I have to ask you a question."

"What question is that?" she teased, and grinned foolishly.

Gabe dropped to one knee in front of her. "Marry me?" he asked, and pulled a small box from his pocket. The lid flipped open and she saw the perfectly cut diamond, which glittered like his eyes. "When you're ready, when you trust me enough, marry me, Lauren?"

Lauren touched his face and held out her left hand and sighed. "I think you've made a big enough fool out of yourself today for me to know I can trust you, Gabe. And my answer is yes. I'll marry you. I love you." She grinned. "And I kind of like the idea of being a doctor's wife."

Gabe got to his feet, slipped the ring onto her finger and kissed her. "I have you to thank for making me see sense, for making me realize how much I've missed my work. I was afraid to go back. I was afraid to try to recapture what I'd lost. But knowing you and loving you has made me stronger. You make me whole."

Lauren returned his kiss with every ounce of love in her heart. "You're the love of my life, Gabe."

His gaze narrowed. "I thought—"

"You," she said, and touched his face. "Only you. I did love Tim, but honestly, anything I've felt in the past feels a bit like kid stuff compared to the way I love you. And want you. And need you."

His eyes glistened. “Thank you. And while I may not be the first man you’ve loved, I’m honored to be the one you love now.”

“Now and forever.” She pressed against him and smiled. “But, Gabe, where are we going to live? Your place or mine?”

“How about neither?” he suggested. “How about we find somewhere new? A new home for a new beginning.”

“I like the sound of that,” Lauren said, and accepted his kiss. “And I’d like to get a dog,” she said breathlessly when the kissing stopped.

He grinned. “Anything you want.”

Lauren curved against him. “And babies?”

His arms tightened around her, and he smiled. “I’ll see what I can do.”

She sighed. “I’m not worried, Gabe. I want to marry you and have your baby. But if there’s only ever us, that will be enough.”

“You’re sure?”

“Never surer.”

She kissed him again, knowing she finally had her happy ending.

* * * * *

HER OUTBACK COMMANDER

MARGARET WAY

CHAPTER ONE

Vancouver
Canada

HE KNEW her the moment she moved into the hotel lobby. The doorman in his natty top hat held the door for her, his face wreathed in smiles. Who could blame him? A woman like that inspired smiles. But just why he was so sure it was *she* he couldn't fathom. Gut feeling? He didn't question it, even when it went against all his preconceptions. But then his mental picture had been based on the description Mark had given his mother, Hilary, in a one-off letter sent months after he had married the Canadian girl. Nevertheless the feeling of recognition was so powerful it was almost a force in itself. It shook him when he was a man who shielded himself against shock.

For one thing, Mark's description didn't begin to do her justice. She was *beautiful*. No other word would do. She always would be, given her bone structure, he thought. She also radiated an air of refinement—a cool reserve that in itself was unusual. Not Mark's scene at all. She was immaculately groomed, her stylishness understated. She was a recent widow, after all, he thought grimly. Obviously her lovely outward appearance camouflaged the shallowness of the woman beneath.

He had chosen the most inconspicuous spot he could find to wait for her. He reasoned it would give him a slight advantage, observing her before she had a chance to observe him. That way he might be able to form a better idea of what sort of young woman Mark had married. Right now he found himself unable to grasp the reality when set against his half brother's description. Where, for instance, was the blonde hair? And surely she was supposed to be petite? But then she was wearing high heels, and women moved on, changing their hair colour as fashion or mood dictated.

He knew in his bones he hadn't picked the wrong woman, despite the many discrepancies. He was supposed to keep an open mind. This had to be Mandy—Mark's widow, Amanda. She didn't look like a Mandy, or even an Amanda. Pretty names, but they didn't suit her. Perhaps it was one of Mark's little jokes? From boyhood Mark had revelled in deception, spinning an elaborate web of fantasies, half-truths and shameless lies that had tied everyone in knots. Their father had once confided he was worried Mark was becoming something of a sociopath. A harsh judgement when their father hadn't been a judgemental man. But it had to be admitted Mark had barely registered the difference between right and wrong. Nothing had stopped him when his mind was set on something. He certainly hadn't *cared* about people. His self-interest had been profound. That hadn't been an easy truth for either his father or him to accept.

As for his tastes in young women? Mark had only been interested in pretty girls who had all their assets on show. Other qualities a young woman might offer, like warmth, companionship, spirituality or intellect, came right down the list. Mark's type had always been the stereotypical glamour girl. "Air-heads" Marcia, his twin, had always called them acidly, with the exception of Joanne Barrett, the fiancée Hilary had picked out for her son and whom Mark had so callously abandoned. This woman he had finally chosen to marry presented a striking departure from the norm.

As she stood poised a moment, looking about her, he rose to his feet to hold up an identifying hand. Poor Joanne wouldn't have been in the race beside this young woman, he thought, with regret mixed with resentment. There was no comparison. At least in the looks department.

No welcoming smile appeared on her face.

Nor on his.

His heart was locked against her like cold steel.

She walked towards him, a willowy figure, glancing neither to left nor right. She seemed to have little idea of the admiring glances she was receiving, from men and women alike. But then a beautiful woman would never escape constant attention. She was probably so used to it she didn't notice.

His trip to Vancouver, beautiful city though it was, surrounded by mountains and sea, unfortunately wouldn't entail pleasure, or even time for some sightseeing. He regretted that. But he would have to say he wasn't at home in such cold—let alone the rain. Outside the centrally heated hotel it was *freezing*, with a biting wind. He had never known it to be so cold, even when wintering in Europe. He had been born and raised on a vast Australian cattle station on the fringe of one of the world's great deserts, the scorching blood-red Simpson. But he was here for a specific purpose: to arrange for his half-brother's body to be taken home and to invite Mark's widow to return with him to Australia, to attend the funeral and finally meet the family. The family she had chosen to totally ignore for the two short years of her marriage.

He didn't think she would ignore them now. There was a sizable legacy he wished to give her, for a start. Very few people knocked back money. Besides, a few deserving people had a right to know why Mark had acted the way he had. First and foremost his mother Hilary, his twin Marcia, and the cruelly jilted Joanne. *He* needed no explanations. Mark's actions had *never* shocked him. And they had never shocked their late father, who had spent the last two years of his life as an invalid, his spine fractured so badly that two operations hadn't helped at all. The titanium pins simply hadn't been able to hold. To make matters so much more devastating, their father had suffered a rare type of amnesia since his near fatal accident. He remembered nothing of the day when he, a splendid horseman, born in the saddle, had been thrown violently from his favourite mare Duchess.

She walked towards him quite calmly, when inside she was anything but calm. This was Blaine Kilcullen. Mark's brother. She would have recognised him even if he hadn't raised that signalling hand. It was an authoritative hand—the hand of a man well used to getting instant attention. Yet the gesture didn't strike her as arrogant. More a natural air of command. He was very tall. Much taller than Mark. Six-three, she guessed, with wide square shoulders, long lean limbs. Superbly fit. He cut an impressive figure. But then Lucifer had been a splendid angel before the Fall.

Memories shunted into her mind: Mark's damning condemnation of his brother.

Handsome as Lucifer and just as deadly.

It had been delivered with a kind of primal anger, even hate. Mark had had a big problem with anger, she remembered. Indeed there had been quite a few aspects of Mark's personality she had found jarring, and had done so right from the start. Charming one minute, and within the space of another he could turn oddly cold, as if the shutters had come down. Impossible to pinpoint the exact reason for the abrupt change.

Mark had claimed his brother was the cause of so much of the unhappiness and pain in his life. He might well have contributed, she reasoned, given the strength of Mark's bitterness and his sense of abandonment.

"Blaine is the reason I had to get away. Leave my home, my own country. My dad died, but long before he died he rejected me—because of Blaine and his manipulative ways. Blaine was out to eliminate me and he did it in the worst possible way. He bitterly resented Dad's love for me. In the end Dad pushed me away. I was never good enough. I could never measure up. Snow will blanket the Simpson before I speak to my brother again."

Alas, Mark had got his wish. At least in part. He *had* been fated never to speak to his brother again. He had died in snow. A skiing accident after he had, despite warnings, left the trail they had been taking and not long after crashed headlong into a tree. She and Amanda had been watching at the time. It had been a horrible experience, one that could never be forgotten. But Mark had enjoyed playing the dare-devil, like some macho adolescent. Perhaps his former life, the never-ending efforts to prove himself against a superior brother, had dictated his attitude? At times she'd had the awful dread he might be borderline suicidal. He'd definitely had issues. But then she had managed to convince herself she was most likely overreacting. She was no psychiatrist, after all.

"Amanda?" The cattle baron extended a lean, darkly tanned hand.

Time for her to unfold another one of Mandy's stories.

She had spent so many years covering for her cousin she was starting to feel drained.

"I'm so sorry, Mr Kilcullen." His handshake was firm, brief, but she felt a very real *frisson* of reaction—a kind of shock wave produced by skin on skin. She tried to hide her involuntary reaction, launching into an explanation. "There wasn't time to let you know, I'm afraid. I'm Sienna Fleury, Amanda's cousin. Amanda asked me to take her place. A migraine. It came on quite suddenly. She suffers from them."

"I see."

Exquisitely polite. But she had no difficulty reading his mind. More cold indifference from the woman Mark had married. More rejection of the Kilcullen family of him as the family envoy.

"Please allow me to offer my most sincere condolences." She spoke gently. "I was fond of Mark." It was far from the truth, but then it never did seem right to speak ill of the dead. At the beginning she had made a super-human effort to like Mark, but there had always been something in his eyes that disturbed her. Amanda, however, had fallen madly in love with him, so in rejecting Mark the family had known it would be as good as rejecting Amanda. Something she could not do, having looked out for Amanda for years like a surrogate big sister.

"Thank you, Ms Fleury." He felt his grim mood softened by her lovely speaking voice. The musical Canadian accent fell soothingly on his ear. Looking back at her, he felt something click in his mind, pretty much as if a light switch had been turned on. Hadn't Amanda's *bridesmaid* featured quite a bit in Mark's letter to his mother? At the time Hilary had confessed she found the talk of the bridesmaid quite odd. Could *this* be the anonymous bridesmaid? From believing she was Mark's widow, he was now convinced she could be Amanda's bridesmaid.

Sienna, quietly observing him, detected the shift in his attitude. She wondered what had caused it. From Mark's account the brothers had been mortal enemies. Believing her husband implicitly, Amanda had made no effort to contact her late husband's estranged family, no effort to effect some sort of reconciliation. She had even been obdurate in not wanting to advise them of Mark's fatal accident. But that had been against the right code of behaviour. Sienna had contacted her father, Lucien Fleury, one of Canada's most highly esteemed artists, and begged him to make the call as Amanda couldn't or wouldn't.

"Always been problematic, hasn't she? Poor little Mandy." An understatement from her father, who rarely bothered to mince words.

Amanda was his niece. His sister Corinne and her husband had been killed in a car crash when Amanda was five. Sienna's parents, Lucien and Francine, had taken in the orphaned Amanda, raising her with Sienna, eighteen months older, and Sienna's adored older brother Emile, now a brilliant architect and interior designer working out of New York.

Blaine Kilcullen's deep voice, with its clear cutting edge, broke into her thoughts. No discernible Aussie accent. More a cosmopolitan voice. "Shall we have a drink before dinner?" he suggested, his diamond gaze revealing nothing of what he thought of her and her unheralded role as stand-in for his half-brother's widow.

"I'd like that." What else could she say? She actually found him every bit as daunting as Mark had said. But then she had to give him a little leeway. These were unhappy times.

* * *

Inside the luxurious lounge, he helped her remove her cashmere coat, laying it over the back of a chair along with the deep yellow scarf she had worn around her throat. It was quite a while since she had been inside this downtown Vancouver boutique hotel. She glanced appreciatively around her. The hotel was famous for its European style: glossy, warm dark timbers, richly upholstered furniture, fine antique pieces, lots of lovely flowers, and beautiful works of art that adorned the public areas as well as the luxurious suites.

He held her chair. She sat down, smoothing back the long hair that had been caught into her woollen scarf.

"What would you like?" He diverted his gaze from the shining waterfall of hair, turning his attention to the ceiling-high, well-stocked bar.

"Perhaps a brandy cocktail?" She didn't really want anything.

He settled for a fine cognac.

Careful not to stare, she was nevertheless making her own assessment with her artist's eye. At twenty-six she already had several successful art showings behind her. She was also a talented photographer, with a good body of work. Her primary job, however, was managing her father's gallery in Vancouver, and overseeing two others—one in Toronto, the other in New York. What was her take on the man in front of her? Blaine Kilcullen, Australian cattle baron, was without a doubt the most striking-looking man she had ever seen, even allowing for the severe expression on his handsome face. But then he would be in mourning for his brother. Bitter regrets, surely? Thoughts of "what might have been"?

He was wearing a beautifully tailored dark suit with a silk tie she very much liked: wide cobalt blue and silver stripes, the blue edged with a fine line of dark red. He would probably look just as elegant in traditional cattleman's gear, she thought. The leanness and the long limbs made an ideal frame for clothes. The surprising thing was the Mark hadn't resembled his brother in the least. Mark had had golden-brown hair and mahogany dark eyes, and he'd been around five-ten. This man was darkly handsome. His thick hair had a natural deep wave, and his strongly marked brows were ink-black. In stunning contrast his eyes had the glitter of sun on ice.

Their drinks arrived. She readied herself for what was to come. Conversation would be difficult. The great irony was that it wasn't her affair at all. *Amanda* was Mark's widow. It was *Amanda's* place to attend this crucial meeting with a member of Mark's family, albeit estranged. Only Amanda had pulled the old hysteria trick. Over the years she had turned it into an art form. The sad fact of the matter was Amanda really could make herself ill, thus giving her the upper hand. They had all bowed to her tantrums, acutely sympathetic to the fact she had lost her parents, but by the time she'd reached her teens it had become apparent that Amanda actually enjoyed wallowing in her feelings. Earlier in the day she had maintained, with tears gushing, she couldn't *possibly* meet Mark's cruel, callous brother.

"We're talking about the brother who tried to wreck his life, Sienna. You expect me to head off to a pow-wow, smoke the peace pipe? Not likely!"

Mark had impressed upon Amanda and the family that he had *hated* his brother, blaming him for his banishment from the Kilcullen ancestral home—although he had been very sketchy about that. It was a desert fortress, apparently, set down in the middle of nowhere. She had checked the Simpson area out on the internet, reading about the breathtaking changes that occurred in the wilderness after rain. It sounded quite fascinating.

Mark had thought differently. “Canada suits me fine. God knows it’s far enough away—the other side of the world.” From time to time there had been such abrupt surges of anger, amounting to rants, flushed skin, darting eyes. She’d once suggested Mark might need professional help to Amanda, falling back defensively against Amanda’s hysterical tirade.

“How dare you? Dare you? Dare you?”

Sienna had never mentioned it again.

The odd thing was Mark hadn’t met Amanda in their home city of Vancouver. He had met her when she and Amanda were holidaying in Paris. Mark had been working behind the bar of their luxury hotel at the time.

“Just a fun job, and I get to meet all the beautiful girls.”

Mark had lived for fun, taking casual jobs here and there in the hospitality industry where—surprisingly—he had shone. But then Mark had been physically a very attractive man. Only he had committed to nothing. Amanda was a born flirt, who’d had a succession of boyfriends, but she had fallen for him good and hard—and in a remarkably short time. As for Sienna herself, the sensible one, she hadn’t taken to Mark—despite his good-looks and superficial charm. But he’d been the type Amanda had always been attracted to.

It hadn’t come as much of a surprise when Mark had followed them home less than a month later. He’d met the family, who had recognised an imbalance there, but felt compelled for Amanda’s sake to be tolerant. Amanda paid attention to no one, but in retrospect it would have been an excellent idea for her to listen. She would have no other. Within six months she and Mark had been married, at a small but lavish affair Lucien had turned on for them. There had been no one on Mark’s side, although there had been a goodly sprinkling of Fleurys and friends to swell the numbers and make an occasion of it. It had later been revealed Amanda had been pregnant the time—something she had kept from them—but sadly she had miscarried barely a month later. She had not fallen pregnant again for the remainder of their short and, as it had turned out, largely unhappy marriage.

Sienna had often wondered if that was the reason Mark had married Amanda—although to be fair Amanda was very pretty and she could be good company when the mood took her. It had never seemed to Sienna that Mark had been in love with her cousin. Using her, maybe? Their family was wealthy. Her father was an eminent artist, her mother a dermatologist and her brother was becoming quite a celebrity designer. For that matter she was doing pretty well herself. Only Mark had never seemed short of money. He'd appeared to have private means. The jobs he'd taken had seemed to be no more than hobbies. At one time he had tried to talk her into allowing him to join her at the gallery. No question of that. She hadn't wanted Mark anywhere near her. He made her very uneasy. Barely a year into the marriage Mark had finally shown her why. She couldn't bear to think about that awful, shameful evening. It still haunted her. From that night on she had *loathed* him…

Blaine Kilcullen was speaking, drawing her out of her dark, disturbing thoughts. "I do hope your cousin is well enough to speak to me tomorrow, Ms Fleury. I need to see her."

"Of course you do," she hastily agreed, thinking there would be world peace before Amanda got out of bed.

"What is the real reason for her not coming, Ms Fleury?"

"Please—Sienna." She took a sip of her cocktail. It perturbed her, the effect this man was having on her. It was as if he had a magnetic power. She was usually composed. Or that was her reputation. Amanda was the bubbly one. At least before her brief marriage had started to disintegrate.

"Sienna it is." He smiled briefly. That was enough. The smile lit the sombreness of his expression like an emerging sun cut through clouds. "Sienna—a significant name. Was it inspired by the colour of your hair?" He let his eyes linger on her long, lustrous mane. It was centre-parted no doubt to highlight the perfect symmetry of her oval face. The colour was striking: a blend of dark red, amber and coppery-brown. Her large beautiful eyes were thickly lashed. The colour put him in mind of fine sherry when held up to the light.

"My father named me," she said, a smile playing around her mouth. "Apparently even as a newborn my fuzz of hair was the colour of burnt sienna. That's a paint pigment. My father is quite a famous artist here in Canada. Lucien Fleury." She spoke with love and pride.

"It was *your* father, then, who rang Mark's mother to let her know of the accident?" Things were starting to fall into place.

Mark's mother. Why not *our* mother? "Yes, Amanda was so distraught she had to be sedated." Not true. Amanda had been drunk. Another cover-up. Amanda had taken to alcohol big-time.

"I feel I should see your father's work," he said, surprising her. "My family have been great collectors over the years. I have a great-aunt—Adeline—living in Melbourne, whose house is like a private museum. Paintings, sculptures, antiques, Oriental rugs, the most exquisite Chinese porcelains behind glass. She tells me every time she sees me she's leaving me the lot."

"Does that please you?" He was a cattle baron, a man of action, of the Great Outdoors, though his whole persona was that of a cultured man of the world. "Not everyone likes such things." She had friends who had little taste for art and antiques though they had the money to possess both.

His handsome mouth was compressed. A sexy mouth, very clean cut, its edges raised. She knew he wasn't married. That had emerged during the course of the conversation between Mrs Hilary Kilcullen and her father. "In my case, I do. But God knows where it will all go. My current plan is to give the lesser stuff away. There's quite a large extended family. But you wouldn't know about that."

"Unfortunately, no." She lowered her gaze. "I should point out it's *Amanda* who is your brother's widow."

"Half-brother," he corrected a shade curtly, again surprising her. Mark had never said. "My mother died of the complications of malaria when I was going on six years of age. She and my father were staying at a friend's coffee plantation in New Guinea at the time. Both of them had had their shots, but in my mother's case the vaccine didn't take. My father, our New Guinea friends, the entire family were devastated by the loss. I still remember my beautiful mother, though those memories have kept changing over time. Hard to forget what she looked like, however. My father commissioned a large portrait of her by a famous Italian artist to celebrate their marriage. It hung in the Great Room. It never came down."

Not even when the second wife, Mark's mother, took her place? That couldn't have been easy for Hilary Kilcullen. Come to that, this cattle baron himself was eminently paintable. She knew her father could do a wonderful portrait of him, but she very much doubted whether he would be up for a commission.

"So you have a permanent reminder of your mother," she said with gentle compassion. "I'm so sorry for your loss.

The feeling of being deprived of your mother must never go away. I'm very close to my mother. I can't imagine life without her."

"Then you're blessed," he said, looking across the small circular table and right into her eyes.

Really looking—as though she was in some way important to him or his agenda.

"And you have both your parents," he continued. "My father died a few years back."

Just as Mark had said. She'd concluded Blaine Kilcullen was a man of iron control, but a flash of pain crossed his chiselled features.

"Dad remarried, according to Adeline, to give me a stepmother." He didn't tell her Adeline had actually said a ready-made nanny. Everyone in the family knew his father's marriage to Hilary had been one of convenience, although Hilary, daughter of a pastoralist friend of the family, had long idolized Desmond Kilcullen from afar.

"Mark never made it clear you and he were half brothers. He always talked about you as though you were—well… full brothers."

"Did he?" He took care to keep his tone even. He could well imagine what Mark had told them all, the damage Mark had done. Not only to him, but to the rest of the family. Mark had near destroyed himself with bitterness and resentment. "Mark was still engaged to a very nice young woman when he took off without a word to anyone," he said, just to put part of the record straight. "He jumped on a freight plane that had flown machinery into the station, as it happened. From the look on your face you didn't know about that either."

"Remember, please," she said again, "I'm Amanda's cousin." She needed to explain her lack of knowledge.

"But you are close?" He resumed his piercing silver-grey scrutiny.

She hoped she didn't flush. She and Amanda had co-existed rather than ever growing close as she had hoped. The closeness simply hadn't happened. "Amanda's parents were killed when she was five. Her parents were returning from a long trip and her father apparently fell asleep at the wheel. *My* mother and father opened up their home and their hearts to Amanda. Amanda, my brother Emile and I all grew up together. He's a highly gifted architect and interior designer."

"So the artistic gift runs in the family?" he said. "May I ask what *you* do?"

He actually sounded interested. "I manage one of my father's galleries, and I paint myself. As you say, it's in the blood."

"Do you show your work?"

She gave him a sparkling glance. He knew the sparkle was unconscious, but a man could find it powerfully seductive. "I've had four showings up to date. Each time they become more successful. I specialize in landscapes, the occasional still-life. My father's speciality is portraiture, though he can paint anything. Many of his subjects have been very important people, and of course very beautiful women. My father worships a woman's beauty. I'm not in his league—" she smiled "—but Lucien is wonderfully supportive. Which is not to say he isn't highly critical when he feels the need. My brother loves Dad but he took off to New York to make his own way in the world. When Emile is home it's like being around twins—Dad and Emile are so much alike." She changed the subject, although she could see his interest was unfeigned. "Did you know Amanda and Mark actually met in Paris, not here in Vancouver?"

He gritted fine white teeth. "Sienna, it was Mark's plan

to vanish into thin air. At that time he was a very disturbed young man." No need to add that he'd had chips as big as desert boulders on both shoulders.

"You don't want me to press you about Mark?" At her question he gave her a searching look. It was as though he wanted to know everything that went on inside her.

"I think I have summed it up," he said in a clipped voice.

"Perhaps you should know what he thought of *you*?" Unforgivably, she was returning his brusqueness.

"Not right now," he said. "Mark was family. His death matters."

He had turned the tables on her. She felt ashamed of herself. "Of course it matters. Please forgive me. I only thought it would explain so much about Amanda if I could tell you—"

"That Mark hated me?" His black brows rose. "Sienna, I *know*. It was a very bad case of sibling rivalry. We all live in isolation on a vast Outback station, yet Mark and I never really connected. We never did things together. It's hard to explain."

Not to me, she thought. It was almost exactly her experience with Amanda.

"I was my father's heir. His firstborn. Mark grew up knowing I was the one who would inherit Katajannga. That's the name of our cattle station. Not that he had any interest in being or becoming a cattle man."

Her interest had soared. "That's the name of your station? Katajannga? How extraordinary Mark never mentioned that."

"Mark kept a lot of things locked up," he said sombrely. "There's a long story attached to the name. It more or less means 'revelation', or sometimes 'many lagoons' when translated from the aboriginal. One can understand why. After good rains the desert is indeed a revelation."

Her beautiful eyes, fixed on his, revealed her fascination. "I'm here to listen."

"When Mark's wife is not?"

She sat back abruptly, trying to interpret the question. "You said that as though you're trying to catch me out?"

"Did I?" He didn't back down.

"I can't be held responsible for Amanda, you know."

"Of course not. But I have the feeling you're covering for her now."

She released the breath she'd been holding. "Amanda just can't deal with this now, Mr Kilcullen. Surely you understand?"

Heightened feelings were contagious. "How well did you know Mark?"

A flash of temper put fire in her deep golden eyes. "As well as anyone knew him."

"An odd answer, surely? Or do you mean his wife aside?"

"Please don't hassle me, Mr Kilcullen," she said, sitting straighter.

"God forbid!" A smile tugged at his mouth. "And I insist you call me Blaine. After all, you invited me to call you Sienna. I'm not a monster, you know."

"Aren't you?" Mark had really hated him.

He read her mind. "Probably Mark's *exact* word. Monster. Should I be offended?"

Colour rose beneath her lovely creamy skin. "I'm just seeking the truth."

He lifted his brandy balloon, took a mouthful, savouring it before responding. "Sienna, Mark may have seen me that way," he said tersely, "but I'd like *you* to keep an open mind. You won't find anyone from where I come from to hang a label like that on me. In fact anyone who tried to would be in for a hard time. My father was a greatly respected man. 'The Kilcullen' he was always called, as his father, his grandfather and great-grandfather before him. He was my role model. I could never let him down."

Had that made less room for Mark? "I would think your father regarded you as the perfect son. Would you say Mark let him down?" Mark, being Mark, would have done just that. He had certainly let his wife down. "You would have been your father's golden boy." She pinned that silvery gaze, knowing she was acting out of character but she couldn't seem to help herself. He was a very provoking man.

"Wrong colouring, surely?" His handsome face relaxed into another half-smile. "Golden boy fitted Mark much better."

He should smile more often, she thought. It was a stunning illumination. "This *has* to be confusing." She focused on a beautiful arrangement of flowers nearby. They would all have to rethink everything damning Mark had uttered about his family.

"It will be confusing when one feels compelled to change one's opinion. I have a fair idea of what Mark told his wife. And *you*. He would have told you, of course."

She took a full minute to answer, not ready for this. "Why 'of course'? What could you be implying?" She hoped to God she hadn't flushed. She wanted to keep her explosive memories of Mark private—especially from his half-brother.

"Let's call it a desire to know what happened to my half-brother. As far as my family is aware you were the one person outside Amanda that Mark didn't hate or resent in some way. Mark fed on resentment."

That was her own judgement, yet she felt as if she was

being dragged into a deep, murky pond. "Let's get this straight," she said. "When exactly did Mark talk about me? More to the point, *why*? I didn't see Mark all that much." *Made sure I didn't.*

He tossed back the remainder of his cognac. "Don't let me upset you, Sienna. None of this is easy. I only mean Mark obviously thought very highly of you. He wrote about you to his mother. That's if you were Amanda's bridesmaid and her best friend?"

"I *was* my cousin's bridesmaid." She frowned in perplexity.

"As I thought. Only Mark failed to mention you and Amanda were related. Knowing Mark, I would say it was a deliberate oversight. Hilary insisted on showing me his letter, although I didn't particularly want to read it or even know what Mark had to say at the time."

"Well, you could tell me *now*." She settled her gaze on him. "The notion that he bothered to write about me at all doesn't make a whole lot of sense. What *did* he say? Mark had good-looks, and an easy charm when the mood took him. That would be no surprise to you. But to be painfully honest we didn't get to be friends."

"Except Mark didn't see it that way." His shapely hand gently rocked his empty brandy balloon. "Not so surprising when one thinks about it. Mark believed what he wanted to believe."

"Which, in my case, was what?" she asked, with more than a touch of asperity.

"Well, you *are* a very beautiful woman. And you seem to have been important to Mark."

She gave an exasperated groan. "If I *was*, he didn't share that with me." She had no alternative but to lie. "What has that got to do with anything anyway?" she asked. "Mark fell in love with *Amanda*. Mark married *Amanda*. End of story."

"Only you know the story, Sienna. We don't. But I'm more than prepared to listen to anything you want to tell me. The marriage was happy?"

"Why wouldn't it have been?" she parried. She wasn't about to tell him there had been lots of crises, rows, Amanda in floods of tears. What good would it do?

He studied her. "The simple answer. I *knew* Mark."

She had known him too. "It was happy enough," she answered, caught up in a swirl of emotion. Even the air seemed charged.

"You were there when he had his fatal accident?"

Memory swept over her. She lowered her head, unaware the light was bouncing off her rose-gold hair. "Yes. Amanda had invited me along." She had only relented and gone because Amanda had seemed desperate she join them at the ski resort. She still didn't know why Amanda had appeared so distraught. "I don't need to tell you Mark had a reckless streak. Amanda and I are experienced skiers. We've been skiing all our lives. Mark, very tragically, thought he was a lot better than he actually was. It was a terrible day. Amanda went totally to pieces."

"But *you* didn't?"

Her eyes flashed. "That sounds remarkably like an accusation of sorts." Her response was just as terse as his question. "I was deeply shocked and saddened, of course, but I was glad I was there. Amanda needed me." Amanda was one of the neediest young women in the world. But no need to tell him *that* either.

His eyes lingered on her beautiful face, now flushed with colour. He had angered her. But it couldn't be avoided. "You do know I'm here to arrange for Mark's body to be shipped home? I also want to invite Amanda to return with me. She must want to attend Mark's funeral, surely? And she can finally meet the family. We will, of course, meet all her costs. Do you think she would do that?"

Sienna had to take time before she could answer. "Blaine," she said in a subdued voice, "Amanda is rather a fragile person."

"And you're her anchor?"

"I've always looked out for her," she admitted. "We've all deemed it important to look out for Amanda. She lost both her parents at such an early age. I must tell you she couldn't have found better foster parents than my mother and father. There were and remain kindness itself."

"I'm sure of that," he said. "Hilary said your father sounded very kind and compassionate. But you don't think Amanda will meet me, let alone come back to Australia with me?"

She stopped him by placing the tips of her fingers very briefly over his. It was a totally spontaneous action born of compassion. "I'm so sorry," she said.

Her skin was warm and as soft as silk, yet it sent tremors shooting down his spine. "I don't want to go back without her." His expression tautened. "She should *want* to attend Mark's funeral, surely? She did agree to our taking his body home. And as Mark's widow she stands to inherit money. I administer the Kilcullen Family Trust now my father has gone. I can make it easy for Amanda to access her inheritance or difficult for her to gain control of the funds. I don't think she should escape meeting her late husband's family at long last. Hilary will welcome her. So will Marcia, Mark's twin." He was far from sure in Marcia's case. Both Mark and Marcia had inherited difficult natures. Not from Hilary, herself but Hilary's family.

Mark had left them right out of the loop, Sienna inwardly

lamented. "Mark never once said he had a twin. He could only be drawn on you."

Blaine shrugged an impeccably tailored shoulder. His tone was ironic. "I expect there's an avalanche of things you don't know. Do you think the trip back to Australia would be made easier if you accompanied your cousin?"

His suggestion rocked her. It also gave her a totally unprepared for thrill.

"That's if you could possibly spare the time?" he said. "I could hang on for a day or two. As an artist, I think you'll find our Channel Country has a lot to offer. At the moment it's boom time. We've had record rains over the past couple of years. The desert dunes are thickly clothed in green. There are wild flowers as far as the eye can see. Flood waters have even rolled into Lake Eyre, turning it into the fabled inland sea of pre-history. A number of Australian landscape artists have stayed with us on the station of recent times. And Hilary and Marcia love company."

"You've quite astonished me." She was unable to free herself from his gaze. It was downright mesmerizing.

"But the idea isn't entirely unacceptable to you?" Brackets framed his mouth. Amusement? Triumph? She couldn't tell. He was a man of contradictions.

"Perhaps…" She found herself admitting, "But you don't know me! I'm a stranger."

"Oddly enough, you don't seem like a stranger to me." The remark was delivered without his thinking, yet it had sprung from deep inside him. More than one switch had been turned on, he thought with a degree of self mockery. He had more than enough problems, yet he *wanted* this woman to come. He wanted to see her on his own land. He had never remotely expected this. being exploited, perhaps, by a beautiful woman wasn't on his agenda.

Sienna, ever perceptive, had caught the subtle nuance.

The level of intensity between them had gone up several notches. She dropped her eyes, startled to discover she was powerfully attracted to Mark's 'Lucifer'. Attraction was beyond anyone's control, she excused herself. It simply *happened.* Often when one least needed it to happen.

"So many things we've lived with without knowing," she said ruefully.

"There are things that you *need* to know. Amanda, you, your family who raised her. Surely you all thought it extremely odd that Mark didn't reach out and at least invite his mother and his twin to his wedding?"

There was a fraught pause. Sienna stared back at the beautiful flower arrangement, seeking a moment of calm. "Of course we did!" Her tone showed more upset than she'd intended. "Especially in relation to his mother. We didn't know about Mark's twin. But it was Mark's decision. Amanda did everything he asked of her. She fell blindly in love with him. As you've guessed, things changed."

"And they've changed even more drastically now Mark's dead," he said, his expression sombre. "He can no longer dictate his widow's actions. She'll be given an opportunity to find out what Mark's family is really like. As you're so close, I'm hoping you'll be able to persuade her, Sienna. And there *is* the money," he added somewhat dryly. "What exactly does Amanda do? I'm assuming as she and Mark were childless she has a career?"

She could hardly say, as was actually the case, that Amanda shared Mark's aversion to work. "Mark didn't want Amanda to take a job during their marriage. She had to be there for him at all times."

"I see." He didn't look surprised. "And what did Mark work at?"

She took a deep breath. "This and that," she said evasively. "He found jobs easily in the hospitality industry.

That seemed to suit him. What does it matter now? Mark always had money. We assumed he had private means."

"He had a bottomless well," Blaine announced in a very crisp voice. "His mother. The mother he didn't want to see. But he was quite happy to take her money. As far as I'm aware—I could be wrong—my stepmother kept in fairly constant touch with Mark."

"She would have wanted to, as his mother. The whole situation defies belief! But it's really none of my business."

He made a jeering sound. "Oh, I think it is. You're *here*, aren't you? You're standing in for your cousin. You obviously protect her. If Amanda needs to be talked into coming back with me, I would say you're the one to do it. You'd be very welcome to come too—as in Amanda's case, with all expenses paid. You would be doing us a huge favour. The past has to be washed clean. All the things that were kept secret brought out into the open. Much healthier that way."

"I can't work miracles," she said, averting her head.

Her profile was exquisite. She was a very beautiful woman. But there was nothing threatening in her style of beauty. She had been born with natural charm. "So much for the migraine!" he returned, very coolly.

She felt hot blood flushing through her. "She's in *pain*," she burst out. "She did love him, you know."

He responded bluntly. "Only—very sadly for Amanda—he fell out of love with *her*. If indeed he was ever in love with her. Mark lost interest in most things very fast. He left behind him a young woman who believed he loved her. They were engaged to be married. Mark's mother was convinced Joanne would be the ideal young woman to lend Mark much needed strength and support. He rejected it from the rest of us. Joanne is a fine young woman. Our pioneering families have always been close."

"So chances are Joanne will hate Amanda? If she comes to the funeral they will come face to face."

"Time has passed, Sienna," he offered, with a spread of his elegant tanned hands.

"Not enough time, I would think. A wounded heart can't heal overnight."

He studied her wonderfully expressive face. "You sound very sure. Has anyone wounded *your* heart?"

"Of course. A little," she said lightly. "I'm twenty-six, but no real heartache to speak of. I'm prepared to wait for the right man to come along. And what about you, Blaine? You're good with the questions. What about a few answers? You're not married?"

"Finding the right wife would be a whole lot easier if I had more time," he said. "If you visit the station you'll realize I have a big job on my hands. We all thought my father was going to live for ever. He was such a force! So strong and powerful. It was unbearable to see him struck down. It changed my life. It changed all our lives."

"Can you speak about it?" she asked gently.

"Mark never did?"

His light eyes really did *glitter.* He must have inherited those remarkable eyes from someone. Father? Or the mother who had died so young? "Not beyond the fact your father had died. He wasn't forthcoming about *how.*"

"I imagine not," he said grimly. "It was Mark who found him lying crippled and unconscious out in the desert." The vibrancy of his voice had been damped right down. "It was the big muster. Somehow Dad and Mark became separated from our group. We all thought Mark had packed it in. He had a habit of doing that. Dad had probably gone after him, to pull him back into line. Anyway, Mark galloped frenziedly into the lignum swamps, where we were flushing out unbranded cattle, yelling near incoherently that Dad was dead. Duchess, my father's very special mare, had thrown him and then trampled him into the ground. Mark had taken his rifle and shot the mare in a fit of grief and rage."

He remembered how wave after wave of waterfowl had risen in fright and outrage at the racket Mark was making. How every last man had stood in a devastated gut-wrenching silence at the drastic news. Everyone had confidently expected Desmond Kilcullen to live for many more years, liked and respected by the entire Outback community.

His pain was so palpable it stabbed at her. "How horrendous!" Sienna was about able to visualize the tragic scene.

"Horrendous, indeed." He underscored her comment. "I damn nearly dropped dead myself from shock. According to Mark, Duchess had kicked Dad in the head. Accidents always will happen around horses, but my father was a consummate horseman. And Duchess was a wonderful one man horse. Something unexplained must have freaked the mare out. If terrified she would have reacted convulsively, throwing my unprepared father. Mark shot the mare on the spot. Dad spent the few remaining years of his life in a wheelchair, his memory of that terrible day blasted from his mind." He didn't add that any semblance of family life had been shattered.

Sienna sat horrified. "I'm so sorry Mark mistook your father's condition."

"I don't know how, but he did," he told her bleakly. "He was in a massive panic."

"It's such a terrible story." She considered a moment. "Do you think it could have caused Mark's subsequent behaviour? Could he have felt some measure of guilt? I mean in the sense that he was the one to find your father.

He had to shoot the mare. Was the mare a very temperamental animal?"

The handsome features visibly tightened, highlighting his fine bone structure. "Duchess was a very special horse, so of course she was a spirited animal. Something must have badly spooked her, as I've said. Mark was nearly off his head at the time. No one could get much sense out of him—*especially* me. He acted like I was accusing him of something. Dad could recall nothing of that day, although much of his past memory came back over time."

"So you never could piece the exact sequence of events together?"

"No." His expression grew darker.

Two tragic accidents that had claimed father and now son. "When did Mark abandon his family and fiancée, exactly?"

"Far too soon." He didn't tell her Mark had shied clear of visiting their father in hospital. Mark had been long gone before their father's second unsuccessful back operation.

"Mark must have been crushed, given what had happened," she offered, as some sort of mitigating circumstance.

"It was my father who was crushed."

"Sorry, sorry—wrong word," she apologized. "But Mark could well have felt guilt. Would *you* have shot the mare?' She waited, wanting his answer.

"No." His reply was emphatic. "My father wouldn't have wanted it. I have to see it this way: something spooked the mare. An encounter with a camel in heat is a possible explanation. They can be ferocious. Male camels come on heat, not the female. They can't be avoided. They're part of the Outback now. They were brought in by Afghan traders in the early days of settlement. They thrived."

"So it could have been a rogue camel, then?" she asked.

He shot her a searching look. "There was any number in the area. But we were all well aware of that. Dad had handled plenty of rogue camels. I have myself. One doesn't waste a moment getting away. Or, if forced to, one takes the camel out. They come at full charge."

"So there remains a question hanging over that dreadful day?"

He took his time to answer. "A question that will never be answered, Sienna. Dad is dead. A disaster that fell like an impenetrable fog over our lives. It has never lifted. Now Mark is dead too."

"How much sadder could that be?" She bowed her head.

"Sienna, I must appeal to you to speak to Amanda on my behalf." He spoke more urgently. "This is no time for inaction. Mark was her husband. I want her to come back to Australia with me. She won't be alone in her grief. Hilary loved her son. She missed him every single day he was gone."

"Of course she would, as his mother." She well understood the strength of the bond. She was very close to her own mother. "And he did write to her, if only to inform her of his marriage. But his twin? Marcia? You seem to have avoided mentioning her much?"

She was proving very insightful. "Strangely enough, the twins didn't get on all that well. They could be antagonistic, although they understood one another completely. Marcia isn't feeling her twin's loss like their mother. Which is not to reduce the close bond entirely—Marcia is deeply distressed. I'm afraid Mark's behaviour put us all off side. Marcia and Joanne remain good friends. Marcia felt Joanne's pain of betrayal. If Mark thought he was abandoned it wasn't true. Leaving was Mark's choice. It was his family and his fiancée who felt abandoned. I think it's time now to bring closure. If Amanda can't do it on her own, you're the one who can help her."

Some strong communication was passing between them. She couldn't begin to speculate on what it was. All she knew for sure was that he had made it sound as if her very destiny hinged on her going to Australia.

CHAPTER TWO

SIENNA was hardly inside the door of her apartment when the phone rang. She didn't hurry to answer it. It could only be Amanda, wanting a second-by-second account of how the evening had gone. That was Amanda! It was well after midnight. But time—everyone else's time—meant nothing to her cousin. Maybe some time soon the family could start treating Amanda like a woman instead of an ever needful little girl. It was a role Amanda had settled into as the best and easiest way to get her through life. Now her husband's tragic end. No one could have foreseen that. Amanda needed support. It always had been Sienna's job to prop her cousin up. At such a time as now it would be cruel not to.

"Hell, Sienna, have you only just got home?" A slurred and highly irritable voice greeted her.

Amanda's modus operandi was to put her on the back foot. Sienna drew a calming breath. "Hi, Mandy. Calm down, now. I fully intended to ring you first thing in the morning. Can't it wait? It's well after midnight." Blaine Kilcullen had insisted on seeing her home. They'd had to wait for a cab. Despite all her earlier misgivings time had flown. One could even say *on wings*. The man was so charismatic a woman might well need to build protective walls.

"No, it can't!" Amanda retorted. "I'm ill with grief."

Of course she was. Sienna softened her stand. "I'm sorry, Mandy. I truly am. But drink won't help."

"Always the role model!" Amanda warbled. "As if that's all there is to life—being a role model. My wonderful, clever, oh-so-beautiful cousin." A pause while she took another gulp of whatever drink was to hand. Vodka, most likely. Amanda had started bending her elbow not all that long into her marriage. Now it was getting out of hand. "Tried to take him off me, didn't you?" Amanda was back to her sickening accusations. "It wasn't me who made my dear husband's hormones soar. It was *you*—and I was powerless to do anything about it."

It had taken Sienna many years to recognize Amanda's jealousies and deep resentments. People had pointed it out to her over the years but she had chosen not to listen. "Amanda, please stop this" She tried to ignore the sick lurch in her stomach. "We've been over it too many times. I was *not* attracted to Mark. Mark was *your* husband. If he'd been the sexiest man in the world—which he wasn't—he'd have been totally off-limits. I refuse to be drawn into any more discussions on the subject, much as you're compelled to bring it up."

Amanda must have made a wild sweep with her hand, because Sienna could hear glass breaking. Probably the glass she'd been drinking out of.

"Aren't you forgetting I discovered the two of you together?" Amanda raged on, in that upsettingly slurred voice.

"Face it, Amanda. You *know* the truth." Yet irrational guilt settled hard and heavy on Sienna's shoulders. Her conscience couldn't have been clearer in regard to that appalling evening. Still she felt a measure of guilt for the pain that had been caused to her all too vulnerable cousin.

"He *loved* you—don't you realize that?"

Sienna held the phone away from her ear. "What Mark loved was creating great disharmony. You're upsetting us both with this talk, Amanda. My sole loyalty is to you. Look, I can't talk to you while you're in this mood. I'm going to hang up now. Get some sleep. I promise I'll ring you in the morning."

"You'd better!"

The force of the threat stopped Sienna in her tracks. "Don't make me withdraw my support, Amanda," she said quietly. "And by the way, Mark's *half*-brother—he didn't tell us that, did he?—is nothing like Mark tried so hard to present him. He's a very impressive man." The polar opposite of everything that had been Mark.

"Such camaraderie in a few short hours!" Amanda hooted. "Just tell me this. Is there any money? Did he look like he's got pots of money? God knows, Mark left me with nothing."

But Amanda had always had a safety net in the family. They would have been expected to pick up the shambles Amanda had made of her life. But now there was Kilcullen money. "To be fair to Mark, he did keep you both in some style. Apparently his mother proved to be a bottomless well when he needed topping up. She must have done it pretty regularly. And just look how he treated her! I'll tell you another thing, so you can sleep on it. Blaine—"

"Blaine?"

Sienna moved the phone away from her ear again. "I can hardly refer to him as Mr Kilcullen," she said, suddenly sick to death of her cousin. "Your late husband's *half*-brother very much wants you to accompany him back to Australia. He's assured me you will be welcomed. Mark has a twin, by the way, name of Marcia. Apparently they weren't all that close—unlike most twins." Now definitely wasn't the time for Amanda to learn about the scorned fiancée.

"Mark wouldn't have deliberately lied to me," Amanda asserted in a thick voice, when her normal tones were soft and breathy.

"Mark had a twin, Amanda," Sienna said. "The truth was an alien concept to him. He lied to us all the time. He kept his true self and his true life well under wraps. Probably he was laughing at us. He had a cruel streak."

"He was a *fabulous* husband."

Clearly Amanda was in denial. "Mandy, you contradict yourself all the time. Why were you always so desperate for me to join you and Mark? You never did explain. Was the marriage all but over? Was that what it was all about, Mandy? Do you *ever* come clean?"

Silence for a moment, then Amanda's harsh reaction. "I need you to understand something, Sienna. If my marriage was over, it was because of *you*. You had to take the one thing I had."

Sienna was too appalled to continue. Drink turned some people happy. It turned others abusive. "I'm hanging up now, Amanda," she said, thinking things would never get better. Amanda would most probably worsen. "You've been drinking. You don't know what you're saying. You're exhausting my good will. In case you're thinking of ringing back, I'm taking the phone off the hook."

"Do it. Go on—do it!" Amanda urged, her voice rising to a crescendo.

Sienna did, wrapping her arms around herself. There were only two ways to deal with Amanda. Put up with her, or remove her from her life. After all these years since decided she could never do that. Maybe a good man would come along to take care of her cousin.

* * *

Sienna was upstairs, talking to valued client and family friend Nadine Duval, when Amanda walked through the front door of the gallery.

"Sienna, where are you?"

Her voice was pitched so high and loud it was startling. It echoed right through the large open space, its white walls hung with stunning paintings from her father's last sell-out showing. In the last fifteen years Lucien Fleury had moved on to international eminence with numerous critically acclaimed exhibitions. Sienna was enormously proud of him. He in turn was enormously proud of both his children. Both had been hailed as major talents.

"In the genes, Sienna, my darling."

Of course he took the credit.

Nadine Duval, an extremely rich woman, who had paid a fortune for arguably her father's finest canvas in the showing, gave her an understanding little smile. "That will be Amanda, poor girl. We all feel so sorry for her, but I just bet she's giving you a bad time. You have to get free of her, Sienna," Nadine warned, not for the first time. "The girl is trouble."

"Well she's suffering now," Sienna explained, beginning to walk Nadine down the spiral staircase.

"Of course she is." Nadine's response was vaguely ironic.

"I'll have the painting delivered this afternoon," Sienna promised, when they arrived at the bottom.

Nadine reached for her hand. "Thank you, my dear. Tell Lucien I want to see him. Maybe lunch?"

"Will do."

They exchanged kisses.

Amanda looked far more fragile than the strength of her voice had suggested. Indeed she looked waif-like. She had lost weight when she couldn't afford to do so. Her skin, her best feature, was so pale it was almost translucent. She had violet half-moons beneath her eyes, and the silky curls of her pretty blonde hair had lost their lustre and bounce.

"I really don't like that woman," she growled.

It was a mercy Nadine had gone through the door to her waiting limousine.

"Your loss, Mandy. Nadine has so much character."

"And of course she loves you too." Amanda was looking hung over, and haggard for her years.

"I hope you haven't come here to make a scene, Amanda." Sienna was worried that just might happen. It was fortunate that, with the exhibition over, all that remained was for her to have the paintings delivered to their clients. That meant fewer visitors to the gallery.

"Nothing matters. Nothing matters any more," Amanda said, face and voice full of woe.

Sienna's tender heart smote her. "Come through to the office. Would you like a cup of coffee? You don't look good, Amanda. I know this is a terrible time, but you have to take care of yourself."

"*Why*, exactly?" Amanda asked bitterly, sinking her fingers into the skin of her face and dragging her eyes down. "I know I look awful. No need to rub it in."

"I hope I wasn't doing that. I care about you, Mandy. We'll *all* help you work through your grief."

"Who's *all*?" Amanda shot back, as if she had been fiercely rejected all her life instead of cosseted. "I hardly see Aunty Francine."

"She works, Amanda, as well you know. But she does ring you often," Sienna reminded her. Like the rest of them, Francine had tried hard to take to Mark, but found she couldn't. Consequently, as often happened, it had put distance between them all. "The family are busy people with busy lives, Amanda. But we're all there for you when we're needed. Come and sit down," she urged, putting out a sheltering arm. "I have things to tell you."

Once seated in the office, Amanda began to gnaw on her nails. "It's taking all my energy just to stay alive."

Sienna risked another caution. "You have to stop drinking, Mandy."

"I need something to get me through,' Amanda maintained doggedly.

Sienna made coffee from her excellent little machine, adding cream from the refrigerator and two teaspoons of sugar. "I have some cookies if you want them?"

Amanda laughed shortly. "I can't get a thing down my throat.' She looked up, her blue eyes moist, her expression wretched. "What am I going to do, Sienna? What sort of a job am I going to get? I was never a good student. Not like *you*. I didn't make university. Not only did you get all the looks, you got all the brains and a gift for painting."

"From Lucien," Sienna acknowledged, taking a seat behind her mahogany desk. "Drink up, and I'll tell you what Blaine Kilcullen had to say."

"It had better be good," Amanda warned. "What a shocking lot those people are. How cruel they were to Mark."

"There are two sides to a story, Amanda," Sienna said quietly, not wanting to provoke her cousin. "Mark did his level best to put us off his family."

"He had good reasons." Wrath registered on Amanda's white face.

Mark had seen himself as a victim. It struck Sienna that was the way Amanda saw herself too. It showed a link between them. All the bad things that happened in life were never *their* fault. The fault lay with others. Both had dark places.

"Oh, my God, Sienna!" Amanda cried, when Sienna had

finished outlining Blaine Kilcullen's proposal. "There's money!" She gave a great cry of relief.

"The Kilcullens aren't going to see you in financial trouble, Mandy." So much for the Fleury family's generosity! She recalled one of her father's recent comments.

"She's not you, my darling, frail little creature that she is!"

"I don't know exactly how much, but I'd say a substantial sum. Blaine administers a family trust. After meeting him, I have to say I don't see him as the ogre Mark made him out."

"Lucifer, don't you mean?" Amanda cried, not about to put all the things Mark had said behind her. "The fallen angel. Does he look like Mark?" she asked. "I don't know if that would make me feel better or worse."

Sienna shook her head. "You wouldn't spot the relationship, but he is a half-brother. He's dark, with the most remarkable light eyes."

"So he got to you, did he?" Amanda shot her a look full of malice. "Did you get to *him*? That's your speciality, isn't it? Getting to guys, fascinating them."

Sienna threw up her hands in defeat. "You'd use a sledgehammer on me if you could, Amanda. At the same time you *use* me—and I allow it. Not for much longer."

"Okay, I'm sorry." Amanda backed off when she saw her cousin really meant it. "I'm just so sick with worry and grief." Tears oozed out of her eyes.

"I understand that." Sienna relented, as usual, although she knew Amanda could turn tears on and off at will. "Would you consider going to Australia?"

Amanda quelled the tears. "I could never go without you," she declared flatly. "You've looked after me since we were kids. I need you, Sienna. Only you could get me through."

Sienna felt a rush of warmth. Not at what Amanda had said, but at the involuntary exhilaration she felt at the idea of going to Australia. "Time is of the essence," she said. "He has to fly back home. He has a vast cattle station to look after, big responsibilities."

"And he doesn't feel *guilty*?" Amanda with one of her lightning changes of mood, banged the table. "He got through to *you*, all right, but *I'm* a different story. I'm Mark's widow. Mark told me everything, how his brother ruined his life."

"Half-brother," Sienna corrected. "There was a tremendous amount of conflict in Mark."

"It's not the first time you've tried to malign Mark." Amanda made it perfectly plain Sienna's observations were unwelcome.

"I'm not maligning him, Mandy. I'm trying to point out some reason for all the discrepancies. He never told you about his twin. He never told you he was getting money from his mother. Mark's account of his past life was all we had to go on up until I met Blaine Kilcullen. If you agree to meet him you can make up your own mind. It's your decision, Amanda."

"Why can't he just give me the money?" Amanda suggested, looking hopeful. "I'm entitled to it."

"And Mark's mother and sister are entitled to meet you," Sienna said, more sharply than she had intended. "You gave permission for his family to ship his body home. Surely you can find it within yourself to meet them and attend Mark's funeral?"

"I don't *want* to." Amanda started to work herself into one of her rages. "I hate them. I hate Mark for the things he did to me."

"*What* things?" Sienna trapped her cousin's darting eyes. "What is it you're keeping to yourself? The reason you wanted me at the ski resort? I thought it very odd, considering the number of times you'd warned me off."

"I wanted to have it out with him. I wanted you there."

Sienna released a long breath. "You're lying. You've been lying all your life—" She broke off abruptly. "I'm sorry. I shouldn't have said that. But you're not telling me the truth."

"The truth will go with Mark into his grave," Amanda said bleakly. "When does this man want me to meet him? I can't do it today. I have to have my hair done."

"Does this mean you *will* go, Amanda? If you want me to go with you I have to make urgent arrangements."

"Really? The only thing you need to do is tell your father," Amanda sneered. "He'll find a stand-in. Lucien *adores* his beautiful Sienna, with the marvellous hair and the matching amber eyes. He's told everybody *you* are his favourite model."

"After my *mother*," Sienna contradicted. "I am no way as beautiful as my mother."

"Who would believe you?" Amanda's voice was brittle enough to break.

Sienna sat back, feeling defeated. "Amanda, we've all done our best for you, yet you keep slamming us with insults even when you put your hands out for money. I do care for you, Amanda. But I need your definite answer now."

Tears sprang into Amanda's eyes. "Do you have to be so dictatorial? You have to give me time."

Sienna shook her head. "There's little time available." She rose as she heard the buzzer signalling someone had entered the gallery.

"If that's another client get rid of them," Amanda's tears miraculously dried up.

"It might take a minute or two. Stay here."

She walked out into the main room, startled to see the visitor to the gallery was none other than Blaine Kilcullen, cattle baron. She couldn't help noting he looked marvelous: handsome, powerful, successful—someone very special. He had been studying her father's remaining paintings—many had already been delivered—and now he turned his raven head to her. "Good afternoon, Sienna."

She felt heat sweep her body when all he had done was say good afternoon.

"I thought, while I could, I'd take a look at the gallery," he explained. "Your father has an international reputation, I understand? Looking at these paintings, I can see why. This portrait of you is stunning!"

He stood directly in front of the bravura portrait—a homage to a young woman's beauty. The canvas shimmered with light. The treatment of her flesh was so good he had an urge to stroke, to check if the bloom was real. Her long hair had unfurled all around her face and cascaded down her back. The *exactness* of the colour of hair and skin was amazing. She was posed tucked into a roomy gilded armchair, clearly French, so the lovely pattern of the silk upholstery added to the arrangement. One bare arm hung over the side, her fingers curving over the gilded wood. She was wearing a long strapless dress in palest gold. Citrine and diamond drop earrings picked up the colour, as did a matching citrine and diamond pendant enclosed in swirls of gold that drew his eye to the high, youthful curves of her breasts.

"It's not for sale," she explained. "My father won't part with it."

"I don't blame him."

She felt the flush that came to her cheeks. "He looks on it as a lucky talisman for opening nights. I was about to turn twenty-one when he painted it. The earrings and pendant were my parents' gift to me. I should tell you my mother is the real beauty in the family. I thought the portrait was going to be a present for me, but he kept it himself." She laughed at the memory. "One never knows what to expect with Lucien. It flatters me."

In no way was she fishing for compliments, he thought. She genuinely believed the portrait *did* flatter her. "I disagree." He remained in place, studying the luminous canvas. "Have you had an opportunity to speak to Amanda?"

"I have, actually."

"And?" He turned to her with his diamond-sharp gaze.

It was at that precise moment Amanda chose to appear—an actress entering from the wings to take centre stage. In the interim she had somehow managed to transform herself. From looking like a rag doll she was now looking almost perky. She had fluffed up her blonde curls and applied some make-up to good effect. She might even have used eyedrops because her blue eyes were wide and strangely bright.

"Blaine, at long last we meet!" She came forward with not one but two arms outstretched.

Award-winning material, Sienna thought. Not that she hadn't seen such transformations in the past.

Blaine Kilcullen towered over the petite Amanda. "Amanda." He took one of her hands and held it in his. "My family is hoping you will come back to Australia with me," he said. "We have a real bond through Mark."

"Of course we do!" Amanda said with a little emotional heave of her chest. "Sienna has been begging me to come too."

"I couldn't be more pleased if you would," he replied.

Having had the benefit of hearing the various nuances

he employed in his voice, Sienna thought there was a possibility he wasn't being taken in by Amanda.

"That just leaves us to decide which day it will be," he said.

Amanda laughed gently. "I can't pack up just like that, Blaine!"

"No need to go to a great deal of trouble," he assured her. "Anything you need we can get for you at home. Just name it and it will be flown in."

Amanda allowed herself a poignant smile. "You're so kind. And I will have Sienna to help me. Would Wednesday suit?"

He inclined his handsome dark head. "Now that we have the day I can make all necessary arrangements." He turned to the silent Sienna. "I hope that suits you too, Sienna?"

"It's okay—don't worry," Amanda broke in. "Sienna can do whatever she likes."

"That isn't true, Amanda." Sienna couldn't help a note of reproof.

Amanda actually giggled, as if Sienna had told a fib. "It is so."

Sienna dropped a warning hand on her cousin's arm. Wasn't she supposed to be a grief-stricken widow? The trouble was Amanda was a dizzying combination of behaviours. "Just tell us what you want us to do, Blaine." She knew she spoke a little stiffly.

He quickly scanned her face. "I'll give you a ring the moment I've got everything worked out."

"We should have been good friends long ago," Amanda burst out, sounding as if she wanted to weep. "I'm so sorry about that." Her voice caught in her throat.

"We'll have time to make up for it, Amanda," the cattle baron assured her.

Sienna thought it came out a mite too suave. But she could have been wrong.

"I'll let my stepmother know immediately. She'll be greatly heartened to know you'll be coming back with me."

"Anything to soften the blow," said Amanda, fully prepared to go with the flow.

A short time later Kilcullen took his leave.

"What a hunk!" Amanda crowed. She sped back into the office, dropping into her chair. "Be still my heart! I thought Mark was good-looking, but this guy! He's a real heart-throb!"

"Who, pray, could deny it?" Sienna only half joked. Should Amanda be so focused on another man at her time of bereavement? From being prostrate with grief Amanda was now acting as if she was on the brink of an adventure. But then Amanda was prone to see-sawing emotions.

"Well, he's a lot nicer than I expected, thank you very much," Amanda said tartly. "Course, I don't know him."

"And he doesn't know *you*, Amanda. That was a great act you put on."

Amanda glared at her cousin. "Why do you always have to think the worst of me?"

"Maybe it's safer than thinking the best," Sienna offered wryly. "Do you want me to run through some of your stunts from the past?" Amanda had tried hard to break up a few of her relationships—girl friends, boyfriends—utilizing outright lies.

"You never fail to remind me," Amanda hit back with disdain. "That's the trouble with you, Sienna. You think all the good things in life should be dished up to you on a silver platter. You've had a charmed life. You don't know what it's like to feel insecure, unloved, distrusted by the people around you. You wouldn't even let me settle into my marriage."

Sienna felt a powerful wash of anger, yet she made a superhuman effort to keep calmly afloat. "Maybe it's high time for you to consider whether it's *you* who can't relate to *us*. It's *you* who doesn't see things straight. But you've told Blaine Kilcullen you'll return to Australia with him. You've made the right decision. Indeed the only decision. You are Mark's widow. You married him. Now, very tragically, you have to bury him. That's what widows do. I'm convinced the Kilcullen family will offer you every support. And there is the *money.* As for me? I think I've run out of patience. I'm your contemporary, Amanda, not your long-suffering aunt. I'm tired of you taking out your anger and frustrations on me. You'll have to go without me."

She would make a call to Blaine Kilcullen's hotel.

Amanda jumped up like a desperately panicked woman. "No, no—you can't possibly shut me out. What would I ever do without you? You can handle people. I can't. I need someone to act as a barrier between me and these people. They'll be judging me, whatever you say. I loved Mark, but he turned out to be a real bastard. Our marriage would never have lasted. He only married me to be closer to *you.* He told me." She rounded the desk, shoving her small face into Sienna's.

Sienna pushed away in disgust.

"If you won't come with me I can't go through with it. I can't believe you'd desert me at such a terrible time.'

"And it *is* a terrible time. I accept that," Sienna returned quietly. "But it all comes down to whether I can tolerate your attacks on me."

"I don't *mean* it," Amanda cried.

Sienna closed her eyes for a moment. "You do mean it, and you enjoy it in a weird kind of way. The attacks in front of me and behind my back didn't start with Mark, either. I've only ever wanted one thing, Amanda. That was to be your *friend*. But you wouldn't let us connect. I know we have very different personalities, but you have to admit I've always been there for you."

"Of course you have!" Amanda put her hands to her aching head. "I should have died with my parents."

Sienna was overcome by remorse. "Don't say that!"

"I've been injured all the same. You don't understand. You never will. All the good fairies attended your birth. They never came to mine." She began dragging in her breath.

It was an old trick. "Relax," Sienna murmured soothingly. "You're so young. You have a lifetime ahead of you. You're very pretty and you have the brains to acquire more skills. I'll help you."

Amanda's expression sharpened. "Only I won't *want* any extra skills if I'm about to come into pots of money.'

"Oh, Amanda!" Sienna cringed.

"Blaine is much taller than Mark, isn't he?" Amanda disregarded her. "Broader in the shoulders, very handsome, and seriously sexy. A woman would feel secure with a man like that. I never thought I would say this, but I could take to Blaine. He's not married, is he?" She shot Sienna a swift glance.

Sienna just stared back. Amanda wasn't going to develop a *thing* about Blaine Kilcullen, was she? Bury one husband, plan the next? "It doesn't mean he hasn't got some very suitable woman in mind," she said firmly. "Don't daydream about Blaine Kilcullen, Amanda. He's off-limits."

Amanda smirked. "For *both* of us."

"Amanda, I'm taking that for granted," Sienna replied. "I'd like you to go now. I have things I must do."

"Okay, I'm out of here." Amanda picked up her tote bag,

then slung it over her shoulder. "If you're not going to come with me I'll ring Blaine and tell him I've thought it over, but I'm so upset it will be impossible for me to make the long flight."

"Suit yourself." Sienna pretended to search for some papers on her desk

Amanda's blue eyes darted back to her. "Stop kidding around. I can't go through with this without you. This is the last thing I'll ask of you, Sienna. Be with me now. I promise I'll be on my best behaviour."

"It's not looking that way now," Sienna said ruefully.

Amanda continued as if there had been no interruption. The fine skin of her face was mottled and she was waving her hands about as if she were under attack from a swarm of insects. "There's no one else I can ask." She swung back to Sienna, looking incredibly forlorn. "You're the one I always fall back on."

"At least you've noticed." Sienna decided not to push her cousin any further. "All right, Amanda. We really can't go back on our promise," she said quietly. "But I have to warn you—if things start to go wrong between us once we're with the Kilcullen family I can and will fly back home. Is that understood?"

Amanda's small features started to glow with inner excitement. "But they won't go wrong. There are going to be big changes. I can feel it in my bones."

Sienna wisely remained silent.

CHAPTER THREE

THEY flew from Vancouver to Sydney—a non-stop fourteen-hour flight. Travelling first class made the long journey bearable, as did the fact they were flying southbound and westward. They had left a freezing Vancouver around midnight and arrived at Kingsford Smith International Airport mid-morning two days later, due to the time zone differences.

Blaine had organized an overnight stay at a city hotel, to give them some little time to adjust to the dreaded jet lag because their biological rhythms would be disrupted. Amanda, in particular, was showing many of the symptoms associated with flying across multiple time zones. She complained of a bad headache, and feelings of disorientation that she claimed were severe. Sienna had warned her against downing champagne during the long flight, but Amanda had rejected the fruit juices Sienna had accepted. Amanda was a grown woman, and she had become unusually aggressive since Mark's death. Sienna too was feeling below par, but as a frequent long-distance traveller she was able to cope better. She had far better tolerance and was physically fitter than her cousin who, for all her petite figure and feather weight, didn't much care for exercise.

Their passage through Customs was relatively smooth and easy. Blaine had a limousine waiting to take them to the hotel. Sienna felt very grateful for that. They were to leave for Brisbane the following morning. She understood that would involve a flight of just an hour. From Brisbane Blaine was to fly them in his own plane, a Beech Baron, to the Kilcullen cattle station in Channel Country. Sienna already knew that was in the far south-west of the huge state that was Queensland, with a population a bit smaller than the population of British Columbia but in double the area—so there had to be a vast uninhabited Outback.

Sienna stood with a quiet, humming excitement, trying to pacify a very sluggish and querulous Amanda.

"I told you I didn't want to come," Amanda moaned. "It's too damned *far*!" She managed to make it sound as thought they had landed on Mars. "And the *heat*! It's bouncing off the pavements."

Sienna was mortified. Surely her cousin would be overheard? Blaine was standing with the limousine driver as he loaded their luggage into the boot. She was certain Blaine would have exceptionally good hearing as well as so piercing a regard, and would be able to suss out just about anything.

"Okay, I'm sorry,' Amanda apologized. "It's just that I feel lousy."

Sienna put her arm around her, offering support. "Hang in there, please, Mandy. I'll make you comfortable as soon as we reach the hotel."

"And we're nowhere near the Kilcullen station! I need sunglasses. The sunlight is *blinding*!"

It was, but Sienna found herself entranced by its quality. It was a very different light from back home, indeed from Europe, she thought. It had a radiance, an intense luminosity, that captured her artistic eye. The sky above them was a glorious cloudless blue with a shimmering veil of lavender. When they had left home the temperature at the airport had fallen dramatically even from the daytime thirty-four degrees. Here in Sydney, the largest and most cosmopolitan city in Australia, they had been informed by the plane's captain that the temperature was a fine twenty-four degrees Celsius. She knew enough about the differences between Fahrenheit and Celsius to realize the daytime temperature in Vancouver would be pretty well around zero. But then November was the end of spring in Australia. Blaine had warned them to expect heat and *more* heat as they moved north into Queensland. The Sunshine State, as it was called, straddled the Tropic of Capricorn.

Their drive into the city was undistinguishable from the drive into many other cities. Except for the fact that light summer clothing was the order of the day, the people along the way looked pretty much like everyday Canadians going about their business. Sienna remembered that a world-famous British journalist had once described Australians as the "Canadians of the South". She was really looking forward to catching a glimpse of the iconic Sydney Opera House and the Harbour Bridge. Sydney Harbour was said to be arguably the most magnificent harbour in the world. If only tragedy hadn't brought them Down Under she would have thought herself on the cusp of a great adventure…

It took a while to get Amanda settled in their beautiful luxury hotel. To Sienna's delight their suite commanded a superb vista that took in the Opera House, the Harbour Bridge and Sydney Harbour beyond, so they didn't actually have to go anywhere to see the Harbour. They had Blaine to thank for that. Making them comfortable was obviously his priority. She realized the hotel had to be in one of Sydney's most spectacular locations.

She later found out the historic Rocks area where they were was only minutes from the Harbour foreshore. Like her beautiful Vancouver, the city was set between the blue ocean and mountains, though she already knew the rugged Great Dividing Range that ran down the Australian East Coast in no way rivalled the height and majesty of the snow-capped peaks of the Canadian Rockies.

Amanda fell asleep as soon as her head hit the pillow. Sienna took a long, luxurious warm shower, and then dressed in sightseeing gear—slim jeans, a white Herringbone cotton shirt, a fancy belt, and comfortable leather flats. She knew she had to pack sunglasses to protect her eyes, so she popped them into her tote bag. A yellow and white silk scarf tied back her long hair, topped off with a slouchy straw hat. She was to meet Blaine downstairs in ten minutes.

She had agreed with him that staying awake for a few hours after their long flight and walking around would speed up their adaptation to their current time zone. She had found in her many long travels that she suffered the worst degree of jet lag a couple of days *after* a long flight. In the meantime, she meant to make the best of her time in Sydney. The excitement she was feeling was overriding her tiredness.

Blaine Kilcullen was waiting for her in the lobby: tall, lean, and truly imposing, with his remarkable colouring, coal-black hair and brows, and silver-grey eyes. His attire was pretty much like hers—except he wore a blue cotton denim shirt with his jeans and was minus a hat. He did, however, have a pair of sunglasses tucked into his breast pocket.

His gaze swept over her as she moved towards him with a pleasant, expectant look. She had drawn her beautiful hair back tightly from face into a thick ponytail. No place to hide there. Her beauty was right on show: natural and classic. It occurred to him she didn't appear to give a lot of thought to her enviable looks. But then she *had* grown up with a very beautiful mother. He didn't doubt it for a moment.

"All set?' he asked.

"Looking forward to it." She could feel the warmth in her cheeks. Despite jet lag, she was feeling electric, her nerves buzzing inside. Meeting "Lucifer," she had to say, was the surprise of her life.

"Great. But I can't let you overdo it. We'll have a cup of coffee and a sandwich before we go. We can have it here in the hotel." He took her arm, leading the way.

"I have to thank you for going to so much trouble and expense to make Amanda and me comfortable," she said as she walked beside him. "The suite is superb. I never expected such views."

"You'll see a great deal more before you go home."

"You made that sound like a promise?"

"It is. I take it Amanda is safely tucked up in bed?"

She almost cringed. Amanda had made her irritations felt. In fact she had kept up her complaints all the way into the city. "Amanda's not a good traveller at the best of times," she explained.

"Not a good idea to drink alcohol on a long flight," he pointed out dryly.

"Amanda feels alcohol reduces the pressure she's under," she offered defensively.

"And…you have told her differently?"

"Of course I have. But who listens?" She looked up at him, revelling in his much superior height. She was taller than average. It felt good to look up to a man. "Besides, Amanda is a grown woman."

"Who is extremely fortunate to have you for a cousin."

"Is that a question of sorts?" She was trying to weigh up his inflection.

"A statement, surely?" he answered smoothly.

A current that wasn't really friction crackled back and forth between them. It was as if both thought it essential to maintain a certain distance. "I'm here as back-up," she said. "Have you given any thought to what it's like for Amanda, Blaine? Losing Mark the way she did."

His reply was swift. "Let's forget Amanda and Mark for an hour or two," he said. "Come and have that coffee."

He began to walk on—one of those men who moved with absolute self-assurance. Women turned to look at him. Why not? *She* was torn between admiring him and speculating on the inherent danger of getting any closer. She hurried to catch up. "Can you really compartmentalize your feelings so easily?" she asked.

He paused to look down at her with his piercing regard. "Call it an acquired skill, Sienna. I've learned to put unpleasant and downright disturbing things out of my head so I can get on with the job at hand. I've *had* to. I never expected to take over Katajangga for many more years, but it didn't turn out that way. Mark's death is a tragedy. I feel for Amanda. I feel for *you*."

"Why me?" Her brows peaked. "Look, Blaine, I have to dispel this notion you seem to have that Mark and I had some sort of rapport."

"If that's not the case, why did he speak of you the way he did?" he countered. "Let's move on." He drew her away from the flow of hotel guests.

"Perhaps Mark found it essential to pull the wool over people's eyes," she suggested with a touch of heat. "I really don't know, and I really don't *care*."

"Okay. Don't get angry on such a balmy day. I know Mark would have tried to convince you and Amanda and all who would listen I was his enemy. *He* chose that way.

Mark took off without a backward glance. The rest of us had to survive."

She made a soft sound of apology. "What say we call a time-out?"

He gave her a glimpse of his transforming smile. "Sounds like a good idea to me."

The following day Amanda's ill temper was directed entirely at Sienna. With Blaine she played the grief-stricken young widow, desperately in need of his strength and kindness. Amanda was never really honest with anyone. Another trait she had in common with Mark. It was hard to explain, but neither of them had wanted or indeed sought to connect with people—even the people closest to them. Bizarre as it seemed, Amanda had now turned her attention to Blaine. Maybe it was only until she got the money?

"Grieving doesn't pay the bills, Sienna. There are bills all over the place. Mark avoided paying them like the plague."

Amanda, truly exhausted and under the weather, slept on the flight to Brisbane. Sienna took ten-minute catnaps. Far from feeling severe jet lag, she was in a state of mild euphoria. Her walk with Blaine Kilcullen around Sydney Harbour's foreshores had been wonderfully exhilarating…

"The best possible way to see Sydney is from the water, of course," he'd explained, with a look of genuine regret. "Unfortunately we don't have time right now. But who knows? Some time in the future…?" He had shifted his dazzling gaze to meet hers. Pinned it as though her eyes held every answer he was looking for.

She had felt excitement ripple down her throat. She might have been a teenager on her first date instead of a sophisticated woman, such had been her feeling of being held spellbound. She'd been increasingly aware he was having that effect on her. Surely it was an unfair advantage? And he'd had it from the first moment, when she'd walked towards him quite calmly when her thoughts had actually been chaotic. She had never expected this. She had never met a man to match him.

She had pretended to brush a strand of hair from her forehead. "I'm only sorry I didn't have time to unpack my camera. This is a truly beautiful city."

"It is that," he agreed. "I've travelled the world, but nothing beats the natural beauty of this harbour. We'll start our tour with the Harbour Bridge. It's the most logical point. It has a pedestrian footpath, and the south-east pylon is a great vantage point for spectacular views of the city, the Opera House and the Harbour. Come along now, Sienna."

He took her arm in gentlemanly fashion, but he might have grabbed her such was the heat of contact. It sizzled through her body. She only hoped he wasn't monitoring her reactions. She would die of mortification. In a way her meeting the cattle baron seemed quite unreal. Or surreal?

A beautiful cruise liner was moored at the Sydney Cove Terminal—the same location, Blaine told her, taken by the ships of the First Fleet when they dropped anchor in the cove in January 1788. As they stood together companionably and watched another big liner approached. One of the Harbour's "jetcats", on its way out from Circular Quay to Manly on the other side of the Harbour, was passing Sydney Opera House—an unforgettable sight. Its iconic white sails glittered in the brilliant sunlight, the three sides of the World Heritage listed building surrounded by sparkling blue water.

"You probably know it was the renowned Danish

architect Jorn Utzon's design." Blaine glanced down on her face, one side half hidden by the dip of her very attractive straw hat. She looked as cool and delicious as ice cream. "Although Utzon's splendid vision was chosen, the irony was that the design was beyond the engineering capabilities of the time. It took Utzon a few years to work out his problems while the costs were blowing out monumentally. There was a stage when the NSW government was tempted to call a halt."

"Thank goodness they didn't!" Sienna exclaimed. "It's a magnificent construction. I would say to a Canadian this is the most recognizable image of Australia."

He nodded. "It's site reaching out into the Harbour makes the building even more spectacular. Utzon must have been thrilled when he heard his design had been chosen. What a site for his building! Could any architect ask for more? There are around a quarter of a million guided tours for visitors every year. Again, we must wait for another time. I'd like to take you to see the Royal Botanic Gardens as they're only a short walk away. I have the feeling you love gardens?"

"Who doesn't?"

"Not all would have your eye for beauty, I imagine, Sienna. Sydney is fortunate to have a thirty-hectare oasis right in the heart of the city. There's a walkway around the harbourfront at the lower part of the gardens we can take."

"What a breathtakingly beautiful setting!" She knew a part of her euphoria was her enormous pleasure in his company, the stimulating way he pointed out everything of interest along with its historical context. She was more than happy with their tour.

"The gardens themselves are splendid, as you will see,"

Blaine said. "Not tiring on me, are you?' He tipped the brim of her hat so his eyes could move over her face.

He appeared to focus on her every feature in turn. It was stunningly sensual. "Do I look it?" she asked, a faint catch in her voice.

He shot her a sideways smile. "You're the most beautiful woman I've ever seen."

"That sounds faintly mocking."

He laughed. "Also a woman to be approached with a good deal of care."

"And yet here we are!" she challenged.

"And making quite a connection," he offered dryly. "It's very liberating, not having to worry about anything else but enjoying one another's company."

Impossible to disagree. "You *knew* I'd come to Australia, didn't you?" she asked, sweeping off her wide-brimmed hat and fanning herself with it.

"I have to admit it," he said. "You're not going to tell me you're sorry?" Very gently, like a brush of velvet, he reached out to tuck a loose strand of her amber hair behind her ear.

"No way!" It was a measure of how dazzled she was that she gave a little shiver. She was beginning to fear her physical reaction to him—this crazy, near uncontrollable desire for him to touch her. It was a reason for considerable concern. But there it was. And not much she could do about it. "I'm not sure I can predict what's ahead of us, however," she said, a sigh escaping her.

He took her hand and tugged her along almost playfully. "It's enough you're here, Sienna," he said.

She was destined to remember that precise moment for a long, long time…

* * *

They flew into the Kilcullen desert stronghold towards late afternoon. It had been a smooth, uneventful flight—although Amanda had professed her nervousness of light aircraft.

"They crash all the time."

"A bit extreme, Amanda," Blaine had soothed her. "You'll be perfectly safe with me. Flying is a way of life in the Outback."

On their flight to the vast arid lands of the remote south-west he had shown himself to be an excellent pilot. Now he was flying low over Katajangga station, so they could get a closer look at the incredible landscape beneath them. Sienna's whole body seemed to be atremble, with a mix of exhaustion and excitement. It was bringing goosebumps to her bare arms. She wanted to wake Amanda, so she wouldn't miss out on their momentous arrival. Katajangga Station the great land mass that lay beneath her, appeared as a fairly large settlement of many buildings, constructed in an area of absolute wilderness. There was no other sign of human habitation to the horizon—only herds of cattle in holding yards, and thousands of head roaming free across the plains, bisected by fiery red sand dunes that ran in almost exact parallel lines.

Blaine thought better of waking Amanda. "Let her sleep," he advised. "She needs sleep badly."

Sienna turned her head towards her sleeping cousin. Amanda was curled up, looking little more than a child, she thought with a pang of the heart. Amanda would always be her little cousin who had so tragically lost her parents. To compound Amanda's trauma she had now lost her husband, in one mindless act of bravado, even if it appeared her marriage had been well and truly on the rocks. Hadn't the family feared it would happen sooner or later? But when Amanda wanted something she wanted it right away, allowing no time for thought. What she had wanted was a *man*. Not a father figure—that would have been easy enough to understand—but a man to keep her close. No woman could possibly offer her the right reassurance, let alone the sense of being cocooned. Amanda had a rather worrying history of attachments that came unstuck when she became too clingy. According to Mark—probably an excuse for his own behaviour—she had got to that point overnight.

"It's got nothing to do with love, Sienna. Mandy suffocates a man like some parasitic vine."

Loyal as she was to Amanda, she had to recognize the essential truth in that statement.

Sienna blew out a small breath of air. "So why do *I* feel so good?" she asked the cattle baron.

"Now, that's a question," he said in a lightly mocking voice. "I'm awed by your energy." Quite true. Her physical fitness added another dimension to her beauty, making it so much more compelling.

"So am I," she laughed. "It's a mystery to me."

She stared out at the western sky. Such a spectacle was unfolding before her—a spectacle growing more glorious by the minute. "Just look at that sunset! From sapphire-blue crystal to *this*!"

On the western horizon incandescent clouds were building: crimson, bright pink deepening into rose, streaks of palest green, molten gold. To her fascinated eye, a silvery cyclamen ring appeared to surround the pulsing setting sun.

"You'll see plenty of those," Blaine told her with a casual white smile.

"I had thought to see a great *brown* land. This is the most ancient continent on earth, after all. How do I go about describing the colours? There's so much unexpected *green*—especially the dense borders along the water courses. It's like a giant maze of wetlands, with streams and lakes."

"Billabongs, we call them," Blaine said, briefly turning his head. "Billabongs, lagoons, clay pans. Plenty of lignum swamps—that is to say eucalypt wooded swamps. What we call the Mulga Lands. The trees can be more than forty feet high. They have lots of hollows that provide shelter and breeding sites for anything from mammals through reptiles to frogs and waterbirds. What you're seeing is far from the norm. But we've had the best rainfall for many long drought-stricken years."

"Hence all the flowing water?"

He nodded. "The Channel Country is actually a series of ancient flood plains. Most years the rains are soaked into the earth and evaporate. But this rainfall has been so heavy, with flooding intensified by heavy monsoonal rains coming down from the tropical North, that flood waters are flowing into Lake Eyre—which you might know as the largest salt water lake in the world. It only fills up about two or three times in a century." He laughed briefly. "We have a group of eccentrics called the Lake Eyre Yacht Club, who set sail on the lake when it's in flood. They're there right now."

"Truly? What fun! I'd love to see it."

"Maybe you will." He cast her another one of his glittering glances. The ones that nearly stopped her breath.

She had to wait a moment to clear her head. "Didn't Sir Donald Campbell attempt a land-speed record on Lake Eyre, or am I wrong about that?"

Blaine too was feeling little darts of excitement that pierced his skin. He was having seriously divergent thoughts about this beautiful young woman. He felt a certain lack of trust, like watching a sleeping serpent, coiled around a spinifex bush yet always ready to strike. And at the other extreme the deepest possible pleasure in her company. She looked entirely innocent of any wrongdoing in connection with Mark, yet his gut feeling told him he had to face the possibility she was lying—or at the very least hiding their connection. There were fine distinctions between married men and single men. Had she bothered to make them? Whatever the character flaws in Mark, he'd never had any trouble attracting women. And Mark, when he had been focused strongly on something, had made it his business to have it.

Blaine knew he would have to separate the truth from the lies. Her voice released him from his disturbing thoughts.

"I take it I'm wrong?"

"No, you're absolutely right." He was somewhat surprised she knew about the extraordinary Sir Donald, let alone his attempts on Lake Eyre. "The *Bluebird-Proteus*. My father and my grandfather were spectators at that event on the salt flats. The Channel Country lies in the Lake Eyre basin. They were there, too, when Sir Donald broke the speed record on water at Lake Dumbleyung in West Australia. Just over 276 miles per hour. He won the land and the water speed record in the same year. Quite a feat! According to my father, Sir Donald had charisma in spades—a great bloke, but he wouldn't have anyone wish him good luck. He hated it. Apparently he was very superstitious. Sadly, but I suppose not unexpectedly, he died at the wheel a few years later. He was only around forty-five, I believe. There are some photos of him at the house you might like to see."

"I certainly would. What a connection!"

"Over the years we've had plenty of VIPs stay at the station," he said, turning his head to her.

All of a sudden they seemed disturbingly close. She had the feeling he was about to say something, then thought better of it. Either way, her heart was beating high and light in her breast. She did the wise thing. She turned her attention back to the infinite landscape. "It's daunting, isn't it? I'd hate to get lost down there."

"You'd never get out alive," he told her dryly. "Probably our most famous explorer, the great Ludwig Leichhardt, a German, disappeared down there in 1848, along with his entire party of men and animals. He was attempting to cross the continent from east to west. He'd already concluded a triumphal three-thousand-mile journey from Brisbane to Coburg Peninsula, north-east of Darwin in the tropics. But the desert brought him to his death. What happened to Leichhardt is one of the great mysteries of the Outback. Our Nobel Prize winning author Patrick White wrote a book based on him, called *Voss*. There are several copies at the house if you want to read it."

"I'd like to," she said, thoroughly intrigued. "Surely search parties were sent out to find him?"

"Of course—several. But all of them failures. Only a couple of trees marked 'L'. What Leichhardt saw, as you're seeing now, is some of the most rugged country on the planet. But it's also the home of the cattle kings. We produce the best beef."

"So I've read. We also have a thriving beef industry in Canada.'

He nodded. "Large-scale cattle and sheep ranching in Alberta—the Canadian Texas, don't they say? But think of its huge oil reserves! Has to make it one of the most financially important places on earth. Our traditional beef markets have been the USA and Japan, but Canada is a notable export destination, along with South-East Asia. Both our countries experience the same problems with enormous distances to get the product to market. We use huge road trains here in the Outback—and as you know, we call your ranches stations."

"Yes." She nodded. "I've been doing a little research for the trip. It's a very British term—*station*."

"Well, it would be. All of our historic stations, sheep and cattle, were founded by men of vision and adventure from the United Kingdom—including my own forebears. You have a French background?"

"Very much so. Sometimes fiercely so. My father's family hail from Quebec, easily the most Francophile province. My mother's family has been long settled in BC. They actually met in New York, at an art showing. My father loves British Columbia—its beautiful landscapes, the Rockies and the forests. My parents are long divorced, but they both still live in Vancouver. Dad travels widely, of course, but Vancouver is home."

"I expect he wants to be near his daughter."

"We're very close." She gave him a quick smile, her gaze returning to the gigantic landscape. "I did read about the wild flowers after rain, but I never expected to see the land awash with them on my arrival. That's incredible." Below her, vast areas were covered in white wild flowers, adjacent areas were yellow, with big areas of pink mixed with purple, and only small spaces of the rust-red carpet of earth in between.

"I stress you're seeing the *good* times," Blaine said. "The entire character of the landscape has been transformed by 'the white and golden glory of the daisy-patterned plains,' to quote one of our Outback poets. The yellow and white are all paper daisies—everlastings. Bachelor buttons, we call them. The pink and pale green areas are *parakeelyas*—succulents the cattle can feed on. The divine blessing of rain has truly been with us. As an artist, you're seeing our

Channel Country at its very best. Though I would have preferred for you and Amanda to see it at a less grievous time, naturally. Hilary will be waiting to greet you. Marcia too, of course. You didn't tell Amanda about Joanne?"

Sienna shook her head. "The timing didn't seem right. I take it Joanne will be at the funeral?"

"Joanne and her entire family," he said. "But don't worry about Joanne. She was very deeply hurt, but she knows how to behave."

"And are you asking me if *Amanda* can do the same?" she responded with a challenge.

"Sort of." He kept his voice impassive. "She's in shock—as she would be. Aside from the long flights, she doesn't appear to be coping all that well."

"Why would she be? She's in a deep state of shock. But there's something that bothers me," she confessed.

"Let's have it." He flashed his diamond-hard glance at her.

Instead of freezing her out, it had the opposite effect, spreading a trail of sizzling warmth. The two of them were cut off from the rest of the world. It seemed the most remarkable thing to be with him at all—like a dream sequence. "You've spoken of how Mark mentioned me in his letter to his mother," she began tentatively, "telling her of his marriage?'

"Is there something else?" he asked, more sternly than he'd intended.

"Something else?" She felt a jolt of simple despair. "There you go again. Of course there isn't something else. I'm concerned she too may have the wrong impression."

"Maybe Mark had a huge crush on you," he suggested, with another searing glance.

"Hardly likely, when he was marrying someone else—

my cousin Amanda." She injected outrage into her voice, all the more because it was shockingly true.

"Who knows with poor old Mark?" The expression on his dynamic face darkened. Who knew what secret sins? Betrayal? Adultery with this beautiful creature? She appeared above such behaviour—but a man and a woman? Always temptation. Always was. Always would be. She might be very far from being Mark's "type", but he had no difficulty seeing Mark letting her into his life. Maybe Mark had finally lost his taste for bubble-headed girls.

"You're not thinking straight, Blaine!" she warned him.

"No?" He fixed his eyes on her.

She couldn't look away. Usually she was adept in controlling man-woman situations. Not with him.

"There's not a man alive who couldn't be caught up in the web a beautiful, highly intelligent woman can spin."

"Oh, yes, there is," she returned with biting sarcasm. "*You.*"

When this was all over she might just collapse and have a good cry. For now she had to be strong for Amanda. She had to see her cousin through this traumatic trip to meet her late husband's family. The smartest thing she could do for herself was keep a strong defensive wall in place. She recognized the powerful dangers of getting to know this dark and edgy cattle baron any better. She would be wise not to expose herself to those dangers.

They made a perfect touch down ten minutes later. "We're here at last!" Sienna cried, unable to fully contain her excitement.

"Welcome to Katajangga," Blaine said, taxiing the Beech Baron towards a huge silver hangar.

"This is unlike anything I've ever seen! A small country

town in the middle of an endless ocean of red sand and rioting miles of wild flowers."

He had to admit her enthusiasm was giving him an adrenalin shot of pleasure. But then she was an artist, with a finely honed eye for beauty in all its forms. "Glad you like it," he said. "How are *you* feeling, Amanda?" he asked, with a half-turn of his head.

"Exhausted," she croaked, starting to sit up straight.

"You'll feel a whole lot better when you've caught up with your sleep."

"I hope so. I feel dizzy and nauseous. I must look a fright."

"Just a little pale," Sienna said.

A flash of the bitter, irrational resentment that had plagued Amanda for most of her life surfaced before Amanda had time to recall it. "Oh, shut up, Sienna," she said resentfully. "We can't all look like *you*."

No, indeed! Blaine made no comment on Amanda's rudeness, but he privately agreed. Sienna, despite their long travels, somehow managed to look as fresh as a rose.

He had long awaited his meeting with Mark's widow, but now he realized she was a young woman with serious issues. Not the least of them jealousy of her cousin. He had taken account of the way she practically bit Sienna's head off every time she opened her mouth. In fact there was something of a manic edge about Amanda that put him in mind of his half-brother. The odd time, however, Amanda showed considerable dependence upon her cousin. So there she was, sending out an ambivalent set of signals.

Love-hate. Sometimes the strong suffered poor treatment from the more vulnerable members of a family, Blaine mused. There had always been tremendous strain between him and Mark, though he had tried his level best to be as supportive as he knew how. Only Mark had chafed endlessly at what he saw as his secondary status. It was emerging Sienna was suffering a fate similar to his own.

The sun, having turned on another glorious display for the day, was sinking fast onto the horizon, leaving a lovely mauve world. It was one of the colours Sienna would always associate with the Outback. They were being met by a station employee, a rangy individual, running the brim of his akubra through his fingers and saying, "G'day!" before driving them to the homestead—a good mile from the hangar that housed the Beech Baron and what looked like a state-of-the-art dark grey helicopter. Two yellow helicopters sat on the broad concrete apron. Sienna assumed correctly they were used for mustering.

They drove along a broad gravel track bordered by soaring gums. Ahead was a terracotta wall some eight feet high. It was draped in the long overhanging arms of a prolific flowering vine, with masses and masses of cerise blossom that made a dramatic splash of colour. Bougainvillea. In the wall a massive black wrought-iron gate stood open. Flanking it were two magnificent date palms such as Sienna had always associated with the deserts of the Middle East.

"The wall is to protect the homestead from dust storms," Blaine threw over his shoulder. "And to protect the garden too, of course. Hilary loves her garden. It's a dry region garden, watered by sunken bores. We're over the Great Artesian Basin. We couldn't survive without it. Don't worry about any lengthy greetings tonight, Amanda. Everyone appreciates you'll be exhausted after so much travelling. A hello, then you'll be shown your room. Anything you want to eat will be sent up to you. Okay?"

"Thank you for being so thoughtful, Blaine." Amanda

leaned forward in her seat to say sweetly, "You're coming with me, aren't you, Sienna?"

Sienna shook her head. "I'm not ready for bedtime yet." Her fascinated gaze was on the fortified Katajangga homestead. It made her think of some wonderful hidden desert retreat. The sky was darkening to purple, so the interior and exterior lights were turned on. She could hear the cooling sound of running water. Where better than from a splendid stone fountain that was the focal point in the enclosed courtyard? Light caught the water, forming rainbows. It splashed and cascaded over three graduating basins held aloft by rearing horses with flowing manes into the circular pond beneath.

Her eyes ranged over the soaring palms to flowering shrubs she recognized as oleanders. Their heady perfume permeated the air. In triangular boxed beds grew great sunbursts of ornamental spiky grasses. In other beds the gigantic leaf rosettes of Mexican agaves. Both species would resist a searing desert sun. In different places a range of boulders lent a stunning sculptural effect.

"This is a magical place," she said, with genuine delight.

"You ought to dress up as a sheikh, Blaine," Amanda suggested, not wanting to be left out. He would make a gorgeous sheikh. So dark and so damned sexy!

"I think I'll stick to being a cattle man," he said. "But, speaking of sheikhs—or dress-up sheikhs—I've seen some garments worn by Lawrence of Arabia in the Canberra war museum. The caftan would be about your size, Sienna. He must have been a very slim, small man, with big ideas."

"But, hey, Peter O'Toole was *tall*!" Amanda piped up with this *non sequitur*. "We'll have to smother ourselves in sunblock, Sienna. It's evening, but I can still feel the heat in my skin."

"We'll look after you, Amanda," Blaine assured her, relieved she was sounding a little more cheerful. One aspect puzzling him was that Amanda gave off no real sense of grief. In fact he didn't identify her with the image of a grieving widow at all. He had to compare Hilary, on the terrible day of his father's funeral, sedated and held together for a short while, before the inevitable collapse. Hilary had idolized his father.

"I cannot imagine how I'm going to get through life without him, Blaine."

At the time he'd felt pretty much the same thing—grief at the loss of a beloved parent and life mentor; the shock of being catapulted into one tough job many years in advance.

Sienna, catching his expression, wondered what he was thinking. Probably he had already formed his opinion of them both. Amanda, Mark's widow, who wasn't displaying much in the way of sorrow; and her, the shadowy figure in the background, who might or might not have embarked on some sort of affair with her own cousin's husband.

Anyone who knew her would know there wasn't a skerrick of truth in it.

Blaine Kilcullen didn't know her at all.

CHAPTER FOUR

KATAJANGGA homestead fitted perfectly into its extraordinary desert landscape. Like the massive fortifying walls, the stone house had been rendered and washed with a deep terracotta colour. There was a two-storey central section, with a hipped metal roof and a long run of covered deck supported by massive stacked stone pillars, and a central core flanked by single-storey wings set at a forty-five degree angle from the main house. Sienna guessed these were additions that had evolved over time, turning the original homestead into something quite grand.

"I'm going to be sick," Amanda muttered out of the side of her mouth.

"No, you're not!" Firmly Sienna took hold of her cousin's small hand. "No one will be expecting you to do much talking. We'll be greeted, and then, as Blaine says, we'll be shown to our rooms."

Amanda posted a clear warning. "They'd better be nice to me."

Sienna pressed her hand supportively. "Everyone wants to be nice to you, Mandy. Just remember to be nice to *them*."

There was no entrance hall, as such, but the Great Room was spectacular for its sheer size alone. It took in almost the length and breadth of the house, with staircases leading to the upper floor on the extreme left and right. There was a massive ceiling-high fireplace made of slabs of stone, big and small, wide-planked timber floors with a dark stained glossy patina, comfortable seating areas arranged around the room, and an area for dining with a mahogany table that could easily seat twenty or more. Splendid rugs with muted desert colours and elements of Asia lent an exotic touch. She was familiar with the arts of Asia. Her own beautiful British Columbia boasted the largest Asian population outside Asia, and her mother had a magnificent collection of Chinese porcelains and jades. A decorative timber railing enclosed an upper gallery, which Sienna could see was hung with paintings.

In many ways the interior was like that of a huge prairie house, except for the great crystal chandeliers that instead of appearing incongruous captured the imagination. She knew there had to be a story to those antique chandeliers. They were as beautiful and extravagant as she had ever seen.

Amanda too was staring about her, her blonde head tilted to the gallery which overhung the Great Room by ten or more feet. "Where is everybody?" she asked, one minute desperate to dodge Mark's family, the next put out that there was no welcoming party.

Before Sienna could formulate a single word—nervous about what Amanda might say next—a tall, middle-aged woman in a dark blue dress, with a wealth of greying hair almost to her shoulders, suddenly appeared to their left.

"Ah, here's Hilary now," Blaine said. He waited a moment to see if Marcia had accompanied her mother and was hanging back. No such luck, even though Hilary's deep suffering would have aroused pity in the hardest heart.

Hilary approached them, holding out her hand. "You,

of course, are Amanda," she said in a soft wavery voice, her eyes fixed on Amanda's pretty face and petite figure.

"I am," said Amanda, her graciousness all dried up.

Blaine stood back so he could observe this long overdue meeting. Amanda made no move to go into her mother-in-law's arms, although it was painfully obvious that was what Hilary wanted and perhaps expected.

Sienna too stood well back, in deference to her cousin. Amanda didn't like being touched and was making that apparent. Not even a smile!

"Welcome to Katajangga, my dear," Hilary was saying. "We are so grateful you could make the long journey."

"I fully planned to," Amanda lied. She submitted to a handshake with a look of surprise on her face she didn't bother to hide. *This* was Mark's mother? What a turn-up! No matriarchal figure here. Not by a long shot. She was no looker, either. In fact she was downright plain—and that wavery voice! Hilary was a far cry from the handsome, intimidating woman Amanda had conjured up in her mind. According to Mark his mother had always been very tough on him. She had failed him, letting him down, siding with her husband and Blaine.

"A traitor she is, my mother!"

Amanda was seriously astonished, and at the same time relieved. This woman would be a push-over. And she looked so *old* when she couldn't be. Aunt Francine, for instance, at fifty, looked marvellous!

Blaine watched his frail stepmother turn to Sienna. "And you must be Sienna," she said, with a heart-wrenching smile.

"How do you do, Mrs Kilcullen?"

He watched with critical appraisal as Sienna stepped forward. She was now beneath the direct light of a chandelier that set her glorious hair on fire. He saw her take his stepmother's thin hand, not in a conventional handshake but in what appeared to him to be a warm clasp. "It's a pleasure to meet you," she said, in a charming voice that had a gentle *hush* to it as she addressed Hilary. "I only wish the circumstances weren't so very, very sad. Please allow me to offer my deepest sympathy."

Blaine found himself releasing a taut breath. In truth, he was enormously grateful Sienna had had the sensitivity to read the lines of suffering on Hilary's face, the double dose of tragedy and her subsequent grief.

To Sienna's surprise Hilary reached out and patted her cheek. "Sometimes really bad things can lead to good things, my dear," she said. "You're very welcome here, Sienna. Please, do call me Hilary." There had only ever been one Mrs Kilcullen, and that had been Blaine's late mother, Hilary thought—entirely without rancour.

With a hint of impatience Amanda jerked her blonde head up once more, looking to the gallery. "Where's Marcia? I'd like to meet her. I suppose she looks just like Mark?"

Blaine cut in smoothly. "Not all that much, Amanda. They're not identical twins. But there are many likenesses you can decide on tomorrow. Marcia is giving you time to settle in. Isn't that so, Hilary?" He looked towards his stepmother.

His glittering light eyes highlighted the black of his hair and brows and the polished bronze of his skin, Sienna noticed. She was fully aware that Amanda and she were under close scrutiny. Like Amanda, she was surprised by Hilary Kilcullen's appearance and the shyness of her manner. But she found it understandable, given the deep grief Hilary must be suffering. Perhaps her life's role as the second Mrs Kilcullen hadn't been much of a confidence-booster.

Hilary picked up on Blaine's hint, grateful as ever for her

stepson's unending support. "We knew you'd be desperately tired."

"Actually, I'm not as tired as I would have thought," Sienna said in some surprise. "I expect it will hit me tomorrow."

"Then perhaps you would join us for dinner?" Hilary turned to Sienna eagerly, looking her full in the face. She was feeling far more comfortable with Amanda's cousin than with her son's widow. Amanda was very pretty, or she would be when she was rested, but her cousin—*the bridesmaid*—was uncommonly beautiful, with extraordinary colouring and a grace of manner. Even more importantly, Hilary knew instinctively this young woman was genuinely kind.

She recalled in detail every word her son had written about his wife's bridesmaid. At the time she and Blaine had found it extremely puzzling, but she didn't find it puzzling now. Mark had found a woman—not his wife—who had deeply moved him. Mark, who was no longer with them. Mark, who would be buried in two days' time.

A big blonde woman—not fat, but solid—came down the staircase to the left. She crossed the polished timber floor to where they were assembled.

"This is Magda." Hilary introduced their housekeeper with a fond smile. "Magda runs the house for us. Most efficiently, I should add. Magda, this is Amanda, Mark's wife, and her cousin Sienna."

Magda nodded her large blonde head in what was intended to be a salute. "Please to come with me," she said in a strong, deep voice, feminine none the less. It still held the trace of a Polish accent. "I will show you to your rooms."

"Thank you, Magda." Blaine took over from his stepmother. "Dinner is at seven if you feel up to it," he addressed Sienna.

"Don't worry. We're going to crash," Amanda cut in, her feathers already ruffled. The limelight that should be on *her* had shifted to Sienna.

Yet *again.*

They moved down a long grand corridor in the tall housekeeper's wake. Magda showed Amanda into her room first. The large, elegant guest room with its soft hues and furnishings was intended for a woman, Sienna thought, following the other two in. A big, romantic four-poster bed immediately caught the eye. It was placed between ceiling-high timber doors that led out onto a balcony that would have views over the extensive rear grounds. She caught glimpses of tall palms. The palette was predominantly blue and white, and a dazzling abstract flower painting hung over the bed to liven things up. She would have liked to study it further. It didn't look European. Aboriginal? There was a pretty desk and chair, and some exceptional pieces of furniture—a daybed upholstered in blue silk, with two matching armchairs.

"This is lovely!' she said, always one to make a warm remark. Amanda, however, was embarrassing her by appearing more than a tad underwhelmed. Where had her good manners gone? Sienna agonized. She had to take into account that Amanda was exhausted, but she hoped her cousin would pick up for the remainder of their stay. There was the funeral to face; doubtless a wake to follow. And, God help them, there was Mark's ex-fiancée, Joanne, to confront. And her parents. Plus all the friends of the Kilcullen family. Most probably it would be a huge affair.

"I will show you to your room now, Ms Sienna," said Magda, pivoting surprisingly lightly on her rubber-soled shoes.

"Thank you, Magda. Do you want to come and see, Amanda?" Sienna asked.

But Amanda was sucking in her cheeks. A familiar mannerism. "I can see it tomorrow," she said flatly. "Can you help me unpack? I tell you, I'm *whacked*."

"Of course you are," Sienna soothed. "I'll come back."

"Is my job to do unpacking," Magda intervened.

"I prefer my cousin," Amanda replied, like a rude child. "And I will want something to eat."

"It will be done," said Magda, showing no sign of disapproval at Amanda's sulky schoolgirl retort.

Sienna's room, two doors down along the wide painting-hung corridor, was very different. For one thing the colour scheme might have been designed with her specifically in mind.

"Thank you, Magda. I'll be very comfortable here," she said, smiling at the housekeeper.

"Mr Blaine chose your room," Magda replied. "It is *sunshine*." She threw out her arms.

"It *is*." Sienna felt a quick lift of the heart, like a bird taking wing. *Blaine* had personally chosen which room she was to have? Like Amanda's room, there was a centrepiece four-poster bed, but hers was ebony, with brass finials and a hand-painted gold trim. Not surprisingly with her colouring, she loved the colour yellow—which had been used generously in the beautiful room. The bedcover and pillows were of yellow silk, but there was a tangerine, scarlet and gold coverlet lying at the foot of the bed. A single yellow rose stood in a vase, beneath a lamp on the small bedside table.

"Dressing room and bathroom beyond." Magda gestured. "Would you like me to unpack, Ms Sienna?" she asked, indicating the two pieces of luggage that now stood at Sienna's door.

"That would be lovely, Magda." Sienna would have preferred to do the unpacking herself, but she was anxious not to offend the housekeeper. She had spotted the fact that Magda was something of a personage in the household, and very probably indispensable to Hilary.

"I'll do it now, while you comfort Mrs Kilcullen," Magda said.

"My cousin has never been a good traveler." Sienna thought an excuse was in order. "I'll find out for you what she would like to eat. I think *I'll* have dinner downstairs. I have my own methods of getting over jet lag. Thank you, Magda."

When she returned to Amanda's room she found her cousin lying limply on the four-poster bed. Sienna turned back to shut the heavy door and block any sound.

"What are you *doing*?" Amanda lifted her head in amazement.

"Shutting the door—obviously," Sienna said. "Anyone would think I was locking you in a prison cell. Magda is just down the corridor, unpacking for me." Mandy was turning into something of a loose cannon.

Amanda choked on a dry laugh. "It makes you happy, doesn't it—sucking everyone in?"

"It would make me a lot happier if *you'd* try," Sienna retorted.

"I can't try. Not *now*." Amanda's large blue eyes welled with tears.

Sienna sank down onto the bed, pushing away her own irritations. "Mandy, I know you're grieving *inside*, but Blaine and Mark's mother could be missing it. They don't know you like I do."

"So you want me to shed buckets all over them?" Amanda was pushing her loose wedding ring and diamond solitaire engagement ring rather manically up and down on her finger. "Mark didn't love me. End of story. End of grieving. The man didn't love me."

"Did you love *him*, Mandy?" Sienna asked very quietly. "I mean really love him? Not the sex."

Amanda stared up at the ceiling. "I've been thinking a lot about that. It's like you once said to me— 'Mandy, you fall in love with *love*, but love means committing to one person.' I know what you're going to say. I *committed* all over the place. Maybe I was a bit promiscuous—which you did your best to hide from the family. So thanks for that. Anyway, I don't want to talk about Mark. Our marriage broke up long ago. *You* know."

"You'll never abandon your groundless accusations, will you?" Sienna asked with weary resignation. "Better to blame someone other than yourself. You might want to think long and hard about where *you* went wrong instead of always trying to fix the blame on me."

"Okay, okay!" Amanda cried, extending a conciliatory hand to Sienna, who took it from long habit. "So what's with the housekeeper?" she asked. "God, she's nearly as tall as Blaine."

"She is tall, yes. But she's rather a fine-looking woman. Mandy, you need to consider that Magda is an important person around here."

Amanda rolled her eyes. "You're joking! The housekeeper? *Important*?"

"Believe it," Sienna said. "Now, what would you like sent up on a tray?'

"You're *not* going downstairs?" Amanda cast Sienna's hand away, as though deeply disappointed in her. "You're *not* leaving me?"

"No need to get worked up." Sienna rose to her feet.

"My metabolism is clearly different from yours. I'll have dinner, then an early night."

"Don't give that!" Amanda snorted in disgust. "It's Blaine, isn't it? I mean, he's a *really* sensational guy."

Sienna just smiled. "With, I expect, a conga line of suitable prospective wives lined up. Why wouldn't he—a man like that?"

"Maybe you're after a fling?" Amanda's blue gaze was as sharp as a razor.

Sienna started to walk to the door. "I don't go in for flings, remember?"

"No, you're such a self-righteous person—always in control. But you haven't met a guy like this to date."

"This conversation is entirely inappropriate, Amanda," Sienna said. "We're here to bury Mark, remember? It's a sad and solemn occasion."

"Sure it is!" Amanda snapped. "But *my* legacy as Mark's widow is the *big* deal." She thrust her curly blonde head back into the pillows, folding her arms across her chest. "What do you reckon I'll get?"

"Mandy, I wouldn't know."

"Better be substantial," Amanda said. "These people are filthy rich. If I'm not happy with what I'm offered I'm going to demand more."

Sienna turned back, appalled. "I wouldn't go *demanding* anything of Blaine Kilcullen, Amanda. It would be a big mistake. Can't you see how tough he is?"

Amanda smiled up at the ceiling. "I love the way he kinda *smoulders*," she said. "Mark always did say he was ruthless. Anyway, enough of that. What I'd really like to eat is a burger with fries. No ketchup. A glass or two of white wine. They should be able to rise to that."

"That's not much of a choice," Sienna said.

"*My* choice, sweetie. I think they were lying about Marcia. I don't think she wants to meet us."

Sienna didn't answer, but she supposed Amanda might very well be right.

The day of the funeral.

Since her arrival Sienna had found it impossible to sleep in. The light woke her, and the tremendous outpouring of birdsong—such a melodious din she thought the rising sun might still be surprised by it. Today was one of brilliant sunshine. Golden rays were already starting to slant across the wide timber deck with its fifteen-foot overhang. No tears from heaven for Mark, she thought. She turned on her back, seeking solace in the birds' piercingly sweet music played at a full *fortissimo.* Now and again the sweetness was underscored by a loud cackling—no other word for it—that cut through the orchestration. She would carry the memory of this wild bush chorus for a very long time.

Moments later she rose, pulling on her pale pink satin robe, leaving the sash untied. Strangely enough, the highly irritable Amanda slept through the dawn orchestra—which was all to the good for today. Amanda's mood swings were legendary. She hoped and prayed they would get through the day without incident. Releasing her long hair from its loose night-time plait, she let it slide over her shoulder, padding across the carpet and out onto the huge deck. It ran the entire length of the first floor, with rattan and bamboo outdoor settings at intervals. The double rooms were screened to some extent by the graceful sweep of palm fronds from the palms growing in huge Asian planters.

At this time in the morning the atmosphere was pleasantly cool, although she knew it would soon build up to real heat. The scents from the extensive open garden were incredibly heady, even hectic, compared to what she was used to. Sweetness mingled with strong aromatic and citrus-type perfumes. The rear garden was a virtual oasis, with a meandering route through banks and banks of small flowering trees and amazingly colourful bushes. The fragrance from the white and violet lilies used as a massed bedding plant wafted to her easily. The lilies were unfamiliar to her. She supposed they were native, since they were thriving so lavishly in such dry conditions.

Moving across to the timber railing, she held onto it with both hands, allowing the glory of the morning to soothe her troubled spirits. Mindful of the day ahead, she closed her eyes and tilted her head to the sapphire sky.

Please God, keep us from harm. Show mercy to Mark. Show mercy to us all. Get Mandy safely through this sad day...

That was how Blaine came on her. He was transfixed by the sight. He even felt a charge in the air. He had to be aware his usual tight control was slipping further and further with this woman. At this hour, and after their long flight, he hadn't expected to see sight nor sign of his guests. They would be sleeping in, gathering their strength for the day ahead. He'd been tucking his bush shirt into his jeans as he'd walked to the French doors of the master suite, glancing out on the day and wondering what it might bring.

Since his father had died he had moved into what had traditionally been the master suite; prior to that he had occupied the entire west wing, which he still retained. Hilary, quite naturally, on her marriage had not wanted the suite of rooms always associated with his mother, the first Mrs Kilcullen, mistress of Katajangga. She had chosen the next largest room. There were seven double bedrooms strung along this upper floor. In the old days they'd always had plenty of guests, some of them important people. These days Hilary and Marcia occupied the east wing.

Moving into the master suite had somehow made him feel closer to the mother he had lost. That was the telling thing. To lose a parent when young, especially a mother, had the after effects playing over and over right through one's life. He had never hated Hilary, who had supplanted his mother. How could anyone hate Hilary? But it had taken him many years to warm to her. Now, thankfully, they were close.

Even from a distance he could see Sienna's lips moving. He sensed she was saying some prayer on this day of days. For Mark? For poor, troubled Mark to be at rest? He waited a moment, then on impulse called to her. Maybe he shouldn't have. She was still wearing her nightgown and robe, her long beautiful hair flowing down her back. He would be invading her privacy. But that didn't stop him.

"Sienna?"

He kept his resonant voice low, but it would carry to her ears. The last thing he wanted to do was wake Mark's young widow, who herself was full of demons. Amanda kept mostly to her room, clearly unable to find it in her heart to offer sympathy and support to her mother-in-law, let alone friendliness. Maybe she had good reason not to take to Marcia, who had made her first appearance at yesterday's lunch. Marcia, though polite enough on the surface—he had demanded that of her—had spoken to him afterwards, in one of her private little rages that could be so like Mark's.

"I don't like her, Blaine. She looks like butter wouldn't melt in her mouth, yet you must have noticed she has a serious grudge against Sienna. I bet she's had it for years. Mark let us down. She's let us down. You can bet your life

she's here for the money. I like Sienna. She's very different. But I don't like or trust Amanda."

Hilary hadn't risked shocking the young, impressionable Marcia by showing her the letter Mark had sent to her after his marriage. For a married man to fall in love with another woman could have terrible consequences. Blaine's instincts told him Mark had been very much in love with or at least torn over his feelings for his wife's bridesmaid. When had Sienna discovered that? For that matter, when exactly had Amanda, his wife, ceased to interest him?

Sienna awaited Blaine's approach with a touch of trepidation. Perversely, she was also revelling in that sense of high excitement and danger he carried with him. He was half dressed, his shirt unbuttoned almost to the waist. She realized he could have worn anything at all and still caught the eyes of women. He had a superb body. One was constantly aware of the musculature beneath his polished bronze skin, just as one would be conscious of the musculature beneath the pelt of a big cat. It added to his already intensely sexual aura. She had never experienced anything approaching what she felt with this man. That alone set off the alarm bells.

"Couldn't sleep?" He reached her, staring down at her, warding off the quite lunatic desire to pull her into his arms. Physically reaching out for her was out of the question. He had thought he could handle just about anything. Hell, he *was* handling a multitude of things. But he was seriously starting to doubt his ability to handle this woman. Her allure was fantastic—that delicate femininity. It was like a gauzy web that whirled around her, drawing him in whether he wanted it or not: another powerful weapon in this beautiful woman's arsenal. No wonder Mark had found her irresistible.

For God's sake, answer. Make your voice work.

Sienna needed that jolt from her inner voice. Even so, she was amazed at the friendly calm of her response. "The birds woke me. I've never heard such a glorious din in my entire life."

He laughed, turning his head away from her to look out over the vast vistas. "In an hour or so the mirage will be up and abroad. As for the birds—they wake me every day of my life."

He risked turning back to look at her. Her skin in the dazzling morning light was flawless, so lustrous he wanted to stroke it. There were intensities and *intensities* in life, he thought. He'd had his share of relationships, very pleasant for the most part, but the power this woman had was almost a threat. He had known her too short a time, yet he had to strain to maintain some sort of distance between them. At that minute he wanted to pull her to him by her long amber hair. He could see the faint rise and fall of her breasts. Her heartbeat was making the lace that dipped low into her cleavage tremble.

He braced his arms against the railing, making a real effort to recapture distance. "Have you heard the ringnecks yet? You must have. There's a whole colony of them out there." He waved in the direction of the banks of blossoming trees. "They're large birds, mostly emerald-green, with a distinct yellow collar and a red band across the top of their bills."

Sienna followed his lead. She too was at pains to hide how his presence was affecting her. From the very beginning she had sensed the heat in him, the heat he covered with severity, yet perversely it stirred turbulent sexual feelings. "Would they be the ones who give that whistling call when they're in the air?" she asked. "I've never sighted so many parrots."

"This is the land of parrots. Ringnecks can be very boisterous."

Just a jumble of words—a good safe topic when what he was thinking was: *Just you and me.* Neither of them was moving, as though they couldn't bring themselves to do so, yet he knew she found just as much danger as he did in their closeness. He didn't want this woman soothing and exciting him in turn. A man in his position could never keep hold of a woman like that, bred to the high life. It would be like keeping a gorgeous bird of paradise in a cage.

Sienna studied his handsome, resolute profile, sensing the perturbation in him.

"What thoughts were going through your head when I called to you?" he asked.

She took in breath at a rush. "A prayer to get us all through the day. I'm so, so sorry for Hilary. Marcia too, of course. But she's young and in far less pain than Mark's mother."

"You're not sorry for me?"

"You're wonderfully blunt."

"That doesn't answer the question."

"No." She dared to turn her body sideways. His coal-black hair was tousled into deep waves, with one stray lock resting on his broad tanned forehead. The sun was picking up bluish highlights. He looked incredibly vibrant, and as much a man as she could ever imagine. "I *hope* I am."

For some reason that amused him. "You haven't mentioned Amanda, which has to be a bit odd?"

Her sigh was impatient. "I know you're very observant, Blaine, and you've had Amanda and me under close observation from the start. Amanda losing both her parents so young has left its imprint, like a kind of desolation. She wards off pain. She thinks of it as an actual invader. She won't let it in. But the death of someone very close to us, even when we're estranged, always brings pain. Amanda is in her own kind of despair. She and Mark weren't all that happy towards the end. Perhaps the marriage wouldn't have lasted—who knows? But don't judge Amanda too harshly. I know you've been doing that."

"Then how would you have me see her?" he asked tersely. "Mark's mother doesn't exist for her. Marcia either."

"Well, they've been strangers up until now," she countered.

He blew out a derisive breath. "How come *you've* managed to make friends with Hilary and Marcia? Magda too for that matter. You have an amazing physical ease with people. It comes across as pure warmth."

"What do you think it is?" A flash of anger heightened the colour of her eyes.

"A great asset, Sienna," he returned smoothly. "It's very beguiling."

"And you think possibly a learned social skill?"

"Your eyes spark fire when you're angry," he said, looking deeply into them.

"And you enjoy leading me on."

His firm, sensual mouth twitched. "Guilty as charged. Let's call a truce for today. I was only pointing out that Hilary and Marcia, and include Magda, are hoping you'll stay on for a good while."

"But, Blaine, Amanda will want to go home very soon."

He laughed without humour. "What has that got to do with you? Amanda's a grown woman. And she's already raised the subject of money."

That shocked her. "Has she r-r-eally?" she stumbled. "When?" Amanda had never breathed a word.

She was staring up at him, her lovely lips parted. He felt like an explorer who had happened upon a gold mine.

Another time he wouldn't have hesitated. He would have pulled her to him and kissed her hard for as long as it took to have her melting in his arms. He wondered if she knew it. He wondered if she would stop him. Only today wasn't the day for a display of serious lust. He had to call it that. *Lust.* Even though he knew it for what it was. A powerful attraction at all levels. Attraction of the mind was as alluring in its way as sexual desire for a woman's body.

"When did she mention it?" Sienna asked again, picking up the sensuality in his expression. Did he see the response that swept through her?

"She found a minute last night." He shrugged.

"She never said a word."

"According to Amanda, *you* advised her it was about time she started speaking up," he said.

She threw back her head. "I absolutely deny that!'

He couldn't withdraw his hand. He reached out and caught a handful of her thick silky hair. "Oh, dear—you're saying Amanda was telling fibs?" he taunted.

She jerked back, more disturbed by his hand on her hair than Amanda's all too familiar malicious lies. "Believe what you want to believe, Blaine. I know you do. Did she mention how much I'd told her she should expect?"

"Far more than she's going to get."

"Are you serious?" She bridled at his grand, insolent arrogance. Even so she wanted to *touch* him—run her fingers along his clean chiselled jaw...move her fingers to trace his raised lip line... He was more *real* to her than any man she had ever known. She had to internalize that.

"Very serious," he replied.

"Okay, how much does she want?" She threw down the gauntlet, taking an involuntary step nearer.

"A lot less than she first thought." If she took one more step he really would lose it. He watched her flip the long lock of hair he had taken hold of over her shoulder. It rippled sinuously down her back. Beautiful hair truly was a woman's crowning glory, he thought, realizing he would have to proceed very carefully.

"At least you're saying *she*."

"Suppose we stop now," he said. Was it common sense, a natural caution, or every male's inbuilt fear of a woman's power?

Suddenly she looked contrite. "Of course. But you really do like to stir things up."

"*You* play that game best."

Her head came up to stare into his lambent eyes. "I really don't know what you're talking about."

He laughed and turned away. "Give me some credit, Sienna," he said, dry as ash. "By the way, everyone should be here by ten o'clock. Most are flying in. Some will come cross-country. It won't be a big funeral, like Dad's. But we can expect around one hundred people."

"Joanne and her family are coming, as planned?" She suddenly realized the sun must be shining through her satin nightgown. She should have tied the sash, but too late now. It was the tingle of electricity she got with his eyes on her that reined in her will.

"Yes, they are." Blaine speared his fingers into his hair. "Do your best with Amanda."

"What is that supposed to mean?"

"Oh, God, Sienna!" He gave a wholly unexpected groan. "You must have spent years keeping your cousin out of trouble, even if you couldn't stop her marrying Mark. My first thought, my main loyalty, is for Hilary. Losing Dad nearly killed her. Now she has to bury her son. She loved Mark unconditionally. I have to admit I set conditions. Conditions that were never met. I don't want Hilary subjected to any untoward outbursts from Amanda. I'm sorry if it pains you, but I think regular outbursts power Amanda, just like they powered Mark. They had that in common if nothing else."

This Sienna already knew.

She knocked on Amanda's door at around nine o'clock, waiting for her cousin to call for her to come in. Amanda hadn't come down to breakfast. Sienna, Hilary and Marcia had breakfasted together in a surprisingly companionable fashion. Magda had taken a tray up to Amanda.

She was standing in the middle of the room, wearing only her bra and knickers, but she had her make-up on and her freshly washed blonde hair was curling softly around her gamine little face. She looked very pale and peaky, however.

"Feeling a little better?" Sienna asked, with a rush of concern.

"I feel awful, if you must know," Amanda said irritably. "Really nauseous. I threw up my breakfast."

"Good grief." The thought that Amanda might be pregnant sprang into Sienna's mind, but she immediately rejected it. Amanda would have told her.

"Those damned pills the doctor gave me after the accident. They helped, but they don't agree with me."

"You're not supposed to mix medication with alcohol, Mandy," Sienna said, as gently as she could.

"Oh, don't start!" Amanda was at once affronted. "I need it at the moment."

"Okay, just try to relax." Sienna endeavoured to be as soothing as possible. "Where's your dress?" She glanced towards the pretty blue dress lying on the bed. Was Amanda thinking of wearing that?

"I'm not wearing black, like you," Amanda burst out, obviously a bundle of nerves.

"Okay, okay—don't upset yourself. Not today. So you're thinking of wearing the blue? It's a little bit—"

"Mark *loved* me in it." Amanda said, pushing Sienna's efforts at soothing her aside. "He loved me in blue."

"All right. I understand. You don't have to wear black. What about your hat?"

"*What* hat?" Amanda screeched, pouring a overload of bitter resentment into it. "I don't have a hat." She flopped into an armchair, looking very tense and wary.

"It's the sun, Mandy. You'll get burned," Sienna explained. "Both of us need hats, as well as sunscreen. The family plot is a good distance away We'll be travelling by car, but we still have to stand in the sun."

"I don't care about the sun," said Amanda. "I've a good mind not to go at all. No one wants me there. *I'm* Mark's widow, yet they're all falling over like ninepins around *you*. It's really weird. Blaine thinks you do it deliberately."

That struck an exposed nerve. "Do what?" Sienna asked shortly.

"Sew people up." Amanda gave an explosive little laugh. "He's right on to you, my girl. I just love your little black dress, by the way. Cute little sleeves. You know, you're very special in your way. And I bet you went out and bought yourself a terrific black hat." She gave a honeyed smirk that really perturbed Sienna.

"Amanda, I shouldn't have to remind you that Mark is being buried today," she told her cousin quietly.

"Come to think of it, Mark *was* a bit suicidal." Amanda sprawled even further down in the armchair, her slender legs outstretched.

Sienna felt her face drain of colour. "He never said such a thing to you, did he?"

"More likely he said it to *you*." Amanda jumped up. "My husband *loved* you, Sienna. He didn't care where he lived as long as it was near you. He was going to dump me for you."

Sienna felt shock allied to very real pain jack-knife through her body. "How many times must I tell you? I was *not* attracted to Mark. Mark was *your* husband."

Amanda looked at her with jaundiced eyes. "He fell in love with you the moment I introduced you."

"Dear God!" Sienna put her hands to her reeling head. "I need to understand this. Mark married *you* when he was in love with *me*?"

"Stranger things have happened, cousin," Amanda drawled. "He used to dream about you."

Sienna whirled about, desperate to get out of the room. "Even if it were true—and it's absolute rubbish—you have to stop this, Amanda. You're determined to hang me for a crime I did not commit."

"You said it. Not me."

Sienna turned back. "You're destroying our relationship, Amanda. Do you realize that?"

"Maybe. But I know what I know." Amanda, for a petite young woman with big blue eyes and a cap of blonde curls, looked as street-tough as they came.

"Then I hope you also know that if you continue to behave badly I'll leave you to fend for yourself. It's high time you did."

Some sense of self-interest clicked inside Amanda's head. "In that case I *will* behave myself. I'm sorry. I'm just your dumb cousin."

"You're dumb, all right—speaking to Blaine about the money you think you're due." For once Sienna lost control. She was finding it harder and harder to connect with Amanda. "And I consider your telling him *I* put you up to it a real betrayal."

Red flags of colour flew in Amanda's pale cheeks. "He's lying. I told him no such thing. Why would I?"

Sienna made a huge effort to pull herself together. "I'm sorry, Amanda," she said tightly, "but it's the sort of thing that carries your signature. Pulling the rug out from under me is something you consider an achievement. I can't bear to ask what you were trying to get out of Blaine, but if it's way too much you won't get it. Now, I'm going to ask Hilary if she or Marcia have a wide-brimmed hat you could borrow. You don't want to damage your skin. You have such lovely skin."

Amanda brushed away an angry tear. "I can just imagine the sort of hat poor old Hilary could come up with. You might come back with a pith helmet."

"I mightn't come back at all," said Sienna, her hand already on the doorknob.

CHAPTER FIVE

THE graveside service conducted by an Anglican minister was mercifully short. A visibly weak and wilting Amanda stood between Sienna and Blaine, with Hilary, Marcia and other members of the Kilcullen clan to the right of Blaine. A mixed bag. A professor of physics, a federal senator with his wife and daughter, a supreme court judge and his wife, a prominent Kilcullen pastoralist and his family, and another member of the extended Kilcullen family—a wheat and wine grower from somewhere called the Darling Downs.

Sienna later found out it was a wonderfully fertile district on the western slopes of the Great Dividing Range—the mountain barrier than ran down the eastern seaboard and divided the lush coastline from the rolling central plains of Queensland and, beyond, the true Outback.

On the opposite side of the open grave the mourners were packed. They had come to pay their respects more to the family than poor Mark, Sienna thought, with real sorrow in her heart. She had been experiencing a good deal of torment over Amanda's out-of-the-blue remark that Mark had been suicidal. There *had* been something very worrying about Mark. Now she had to wonder. He had not been an experienced skier, and they had begged Mark to stay on the recognized track, but he had taken off in such a strange way—heading into the trees, one of which had caused his death.

She recalled a moment she had almost forgotten, when Mark had told her he was "worthless" and then immediately laughed it off. Had he really thought himself worthless? If so, why? Having met Mark's family, she couldn't see any one of them working to strip Mark of all self-esteem. Although she could see how it might have felt walking in his half-brother's tall shadow.

Light aircraft had been flying in all morning, causing Amanda to ask irritably, "What is this? An air show? They've been coming in for ages."

"They're Outback families, Mandy. This is a way of life out here. Don't let it bother you. You have to keep calm."

"Tell me about it!" Amanda said, sounding angry. "I hate this blasted hat."

"Just let me adjust it a little." Sienna tilted the ribbon-decorated, wide-brimmed straw hat further onto Amanda's forehead. "Actually, it looks good on you."

"You can't mean that!" Amanda pushed the hat back again. "I've had to slap sunblock all over my face."

Sienna didn't respond. She was finding it impossible to say the right thing. Amanda would be on show. Everyone would be looking at her, probably judging her. But Sienna thought it more than her life was worth to point that out. Amanda could just as easily decide she wasn't going to the graveside service at all. Amanda was becoming more and more of a mystery as she got older.

The Barrett Family had flown in, in their Cessna, accompanied by their only daughter, Joanne—Joanne who had been Mark's fiancée. Blaine pointed Joanne out very briefly as she and her parents alighted from a station Jeep.

An attractive, athletic-looking young woman, sombrely dressed.

A procession of vehicles had been coming and going, ferrying the funeral guests to the Kilcullen family plot set on a low ridge. The area was quite large, surrounded by an arrow-capped, six-foot-high wrought-iron fence painted black. Massive date palms, probably the most ancient cultivated tree in the world, lent some shade, but the chief mourners would be standing directly in the harsh sun.

"That's Joanne, with her mother and father," Blaine told her in a quick aside. "Rachael and Allan Barrett. Amanda doesn't know about Joanne?"

"Not as yet. If I'd told her I don't think I could have got her here."

"Right!" He nodded crisply, leaving her side to speak to another arriving group.

Sienna looked around her quickly, shivering with tension despite the brilliant sunshine. Amanda too was trembling. Amanda had never liked graveyards at the best of time. She had refused point-blank to visit the famous Cimetière du Père-Lachaise when they were in Paris, as though the souls of the writers, artists, poets, composers and other notable figures buried there might rise up and hurt her. Sienna had always found Père-Lachaise a serene place, while Amanda claimed graveyards gave her the creeps.

The true pain was for the living, Sienna thought. Mark's pain was over.

There were too many headstones for an easy count. Blaine and Mark's father lay at rest here. So did Blaine's mother, Marianne. None of the headstones, granite and stone for the most part, could be called in any way a monument—except for one seated marble figure that Sienna assumed was the Kilcullen ancestral figure. Children had been buried there, their graves marked by little guardian angels with spread wings. One showed a small child, a girl with long hair and wearing a dress, lying as if asleep on top of the broad headstone. Sad and touching.

Beside her, Amanda sucked in her breath. "This is too much for me."

Sienna put her arm around her cousin and held her close—if only to muffle her voice. "I know you feel terrible, but we'll get through this together."

Amanda was perspiring profusely. Heat coloured her very fair skin, and she was stumbling on her feet by the time it was over. Blaine was fully occupied supporting his stepmother, who was grief stricken and not holding up at all. Senator Kilcullen, delegated by Blaine, came swiftly to assist Sienna in getting Amanda back to the waiting Jeep.

"A very difficult time for us all," said the Senator, opening the rear door and gently handing Amanda into the vehicle.

"Thank you, sir." Sienna held out her hand. The Senator took it between both of his, staring in rather a rapt fashion into her face, shaded by the broad brim of her hat. "Sad business, my dear. You're Mark's young widow's cousin, isn't that right?"

"Yes, Senator," she responded gracefully. "Thank you so much.'

"We'll talk more at the house," he promised.

"He won't be talking to *me*," Amanda said behind her hand, all worked up. "I want to be free of all this. I want no grief." The last word was almost spat.

By the time they arrived back at the homestead a number of people were already gathered in the Great Room. There was to be a buffet lunch for the funeral guests, many of whom had travelled long distances. Hilary herself was stoically receiving people, with a white-faced, unsmiling Marcia standing at her side.

Sienna would have picked Marcia as Mark's twin out of a large crowd. True, the resemblance wasn't as strong as in many other sets of twins, but Marcia was clearly Mark's sister, with the same thick golden brown hair and dark eyes, plus something of his manner. Marcia had been ignoring Amanda—if not pointedly then near enough to it. Sienna was starting to feel very bad about everything.

With good cause.

Amanda was looking around the Great Room aghast. "They needn't think I'm going to be a part of *this*," she said, sweeping the straw hat off her head and throwing it on the nearest chair. Damp blonde curls were stuck in little clusters to her white forehead. "I wouldn't be surprised if I fainted."

"You won't," Sienna said, fearful Amanda might just do that. She really did look ill. Sienna hoped it would be interpreted by the funeral guests as a very natural grief. Amanda *was* the bereaved widow, even if it appeared in private she had moved to a point where the money coming to her was claiming her attention.

The instant Blaine came through the door, physically so impressive, and so much more than that, Sienna knew she had to tell him she had an emergency on her hands.

"What is it, Sienna?"

He broke away from the distinguished, middle-aged couple he'd been escorting into the homestead to come towards her, staggeringly handsome in funeral clothes relieved by a snowy white shirt. She was aware that beneath the iron control he was feeling his own kind of anguish. The eternal "what might have been".

"I'm sorry, Blaine, but Amanda isn't feeling at all well," she explained quickly. "I'm afraid there are just too many people for her to contend with. I hope you and Hilary won't mind, but I'm taking her upstairs. She's desperate to lie down."

His striking face showed no emotion at all. "Whatever she wants. I could tell she was finding it a tremendous strain. You're coming back again?"

"You want me back?"

"Of course I want you back," he said, as though she had said something out of order.

"Then I'll *be* back. I'll just get Amanda settled."

"Okay," he nodded shortly. "I want you to know I'm giving Amanda enough money to make her secure. So there will be no need for you or your family to offer financial support in the future."

Anger flashed, but she kept her tone level. "Blaine, we've been happy to."

"There's such a thing as being *too* kind," he said tersely, staring down into her upturned face. Like the rest of them she had been standing in full sun, yet she looked as cool as a lily. He had been moved to speak because he had been observing Amanda closely. She had really jumped the gun, questioning him about her legacy. It revealed a decidedly mercenary streak.

On this very day when they had buried Mark he still wasn't sure what had happened that terrible afternoon when their father had suffered his crippling accident. What part had Mark actually played? Mark had been capable of just about anything, Blaine acknowledged, when he was seriously off balance. But he had never been able to speak to anyone of his fears. And his father had lost all memory of the day. Secret fears had to be borne in silence.

By the time Sienna went downstairs again the large crowd of mourners were all but feasting on the lavish buffet lunch, as though any day now they could expect famine. It was no different back home. People seemed to relish a free meal. The buffet had been prepared by Magda and her trained helpers, part-aboriginal girls who worked around the very large homestead. Long mahogany tables were laden with sliced beef fillet, hams, roast pork, pink lamb. There were all kinds of salads, mountains of freshly baked bread rolls. On another table there were bottles and bottles of Scotch, bourbon, red wines and chilled white wines in buckets of ice, frosted glasses.

The mourners were beginning to arrange themselves in little groups. Apart from the family and the Senator, Sienna hadn't met anybody, but gallery work for her father and her own family's position in society gave her an easy self-confidence.

Blaine had been keeping an eye out for her while not appearing to do so. She calmed him in a way he had never experienced with another woman outside his beautiful mother. Burying his half-brother had been a harrowing experience. He deeply regretted their estrangement even if that estrangement, hadn't been of his making, and he mourned Mark, dead so young. The dead didn't age. Only the living could do that.

Just about everyone had offered some comment about Mark's pretty little widow in her blue dress. Most had genuinely found the blue dress touching, others maybe not. He didn't have an opinion himself, although he knew Hilary had been taken aback. All were in agreement, however, about Amanda's stunningly beautiful cousin.

"Prettiness is one thing. Beauty is something entirely different, isn't it?" Joanne had remarked. "I knew straight away which one was Mark's wife. Mark was intimidated by strong, confident women. I'd say the cousin is both."

And a weaver of spells, Blaine thought. She had cast

one over Mark. Having met her, he could understand. If he was going to be completely honest she had cast one over him. It brought home to him the powerful reminder that underneath his outward persona he was a sensual man.

Mourners watched in fascination as Sienna made her graceful way to Blaine's side. "Amanda is resting," she said, her eyes moving automatically to his companion.

"Sienna, I'd like you to meet Joanne Barrett." Blaine introduced them. "I've spoken of Joanne."

"Of course. How do you do, Joanne?" Sienna extended her hand, her charming voice gentle and polite. "This is a sad day for you." She could see the flickering disturbance in the young woman's face.

Joanne looked her straight in the eye. "It is indeed. I loved Mark, you know."

Sienna had bargained on hearing this. "Then you must know you have my deepest sympathy, Joanne."

Joanne stood for a moment, as if trying to come to a decision, then said, "Thank you, Sienna. You must meet my parents. Then we should get you something to eat."

"I don't know that I'm hungry," Sienna told her wryly. She was trying to deny her own distress.

"Have something all the same." Blaine realized Sienna too was striving to keep her feelings at a distance, but he was obliged to turn his head away from her as the Senator called his name, clearly wanting him to join him and his whisky-drinking mates. Drink was always more important than food to those guys, he thought.

"I'll take care of Sienna," Joanne told him, linking her arm through Sienna's. "There's so much I want to know, Sienna. Could you find it in your heart to tell me? I've never been reconciled to Mark's leaving me."

So Joanne hadn't moved on? That was sad. "I'm so sorry,

Joanne. I'll tell you what I can, but I never got close to Mark, you know."

"Did anyone?" Joanne asked, grief in her fine hazel eyes. "Did anyone know the *real* Mark?" She choked back tears, sinking her teeth hard into her bottom lip. "He was born to upset people. God forgive me for saying it, today of all days, but everyone here knows about Mark. What happened to the family. What happened to *us*."

"Joanne," Sienna said, very earnestly. "To this day Amanda doesn't know Mark had a fiancée back home."

Joanne's hazel eyes seemed to glaze over. "He never *told* her?"

"He never told anyone. I only found out myself from Blaine when he came to Vancouver. I haven't told Amanda what I know because she's barely holding it all together."

"But what *is* it she's holding together?" Joanne asked in an abruptly cold voice. "I know Amanda is your cousin, and you appear very protective of her, but I don't believe she's the sad and vulnerable little person she makes out to be."

"Why ever would you say that?" Sienna turned on the other woman in surprise, wondering if Blaine had supplied Joanne with only a few facts and left out others. Such as Amanda being ignorant of any fiancée. "Has Blaine said something to you?" She hated the idea of Blaine's discussing her and Amanda with other people, however well-known to him.

Joanne's voice dropped a tone. "Blaine has said very little. It's my friend Marcia who has given us her unsolicited views. Marcy is wound very tight. She had a love-hate going with Mark. Which is to say she was always desperate for a loving brother, but got Mark instead. *Blaine* is her hero figure. But Blaine is her half-brother. Mark was her *twin*, though he spent most of his time ignoring her."

"I'd say that was Mark's loss, wouldn't you?" Sienna murmured quietly. "How did you come to fall in love with Mark?"

"God knows!" Joanne shrugged. "I didn't ask to. I knew he was cruel, and I can't say he ever made me happy. I knew he was hellishly jealous of Blaine, but he *was* handsome. He could be fun when he was in a good mood. And he was a Kilcullen. Plenty of girls wanted Mark for that reason alone. They knew they couldn't have Blaine."

Sienna found herself asking what she dearly wanted to know. "Does Blaine have someone special?"

Joanne leaned closer. "Blaine could choose a wife from any women he wanted in this room," she said. "See the tall brunette over there, with the great figure? That's Lynda McCrae. Her family run an Outback airline—McCrae Air. Passenger, charter, freight. Blaine and Lynda were an item at one time, but nothing came of it. Not that Lynda isn't still in there trying. Then there's Kerrie Henmann, and I guess Camilla Marsh. All in with a chance. But Blaine lost his father. Blaine worshipped his father. The horrendous accident hit him hard and he had to take over the station, which is a huge job. Mark, of course, took off. That's the sort of person he turned out to be."

Which sadly corresponded to Sienna's own evaluation. "Well, he's laid to rest now, Joanne," she said. "That chapter of your life is closed."

"I hope!" Joanne released a strangled breath. "But I have a funny sort of feeling it isn't. I thought I despised Mark when he took off, but I never wanted him to end his life this way."

"Of course you didn't," Sienna said. "It was a freak accident."

"That's what happened to his father—a freak accident." Joanne paused for a moment, seemingly on the brink of saying more. "My dad didn't like it one bit. Mr Kilcullen was a superb horseman. Dad always says—" She broke off, putting a hand to her mouth.

"Dad says what?" Sienna prompted.

"He wouldn't want me to talk about it." Joanne stared across the Great Room to where her parents were standing talking, plates in hand, to Emily Kilcullen, the Senator's wife. "People couldn't seem to accept what had happened even though accidents happen on stations all the time. We would have known what happened, only Mr Kilcullen lost all memory of that day."

"A terrible thing." Sienna was well able to visualize a strong, powerful man reduced to life in a wheelchair. "People always want to find reasons behind what's happened to those they care about."

"Of course." Joanne sighed. "Dreams don't come true, do they?"

"You're talking about yourself?"

"Yes."

"They won't if you don't reach out, Joanne. There'll be someone for you. I know. But you must put the past aside. You have a future."

Joanne brightened. "How long do you intend to stay, Sienna?"

She could hardly say they'd leave tomorrow if Amanda had her way. "A couple of weeks at least," she replied. "Amanda suffers greatly from jet lag, and we'll be flying the other way—always the worst way to go. So, tell me, what does Marcia have to say about Amanda?"

Joanne moved on, still holding Sienna's arm companionably. "Let's just say Marcy doesn't like her. I hope you can find the time to visit us. Our cattle station, Ettamunga, is only a thirty-minute flight away. It's no Katajangga, of course, but I think you would enjoy the experience. Mum and I would love to hear all about your life, what you do.

Blaine said you're an artist. I have to say you look very artistic. I love your accent, by the way. You have the sort of voice that makes a person want to hang onto every word. Ah, there's Mum, waving a hand to us. Let's go over. Say hello. Then I'm going to get you a cold drink and a plate of something. You are just *so* beautiful!" she exclaimed in genuine admiration. "But I guess you're used to hearing that. Why aren't *you* married? Blaine said you weren't."

So Blaine had volunteered that piece of information. "Hey, now, I'm not drawing my pension yet." She smiled.

Sienna caught Blaine's eye across the room. It struck her as she met his gaze that she had been missing something crucial in her life. Blessed with youth, health, inherited good-looks and her gift as an artist, with a mother, father and brother she adored, there was still that *empty* spot needing to be filled. By a man, by a soulmate. Her loyalty to Amanda remained intact, but she had to face the fact that if Amanda were not her cousin she would never have chosen her for a friend. They were just too different, and becoming even more so.

She had never been short of men friends, when it came to that. She'd had two fairly serious affairs and had considered marriage, but in the end backed off. Why? Both men would have made good husbands and fathers, but in the end she'd had to confront the fact she hadn't *loved* them. Or not enough. She wanted a man to *fill* her up. Fill up her life. She wanted a man she could be passionate about—a man who would be passionate about her. She wanted that *soul mate* she had been beginning to think would never come along. Maybe she was too choosy. But she wanted *total* love.

And into her life had come Blaine Kilcullen.

Beware of what you wish for.

* * *

It was mid-afternoon before the private planes, the charter planes and the fleets of four-wheel drive vehicles left for their journey home. A broken-hearted Hilary had retired to her room, the immense struggle to hold back her grief no longer necessary, and Joanne had taken charge of her friend Marcia. Marcia had gone to stay with the Barretts for a day or two. Everyone knew of Hilary's love for her wayward son. They knew Mark, for all his difficult nature, had been the favourite twin. Sienna had the feeling Marcia had gone off so easily because of that factor, and no doubt to escape Amanda.

In her room, Sienna changed into a tangerine cotton shirt, tucking it into a pair of cream cotton twill pants, and slipping on sneakers. She didn't quite know what to do with herself. She thought she might ask Magda if there was anything she could do to help, although Magda and her girls had already made inroads into the big job of clearing away. Still, she would ask. If Magda refused help she would take a walk around the rear gardens. But first she had to call in on Amanda.

"Well, *you're* late!" Amanda was sprawled atop the four-poster bed, wearing a silk caftan.

"Excuse me?"

Amanda was inspecting her wristwatch for all the world like an employer clocking a recalcitrant employee. "It's half past three."

"Pity you couldn't have made it downstairs, if only for a half-hour," Sienna retorted. "People really wanted to meet you."

"Oh, yeah!" Amanda snorted. "They were looking at me like I was some sort of a freak. And that Marcia! She hates me."

"She doesn't. But you haven't been particularly nice to

her. Anyway, she's gone back with the Barrett family. The daughter, Joanne, is a close friend."

"God, I didn't know she had one. Anyway, that's your job, isn't it? Winning people over."

"Joanne was Mark's fiancée at one time." Might as well get it over. At least Amanda was lying down.

"I knew he had one," Amanda said, casually admitting a long deception.

"And you never said a word?" Sienna was aghast.

"What was it to *you*?" Amanda asked querulously. "Mark said she'd been mad about him since they were kids. His mother more or less forced him into the engagement, but he couldn't hack it."

"He couldn't hack marriage either, could he?" Sienna said with a rush of anger.

"God, you're not going to make a scene, are you?" Amanda half sat up, looking like an innocent under unfair attack. "Can't you see I'm sick?"

Sienna backed off. The habit was ingrained. "I *can* see, Amanda. But you'd feel better if you'd been getting some food into you these past days. You've lost weight and you can't afford to. You're starting to look like a waif."

"That's it! Rub it in." Amanda fell back to thrash the pillows. "Mark and I might have been heading for disaster, but I loved him."

"Some part of you may have. But you wanted Mark, right or wrong. You have to take some responsibility for that."

Amanda's milky white cheeks blotched. "Thanks for your compassion. I'd like to go home, only I don't think I can face the long trip yet. I might go to Sydney. I liked the look of Sydney. I might go when I feel better and Blaine hands over the money."

"The money, the money! Was the sole reason for your coming here the money?"

"You bet!" Amanda gave her a droll look.

"Then I'd strongly advise you to allow Blaine to choose the time," Sienna warned her.

Amanda stretched her slender arms above her hand. "Then I won't have to run to you and Lucien any more."

Sienna stared at her cousin in dismay. She had spent most of her life looking out for "little Mandy". Her parents had been endlessly supportive. Apparently it all counted for nothing with Amanda. "Is that all we've meant to you, Amanda?" she asked sadly.

Amanda laughed. "God, no! Just joking. I love you to bits. But please don't sermonize, Sienna. I've had enough of it."

"Okay." Sienna turned about. "Is there anything I can get you?' Amanda really did look sickly. She wondered if she had a bottle of something secreted in her room.

"A pitcher of martinis?" Amanda suggested.

"Cup of tea and a sandwich? Magda is pretty flat out, but I can get it for you."

"Don't bother," said Amanda. "I'll have something sent up later."

Magda had allowed Sienna to take charge of the crystal glasses. Although coasters had been placed strategically around the Great Room, both she and Magda had paused to cluck over a couple of rings on the gleaming timber surfaces.

"People are so careless." Magda had shaken her heavy blonde head. "Not to worry, Sienna. I have a good trick for removing marks."

Now Sienna was in the kitchen, a huge room with "Magda's Domain" on a brass plaque fixed to the door, accessible from the corridor adjacent to the left staircase. They were talking easily—Magda telling Sienna her story of how as a young Polish migrant she had been taken in by the Kilcullens when her Lithuanian partner had left her penniless and stranded in Darwin.

Magda broke off as Blaine walked in. He was dressed pretty much as Sienna was, in shirt and jeans, only he wore riding boots that made him even taller.

"I've been looking for you, Sienna," he said, sending his sizzling glance in her direction. He crossed to where Magda was standing, placing a hand on her comfortably padded shoulder. "Thank you, Magda," he said quietly.

Magda coloured up. "I do anything for you, Mr Blaine," she said. "You want to take this beautiful young lady off?"

"Got it in one. I need to get out of the house," Blaine said, the strain of the day showing on his dynamic face. "I thought you would too, Sienna. You ride?"

"I'm a Canadian, aren't I?" she said with a lift of her brows.

"Thank God for that. I knew you would. There can't be anyone in the world who hasn't heard of the Royal Canadian Mounties and the Calgary Stampede. Horse-riding must be something of a passion in Canada, just like here. I thought we'd take same horses."

"You go now, Sienna."

Magda waved Sienna off—as though she needed any encouragement. The atmosphere at the homestead had become almost unbearably claustrophobic.

Blaine let her take her pick of mounts, bar his own—a stunning sooty bay called Amir. Its gleaming coat was almost completely black, but it had a bay's points, black mane, tail and legs.

"It looks a temperamental animal," she said, eyeing

the big gelding. It was dancing skittishly, and Blaine was taking a moment or two to control him. It couldn't have been plainer that Amir was raring to go.

"Just what I like."

Blaine glanced across at her with taut approval. Her every movement was so fluid she might have been buoyed by the breeze. She was wearing a cream akubra he had taken from the station store. It was not only a perfect fit, it suited her to perfection. She had secured her long hair in a thick, glowing plait. He was grateful her flawless skin wasn't the milky, very sensitive kind of the redhead that threw up freckles for protection. It was a load off his mind. Amanda's skin was much thinner and whiter, which could be a real problem in the desert sun, but Sienna's was creamy, and didn't burn given adequate protection. In fact she had already taken on a little colour. She'd had the foresight to pack gleaming riding boots, so she had fully expected to ride. It pleased him greatly that she shared his love of horses. He could feel his blood rising—as though *nothing*, not even the grief of Mark's funeral, could snuff out the sexual excitement she engendered.

"So, handsome horses for handsome people," she was saying, throwing him a half-smile over her shoulder. "I think I'll have this one, if I may." She stopped at a stall where a beautiful bright chestnut mare with a white star on its forehead was definitely looking for her attention. The mare clearly liked her, nuzzling her ear while she tickled its neck.

"Tamara. Good choice," Blaine clipped out. "Especially when we plan on galloping to the horizon." His expression was that of a man who needed to get moving. If only away from temptation.

The going ahead looked fast and fair. They rode at full gallop the minute they came to the open plains country, giving the eager horses their heads. Big, sturdy-legged gelding and smaller white-socked mare rose to the challenge. It was impossible to avoid the paper daisies. No help for it! They carpeted the landscape! So the horses' hooves cut wide swathes through their glory. To Sienna it was a tremendous relief, like coming out of a sick stupor.

When they eventually slowed Sienna fancied Blaine's smouldering expression had lightened.

"You're good." He gave his verdict the minute she brought the fleet chestnut mare alongside the taller, stronger gelding.

"Know why? I've been riding since I was a child. Just like you. I love it."

"It shows."

"So nice to have your approval."

It was a mocking little thrust, he acknowledged.

Gusts of heady scent from a patch of velvety red wild flowers were being drawn into her lungs. The perfume was so sweetly, exotically overpowering Sienna thought it could easily make her woozy if she was exposed to it long enough.

"How different the landscape is to my own British Columbia," she mused. They had moved off, heading towards water.

"Well, it *would* be," he said dryly. "Isn't British Columbia renowned for its beautiful verdant landscapes, powerful rivers, forests, lakes, snow-capped mountains?"

She nodded with pride, adjusting her thick plait. "This is another world. It speaks a different language. The language of your indigenous people. This landscape is unique to anything I've ever seen, and I've seen a lot of really fabulous desert country in the US. This is the red planet Mars, only it's covered in wild flowers mile after mile."

"You couldn't get used to it?"

Now, why the hell had he asked that? But mercifully, she didn't appear to attach much significance to his question so far as he could see.

"Oh, *yes*!" she exclaimed. "My imagination is fired to the extent I'm storing away scenes for the future. I can paint from photographs if I have to. There's wonderful inspiration here for an artist. The pervading sense of antiquity must be one of the Outback's greatest attractions. That and its mystique: the lonely wilderness, the extreme isolation, those extraordinary rocks. It's dramatic and lyrical at the same time. And the *colours*! All the dry pigment powders—yellow ochre, Venetian red, burnt umber, raw umber, burnt sienna, bright yellow, the blacks and the flake whites. Incredible. That flat-topped mesa way off in the distance appears a deep violet, and even that tree is simply beautiful, framed by the blue sky."

"Ghost gum." He identified the lovely Outback species, feeling his link to her strengthen by the minute.

"Of course—with that stark white bole. Some great being from your Dreamtime must have scattered those boulders about."

They were heading towards a broad glittering expanse of water, visible through the thick screen of trees. Bright golden spears of desert Spinifex grew in clumps here, circling the ferrous red boulders, big and small, that were scattered over the desert sands at random.

"Devil's marbles." Blaine's silver-grey eyes were steady on her profile as he asked a question. "Are you glad you came along?'

"What, now? Or for the trip?"

"Both."

She took a deep breath. There had been so many emotions unlocked inside her. Emotions she hadn't even known she was capable of. "I wouldn't have missed it for the world."

It was the absolute truth.

Blaine's face grew still. "Then I guess we owe thanks to Mark for that. I suppose there's a hidden purpose in everything?"

"I'm sure there is."

Sienna faced it squarely. If she longed for high romance she had a feeling she was going to get it—if only briefly. They lived in vastly different worlds, separated by a great ocean. But her rising attachment to Blaine Kilcullen, however well she was managing to hide it, was starting to seriously implode on her life. She couldn't be in his presence without her whole body quickening. She couldn't even *think* of him without experiencing shooting thrills. She had come to believe she was a woman in control of her life. She now found she was as vulnerable as the next woman. Falling in love was like being set adrift from one's moorings. Her feelings that were running so strongly seemed quite separate from herself. Or the self she had thought she was. The truth was she was being swept away.

In the wrong place, at the wrong time.

CHAPTER SIX

SIENNA hadn't been expecting to come upon such a very large body of water, covering she estimated at least five acres. It was more like a wetlands, with huge pink water lilies and aquatic plants and grasses massed thickly around the water's edge. The water lilies held their exquisite faces up out of a great lake that looked as if it would be quite deep at the centre. It came to a dead end to the left, and to the right the broad stretch of water narrowed into a channel that disappeared around a tree-lined bend.

The water had taken its colour from the densely blue sky. Overhanging trees preened in their own reflection. The surface was still and crystal-clear.

They had tethered the horses, were walking together in silence down to the pale yellow sand. The air was remarkably pure. Birds warbled in colonies from the trees, or flitted from one side of the bank to the other, their brilliant plumage glistening like jewels in the sun. She had been fascinated by the great flocks of tiny green and yellow birds, the budgerigar of the wild, that had followed them on their ride. Once Blaine had called a halt so she could admire the perfectly co-ordinated flight displays they were turning on, involving swift twists and turns, always in an impressive arrowhead formation.

"I somehow had the idea a billabong was just a pool,"

she remarked. "This is a very large sheet of water." She took off her akubra and threw it so deftly it landed on a flat topped boulder nearby. On impulse she pulled off the covered elastic band that held her plait, shaking her hair free. "Ah, that's better!"

Watching her, Blaine felt a great thrust of desire. Cupid's arrow through the heart, he thought grimly. Her long, magnificent silky mane flew back in the air like some darn TV commercial. He wanted to reach out and take a great swathe of it in his hand, wrap it around his wrist, draw her into him.

She turned back. Aware? Unaware? A woman like that would be able to read men with ease. He removed his wide-brimmed hat, aiming it unerringly so it landed beside hers.

"Billabong is an aboriginal word, most probably from the Wiradjuri." His voice showed no hint of his inner turbulence. "In the early days claims were put forward that billabong was of Scottish Gaelic origin. Who knows? Nearly all our early settlers, especially Outback pioneers, hailed from the British Isles anyway. But I go with the aboriginal. You might know the most famous reference to a billabong—in the opening lines of Banjo Paterson's 'Waltzing Matilda'. It nearly became our National Anthem way back in 1974, only 'Advance Australia Fair' beat it to it."

"So sing it for me," she teased gently. "Try out your voice." He had a very attractive speaking voice, dark and resonant, not dusky-mellow, but very crisp and clean.

"As it turns out, I'm game to sing you the opening lines," he said. "That's if you're not trying to take a rise out of me—which I suspect you are. People in the Outback are fiercely proud of 'Matilda'."

"Okay." She nodded at him approvingly "Let's hear it." He would be a baritone, for sure.

She didn't quite know what she would hear, but found she was swept by a rush of pleasure as he began to sing to her. When she had first met him she had thought him very much on the severe side, even daunting, but plainly he had his lighter moments.

He started off quietly, warmly, with innate musicality. A simple song, yet his rendering of it stunned her. She felt a lump in her throat, the sting of tears at the back of her eyes. Lord knew how she would react if he broke into a love song.

"How's that?" he asked when he was finished, his silver eyes sparkling with provocation.

The moment had turned from a bit of fun into something extraordinarily intimate. "Wonderful!" she said, clapping her hands and thus disturbing birds that shrieked instant protest.

"Great! So what do we do *now*?" he asked very coolly.

The question, allied to the look in his brilliant eyes, threw her completely off guard. "Well, I know what *I'm* going to do," she said after a moment, making a huge effort to quell the excitement he was deliberately creating. "I'm going to splash my face with water."

Cool down. That's the girl! In no time at all you'll be going home.

"Go for it!" he said, his voice now openly taunting.

She chose a spot where clear water pooled in the depression around a big boulder that was half in and half out of the water. Bending, she scooped up handfuls. "Ooh!" She had no idea the water would be so *cold*! But she continued, splashing her face and neck several times. It was so refreshing. The water spilled down over her shirt and ran in a channel between her breasts. She turned to face him.

Her golden sherry eyes were shimmering, her skin radiant, her beautiful hair luxuriously tangled. He was filled with the fierce need to hold her. He had never dreamed of anything like this. He certainly hadn't planned it.

"Want to take a picture of me?" She was only joking, but the expression on his handsome face stopped her. "Blaine?"

"I don't have a camera right now."

He was walking towards her, the most exciting, magnetic man in the world. Close to, he brushed back a stray curl. "You're a very beautiful woman," he said, in a dark brooding voice.

Her reply was tense and guarded. "Sometimes I'm not sure that's a good thing."

"Meaning what?" He stared down into her eyes. He was holding himself tightly in check when the very closeness of her was electrifying him.

"What do *you* think I mean?" she retorted with spirit. "I know you have trouble trying to fit me into the scheme of things."

He nodded. "I can't deny I want to know the answer to one question. Did you have an affair with Mark?"

All of a sudden she felt as if she was suffocating. "Damn you, Blaine." She went to stalk past him only he caught her back, one arm encircling her waist. She was at once inflamed and chilled. "I find you absolutely *hateful*!" she cried.

"Except your body is telling me something very different."

Powerful emotions were rising like a sea creature from the great ocean depths. "This isn't right, Blaine." The moan that issued from her throat was low and plaintive.

"I know."

The trembling in her body had to be betraying her. She was so close to him she could feel his breath on her hair. "Attraction—mutual attraction—is a funny thing, isn't it?"

he pondered. "*Elemental.* You try to fight it but it makes no difference. You're powerless." As he spoke he was pulling her in tight to his lean body, compounding the sizzling sexual tension.

She should have been offering resistance—except one of her hands, as if it had a life of its own, was clutching at the front of his shirt and holding tight. Attraction wasn't just elemental, it was *merciless.*

When his mouth came down hard and deep on hers it was such shattering excitement that, the need that pulsed between them was heightened by a tiny element of violence. It was as though both were at war with the force that had so fiercely and easily overtaken them. When his hand shaped, then cupped her breast, his thumb working the taut, aroused nipple, her mind and body went into a spin. Desire was like a fever coming on her, making her light-headed. He was whispering something into her open mouth, but she couldn't make out the words she was so far gone. She had thought she longed for an overwhelming passion, but passion at this level was a snare. It could destroy her and her ordered life. If he didn't stop kissing her and caressing her she thought she might just offer herself to him like some sort of sacrifice.

When Blaine jerked back his dark head, his voice reflected immense strain. "I needed to do that," he rasped. "I've done it."

"Like it was on your 'Before-I-die' list? You've done what you intended to do all along?" she gasped, her thoughts chaotic. "Is it going to be dangerous to be alone with you? Is that it?" She was angered now, such was the ambivalence of human nature and the ways of woman with man.

The vertical line between his black brows looked ominous. "You *know* there's something very powerful between us, Sienna. It couldn't be plainer. So don't for the love of God pretend you don't."

The sternness of his voice set her teeth on edge. To her horror, she found herself reacting blindly. She struck out with her fist, hitting the hard wall of his chest. "I know *nothing* can come of it," she cried in frustration, and then abruptly all anger drained out of her. She didn't even know how to go on. The strength of her passions had thrown her completely off balance. "I'm sorry—I'm sorry," she apologized. "I shouldn't have hit you. I've never done such a thing in my life. But you make me so *mad*. Lord knows, I've never attacked a man before."

"And it has you shaking." He put steadying hands on her shoulders.

The concern in his voice actually stoked the dying flame. "Ever heard of a romantic nightmare?" she challenged. She had been referring to the situation between *them*—only Amanda's claim that Mark had dreamt of her shot like an arrow into her mind.

"Give it to me straight, Sienna," Blaine said determinedly. "Were you and Mark having an affair that ultimately *you* wanted to break off?"

Her eyes looked enormous in her over-wrought face. "I'm sorry, Blaine. I don't want to get into this. And I won't accept your efforts to try and allot blame to me. You're in no position to judge."

"How can I judge what I don't know?" he retaliated. "You don't think you might at least offer me the truth? What *did* happen? Something did. I'm not a fool. My every instinct tells me Mark was madly in love with *you*. Not his wife, your cousin. *You!*"

She went limp, in need of comfort. "We buried him today, Blaine. He had so little time."

"Do you think I've forgotten that?" His strong hands clenched on her shoulders.

"You're hurting me," she said after a moment. It was awful to fight with him.

"I'm sorry." He released her immediately, but his expression remained tormented. "I don't seem to be able to think of anything else. All these secrets—things kept hidden, held back."

"That happens in every family, I should think," she offered in a toneless voice.

"Far too much of it in my family," he said, his expression bleak. "We might as well ride back now."

Sienna said nothing. She replaited her hair, then reached for her hat. Some part of her desperately wanted to tell him of that ghastly late afternoon when his half brother had tried his hardest to force a sexual response from her. Only even now she felt shamed. To tell him she would be forced to tell him *everything*, to reveal the darkness at Mark's core. What good would come of that? Her conscience was clear. She'd been innocent of any wrongdoing then. She was innocent now.

Yet the shade of Mark was still around to threaten her.

Dusk had fallen before they arrived back at the homestead. Blaine headed towards the west wing, his own private retreat. Sienna pulled herself up the timber staircase, reluctant to call in on Amanda for fear of what she might find. Amanda had well and truly turned to alcohol for comfort. There was the possibility she could be lying in bed drunk. God Forbid. All the devotion Amanda had been offered through the years. Had it ever counted?

Blaine would most probably be speaking to her in the

morning about her legacy. Amanda had better make sure she made a better impression than she had been making so far.

With a feeling she was shocked to recognise as dread, she knocked on Amanda's door, hearing with relief Amanda's voice call clearly, "Come in."

Amanda's blue eyes swept her cousin's willowy frame, down to her riding boots.

"So where have *you* been?" she asked archly.

"Out for a ride."

"Alone?"

"Of course not. Blaine was with me. This is the most extraordinary place. You should see it."

"Don't really want to, sweetie. The desert ain't my thing. Course, Blaine could be—but he's not interested in me, is he?" There was something terribly suggestive in the way Amanda posed the question.

"Ah, give me a break!" Sienna said. "Blaine has just lost his brother."

"*Half*-brother," Amanda corrected. "No two men could be less alike."

Sienna turned away. "Are you coming down to dinner? I think you should."

"No way!" Amanda shook her head. "Do you reckon Mark could have had anything to do with his dad's accident?" she asked as Sienna was almost at the door.

"What?" Sienna was so stunned she stopped in her tracks. "What are you saying?"

"And you're supposed to be the genius?" Amanda vented her jealousy. "Don't you think it was odd the way Mark got stuck into his family, particularly Blaine, but he couldn't be drawn much on his father. No-go territory. I used to get the feeling Mark was guilty of some stupidity, some rash act. You know how he used to go off half-cocked. Maybe he caused his father's accident. Didn't mean to—but that was Mark. Damn it, Sienna, he sort of killed *himself*, didn't he?"

Sienna felt a vibration along her spine. "We'll never know."

"Another one of those great mysteries!" Amanda declared.

"I know Mark carried a great burden," Sienna said. "But there's no use thinking about it. Mark is no longer with us."

"And he never got to have the woman he had the hots for."

"I don't know you at all, do I?" Sienna was labouring to keep calm. "Have you lost *all* feeling for Mark?"

"You have no idea how *hard* it was for me." Amanda's blue eyes flashed. "He'd have sex with me, pretending it was *you*.'

Sienna grasped the porcelain doorknob, desperate to get out of the room. "Do you know how terrible you sound? Please be on your best behaviour tomorrow. That's probably when Blaine will want to talk to you. I know how good you are at play-acting, so try to remember you're Mark's grieving widow."

"Ain't that the truth?" Amanda lifted her blonde head, then slammed it back into the pillows. "Tell the housekeeper I'd like a light chicken dish for dinner. Some white wine. Maybe a scoop of vanilla ice cream for dessert. I'm not keeping things down, I'm so out of whack. Why did you ever persuade me to come here, Sienna?" she wailed, for all the world like a child.

"I didn't persuade you, Amanda," Sienna felt eerily calm. "You came because you thought there was a good deal of money in it for you."

"Afraid for once I'll have more than you?"

"Anything to make you happy," Sienna said, facing for perhaps the first time in her life that deep in her heart Amanda hated her. It stung her like the bite of a hidden viper.

Just the two of them for dinner. Hilary's doctor had given her a knock-out pill, and Marcia had contacted the homestead to say they had arrived safely on Ettamunga. She would stay overnight with Joanne and her family.

"Mum doesn't need me," she had lamented, and for a moment Blaine hadn't known what to say—because there was more than a grain of truth in that. "I could see it in her eyes. She wants to mourn Mark on her own. She has never faced the truth about him. She never will. He was her son. Her daughter got left out in the cold. I don't know what I would do, Blaine, if it wasn't for you."

It was at that point he'd made a decision. Marcia needed help right away. He would send her to stay with the Senator and his wife in Sydney. They would happily take her in. If she liked it in Sydney he would buy her an apartment, with family close by. Marcia had enjoyed an excellent education. Time for her to get on with her life.

He would have to find another solution for Hilary. Not her own family. They had never wanted Hilary, had been amazed and overjoyed to see her taken off their hands by his father. His expression grew sombre as he considered Hilary hadn't had much of a life. But then like Marcia she hadn't taken life on. One had to.

Neither of them was hungry. Magda, knowing this, served a platter of thickly sliced ham with a bowl of salad Niçoise. They shared a bottle of red. It was more than enough. Both skipped dessert, settling for coffee. But because she had baked them fresh, Magda couldn't resist piling several of her peanut butter cookies on a plate.

They moved to the seating arrangement in front of a great stone fireplace. "Do you mean to speak to Amanda tomorrow?" Sienna asked after a while.

Blaine picked up one of the cookies and took a bite. "You mean about the money?" His brilliant eyes lighted on her.

"You know I mean about the money."

"Not the first time it's been brought to my attention," he said dryly.

"Thank God *I* have no interest in your money, Blaine. I have a life of my own. I'm successful, and I intend to become even more so."

"I haven't the slightest doubt you will," he said, with outward suavity and an inner sense of coming deprivation. "Have you ever wondered if your cousin deserves your devotion?"

She set her coffee cup down. "You don't like her, do you?"

His eyes on her were piercingly intent. "At this point I'm wondering what's to like? I realize Amanda is heavily jet lagged—we've all made allowances for that—but she's shown no spark of kindness towards Hilary and Marcia. She's ignored them in their own home. They really were prepared to welcome her. They've had no difficulty taking to *you*. You have great people skills."

"Maybe it's because I *like* people," she returned. "Although I have reason to make an exception of you."

"Ah, don't be like that, Sienna," he mocked darkly.

"Just so you know."

"You have a circle of golden light around your head," he said, studying the effect. "*Are* you an angel?"

She ignored him. She knew he was baiting her. "The chandeliers?" she queried. "It's a superb collection. I've been meaning to ask you who started it."

"Who started it?" He repeated the question, rather forlornly for such a dynamic man. "My dad. He imported the lot of them some time after my mother died. I've grown up with them. Some people think they're completely over the top. I suppose they are."

"Well, I love them," she said, staring up at the great gilt, bronze and crystal chandelier above their heads. "They add a touch of fantasy—magic, if you like. They must be very valuable. They're all antique."

He nodded. "The one over us is Russian—circa 1840. I guess my father's aim was to *light up* the homestead. He wanted to bring brilliance and luminosity back when he thought he had lost it for ever. The light must have reminded him of my mother in some way."

"I can understand that," Sienna said quietly, surprised by the sting of tears in her eyes. "Where *is* the portrait of your mother? You told me it has never been taken down. I would dearly love to see it."

"And you shall, Cinderella. It used to hang in pride of place at the top of the gallery, but after Dad died I changed things around. The west wing had always been mine, but for some reason I can't quite explain I shifted back into the main house—the old master suite. Hilary had chosen elsewhere after their marriage. I had the portrait removed to the west wing. Finish your coffee and I'll take you."

"Will you step into my parlour?" said the spider to the fly.

"Will you, won't you, will you, won't you, will you join the dance?"

Sienna walked with him quite calmly, but as usual she was anything but calm. Her heart was beating faster with every step, her head crammed with snapshots of their afternoon together—that fierce, deeply passionate kiss.

Was it really possible to fall hopelessly in love at a single glance?

She feared the answer was *yes.*

The west wing, bigger than the average house, was exactly *him*: dynamic, exciting, full of surprises. He wasn't just a cattle baron, he was a man of culture. She had realized that from the very beginning.

"Wow!" she exclaimed as she looked at the carved panels—leaves, flowers, fruits, animals—obviously Asian, that surrounded his front door.

"Balinese screens," he said. "I had them cut to fit. Come on in."

"I'd love to. How we decorate our private sanctuaries says a lot about us. Now I can find out more about you."

"Are you sure you want to?"

Her hands trembled, so she linked them behind her back. Unlike in the main house there was a foyer, with a big carved chest with a bronze head on it, a large painting in a heavy gilded frame above it, and a glorious Iranian rug with fiery tones. But what dazzled her eye was the magnificent painting on the facing wall.

"Wherever did you get this?" She moved across the rug to examine the large canvas with a professional eye.

"On a trip to Rome," he said, standing back, the better to observe her. "It's seventeenth century, but unsigned. Even so, it cost an arm and leg."

"I'm not surprised. It's so powerful! Probably the work of a very good apprentice who studied under a leading painter of the time. Clearly your artist was influenced by Rubens. Those are Rubenesque horses. Just look at the long, flowing, curling manes and tails. I've seen a horse like this in the Prado in Madrid. A Spanish grandee astride a white horse. Only these two rearing beauties are doing battle. It's savage in its way, isn't it?"

Very gently she touched the surface of the aged canvas. The horses' coats had a wonderful satiny-pearlescent lustre. The background was a rich orange-red, with broad strokes of gold, a palette that Blaine had picked up with the Persian rug.

"What more treasures do you have for me?"

"A lot of aboriginal paintings," he said. "I collect the best of them. We have some very fine indigenous artists." He led the way off to the right of the central panel, obviously specially constructed to take the painting. "This is the living room. The dining room on the other side. As you can see, I favour our region's colours."

Sienna looked around the very generous space with a rush of pleasure. In some ways it reminded her of a house her father once rented in Marrakech: the strong contrast between white walls and the fiery red-orange-ochre elements. Another splendid Iranian rug in rich tones, with a large ornately carved coffee table atop it, divided two bronze leather sofas with dark red damask scatter cushions. Two deep armchairs were covered in cream leather. One entire was given over to a built-in mahogany bookcase filled with books. There were paintings galore.

"Have you ever been to Marrakech?" she asked.

"I've been most everywhere—including the South Pole," he said. "I have yet to explore beautiful Canada, but I will when I get the time."

"I hope so." Her eyes were on an exotic looking planter's chair made of cane, and a bamboo and lacquer octagonal small table nearby.

"Time enough to look around," he said. "You wanted to see the portrait of my mother? It's in my study. Pride of place. As you can imagine, a bravura painting of a beautiful woman demands its own space. Besides, it wouldn't fit in with all the other paintings. Come along."

"Of course! You're my guide."

He turned back so suddenly she almost slammed into him. "So what are you going to do to pay for your tour?"

The blood started to pound in her ears. He looked extremely handsome and a little daunting "I don't know. What about telling you how clever you are?"

"It will do for a start."

More timber panelling, this time in light golden tones, and a big, very workmanlike desk—masculine design. Midnight-blue leather sofas were grouped around a big square glass-topped table with a very interesting sculpture of an Indian goddess on it. But, as he had said, in pride of place behind his desk was a large portrait of a very beautiful dark-haired, magnolia-skinned woman with the silver-grey eyes she had passed on to her son. She was wearing an exquisite white duchesse satin gown with a silvery sheen. Around her throat hung an opera-length string of large pearls. Diamond earrings with pearl drops fell from her ears. She was sitting in a high backed gilded chair; the background was a muted deep blue.

"She looks quite unforgettable," Sienna said, thinking her father would love to see this portrait and give his private opinion of it.

"Doesn't she? That's her wedding gown."

"It's beautiful. Now I know where you get your extraordinary eyes from. Do you remember her?"

"I remember some things," he said, in a dark sombre tone. "I remember when she died. It was the only time I ever saw my father cry. Grief just burst out of him. He couldn't hold it back. He never got over her."

"It must have been a great tragedy—for you and him."

His eyes remained fixed on the portrait. "My mother's life ended too soon. Now Mark's. Dad married Hilary to give me a surrogate mother. It some ways it might have been the worst thing he ever did.'

Her heart was wrung for Hilary. "But, Blaine, Hilary had their children—the twins."

"I think that was the closest my stepmother got to real happiness," he brooded. "At least for a few years. Dad couldn't have been kinder or more considerate to Hilary. She had everything she wanted. But she always knew he didn't love her."

"She must have known that before he married her?" Sienna reasoned.

"Of course."

"Well, then, it was her decision. She may have got more out of her marriage than you think."

"I'd like to think so, Sienna." He sighed. "I'm fond of Hilary, only it didn't work out. Mark was difficult right from the start. Marcia too. But, being a girl, very much less so. Dad always said he recognized Hilary's family in the twins. The only good thing Hilary ever did as far as her family was concerned was to get my father to marry her."

A look of sad acceptance settled on Sienna's face. "We can't pick our parents, but we can make our own lives, Blaine.'

"Not so easy when one inherits a problematic temperament. It's all in the genes. One should really think about that before getting married."

She turned to him. "So, are you moving on that? Getting married? Joanne pointed out a trio of likely candidates to me."

"Everyone wants to marry me off," he said. "Including Joanne. I have to tell you I've no urge to walk down the aisle right now."

"Well, men like you are obliged to obey the rules. You know—provide heirs. You have a great deal to hand on."

He pinned her gaze. "You're trying to get under my skin, aren't you?"

"Is that possible?"

"Back off, Sienna," he warned.

There was a faintly taunting edge to her voice. "Hey, who has the problem now?" She turned to the door, a willowy figure in her short summery dress printed with yellow and red poppies gone wild. "I love the portrait of your most beautiful mother, but now show me the rest of your domain. It's so very *you*. Why did you ever leave it?"

"Sentiment, I suppose," he said, following her out.

"I thought you might be rather short on that." She spoke with feigned casualness, but the fact was she was deliberately provoking him. Where was the sense in that?

Back off. Back off. He told you to.

The dining room setting was for eight—six Spanish-style chairs and two carvers surrounding a polished timber table. The walls were orange, with two very powerful aboriginal paintings to either side of the French doors that led out onto the grounds. Each painting depicted a different version of an orange-scarlet sunset reflected in the waters of a billabong surrounded by mounds of golden Spinifex, with a low flat-topped mesa in cobalt blue in the background. On the wall above the sideboard hung a long indigenous painting of the Central Desert region, with its rolling fiery red sand hills.

"A woman of the Eastern Arrente people," he told her, seeing her interest. "Self-taught."

"She's wonderful. I could sell paintings like these back home in less than a minute. I could never capture this particular vision—this passion for the land of birth, the intimacy with an incredible landscape and its land forms, the unique way of expressing that passion on canvas."

"The land is everything to aboriginal culture," Blaine said. "Many of our indigenous artists have been taught by white people, but they paint in their own way—not ours."

"That's all to the good."

"I think so. The kitchen leads off here," he said. "When my polo pals fly in for a casual game I entertain them here."

"You do the cooking?" It wouldn't have surprised her if he had said yes.

"Sienna, we have an excellent cook in the house," he pointed out dryly. "Magda does the cooking and the serving. She would be greatly offended if I didn't leave it to her."

"That's the way women are with heroes." Sienna sighed. "'I'm here for you. Just tell me what I can do.'"

His eyes glittered like diamonds. "I caught that note of derision, Sienna."

She looked back at him in feigned astonishment. "I'm sorry, Blaine. I didn't mean anything. I'm being utterly sincere."

"I think you're forgetting I have a devil in me."

"And I don't have the slightest desire to raise him."

There was a stone fireplace in the bedroom—"Desert nights in the Dry can be very cold," he said—and another stunning aboriginal painting, this time with a palette of blues and featuring birds in flight. The huge bed was custom-made, with a carved bedhead and carved side tables. Indonesian, Blaine said. A magnificent carved chest at the foot of the bed held a mix of exotic objects—a Cambodian Buddha head covered in silver leaf in particular—no doubt from his travels.

"For a cattleman you have a great sense of theatre," she said, more fascinated with every passing second.

"I like to use what I collect. Dressing room. Master bath. Want to take a look?"

"Sure. When do you get to wear these suits?" she asked, admiring the rows of tailored suits, the high-quality cabinetry, the shelves holding dress shirts on one side, bush shirts and casual shirts on the other.

"I do have another life," he said dryly. "Katajangga the working cattle station is nowadays only a small part of our family interests. We have substantial mining interests, real estate, vineyards. My grandfather had the great good sense to realize we had to diversify."

"So you get to the cities often?"

"I do. I have a great overseer, which makes things easier for me. You'll meet him when things settle down a little. Zack Mangan. He has a wife, Gail, and two kids—two boys away in Brisbane at boarding school. We send the kids away around ten, so they can get a good education. I was educated at my father's and my grandfather's old school in Melbourne. My son—hopefully sons—will go there too."

"You don't want daughters?" she asked, with a certain charge in her voice.

"Absolutely," he said, and drew a finger down the line of her cheek. "Who wouldn't want a daughter that looked, sounded and acted like you?"

She put up a hand, held it for a moment over his, and then drew his hand down. It was enough to make her breathless. They were still standing in the dressing room—only now she was backed against one of the wardrobes.

"We can't do this," she said, in a strange little whispery voice.

"What *are* we doing?" he whispered back, bending his dark head so it was poised over hers.

"I'm thinking of you as well as myself."

"Why are you so sure I want to make love to you?" He whispered the words in her ear.

She flushed at the mockery. "You're a terrible man!" She plunged forward in flight—only, as he had done once before, he caught her back. This time she put up some resistance, though her excitement was very real. She knew what she wanted even if she acted very differently.

"Stop fighting this." A groan came from deep in his throat, as though all resistance was in vain. "I want you so badly I'm nearly mad with it."

His words expressed exactly what *she* was feeling. It passed understanding, this powerful need. "Is this why you brought me here?"

"Is this why you came?"

She lifted her head to stare into his brilliant eyes. "What do you want out of life, Blaine? *Tell* me."

His expression was very serious. "A woman to love. A woman I've only imagined up to date. A woman who will have my children and raise them with me—a woman who won't ever leave me. But a woman like you—a woman who lives such a very glamorous lifestyle—could slip out of the grasp of a man like me." He broke off, his voice roughening in concern. "Sienna, what are you crying for?"

She dashed a stray tear from her cheek. "God, I don't know." Tears were a natural response to high emotion.

"Are you crying out of grief for Mark?" He stared down at her.

"More out of pity for myself," she said with a poignant little shrug. "I didn't ask for this, Blaine—for what's happening between us."

"Any more than I did," he answered. "But it's not as though you can't make your escape. You get on a plane and go home. You take Amanda with you. I'm sorry to say this, but I think Amanda is trouble."

She couldn't move for the tremors in her legs. "*You're* the big trouble," she said.

"You call falling in love *trouble*, do you?"

She searched his taut face. "You're actually admitting you're in love with me?"

"Oh, stop it. Stop it. *Stop it,*" he groaned. Desire was building like a fury inside him. Their bodies were almost touching, drawing closer as though magnetized. "Kiss me," he said, low-voiced. "Last time I kissed you. *This* time you kiss me."

"That sounds like an order." As if it mattered.

"It is."

"From a man well used to giving orders."

"And being obeyed," he told her very quietly.

Desire was so immense she could barely contain it. "You know where this will lead?"

"What did you come here for, Sienna?" he countered.

"I couldn't *not* come," she confessed. "That's scary, don't you think?" She couldn't endure not touching him. She put up her hands, her heart beating wildly, pulling his head down to her. "I've never felt like this before." *Never, never, never.*

"I hope you mean that." He wrapped his strong arms around her, drawing her in closer, closer, so she could feel his powerful arousal.

"Sexual attraction is such a lure—even when you can't bring yourself to trust me."

"I can't deny what I feel. *Kiss* me, Sienna," he repeated, this time harshly.

She wanted to so badly she felt naked and exposed. She stood on tiptoe…

Her lips touched very gently on his—so sweet, so silken.

Her questing tongue slipped into his mouth, sending off shock waves inside him. Their tongues met in a love dance. He ran his hands down her back, spreading them out to lock over her hips. A moment more and his hands slipped down over the curves of her taut buttocks, lifting her body up to him. His hunger had grown to such an intensity he had to have more of her. Passionate concentration was stamped on his face. With a muttered exclamation he swooped her up like a featherweight and carried her through to his bed.

She lay with one arm flung out, her long rose-gold hair in disarray. He lowered himself onto the bed beside her. There he turned her gently on her side, reaching for the long zipper of her dress. He pulled it down—she helped him—peeling the light, sleeveless dress from her and tossing it away. Then he turned her back to him slowly, his eyes moving over her. Her body was just as beautiful as he'd imagined: the small high breasts, the taut midriff, narrow waist, sleek thighs, and the long, slender length of her legs. She was wearing only bra and matching briefs, as pretty as any bikini. This was a body he didn't yet know. But he *would* know. Oh, *yes*! He wanted desperately to satisfy her. He wanted them both to connect with the moon and the stars. She was a thousand times *more* than his imagination. She was the woman he had been searching for. How could he possibly let her go?

"Make love to me," she whispered, holding up her arms to him. Excitement and sexual hunger radiated from her, unravelling his last scrap of control.

His heart was pounding in his ears. Her voice conveyed the deepest longing, flooding his veins with a kind of exultance. He *would* make love to her. Endlessly. All through the night. Nothing now could stop him.

CHAPTER SEVEN

SOME time in the early hours of the following morning Amanda awoke, feeling an overpowering sense of fright, of things going badly wrong. A glance at the little carriage clock in her room told her it was two-fifty a.m. Wasn't three o'clock some sort of witching hour?

Things she had done came back to haunt her. Things she should have been ashamed of, but hadn't been at the time. The dark side of her ran deep. What was she going to do with her life from now on? She would have to pay for what had happened. Mark was dead. But he had long left her behind. She had been in love with him in the beginning. She would have loved him to the end. Only the woman he'd really wanted was Sienna. She knew—of *course* she knew—Sienna had never given Mark the slightest encouragement. Sienna had gone out of her way to avoid ever being alone with him. But for some twisted reason it gave her great satisfaction to heap blame on her beautiful, gifted, ever-popular cousin. Ever since high school boys had swarmed around Sienna like bees. Was it the honey hair, the honey eyes, the honey voice? She couldn't remember a time when she hadn't felt violently jealous of Sienna.

I love her.

I hate her.

That was the really odd part. She had always relied heavily on Sienna, who had never failed to support her through all her troubles—and there had been many. She felt like talking to Sienna now. Sienna always managed to calm her.

She tossed back the covers like a child desperate for comfort. Sienna would help. She always did.

Only Sienna wasn't in her room. The bed was still made up, the luxurious quilt in place. So where was her sainted cousin?

She's naked in bed with Blaine.

The voice in her head was so loud she had to hold her hands over her ears.

"Bitch!" she shouted into the empty room. "You're going to pay for this."

It was the next day. "Please have a seat, Amanda," Blaine spoke gently, as he showed his half-brother's young widow into his father's old study. She was looking extremely pale. Heartbreaking, really, when he had thought her tough—or at the very least conniving—to the core. Now he felt considerable remorse, looking down at her with a definite softening to his manner. She was such a little bit of a thing, without spark. He supposed she would be very pretty in her way when she was well, but she didn't look well at all, although she should have been pretty much over her jet lag.

What exactly had attracted Mark to her? he wondered, not for the first time.

Amanda was *waiting* to tell him. Her blue eyes lifted to Blaine's face as she began to squeeze tears out of her eyes. It was one of her best tricks. She could sob at will and she was fully prepared to do so. Men melted at a woman's tears. Even Mark had done that when she had accused him of sleeping with Sienna.

"I *wish*!" he had groaned, before getting ready to head out without her.

Some part of her had even been pleased when he had slammed into that tree. He had wronged her, so why shouldn't he be punished? The cruelty of the man! She had never forgiven him for that. She had never even felt a pang when they buried him. Was that *normal*? Mark had been a loser, but his big brother was something else again. Mark's big brother was going to pay up big-time. Why wouldn't he, when he heard her story?

Blaine sat behind his father's massive partner's desk, his eyes trained on Amanda as she literally heaved out a story of treachery.

"Sienna always took what I wanted," she said, the tears pouring down her blanched cheeks. "I know she didn't exactly *mean* to, but it always happened. The day Mark told me he'd only married me to get to Sienna I felt like giving up and killing myself.

"Killing yourself?" Blaine repeated. "How?"

"What?" Why would he speak like that to her?

"How were you going to kill yourself?" he asked.

She hated the fact he looked so *stern*. He wasn't responding as she had hoped.

"I don't know—sleeping pills, a bottle of vodka." She cast about wildly. "You can't image the depth of pain I was in."

"So what you're claiming is that Sienna, who appears devoted to you, was sleeping with your husband?" Blaine asked in a clinically concise voice.

"I know the way it sounds." She shook her head from side to side. "It sounds *terrible*. But I saw them. It was a dreadful affront to my marriage. Sienna didn't love Mark. She was toying with him. She's so beautiful she can have anyone she wants."

"So why would she want Mark?" Blaine asked of Mark's widow, very gravely. "We've just buried him, remember? Do you really want to destroy his image in his family's eyes? Do you want to destroy Sienna?" What *was* going on with this young woman?

Deep in her role, Amanda was incapable of dropping her act. "I *love* Sienna," she said with actual sincerity. "I'll always love her. But she caused me terrible grief. I know she didn't intend for me to catch them out."

Blaine sat back like a judge. "I'm sorry, Amanda, but I can't believe a word of this."

Amanda jerked back in shock. "It's true! It's true!" She was fighting her hardest to convince him. "Why would I lie to you? It wouldn't be right. I have a little more integrity than that. I've asked myself the same question over and over. Why would Sienna do that to me?"

"You mean that which didn't happen?"

She looked at him, so big and powerful. "She's got to you, hasn't she?" She found her most pitiable voice. "She does that—can't you see?"

"No, I can't, Amanda," Blaine said flatly. "I think, very sadly, you've been jealous of your cousin all your life. I know about jealousy and resentment. I know because it happened to me. I had to endure Mark's bitter jealousies and resentments. I bet he filled your ears with all the rotten things I did to him. Jealousy ravaged him like it's ravaging you."

Amanda looked back at him in stunned disbelief. "Are you mad at me, Blaine?"

His eyes on her, he said, "Mad at you? No, Amanda. I think you need help. I do believe Mark treated you badly. I do believe he fell out of love with you. Mark was never a stayer. Sienna's beauty and her warm personality would have attracted him despite himself. He was drawn to her like a moth to a flame. But then, I imagine any number of young men have been in love with her."

"You too," Amanda accused forlornly. "You're a strong, clever man, but you're not seeing straight on this. I don't blame you. I've seen it all before. I swear everything I've said to you is *true*. I can't offer proof. I can only offer you my word. My word on my child's life." Amanda threw up her blonde head as she proclaimed her pregnant state proudly.

For a moment Blaine was too stunned to speak. "You're pregnant?" he asked finally. Some women bloomed, others could look very wan. Did that explain it?

She nodded, using a handkerchief to bravely wipe away her tears. "Confirmed."

"My God! And Mark is the father?"

Amanda showed more hurt than outrage. "Of *course* Mark is the father. What do you take me for? We were still having sex."

"At the same time Mark was having an affair with Sienna?" Blaine asked incredulously. "Come on, now, Amanda."

"Mark and I had sex during that time," Amanda maintained. "Why can't you simply believe me?"

Because it's all bunkum. Instead he asked, "Did Mark know about this baby?"

She shook her head with the saddest expression. "This baby is *our* baby. Hilary's grandchild. Your half-nephew, or whatever the relationship is. There never seemed to be the right time to tell Mark. I hate myself now for not telling him. It might have saved him."

Blaine kept his eyes trained on her. "Are you implying he was suicidal?"

"He couldn't have Sienna, you see."

"Ah, yes," he said, in a voice Amanda didn't much like. "Sienna doesn't know you're pregnant?"

He continued to watch her with those extraordinary diamond-hard eyes. She felt as if they were drilling holes right through her. "I was getting around to telling her," Amanda blurted. "But I've felt such injustice. My own cousin betrayed me. I'll get over it in time. I know I will. But right now—" She broke off. "That's why the money is so important to me, Blaine. I'll have the security and the peace of mind to raise Mark's child. I need someone to love. I desperately need someone to love *me*. My baby will do that."

"You want this baby?"

"Desperately," Amanda said. "I'll have something of my own."

Blaine glanced away, then back at this waif-like little person who clearly needed help. "I had proposed to give you five million, Amanda. That's Australian dollars. You will remarry in time. Invested wisely, five million will keep you nicely."

Amanda sat forward. "Five million for *me*, Blaine? Shouldn't it be a lot more for the baby?"

So she was raising the bar. "Forgive me, but I don't even know if you *are* pregnant, Amanda. I don't even know if the baby's Mark's."

If possible she lost even more colour. "You know it is," she said, sounding unbearably upset. "Sienna will know it's true. Mark may have cast me aside, but I bear his child. I'd like you, Blaine, to take that into consideration."

"And I'd like *you*, Amanda, to keep your very unexpected news to yourself until I have time to sort things out. Can you promise to do that?"

"Of course I'll do that," Amanda said, with tears in her eyes.

* * *

Sienna took shot after shot of the wild flowers, standing in the centre of a great circle of pure white everlastings armed with her camera. She bent to break off several paper daisies, which didn't wilt when picked, thrusting them into her hair and her braid. Lines from a poem of William Blake, one of her favourite poets, sprang inevitably to mind.

To see a World in a Grain of Sand,
And Heaven in a Wild Flower,
Hold Infinity in the palm of your hand,
And Eternity in an hour.

She felt extraordinary, standing in the middle of this Outback ocean of wild flowers on the other side of her own world. The truth was she was in a state of euphoria. What had happened between her and Blaine last night had been a colossal, life changing event. Their lovemaking had gone on and on, utterly ravishing to the senses. They hadn't been able to get enough of each other. Passion was a potent force that swept mere mortals away. He knew *exactly* how to kiss her, touch her, caress her. He knew when to allow her to take the lead, and when he had her on her back mastered her so gloriously. Life was so short. Too short for Mark. She fancied she saw his silvery shadow blend in with the mirage. It had never been discussed, but now she had the totally dismaying notion Mark had only married Amanda because she was pregnant. Or had *claimed* to be pregnant.

Now, where had that come from? No one had doubted Amanda. She had suffered her early miscarriage when she was in her bathroom, alone. Sienna had been with her father in New York. Amanda had had to take herself off to a doctor. Not the family doctor, nor even the clinic where he practised.

Sienna clamped the side of her bottom lip between her teeth, trying to thrust her disturbing thoughts away. Of *course* Amanda had been pregnant. She had a vision of herself comforting Amanda when she'd arrived home.

"You'll be fine, Mandy. Fine. Things obviously weren't going well. You'll be pregnant again in no time at all. A good pregnancy. You have to look after yourself."

You ought to speak to Amanda about this, said her inner voice. *But be careful.*

She had spent a lot of time communing with herself this morning. She knew beyond any doubt that she was deeply in love with Blaine. Neither of them had used the words *I love you,* as though each had been waiting for the other to say it first. A continuing relationship would demand serious decisions. She knew Blaine would never—could never—abandon his inheritance. *She* would be the one who had to make the big life-changes. Could she do it?

What a ridiculous question! The answer, overwhelmingly, was *yes.* No place on earth was too far away in the modern world. She would never lose her family and her homeland. Blaine would gain a family and a second home. She could continue her work. She could see exactly how it could be done.

How do you know he wants to marry you?

How can he not marry me if he won't ever let me go?

He'd had no hesitation in assuring her of that. Over and over...all the while raining down kisses on her face, her throat, her breast, moving down over her body.

Blaine had put a station Jeep at her disposal. She was happy with her photo session for the day, so she drove the vehicle to the pink water lily lagoon. She wanted the coolness there after the heat of that brilliant sun pouring down from an opal-blue sky. She parked the Jeep at the top of the slope, and then walked down their trodden path to the sand. Tiny little lilies crushed underfoot gave off a scent so alluring it ought to be bottled. The scent was everywhere. She had left her hat in the vehicle so the light breeze could blow on her bare head.

There was a wonderful sheen like silk on the water. Off to her right the feathery lime-green branches of trees with pale yellow puffs and plumes were dipping and rising with the breeze; water foamed whitely around the standing red boulders that were set at intervals along the stream; more foam lay like lace upon the sand. Such a far, far away place—so beautiful! Already it caught at her heart.

Still lost in her euphoric thoughts, she picked up a pebble, then set it to skip across the surface of the water.

Dream on, Sienna.

It was a marvellous thing to be in love. It had totally changed her and yet she had never felt more *herself*, more womanly, with an endless capacity to satisfy her man. Love stirred the imagination and set the flesh on fire. Her every need had been met by this one man, even into the dawn…

The moment the pebble hit the water a flock of brilliantly plumaged parrots rose up, scattering and screeching as if a bomb had gone off.

"Sorry!" she called apologetically, marking with some wonder the stunning combination of enamelled colours in the sun. Audubon country, she thought. The great French-American John James Audubon, the father of bird-painters, would have found endless inspiration in Australia's Outback. He'd had such a love and fascination with the beauty and dynamics of all species of birds. She did too.

I could paint this place.

Not in the moving depictions created by the country's indigenous people, but in a white woman's way. The ancient landscape was enormously powerful. And she had only seen what amounted to a postage stamp area. She considered herself a woman blessed to have her own passion for the land—a land that couldn't have been more different from what she'd been born to. But it was a truly amazing world, with each country having something wonderful to praise.

Blaine spotted the Jeep at the very spot where he'd thought Sienna might be. Magda had told him Miss Sienna had gone off to "take lots of photographs".

"She is a photographer as well as an artist," Magda had added, with a touch of awe.

He needed to talk to Sienna, and it had to be right away. He had no great faith in Amanda. No great faith in her keeping her momentous news to herself now that her secret was out. Hilary, he realized, would be thrilled out of her mind to know she had a grandchild on the way. It would lessen her deep grief at losing her only son. The huge problem was that Amanda would be going back home to Canada. Any fascination the Outback might have was totally lost on her. He was certain she wouldn't stay. As soon as he gave her the money she would be on her way. *More* money, as well. He was done with being surprised by Mark's widow. Shallowness and greed weren't a good combination. She would want to raise her child back home.

You couldn't totally know a person *ever,* he thought. No way could he read Sienna like a book. But he *had* grasped the fact that Amanda had the same problems with Sienna as Mark had had with him. Amanda might well be a pathological liar. Even so, pathological liars were often believed. That was the truly bizarre part. He could not, *would* not accept his beautiful Sienna had had an affair with Mark, however short-lived. He would *hate* for that to have happened.

Damn it—it didn't happen!

No way would he believe Amanda over Sienna. Mark might well have tried his hardest to develop a relationship—it was the sort of thing Mark had done—but he couldn't for the life of him see Sienna falling for Mark, let alone betraying her own cousin.

He leaned against the horn to alert Sienna to his presence, then he got out of his vehicle, striding down the coarsely grassed slope. "Sienna!" he called.

She was rushing towards him, electric for him, a radiant smile lighting up her beautiful face, such pleasure in her eyes. "What are you doing here?"

His sober expression brought her up short. "We have to talk," he said quietly, taking her arm.

"What is it? What's wrong?" She had thought he had driven out to the lagoon to meet up with her—marvellous idea. Now it seemed he had something very different on his mind. That was immensely sobering, but sobering things happened all the time. Especially around Amanda.

"It's about Amanda, isn't it?" she guessed, standing very still beside him. "Something was said at your meeting? She's okay, isn't she? She hasn't been terribly well of late."

"I guess that can happen when a woman's pregnant," he answered, his expression more grim than delighted.

For a moment Sienna thought she wasn't hearing right. "Hang on. Amanda told *you* she's pregnant?"

"Such a big event is worth more money. She's pregnant with Mark's child," he said bluntly, wrenched by the thought that Amanda might very well come between them. It could happen. Right or wrong, Sienna was devoted to her cousin.

"Dear God!" Sienna breathed. "I had no idea. Why didn't she say something? She's not taking proper care of herself. That long flight in these early months. Her drinking. Why didn't she say? She should be looking after herself for the baby."

"So there *is* a baby?" he asked.

That struck at her like a blow. "Oh, God, Blaine, you sound so cynical. What's going on here? Didn't she tell you she was? Amanda can be a very secretive little person. She's had one miscarriage, you know."

"No, I *don't* know," he said tersely, relying on his gut feeling that Amanda was a very devious, manipulating young woman. "When was this?"

"Oh, early days!" Sienna threw up a vague hand. "It occurred to me not long after we arrived she might be pregnant—highly irritable, sickly and lying down all the time. But I dismissed it. Then she goes and tells *you*. I don't get it. I never get it with Amanda."

"I'm not surprised!' he said in his most clipped voice. "I think your cousin is a young woman with lots of problems. I find it near unbearable to mention this, but she's holding to her story that Mark was in love with you. That he only married her to get to you."

For a moment Sienna felt like screaming. Turning on a tantrum like Amanda, who was right in her element screaming. Only Sienna wasn't made like that. But she *was* driven to throwing her arms impotently into the air. "He married her because she told him she was pregnant," she said. "Honestly, Amanda might be my cousin, but she's the most appalling troublemaker.'

"There's always a scrap of truth in a mountain of lies," he offered starkly, trying to cope with his own massive upset. The thought in his mind was that Amanda was a liar who was going to cause more problems for his family.

"At least tell me what she said," Sienna begged.

All the radiant pleasure was drained out of her face.

That hurt him. "Perhaps we need to talk about it for it to go away," he said, and drew in a long, determined breath. "Last night meant everything to me, Sienna."

There was no doubting his sincerity. "It meant everything to *me*, Blaine. Yet you can still harbour some element of doubt about me?"

"No, no!" He shook his handsome head vigorously. "I *don't* doubt you. But I still don't know exactly what happened between you and Mark. It's preying on my mind, Sienna. Can't you see that?"

"Are you sure you *want* to know?" Her voice was a challenging mix of distress and deep disappointment.

"Whatever happened, I won't let you go." He turned her towards him, holding onto her shoulders. She had picked some white paper daisies, popped them into her thick braid and the open top buttonhole of her shirt. They still clung to her. Why not? He thought her the most beautiful creature he had ever seen. How could he ever cage such a woman? "Amanda claims she surprised you and Mark," he managed, after a moment.

Sienna closed her eyes. "She *did*," she admitted. She opened her eyes again and fixed them on his brooding face. "I'd gone over to their apartment to deliver a birthday present for Amanda from my mother. I expected her to be there, only Mark was the one at home. Amanda had been delayed, he said, doing some extra shopping. I wanted to leave the present, saying I had to be on my way, only Mark saw it as a priceless opportunity for us to be together. He thought himself attractive to women. He *was* attractive to women. I had seen that for myself. But he was never attractive to me. I spotted something not quite right in Mark from the word go. Amanda isn't a strong person. She needed balance. We knew she wouldn't get it from Mark, nor he from her. But she didn't listen. She's *never* listened, come to think of it. She was—"

Blaine cut her off, steel in his tone. "I don't want to hear about Amanda, only *you*."

"Me?" She gave him a long stare, but she was the first to look away. "Okay, Blaine, you asked for it. Mark was in the mood for games, but my mind was concentrated on getting away. He told me if I could only relax he would make me feel good."

Blaine had to fight hard to control his rush of anger. "But you couldn't have kept silent, Sienna?"

"Of course I didn't. But Mark was determined. I was wasting my breath."

"What sort of a fool was he?" Blaine groaned in despair. "A woman like you, with your family, a father and brother to answer to. Obviously he didn't give a damn about betraying his wife."

Sienna too was struggling to compose herself. "Blaine," she said, more calmly, "you were his half-brother. You knew what he was like. Mark didn't really care about anyone. He didn't obey the rules like the rest of us. He didn't even know them. He genuinely thought he could do what he liked. I think he planned the whole thing. I'd rung *Amanda* earlier in the day to say I would drop the present over. Mark made sure he was there and Amanda wasn't."

"So what happened? "Blaine asked with great insistency.

There was a golden flame in her eyes. "He overpowered me. That's what happened. He slammed me into a wall. He held both my hands behind my back. He manhandled me and took great pleasure in it. He was much stronger—" She broke off, swallowing on a parched throat. She was growing steadily more agitated. What if Blaine didn't believe her? She didn't think she could cope with that. Amanda could be terribly, harmfully convincing. "Look, I don't want to talk about this."

"I don't either," he responded tautly. "But we have to. Let me share your pain."

"*Shame*, you mean!" she cried out from the depths of her wounded soul. When would this finally end?

Blaine felt as if he had swallowed acid. It was burning into his gut. "You're telling me Mark raped you?" he asked, a terrible tension in his face and lean body. "My God, if he were still around I'd strangle him with my bare hands."

"Don't say that! You wouldn't do it. Though I'm sure you'd give him the hiding of a lifetime. It didn't get that far, Blaine. You must believe that—for me, for yourself, even for Mark. Amanda arrived on the scene. Only there wasn't time for Mark to break away. Amanda caught him with his hand down the front of my dress. He had a bruising grip on my breast. When she saw that, Amanda started screaming and raving. Then she started throwing things. She wouldn't stop. She was out of control. She seemed desperate to hurt me. *Me*, not Mark. Can you beat that? He was the predator. I was the victim. But it was *me* she wanted to hurt. Oddly enough, it was Mark who stood between us, turning of all things into my protector. At least he had some remnant of decency left. He *told* Amanda it was all his fault, though she wasn't happy with that. No way! I have to be punished for the rest of my life. Mark told her he lost his head."

"Do you think that exonerated him?" Blaine asked in a white fury.

"No, of course not! But women are always under threat from a man's physical power, Blaine. Look how tall and big and strong you are compared with me. You could overpower me with one arm behind your back. There's a violence in men and boys that's hidden behind their attractive white grins. A dear friend of mine was raped in college by one of our top athletes. She told no one at the time. She only told me years later. She was still traumatized. He's a successful lawyer now, no doubt still taking the women he wants. The thing is, women are always at a man's mercy for that very good reason—their greatly superior physical strength."

He looked down on her bright head, the daisies a pure white contrast to the glowing amber of her hair. He remembered his first sight of her. He had known her then. His physical self and his mind, his spirit. "For God's sake, Sienna, the world is full of good, decent men," he protested. "Caring men, protective men, family men, husbands, fathers, partners. Most men aren't potential rapists. Surely you've learned that? I could never harm you. Do you think I could? I could never harm any woman. Take that as an absolute. How could Mark have assaulted you, even if he hadn't intended something more terrible?"

She gave a brittle laugh. "Well, we don't know that, do we? But Amanda has never let me forget that day she walked in on us. She *knows*—Mark told her—I was the innocent party. She *knows* me. Yet every now and again some demon in her rises up."

"So just think how *women* can and do behave! Women have a different kind of power. They know how to use it like the crack of a whip. Your cousin needs help." Blaine's voice carried outrage, not pity. "Ah, come here to me," he said, his taut expression softening. "I'm sorry. So sorry." He drew her tightly into his arms, resting his chin on the top of her head. "What are we going to do about this?"

She lifted her head to him, all her nerves fluttering. Right at that moment she was only interested in the two of them. Amanda and her pregnancy could wait. God knew how far along she was. It had taken a great deal to force that sickening incident with Mark out of her, but now she was glad she'd told Blaine. It was as though a heavy burden had been lifted from her. Amanda would have to give up her baseless accusations or forfeit their relationship. She knew Amanda would have done her worst to damage her and her good name. It was as though Amanda saw it as her entitlement to bring her down.

A look of remembered rapture was transforming her expression, bringing back her natural radiance. "More to the point, what are we going to do about *us*?"

He took her beautiful face between his hands, amazed the woman of his dreams had come into his life. Had the gods brought her to him? Would she stay? His whole body burned with desire and love. "I want an *us* more than I want anything, Sienna. It's hard to imagine how I could go on without you. But I know there are so many things we need to work out."

"As long as you believe in me?" She stared up into his glittering eyes.

"I believe you're someone rare and precious," he said. "I'm fiercely protective of you. I only hope I can work to dissolve your pain. I have to admit to feeling a degree of guilt because Mark was my half-brother. What he did was an affront to you, his wife, and to our families. It was vicious and cowardly, to my mind. I'm going to do everything I can to make it up to you."

"So kiss me," she implored, drawing his eyes to her softly alluring waiting mouth. "And don't stop. Please don't stop."

They were together. An opal blue sky was above them. The wild fragrant bush was around them. She was where she wanted to be, sealed off and safe in Blaine's powerful arms. She didn't want to solve the problem of Amanda right now.

Nothing mattered but Blaine and his belief in her. She had thought she would never find the love she craved. She had thought she would never find that one perfect-to-her man.

She was ecstatic to find herself blissfully wrong.

CHAPTER EIGHT

SHE drove back to the homestead, her flesh tingling, a smile on her mouth.

Blaine had things to do that afternoon. He had to organize an overdue cattle drive. With Katajangga Station covering some four million acres it was a huge job to chase and then drive out sections of the herd that had sought a hiding place in the wild scrub. Often the cattle travelled over many miles into the desert fringe. He was planning on taking the helicopter up and letting his stockmen on the ground—some on horseback, others on motorbikes—know the exact location of the various hide-outs. A chopper was indispensable on a working station, for mustering and aerial views of the vast area. Driving large numbers of unwilling cattle back to holding yards closer to home territory was a hard and often dangerous job, but his men loved it, he said. This was the place they wanted to be. Theirs was the best job in the world. They couldn't do this one in a few days. Some of the men would have to camp out—most probably for weeks.

When Sienna returned to the homestead she found to her astonishment that Amanda was sitting companionably with Hilary over a light lunch. Would wonders never cease? Amanda was pretty remarkable in her way, Sienna thought, heartened by the way Amanda had pulled herself together.

Amanda could act sweetly, or act badly. There was nothing much in between. Today she had put on a very pretty sundress, no doubt for her interview with Blaine, washed her hair and applied just the right amount of make-up. Make-up made a big difference to her. She looked much more herself.

Hilary looked up with a bright tremulous smile that expressed her pleasure in having Amanda share some quality time with her. "Have you had lunch, dear?" she asked Sienna.

"I'd love a sandwich." Sienna smiled back. "How are you today, Hilary?" she asked with genuine concern. She had thought Hilary might fall apart.

"Coping better," Hilary said, reaching to cover Amanda's small hand that was lying on the table with her own.

"I'm so pleased to hear it," Sienna responded, noting the gesture. "And you, Amanda?" Her eyes moved to her cousin. "You look much better."

"I feel much better," Amanda said, giving Hilary's frail hand a squeeze. So she *did* have a heart! Then she looked back at Sienna, as though waiting for some reaction from her.

One wasn't forthcoming. "I'll go through to the kitchen. Be back in a minute," Sienna promised.

Blaine had told her before they parted company that he had specifically asked Amanda not to mention her pregnancy to Hilary until he'd had time to think things through, and Amanda would have to be seriously deranged to ignore his express wishes. The fact it might *cost* her would act as a deterrent. Amanda had learned early to act appropriately when it was in her own best interests. Obviously she had grasped the fact she had to get the Kilcullen family on side, and it was heartening to know she had already made an attempt. That was a big step forward.

Marcia was due home some time that afternoon—Joanne, who had her pilot's licence, would be flying her in. But whether Joanne intended to stay over she didn't know. Anyway, Amanda had known from the very beginning about Mark's abandoned fiancée. It hadn't worried her then. It wouldn't worry her now. Amanda operated on a different system from most people.

An hour or so later Sienna drove down to the airstrip to pick up Marcia and Joanne. Truth be told, although she'd wanted to do the pick-up, she had found Amanda's newly realized empathy for her mother-in-law a bit on the cloying side. Amanda was acting out of character, but Hilary was clearly taken in. Sienna, however, had her cousin's measure. The show of togetherness was contrived. Of course she couldn't fail to grasp the significance. Amanda was carrying Hilary's grandchild. That put her in a powerful position, and maybe Amanda craved power.

Amanda—a mother! Maybe it would be the making of her. She would have to take responsibility for her life and that of her unborn child. Sienna couldn't ignore the thought that Kilcullen money would help, though her own family would never see Amanda go short or without support. Had Mark known about his child? Surely he had not. How far along *was* Amanda anyway? She was still very slight. No baby bump. At the first opportunity she and Amanda had to talk.

Sienna pushed her sense of hurt away. She had never thought for a moment that Amanda would keep the news of her pregnancy from her. The fact of the matter was Amanda *had*.

Why, exactly? Why had Amanda felt it necessary to keep her pregnancy under wraps? Because she had miscarried in the past and wanted to be very sure before she announced the big event? Or because Mark's tragic early death had delivered a numbing blow? Sienna concluded it was a combination of both.

A white, blue and yellow-striped Cessna was standing like a big bird on the concrete apron. Marcia and Joanne were lolling in the shade of a giant hangar.

Sienna slammed the door of the Jeep and hurried towards them. "Hi!"

They moved towards her as one, no formality between any of them. "Thanks for coming for us," Marcia said, giving Sienna a spontaneous kiss on the cheek.

"No trouble at all. How are you?"

"Getting there," Marcia said.

"I have to return home," Joanne told Sienna, bestowing upon her another friendly kiss. "Always things to do around the station. But I'd love a cuppa."

"Me too." Marcia lightly touched Sienna's shoulder. Despite the odds all three young women were at ease with each other. "How's Mum?"

"She's coping better today," Sienna said, stowing Marcia's overnight bag. "She looks better."

"Amanda up and about yet?" Marcia asked, getting into the front passenger seat, while Joanne clambered in the back.

"Actually, she and Hilary have been enjoying lunch and a long conversation," Sienna said, switching on the ignition. "I've been out taking photographs of the wild flowers, the great gardens of the desert and the amazing landscape."

"I'd love to see them when they're ready," Joanne piped up. "Amanda knows about me? About me and Mark?" she asked.

"Yes, Joanne," Sienna said. "You have no concerns there."

"You *hope*!" said Marcia, in a decidedly unconvinced

voice. "I have my own opinion of Amanda, and I bet I'm right. She's probably come round because she thinks Blaine is going to set her up for life."

"Come on, Marcy, why take it out on Sienna?" Joanne hastily intervened, leaning forward to make a protest.

"Sorry, Sienna," Marcia apologized. "I don't want to offend *you*. I like you. But you know better than I do that your cousin is one big crate of trouble."

"Oh, Marcy!" Another wail of protest from Joanne.

"A harsh judgement, Marcia," Sienna said.

"I know. But it could be the truth,'" Marcia said, in a worried voice. "I know in my bones Amanda doesn't mean well." She actually gave a shudder.

Sienna glanced across at Mark's twin. Marcia wasn't Mark's mirror image, but the resemblance was very strong. Some facets of the manner as well. "Take it easy now, Marcia," she said gently. "I'm here."

"To act as a buffer?" Marcia shot her a wry glance. "I don't know why you do it."

"You know why. Amanda is family. My parents took her in when she was a little girl. I can't just up and abandon her."

"I hope you don't have to." Marcia spoke very seriously. "But watch your back. You're too kind, Sienna. Maybe for your own good."

"Marcy, Sienna knows what she's about." Once more Joanne, well used to her friend and her often alarmingly straight talk, intervened.

"It's okay, Joanne," Sienna said soothingly. "I understand how Marcia feels. Mark and Amanda didn't handle family matters well. But there are a few things you have to know."

"Like what?" Marcy sat bolt upright in alarm.

"Blaine will explain." Sienna kept her voice relaxed.

"Now for the most important thing," she said, as they swept through the open gates of the compound. "A cup of tea."

"Lovely!" Joanne breathed. "When do you think you can come over, Sienna?" she asked. "You can't possibly go home without a visit."

"Sienna is going to stay a good while—aren't you, Sienna?" Marcia stated, as though it were a *fait accompli*. "Amanda might want to fly off just as soon as she can, but you don't have to. Believe me, we've got lots to show you—haven't we, Jo?"

"Plenty!" Joanne smiled. "Like, for example, the Red Centre, Uluru and Katajuta."

"That's Ayer's Rock and the Olgas," Marcia supplied. "Kata means many. We have many rock formations on Katajangga. If you want to see some truly wonderful desert rock formations you have to visit our Ancient Domes. Blaine will arrange it all. I know he wants you to see as much as you possibly can before you go home. I wish you weren't going home, actually. You and Blaine seem to click. I wish I could find someone *I* could click with," she supplied confidentially.

"Me too," sighed Joanne from the back seat.

"It will happen." Sienna used her most reassuring tone. "But first you might have to widen your horizons. At least in terms of meeting people. You'd both be very welcome to visit my country. It's very beautiful, very big, and very diverse. I have a large apartment in Vancouver—three bedrooms: master, guest, and the other I use as my study. But there's also a comfortable sofabed. You could use the apartment as a *pied à terre*."

"That sounds very French." Joanne laughed, fascinated like most people by an authentic French accent.

"I'm bilingual," Sienna replied. "Think about it."

"Gosh, you won't have to ask *me* twice," Marcia's whole face had lit up. It was such a transformation.

"Me either!" Joanne chortled. "Canada, here we come!"

Amanda had settled right into her good behaviour, even exhibiting a few little airs and graces that went over very well with Hilary. Sienna couldn't help noticing Amanda was getting far more attention from Hilary than her own daughter. Sienna's kindly impression of Hilary slipped a bit as a consequence. But she did find herself breathing a great sigh of relief. Maybe Amanda's morning sickness—whatever—had settled as well, and she was on the road to recovery. There was a whole list of questions she wanted to ask her cousin at the first opportunity, but she had the nagging idea Amanda was putting any and all questioning off.

Amanda did, however, apologize very sweetly to Marcia for what Marcia might have thought of as her "stand-offishness". Her nerves had been shot to pieces, she explained. Joanne received an apology as well. Both young women accepted the apologies more gracefully than Amanda might have expected or deserved—although Sienna intercepted a very enigmatic smile from Marcia. She appeared to have summed Amanda up from their first brief meeting, the day after their arrival. Sienna was vividly reminded of how very quickly she had summed up Mark.

Joanne flew home no more than an hour later. Blaine hadn't arrived back at the homestead.

"He'll come in at dusk," Marcia told Sienna. "Dinner at seven. Come down a bit earlier," she invited, before turning to Amanda. "You are having dinner with us, Amanda?"

"Of course I am." Amanda appeared entirely at ease. "I'm feeling very much better."

Under her pretty pink blusher Sienna thought her cousin was still looking pale. But that was only to be expected. She was starting to feel real concern about Amanda's drinking. She felt obliged to speak up as soon as she got the chance.

Walking along the upper floor gallery to their beautiful guestrooms, Sienna took Amanda's hand—much as she had done when they were children and she was the elder, the one in the lead. But Amanda shook it off.

"I don't want to talk now, Sienna," she said.

Sienna laughed in disbelief. "But this is incredible news, Mandy. You're pregnant! Only it's such good news I'm hurt you didn't confide in me. Or Mum—or anyone."

"What's good about it?" Amanda turned on her, all her sweetness and light hardening into an all too familiar resentment.

"I don't understand you," Sienna said. "You loved Mark once. This is his child. You may have been feeling sickly but your tummy will settle. And just think when the baby comes. A beautiful baby to love and cherish!"

"Oh, shut up," Amanda said, in a rude, angry-sounding voice.

Sienna pulled a disgusted face. She saw that her cousin's calm was shattering. "So, do I take that as proof positive you don't want your child?" she asked, very quietly.

"I told you, Sienna." Amanda gritted her small white teeth. "I don't want to talk about it. I want to get out of here as quickly and as painlessly as I can."

"In which case I should tell you I'm not coming with you," Sienna announced. "I'm staying on for a while."

"Blaine, of course!" Amanda sneered. "You're as bold

as brass. You're sleeping with him already. Now, that's what I call fast work."

"Call it what you like, Amanda—and *you* would know." Immediately the words were out of her mouth Sienna regretted them as a cheap shot.

Amanda's brittle tone abruptly broke, and she gave a kind of strangled whimper. "You couldn't let me travel all the way home alone, Sienna. I'm *pregnant*." She ran her hands wildly through her pretty blonde curls. "The very time I need you, you propose to *abandon* me?"

Sienna stared at her cousin in consternation. Amanda was visibly trembling. "Look, don't upset yourself, Mandy," she relented. "I can see you need someone at this time. But we have to strike a bit of a balance here. It won't hurt you to stay on. How far along are you? Hilary has brightened no end, just being able to talk to you. Just think how excited she'll be when she hears the good news."

"Damn Hilary," Amanda exclaimed, her voice full of venom. They were now at her door. "I'm going to lie down for a half-hour," she said. "So don't come in."

"Okay." Sienna was determined not to get into an argument. "But there are a few things we need to clear up, Mandy, before you make your announcement. You still haven't told me—how far along are you?"

"You suspect I'm *not* pregnant?" Amanda's petite body had turned stiff as a board.

"Amanda, I didn't say that." Sienna shook her head, perplexed. "I merely asked how many months. You miscarried once. You have to be doubly careful."

Amanda swung about like a defiant child. "You're supposed to be my cousin—my best friend. Why can't you simply support me?"

Sienna put a hand to her cousin's back, feeling the bones

like little jutting chicken wings. "Mandy, I *am* supporting you. I've always supported you. Settle down, now."

"Just leave me alone!" Amanda opened her bedroom door. "My baby's conception was no act of love."

Sienna froze. "For God's sake, Amanda," she muttered, low-voiced. "You're not going to put the blame on your innocent unborn babe? When *was* this anyway?" She frowned, her instincts suddenly kicking in. "Mark was away for a month or more when he took that hospitality job in Banff."

Amanda didn't answer. She darted away into her bedroom and slammed the heavy door. Sienna heard the key turn in the lock. Chills were breaking over her in waves. She rattled the doorknob, feeling a great sense of urgency, but Amanda ignored her.

"Come on, Mandy," Sienna urged. *"Please."*

She heard Amanda's near-hysterical reply. "Go away!"

Sienna went. She feared making matters worse. Amanda was so unpredictable. And being pregnant she would be at the mercy of her raging hormones. Alarmed on a number of counts, Sienna walked down the corridor to her own bedroom.

The voice inside her head spoke out.

You're right to question this pregnancy.

A pregnancy Amanda had kept secret from all of them. Yet this very day she had confided in Blaine. Could it possibly be a trick to extract more money? She couldn't accept that. Amanda wasn't *that* unbalanced. But she was a very vulnerable little person. Amanda had to take care of herself.

What Sienna didn't realize or take into account was that *she* was the one who needed to take care…

* * *

By eight o'clock they were all assembled in the Great Room. One of Magda's young staff members carried around canapés on a silver tray—delicious little morsels. Blaine had been pouring a glass of white wine for Hilary when Sienna reached the bottom of the staircase, walking across the room to join them.

"A glass of wine for you, Sienna?" he asked, waiting for the exact moment when the light from the chandelier fell over her radiant hair. "This is a Chardonnay, but I can get you something else."

"Chardonnay will be fine." Sienna smiled even though she didn't particularly like Chardonnay. She didn't feel sufficiently at ease to ask for anything else.

Seated beside Hilary on the sofa facing the massive piled stone fireplace, Amanda was watching them both very closely, gauging their reactions.

There she is, making another grand entrance. Yet another man in thrall. And what a man! There's nothing fair in life.

Amanda downed her wine in a single gulp. Sienna had told her many times that alcohol made her face take on a definite pallor, but who cared? She needed a drink. Sienna was wearing one of those silk dresses that looked like *nothing* on the hanger until she put it on. This was in a shade of garnet that shouldn't have gone with her hair, but did. Sienna was just *too* perfect. She, Amanda, was the one who'd had the utterly demoralizing task of growing up with such perfection. She remembered how Mark had always bitterly bemoaned walking in his half-brother's tall shadow. It had been just the same with her. Sienna had actually ruined her life in a way.

She had been feeling okay, buoyed up by the thought of the money she was about to get, but now her mood was descending into the doldrums. She could find no pleasure in the thought of the baby. How could she? She had been careless. Upstairs in the bathroom she had stared at her naked body. Hard to believe she was pregnant, but it wasn't a state of mind. In a few weeks she would be starting to show.

"Are you all right?" Blaine asked Sienna quietly as he passed her a crystal wine glass.

She moved closer to him. They were standing by the long sideboard that held the drinks and canapés. "I haven't had a chance to speak to Amanda," she said, as though that grieved her. "Or rather she didn't want to speak to me. I hope she's not going to make any announcement over dinner. Are *you*?" She stared into his dynamic face intently.

For once she saw him falter, his expression darkening. "*I* won't be saying anything, Sienna. Amanda really ought to tell everyone herself. I'm worried that she hasn't confided in you. That's odd. I'm worried she might just blurt her news out."

"Would it be so bad?" Sienna asked, although she also had a fear of her cousin's bent for duplicity.

Involuntarily Blaine brought up his hand, touched her cheek. "You look lovely," he said, low-voiced. He couldn't help himself. She looked so beautiful, so graceful with her lovely hair pinned up. Her silk dress, in a colour that suited her rare colouring, lightly skimmed her slender body, but anyone looking at her would realize just how beautiful her body was. *He* certainly knew. He had never thought his own body would feel incomplete without being inside the body of the woman he loved. He had the mad urge to leave the rest of them to it and take Sienna off. But he couldn't do that. He hoped Amanda had taken him seriously when he told her to keep silent until the appropriate moment...

* * *

Magda brought in little baked tournedos of Tasmanian salmon for the entrée, a lamb dish for the main. While they waited for dessert to be served Amanda suddenly picked up a spoon and struck the side of her crystal wine glass. The ping startled Hilary, at one end of the long rectangular table, who looked at her in surprise.

"Yes, dear? You have something to say?"

Blaine braced himself. "What is it, Amanda?" he asked, in a voice that would have stopped a more perceptive person.

"Yes, what is it?" Marcia spoke up too. It sounded like a challenge.

Sienna swallowed hard, knowing Amanda had the bit between her teeth.

"I'm having a baby," Amanda announced, straightening up and holding her head high.

"Oh!" Hilary threw up both her hands in absolute delight. "You're having a baby?" she echoed. "My son's baby?"

"Satisfied, Amanda?" Marcia asked, very tightly. "You're the centre of attention now. Did you know about this, Sienna?" She looked across the table at Sienna, who appeared stricken.

"Only today," Sienna confirmed. "Blaine asked me not to say anything. He felt Amanda should make the announcement."

"Oh, I couldn't be happier!" Hilary cried. She pushed her carver chair back and rushed to Amanda, putting her arms around Amanda's delicate shoulders. "This is wonderful news, Amanda."

"It's certainly news," Blaine said.

"I desperately need some good news." Tears of joy had sprung into Hilary's eyes.

"Don't we all?" Blaine leaned back in his chair, an imposing and very sombre figure.

"You don't look too enthusiastic at the thought of becoming an aunt." Amanda threw Marcia her own challenging glance.

"I expect I'll perk up," Marcia said. "Personally, I don't think you should have kept your news secret, Amanda. How far along are you? There's not a trace of a baby bump yet."

"Well, this *is* my first child," Amanda said.

"But you suffered an earlier miscarriage?" Blaine cut in.

"I wasn't going to bring that up, Blaine." Amanda tutted.

"Well, we're very, *very* glad you have now, my dear," Hilary said, returning to her chair. "I think this calls for champagne?" She looked rather glassy-eyed down the table to Blaine.

"Not terribly appropriate right now, Hilary," Blaine told her quietly.

"Well, haven't you turned out the surprise packet, Amanda?" Marcia said, abruptly rising to her feet. "I wonder if you'll all excuse me? I'm not in the mood for a celebration. We've only just buried my twin."

"You weren't all that close, though, were you?" Amanda said. "Life goes on, Marcia."

Sienna tried to catch Amanda's eye. Failed.

Marcia drew in a harsh breath. "Don't we need some *proof* you're pregnant?" she asked sharply. "Don't we need some proof, if you are pregnant, that the baby is Mark's? I'm not getting good vibes about this. My twin's shadow is not at rest."

Amanda gasped. At the same moment Blaine snapped his fingers—hard. His eyes were glittering like diamonds in the dark tan of his face. "That will do, Marcy," he said. "You're excused."

Sienna sat very still, staring at her clasped hands resting on the linen and lace tablecloth.

"What are you doing, Sienna?" Amanda turned on her cousin, her tone almost a taunt. "Praying she'll cool off?"

Blaine pushed back in his chair. "I think we might hold the dessert, Hilary," he said, throwing his linen napkin down on the table, then standing up. "Sienna, let's take a short walk." He put out an imperative arm.

She went to him.

"I never thought my news would cause such a rumpus," Amanda said to Hilary, raising her fair brows.

"No, indeed!" Hilary was staring at Blaine in utter astonishment. "Blaine, whatever is the matter?"

"I'll tell you. He thinks I was mad to tell you without his approval." Amanda leaned towards Hilary confidingly. She was convinced she now had Hilary eating out of her hand.

"*Mad* being the operative word." Blaine looped his hand around Sienna's wrist. He knew she was making a real effort to remain quiet.

Marcia wasn't sure about this pregnancy. He couldn't quite believe in it either. Only Sienna could get to the bottom of things. Amanda might well be delusional. Stranger things had happened.

Sienna had never seen so brilliant a sky. It was packed with stars. In an effort to ease the tension between them, she tilted her head upwards. "I don't find it all that easy to locate the Southern Cross," she said. "It seems to be in a different position each night."

"That's because the stars of the Southern Cross, like all

stars, rotate throughout the night," Blaine explained. "The location depends on what time of night you're trying to find it. I'll show you." He turned her gently by the shoulders, pointing a finger at the great glittering river of stars that made up the Milky Way. "The Cross is in the middle of the Milky Way. It's the most famous constellation in the Southern Hemisphere. Small compared to other constellations, but it's made up of some of the brightest stars in the heavens. That's Acrus up there. See the very bright one? Some people think it resembles a kite more than a cross. See the two bright stars trailing the kite? They're called pointers. That's how you know for sure you're looking at the Southern Cross."

"I see it clearly now," she said. "I was—"

He stopped her by kissing her, his mouth hard on hers, thrillingly passionate. He held her very closely. She clung to him while he buried his face in her sweet-smelling hair. "What's it going to take to get Amanda to confide in you?" he asked.

She stared up at him in a kind of anguish. "She *is* pregnant, Blaine. It's wrong of us to doubt her."

He gave a harsh laugh. "Marcy certainly doubts her. The twins mightn't have got on, but believe me they were *close*. When they were kids one could finish the other one's sentence. You don't think Amanda could be delusional?"

Sienna shook her head. "No! She's pregnant, all right. But there is the possibility she's not all that happy about it. It's a very bad time for her—losing Mark, especially the way she did."

"I'm like Marcy," Blaine said. "I don't trust Amanda at all."

"I'm sorry. Maybe you think I shouldn't have brought her here?"

"Sienna, *I* was the one who asked her here. She was Mark's wife, even if he didn't feel much love for her."

Disturbing thoughts were pressing in on Sienna. "Life. Death. New life. How did I get so deeply involved in all this?"

"Do you wish we hadn't met?"

"No, never. But—"

"There shouldn't be a *but*, Sienna. Your cousin has a plan, and part of that plan is to stop our relationship going any further."

"So what am I supposed to do? Abandon her?"

He pulled her back into him. Kissed her again. "I want you to come to me tonight. Will you?"

There was nothing she wanted more, yet she felt compelled to say, "Maybe I should stay close to Amanda." She looked up at him, and he cursed softly beneath his breath.

"For God's sake, Sienna," he cried in exasperation. "You treat your cousin more like a child than a woman."

"I have a responsibility towards her." Sienna felt very much on the defensive. "More so now that she's expecting."

"Which she failed to tell you."

His tone was so terse she could feel her heart hammering violently in her breast. "I don't want us to fight, Blaine."

"I don't want to fight either." He trapped her in his gaze. "I want to make love. I want to make love to you so much I don't think I could get through the night without you. I won't let your cousin destroy what we have."

"Blaine, Amanda is nowhere near as conniving as you think," she said, sickly aware of the hard glint of scepticism in his eyes. "She's vulnerable and in need of my support. Can't you see that?'

He could feel the hot blood rising; forced it down. "Okay.

I don't want to upset you. Amanda should be very thankful she has you. You might tell her that if she wants me back on side she had better have a long talk with you. You saw how thrilled Hilary was at her news. Is Amanda going to tell us next she's going home and won't be back?"

"She *will* want to go home," Sienna was obliged to point out.

"Is that what you want too?" He was able to mock himself. All he wanted now was to have Sienna. He didn't want a life without her. Only she had to want that too. Otherwise it would never work.

Dreams were abandoned all the time.

Blaine was reluctant to let her go, and Sienna went upstairs feeling terribly torn. But she had a duty to her cousin and she wasn't going to allow Amanda to put her off. They needed to talk. And first she had to establish how far along her pregnancy was. She wondered if Amanda had consulted a doctor—what doctor?—before undertaking the long flight. She couldn't be even three months. She wasn't showing in any way, even when down to her bra and knickers. Sienna had to understand what was going on.

"Amanda?" She knocked on the bedroom door, listening for a response.

There was none. But she knew Amanda was in there.

Pregnancy could be a big upheaval in a woman's life. So many changes taking place in her body. Maybe Amanda found the prospect of raising her child alone very daunting? The fact she had been suffering morning sickness would have affected her moods. Sienna was roused to sympathy. Amanda would have to stay on until a doctor gave her clearance to make the long journey back home. She had, after all, suffered one miscarriage, and she had never had robust health. Sienna felt the weight of responsibility keenly.

Once inside her own bedroom, she made the decision to walk along the deck to Amanda's bedroom. She should have done that in the first place, since Amanda had decided not to let her in. The big question was *why*?

The French doors were open to the night. She stepped into the bedroom to find Amanda lolling on the bed in her nightgown, her fingertips playing some sort of tattoo on her stomach. "Hi!" she said laconically.

Amanda swung her legs out of bed so abruptly she knocked over a crystal tumbler on the bedside table. "How dare you invade my privacy?"

"Get real!" Sienna put up a staying hand. "This is no time to go on a drinking binge, Amanda," she said, eyeing the fallen tumbler. "What are you thinking of? We have to talk. You seem to have a problem. What is it?"

"Problem? *Exactly*. I'm seriously screwed," Amanda burst out bitterly.

Sienna felt a great stab of alarm. "How's that? Come on—tell me. I'll do everything I can to help you. Are you frightened of this pregnancy? I can understand that."

"Did you *see* Hilary?" Now, unbelievably, Amanda sounded amused. "I could live off her for ever."

Sienna stared back at her cousin in astonishment. "Mandy, what are you talking about?'

Amanda laughed. "Hilary, of course. She's thrilled out of her mind. Not that bitch Marcia. Or your big-time boyfriend. Who does he think he is, anyway?"

"He *knows* who he is, Amanda," Sienna shot back. "The question is, who are *you*? I can't believe you told Blaine without telling me. Did you see a doctor before we left Canada?"

"Are you crazy?" Amanda asked, pulling on her robe.

"I'm not crazy. Are you? How far along are you?"

"Goodness, I don't know. Eight weeks, something like that."

"You're not sure?" Sienna asked incredulously.

"I'm sure I'm pregnant, if that's what you mean," Amanda sneered. "I did a home test. It was valid. What's bugging you, anyway?"

"I'm worried about you," Sienna said. "You should stay here until you're three months at least. That's if you want to go home?"

"Of course I want to go home," Amanda retorted, her tone very cold. "And I *am* going—believe me. As soon as I get the money."

"The money? What the hell are you playing at?" Sienna asked. "This isn't making a lot of sense. When was Mark in Banff?"

Amanda turned ashen. "Don't know. My memory isn't all that reliable these days."

Sienna was determined to get an answer. "I was in Toronto, wasn't I?"

"What the hell does it matter?" Amanda snarled.

"It matters a great deal." Sienna was trying very hard to keep calm. "Mandy, this isn't Mark's baby, is it?" She was playing on no more than a gut feeling.

Only Amanda's small face turned stony. "It is as far as the Kilcullens are concerned."

Sienna put her hands to her head. "God, I don't believe this! You were *lying*? You honestly believe you can put one over on them? How stupid can you be?"

"I'm not stupid at all. I'm going to get the money—which seems reasonable as Hilary is the grandmamma. Hilary is going to see to it."

Sienna stared at Amanda as though she were a total stranger. "You can't allow Hilary to go on believing you're expecting *her* grandchild."

"Why not? It happens all the time," Amanda retorted.

"So who *is* the father?"

"Just a guy." Amanda shrugged.

"Do I know him?"

"No. And he's never going to know anything about it. I don't actually want this baby. I don't fancy playing Mummy. But right now a baby is my trump card."

"You have to be losing your mind," Sienna uttered very bleakly. "Amanda, I have to intervene. I can't allow you to deceive this family."

"I'm confident you will, Sienna," Amanda tossed back at her. "You've always looked out for me."

"Maybe that was a huge mistake! Shut up now," she begged. "I have to think."

Amanda did.

Sienna fell into an armchair, trying hard to clear her swimming head. "I can't allow this, Amanda," she said eventually. "It's wrong, wrong, wrong. The family must be told at once."

"You wouldn't do that to me?" Amanda breathed, as though she didn't think such a thing possible.

"Amanda, you *are* crazy. You just don't know it yet. I can't be party to this massive fraud. If you're frightened Blaine won't give you any money I can speak to him. You were married to Mark. You're entitled. Was this what it was all about at the ski lodge? Mark discovered you were pregnant, and certainly not by him?"

"Whoa!" Amanda yelled. "He didn't know. Mark was eaten up by his own sins."

Sienna felt as if she was descending into her own little hell. "Mandy, let me handle this." She didn't realize she was shaking violently. "We'll say we talked it over and you realized it can't be Mark's baby after all. That you and Mark had as good as broken up. You were desperately unhappy. You turned to someone else for comfort. You're dreadfully sorry for your mistake."

"Prove it." Amanda crossed her arms across her chest in what appeared to be a gesture of triumph.

"Oh, don't be silly!" Sienna burst out, appalled. "There's such a thing as DNA."

Amanda looked back blankly, and then swore. "Don't rat on me, Sienna," she pleaded, her blue eyes like saucers in her white face. "I think I'll kill myself if you do."

Sienna groaned. "I've heard all this talk before. It's called emotional blackmail. You will have your baby. You'll be a rich woman. And I haven't the slightest doubt you'll find someone else." Sienna rose shakily, then walked to the door. "I have to discuss this with Blaine, Amanda. This deception can't go any further."

Amanda rushed to her side. "What if I give you some of it? The money?"

"Ah, *please*." Sienna was filled with despair. "You've landed yourself in a mess, and now we have to get you out of it."

Amanda looked both stricken and amazed. "I'll hate you if you do this," she threatened.

"Hate away. This little plan of yours, Amanda, was never going to work. I can't believe how amoral you've become."

They were out in the gallery now, with Sienna making her way resolutely to the top of the staircase. "Stay there, Amanda. I'll work something out."

"Don't do it. Please don't do it," Amanda implored, her voice rising to a wild shriek. "Sienna!" She had to run to keep up. She was beside herself with panic and rage. Her deception exposed, might she have to suffer the consequences?

No money, when she had already adjusted to the idea of being rich and free of them all?

Sienna cast a hurried look behind her, surprised Amanda was so close on her heels, the expression on her small face near feral. "Go to your room, Mandy," she ordered. "We'll get through this. Leave it to me."

"You?" Amanda exploded, unbalanced by fear and her need for malignant revenge. "I've never been happy. Not a single day of my life. And it's all *your* fault."

The violent accusation hit Sienna like sharp-edged stones hurled in her face. She staggered as Amanda, in a blinding rage, prepared to spring.

It had all come together in Amanda's mind. There would be a kind of justice in sending Sienna hurtling down the stairs.

Only Amanda's high pitched shrieks had brought not only Blaine but Magda, who had been in the kitchen, charging to the scene.

"Sienna—look out!" Blaine roared in a voice like thunder.

Instantly Sienna heeded the warning. She fell back against the timber balustrade, collapsing on the step, while the doll-like Amanda went tumbling down the stairs in her stead.

CHAPTER NINE

Vancouver Island. Three months later.

SIENNA walked along the beach in front of her family retreat, feeling the sun on her head. Water sloshed rhythmically onto the shore, where a jumble of driftwood lay like a piece of sculpture at the water's edge. The house rose up behind her, white weatherboards, tiled roof—a substantial holiday home with a large extension that she and her father used as a studio. The house had breathtaking views of the ocean. They had their own sandstone beach. She had been coming here since she was a child. She loved the place. She had always been happy here. Her mother's father had bought the beautiful peaceful property long ago. It even had mooring for their boat, a yellow kayak, which was beached on the jetty.

Things had changed quite a bit over the years. The islands were easily accessible by ferry, private boat and plane. She could walk to the shops, the galleries, and to the other amenities if she had a mind. Only she didn't. She was in retreat. She had come to the island to try to recover from an experience that still rocked her.

She and Amanda had left Katajangga in what she thought of as a cloud of disgrace. She felt she would be tainted by it for ever, although that was an irrational judgement. Her mother and father had been waiting for them when they touched down in Vancouver. Her parents had been as appalled as she by Amanda's multiple deceptions and her father had taken charge of Amanda in no uncertain fashion. Amanda had been admitted to a private and very expensive psychiatric clinic to undergo treatment.

In a matter of weeks Amanda had convinced the psychiatrist in attendance she was as sane as the next person. A week later, without a word to anyone, she had taken off for New York. She had money now. She no longer needed the family who had reared her.

"Good riddance!" her mother had said, totally fed up. "To think she could have killed you, my darling! I don't see how they let her go."

Amanda was a marvellous actress. That was the answer.

Sienna was finishing off a painting in the studio when she heard footsteps on the gravelled section of the rear courtyard.

She put down her paintbrush, wiped her hands on her smock and hurried outdoors. "Hello? Who's there?" She felt no sense of alarm, although the house was very private. At her call, a tall, lean figure came into view. He was dressed in jeans, a blue T-shirt, and a bomber jacket with one side flapping in the breeze.

Blaine.

She couldn't believe it. He had to be a figment of her imagination. She had never stopped thinking about him from the moment they had said a wretched goodbye. She had heard from him, of course, Marcia too—until she had taken refuge from the world on the island. He haunted her, following her wherever she went. She even took him into her bed.

Now the sudden shift from the shade of the studio to full sun had her blinking, covering her eyes with her hand. For a moment she was mute with astonished joy. "Blaine?" A tremendous excitement descended on her, though she tried to calm herself. He wasn't exactly looking ecstatic to see her.

"Oh, good—you recognize me," he said.

The same vibrant voice. The same clipped tone. The same brilliant eyes. She drew in a great gulp of air. "How did you find me?"

"You *knew* I would." He covered the distance between them, staring down at her, studying her intently. "Your father and I have had a number of fruitful conversations. I've spoken to your mother as well. The only person who has made herself unavailable is *you*."

"I'm sorry. Sorry." She hung her head as Amanda's guilt rippled over her afresh.

"Apologies won't do," he said. "Incidentally, your dad told me what *you* failed to. You covered for Amanda right to the end. Why did you do that?'

"Shame," she confessed, a tremor in her voice. "I don't know to this day if Amanda genuinely believed she was pregnant. I was as shocked as you when the doctor told us she wasn't."

"She was conspiring to rob me, Sienna," he said. "That's the brutal truth. A baby meant lots more money."

"You gave her enough," she said, still keeping her eyes lowered.

"Anything to get rid of her. She had it all planned, Sienna. She almost pulled it off. Knowing what I know now, it was detestable of her to pretend she was carrying Mark's child. Even if she believed herself pregnant—which I doubt—it was another man's."

"Dad shouldn't have told you..." She let her voice trail off.

"Your father was right to tell me," he said forcefully. "We understand why you kept quiet."

She threw up her head. "It would only have caused more pain. I was so upset I just wanted to disappear with my awful delusional cousin. Call it irrational, but I felt I shared the guilt and the shame."

"*Your* only crime, Sienna, was loyalty and the desire not to inflict more hurt. But you could have told *me*. You should have told me."

"I know. I wanted to. But I could see Hilary had her doubts about me by the time we got Amanda back from the hospital. If you hadn't broken her fall she could have been badly injured."

"She was quite prepared to injure *you*," he said, showing a flash of anger.

No way to deny it. Amanda *had* meant her harm. "Well, she's taken the money and headed off for New York," she offered very quietly.

"Bless her," said Blaine. "Your dad told me. May we never hear from her again."

"I think I can say amen to that." Her spirits picked up. "Please, Blaine, come into the house," she begged.

"You've been working?" He looked past her into the studio. She was still wearing a paint-splattered smock. "May I see?'

"Of course." She led the way in. Two of her paintings, large-scale botanicals, oil on canvas, were complete. The other, unfinished, sat on the easel.

A look of open admiration broke slowly across Blaine's handsome, dynamic face. "These are really beautiful, Sienna," he said.

"I was searching for something to remind me," she explained, struggling not to reach out and touch him.

"Were you, indeed? It's wonderful what you can do." He made his voice casual when he was all heat and fire. "Tell me. Have you missed me?"

Her face revealed what was in her heart. "I've missed you so much you can have no idea."

"Really? I'm amazed." In a moment Blaine knew all would be motion. His whole body was quaking with his need for her. But for now he valiantly held off.

He continued to study her amazing paintings. The Outback flowers he'd been used to all his life had been treated with a kind of passion. Fantastic huge-scale pink waterlilies grew out of one canvas; an extraordinary representation of dozens of floating blood-red Desert Pea glowed richly from another. The unfinished canvas was of a young woman, clearly Sienna, with long flowing amber hair and wearing a gauzy yellow dress. She stood waist-high in a shimmering wonderland of white and yellow paper daisies. The size of the wild flowers, perfect in botanical detail, had been blown up into fantastic blooms that rose all around her and bathed her in radiance.

"I love you." Sienna broke the silence. "I really love you." She had no choice but to tell him. "I can't explain what I've done, but I love you. I—"

Her attempted explanation was cut off. His muscled arms were around her, his hunger for her fully unleashed. "And being with you is the closest I'll ever get to heaven," he rasped. His mouth covered hers with insatiable yearning. "I love you. I *love* you," he muttered, without once breaking the passionate lock of their lips.

Gradually the fierce, needy pressure eased into a deeply

desirous exploration that had her moaning and arching her throat. Eventually he picked her up, feeling her long slender legs close convulsively around him.

"Which way's the bedroom?" he groaned. "Though I don't think we can get there." His eyes lit on the big leather chesterfield.

Their clothes evaporated, as though their flesh was so *hot* they couldn't bear to have anything touch their skin.

He held her head, staring into her warm golden eyes. "You can't do this to me again. Understand?"

"I knew you'd find me," she said. "I carried the thought of it every day. It kept me going. Helped me to paint. *Blaine will come for me.*"

"I'd come for you if you were holed up in an igloo at the North Pole. But don't think for one moment I'm not mad at you."

"You're right to be—yet you're here. I love you," she said all over again. "I can't say it enough times."

"You can try." His hands covered her swelling breasts, and his mouth descended to take in one rosy budded nipple after the other.

The rapture was immense. She moaned as his hand moved down over the flat plane of her stomach, his fingers seeking and then moving into the cleft of her.

She cried out his name, her voice ragged with desire. Her hands were tracing his wide shoulders, moving down his back. He was a dark tan all over, suggesting he had often swum in Katajangga's lagoons naked. His male body was splendid in its form. She spread her legs wide, her bright head rolling from side to side as he entered her. Her hands curved and clawed around him as she fitted herself to him. She couldn't tell where he started and she began. They were gloriously *one*.

I am with him. He is with me.

Sienna had never felt more loved or more safe in her life.

My soul mate has come to get me.

THE DOCTOR & THE RUNAWAY HEIRESS

MARION LENNOX

To Alison Roberts, author, ambulance officer, mother, dancer, superwoman—a woman I'm honoured to call my friend.

CHAPTER ONE

DR RILEY CHASE was bored. It was his third night in a row with no action, and Riley was a man who lived on little sleep. His medico-legal bookwork was up to date. He was on his third coffee. He'd even defeated the crossword.

He was checking his email for the tenth time when his radio crackled to life.

Two messages in twenty seconds. One was announcing the arrival of a daughter he'd never met, the other was a suicide.

It was enough to make a man spill his coffee.

Only the headlines of Britain's gossip magazines were stopping her drowning.

'Heiress Suicides!'

Pippa was surrounded by blackness, by cold and by terror. Any minute now something would attack her legs. Maybe it already had—she could hardly feel anything below her waist. The cold was bone-numbing. She was past exhaustion, and there was only one thing holding her up.

'Phillippa Penelope Fotheringham, heiress to the Fotheringham Fast Food fortune, suicides after jilting.'

She would not give Roger the satisfaction of that headline.

'Are we sure it's suicide?' Riley was staring intently down at the blackened sea, feeling more and more hopeless.

'Jilted bride.' Harry Toomey, pilot for New South Wales North

Coast Flight-Aid, was guiding the helicopter through parallel runs from the cliff. Harry, Riley and Cordelia, the team's Flight-Aid nurse, were searching north from Whale Cove's swimming beach. Grim experience told them this would be where a body would be swept.

'Do we have a name?' Riley said through his headset.

'Phillippa Penelope Fotheringham.'

'That's a mouthful.' Their floodlight was sweeping the water's surface, but the sea was choppy, making it hard to see detail. Detail like a body. 'Do we know how long she's been missing?'

'Five hours. Maybe longer.'

'Five hours!'

'There was a party on the beach that went till late,' Harry said. 'Kids everywhere. When they left, one of the security guys noticed an abandoned bundle of clothes. Plus a purse, complete with ID and a hotel access card. She could have been in the water since dusk, but we're assuming later, when it was good and dark.'

'Five hours is about three hours too long for a happy ending.'

Harry didn't bother replying. The crew knew the facts. The worst part of this job was pulling suicides out of the water. The jumpers were the worst—there was no coming back when you went over cliffs around here—but almost as bad were those who swam out from the beach knowing they couldn't get back. Desperate people. Desperate endings.

'So how do we know she just didn't have a good time at the party?' Riley demanded. 'She could have ended up back in someone else's hotel room.'

But even as Riley suggested it he knew it was unlikely. The police had called them in, and the cops around here knew their stuff.

'Logic,' Harry said, bringing the chopper round for the next pass. 'She's thirty-one, about ten years older than the party kids. She's staying at the Sun-Spa Resort, in the honeymoon suite no less. The cop who went to the hotel found her passport in the safe. She's English, and when he phoned the contact number in London, her parents had hysterics. It seems her wedding went up in smoke and our Phillippa fled to Australia with a broken heart. Alone. She arrived late. She booked into her honeymoon hotel with no wedding ring, no groom, and we can assume a decent dose of jet lag. Lethal combination. She headed for the beach, dumped her clothes and out she swam.'

'He's not worth it,' Riley muttered, feeling worse. Any minute now they'd find her. They usually did.

He was a doctor. He wasn't supposed to do this.

But, yeah, he was, he thought grimly. This was his choice. He, Harry and Cordelia did routine work, clinics in Outback settlements, flying in and out at need, but they also took Search and Rescue shifts. Sometimes it was incredibly satisfying, saving people from their own stupidity. Sometimes, though, like now…

Sometimes it was the pits.

Phillippa Penelope Fotheringham.

'Where are you, sweetheart?' After this time he knew they were searching for a body, but it was still incredibly important to find her. The parents could bury her, could grieve, could know exactly what had happened.

'So what was happening when the call came in?' Harry asked.

'What do you mean?'

'Who's Lucy?'

'You read my email?'

'Of course I did,' Harry said, unabashed. Harry was a highly skilled pilot, good-humoured and big-hearted, but his downside was an insatiable nose for gossip. 'You took thirty seconds to put your gear on, and you didn't supply alternative reading material. So someone called Lucy's coming on Friday and can you please put her up. You going to tell us who Lucy is?'

Riley thought of all the things he could say. *Mind your own business. A friend. Nobody important.* Maybe it was the grimness of the night, the tragedy playing out beneath the chopper, but in the end he couldn't bring himself to say anything but the truth.

'My daughter.'

My daughter.

The two words resonated through the headset, sounding… terrifying. He'd never said those words out loud until now.

He'd never had reason to say them.

'You're kidding us,' Harry breathed, turning into the next sweep. They were over the cliff now, momentary time out while Harry centred the machine for the next run; checking bearings so they weren't covering sea that had already been searched. 'Our solitary Dr Chase… A daughter! How old?'

'Eighteen.'

'Eighteen!' Riley could almost hear Harry's mental arithmetic. Cordelia was staring at him like he'd grown an extra head, doing maths as well.

'You're, what, thirty-eight?' Harry breathed. 'A daughter, eighteen years back. That's med student territory. Man, you've kept her quiet.'

He had. Mostly because he hadn't known she existed. Three months ago he'd received an email, sent via the Search and Rescue website.

Are you the Dr Riley Chase who knew my mother nineteen years ago?

Names. Dates. Details. A bombshell blasting into his carefully isolated existence.

And then nothing. No matter how desperately he'd tried to make contact, there'd been no word. Until tonight.

I'm arriving on Friday. Could you put me up for a few days?

But he couldn't afford to think about Lucy now. None of them could. The chopper was centred again. He went back to studying the waves, grimly silent, and Harry and Cordelia did the same.

Despite the bombshell Riley had just dropped, every sense was tuned to the sea. Harry was a flippant, carefree bachelor. Cordelia was a sixty-year-old dog breeder with a head cold. Riley was a man who'd just been landed with a daughter. Tonight though, now, they were three sets of eyes with only one focus.

Phillippa Penelope Fotheringham…

'Come on,' Riley muttered into the stillness. 'Give yourself up.'

The floodlight from their little yellow chopper, a Squirrel AS350BA—the best in the business, according to Harry—kept right on sweeping the surface of the night sea.

There was nothing but blackness. Nothing, nothing and nothing.

'Where are you?' Riley asked, but he was talking to himself.

Nothing.

There were lights. The mists cleared for a moment—the fog of fear and cold and fatigue—and let her see further than the next wave.

There were floodlights beaming out from the cliffs, but they were so far out of her reach they might as well be on the moon.

She could see a helicopter moving methodically over the water. Was it searching for her? Had someone found her clothes?

It was a long way south. Too far.

Was it coming closer?

'Just hold on,' she told herself, but her body was starting to shut down.

She couldn't feel her feet at all. She couldn't feel anything.

She was treading water. Up and down. Up and down. If she stopped she'd slip under.

A wave slapped her face and made her splutter.

'I will not give Roger the satisfaction,' she muttered, but her mutter was under her breath. To speak was impossible. Her teeth were doing crazy things. She was so cold…

'I will not be a jilted bride. I will not die because of Roger.' It was a mantra, said over and over.

The helicopter turned.

It was still too far south. So far.

'I will not…'

'If it's suicide she'll definitely be dead by now and probably slipping under.'

'We all know that,' Harry said. 'But it doesn't stop us looking.'

'No, but…' Riley was speaking more to himself than to Harry. 'As a last resort let's think sideways.'

'What?'

The crew hadn't spoken for what seemed hours. They'd swept the expected tidal path and found nothing. Riley's words had tugged Cordelia and Harry out of their intense concentration, but Harry sounded as hopeless as Riley felt.

'I'm thinking,' Riley said.

'So think away. It's gotta be more useful than what we're doing now.'

Riley thought a bit more and then put it in words. 'Okay. If our Phillippa was a normal tourist with no intention to suicide… What time did she get to the hotel?'

'Around seven-thirty.'

'Let's say she's jet lagged, tired and hot. She walks out to the balcony and the sea looks great. She might take an impulsive dip at dusk. Eightish, maybe? The lifesavers would have long gone home, but it's not so dark that the water's lost its appeal. If she got into trouble at dusk, no one might see.'

'The party started on the beach at ten,' Harry said, hopelessness giving way to thought. 'No one noticed the clothes before then. We're working on search parameters based on an entry at ten at the earliest.'

'Sunday night. The beach was busy. One bundle of clothes

might well go unnoticed. An entry at eight, she'd be a lot further north by now. And if it was a mistake she'll be fighting.'

'Her mother's sure she's suicidal.'

'How much does your mother know about you?' Riley demanded.

'I'd hate to imagine,' Cordelia retorted—which was a lot of speech for Cordelia. She was quiet at the best of times, but tonight her head cold was making her miserable.

There was a moment's pause while they all thought this through. Then: 'I guess it's worth a shot,' Harry said, and hit the radio. 'Assuming an eight o'clock entry,' he asked Bernie in their control room, 'can you rework the expected position?'

They did two more unsuccessful sweeps before Bernie was back with a location.

'Half a kilometre north and closer to shore,' Harry relayed. 'Let's go.'

It'd be so easy to slip under.

There will be no headlines. Not.

She was so tired.

The light. Had it turned? Was it coming?

She was imagining it. Her mind was doing funny, loopy things. The stars, the fluorescence of the waves and the roar of the sea were merging into a cold, menacing dream.

If this light wasn't really in her head she should raise her hand. If she could summon the energy. She could just…

Maybe not.

She must.

'Something.'

The Squirrel banked and turned almost before Riley barked the word. Harry was good.

So was Riley. His eyes were the best in the business. But still…the water was so choppy. They were in by the cliffs; any closer and they'd be victims themselves.

'Sure?' Harry snapped.

'No. Ten back. Five left. Hover.'

They hovered. The floodlight lit the water. The downdraught caused the water to flatten.

There…

'Got it,' Cordelia snapped.

They both had it. And what's more… There was a hand, feebly raised.

'She's alive,' Riley said, and he didn't try to keep the exultation from his voice. 'How about that? Suicide or not, it seems our bride's changed her mind. Hold on, Phillippa Penelope Fotheringham, we're coming.'

The light…the noise… It was all around her. She couldn't think.

She also could no longer make her feet tread water.

A shadow was over her. Someone was yelling.

She was so tired.

Do not slip under. Do not.

Please.

Something was sliding into the water beside her. *Someone.*

She was too weak to clutch but she didn't need to. Arms were holding her. Just…holding.

Another human.

She was safe. She could let go. She had to let go. She could slip into the darkness and disappear.

'Don't you give up on us now, Phillippa Penelope Fotheringham,' someone growled. 'I've got you.'

She made one last effort. One massive effort because this was really, really important.

'I am not marrying Roger,' she managed. 'My choice, not his. And my name is not Phillippa. I'm Pippa.'

CHAPTER TWO

THERE were sunbeams on her bedcover. She woke and the sheer wonder of sunlight on linen was enough to make her want to cry.

Someone was standing at the end of her bed. Male. With a stethoscope.

She was in hospital?

Of course. The events of the night before came surging back—or maybe only some of the events, because there seemed to be gaps. Big gaps.

Water. Dark. Terror.

Then in the water, someone holding her, yelling at her, or maybe they were yelling at someone else.

Someone fastening her to him. Large, male, solid.

'You're safe. You don't need to hold on. I have you.'

Noise, lights, people.

Hospital.

'Hi,' the guy at the end of the bed said. 'I'm Dr Riley Chase. Welcome to the other side.'

The other side.

She surveyed the man talking to her with a certain degree of caution. He was…gorgeous. Tall, ripped and, after the nightmare of last night, reassuringly solid.

Beautifully solid.

She took time to take him in. Detail seemed important. Detail meant real.

His face was tanned and strongly boned. His deep blue eyes were crinkled at the edges. Laughter lines? Weather lines? Weather maybe. His near black hair—a bit unkempt, a bit in need of a cut—showed signs of sun-bleaching. That'd be from weather. He was wearing cream chinos. His short-sleeved shirt was open at the throat—this guy was definitely ripped—and his stethoscope was hanging from his top pocket.

Welcome to the other side?

Gorgeous fitted the *other side* description, she decided. Doctors didn't.

'Doctors aren't in my version of heaven,' she said, trying her voice out. She was vaguely surprised when it worked. Nothing felt like it should work this morning.

'It's definitely heaven,' he said, smiling a wide, white smile that made him look friendlier—and more heart-stoppingly gorgeous—than any doctor she'd ever met. 'In the other place the pillows are lumpy and we're big on castor oil and leeches.'

'And here?' she managed.

'Not a leech in sight, we reserve our castor oil for emergencies and there are two pillows for every bed. And because you were soggy the angels have decreed you can have more.' He waved an expansive hand around her not-very-expansive cubicle. 'Luxury.'

She smiled at that. She was in a two-bed cubicle that opened out into the corridor. The nurses' station was on the other side, giving whoever was at the station a clear view of her bed. Luxury?

'And heaven also means your medical care's totally free,' he added. 'Especially as your documents say you have travel insurance.'

Her documents?

There was enough there to give her pause. To make her take her time about saying anything else. She looked at Dr Riley Chase and he gazed calmly back at her. She had the impression that he had all the time in the world.

'Dr Chase?' a female voice called to him from the corridor. Maybe he didn't have all the time in the world.

'Unless it's a code blue I'm busy,' he called back. He tugged a chair to her bedside and straddled it, so he was facing her with the back of the chair between them. She knew this trick. She often wished she could use it herself but it was a guy thing. Guy thing or not, she appreciated it now. It gave the impression of friendliness, but it wasn't overly familiar. She needed a bit of distance and maybe he sensed it.

'You're on suicide watch,' he said bluntly. 'We have a staff shortage. Are you planning on doing anything interesting?'

She thought about that for a bit. Felt a bit angry. Felt a bit stupid.

'We're struggling with priorities,' he said, maybe sensing her warring emotions. Feeling the need to be apologetic. 'Olive Matchens had a heart attack last night. She's a nice old lady. We're transferring her to Sydney for a coronary bypass but until the ambulance is free I'd like a nurse to stay with her all the time. Only we need to watch you.'

'I don't need to be watched.'

'Okay, promise I have nothing to worry about?' He smiled again, and his smile… Wow. A girl could wake up to that smile and think it had been worth treading water for a night or more or more to find it. 'You need to know you're at risk of that cod liver oil if you break your promise,' he warned, and his smile became wicked. Teasing.

But there was seriousness behind his words. She knew she had to respond.

'I wasn't trying to do anything silly.' She tried to sound sure but it came out a whisper.

'Pardon?'

'I was not trying to suicide.' Her second attempt came out loud. Very loud. The noises outside the cubicle stopped abruptly and she felt like hauling her bedclothes up to her nose and disappearing under them.

'Your mother's frantic. She's on her way to Heathrow airport right now,' Dr Chase told her. 'With someone called Roger. Their plane's due to leave in two hours unless I call to stop them.'

Forget hiding under the bedclothes. She dropped her sheet and stared at him in horror. 'My mother and Roger?'

'They sound appalled. They know you're safe, but you've terrified them.'

'Excellent.'

'That's not very—'

'Kind? No, it's not. My mother still wants me to marry Roger.'

'This sounds complicated,' he said, sounding like he was beginning to enjoy himself. Then someone murmured something out in the corridor and he glanced at his watch and grimaced. 'Okay, let's give you the benefit of the doubt, and let Roger and Mum sweat for a bit. What hurts?'

'Nothing.'

'You know, I'm very sure it does.'

She thought about it. He watched as she thought about it.

He saw more than she wanted him to see, she decided. His gaze was calm but intent, giving her all the time in the world to answer but getting answers of his own while he waited. She could see exactly what he was doing, but there was no escaping those calm, intelligent eyes.

'My chest,' she said at last, reluctantly.

'There's a bit of water in your lungs. We've X-rayed. It's nice clean ocean water and you're a healthy young woman. It shouldn't cause problems but we're giving you antibiotics in case, and you need to stay propped up on pillows and under observation until it clears. Your breathing's a bit ragged and it'll cause a bit of discomfort. We're starting you on diuretics—something to dry you out a bit. There'll be no long-term issues as long as you obey instructions.'

'My arms…'

'Harness,' he said ruefully. 'We try and pad 'em.'

'We?'

'New South Wales North Coast Flight-Aid.'

There was an echo—the way he said the name. Some time last night those words had been said—maybe even on the way up into the helicopter.

'New South Wales North Coast Flight-Aid, ma'am, at your service.'

Same voice. Same man?

'Were you the one who pulled me up?' she asked, astounded.

'I was,' he said, modestly. 'You were wet.'

'Wet?' She felt…disconcerted to say the least.

'Six years in med school,' he said proudly. 'Then four years of emergency medicine training, plus more training courses than you can imagine to get the rescue stuff right. Put it all together and I can definitely state that you were wet.' He took her wrist as he talked, feeling her pulse. Watching her intently. 'So, arms and chest are sore. Toes?'

'They're fine. Though I was a bit worried about them last night,' she admitted.

'You were very cold.' He turned his attention to the end of the bed, tugged up the coverlet from the bottom and exposed them. Her toes were painted pink, with silver stars. Her pre-bridal gift from one of her bridesmaids.

Not the bridesmaid she'd caught with Roger. One of the other five.

'Wiggle 'em,' Riley said, and she hauled her thoughts back to toes. She'd much rather think of toes than Roger. Or bridesmaids.

So she wiggled then and she admired them wiggling. Last night she'd decided sharks had taken them, and she hadn't much cared.

Today… 'Boy, am I pleased to see you guys again,' she confessed.

'And I bet they're pleased to see you. Don't take them night-time swimming again. Ever. Can I hear your chest?'

'Yes, Doctor,' she said, deciding submission was a good way

to go. She pushed herself up on her pillows—or she tried. Her body was amazingly heavy.

She got about six inches up and Riley was right by her, supporting her, adjusting the pillows behind her.

He felt…

Well, that was an inappropriate thing to think. He didn't feel anything. He was a doctor.

But, doctor or not, he was very male, and very close. And still gorgeous. He was…mid-thirties? Hard to be sure. He was a bit weathered. He hadn't spent his life behind a desk.

He wouldn't have, she decided, if he was a rescue doctor.

If it wasn't for this man she'd be very, very dead.

What do you say to a man who saved your life?

'I need to thank you,' she said in a small voice, but he finished what he had to do before he replied.

'Cough,' he ordered.

She coughed.

'And again? Good,' he said at last, and she repeated her thank you.

'My pleasure,' he said, and she expected him to head for the door but instead he went back to his first position. Perched on the backward chair. Seemingly ready to chat.

'Aren't you needed somewhere else?' she asked, starting to feel uneasy.

'I'm always needed,' he said, with a mock modesty that had her wanting to smile. 'Dr Indispensable.'

'So you save maidens all night and save everyone else during the day.'

'I'm not normally a duty doctor but we're having staffing issues. Plus I haven't finished saving this maiden yet. You want to tell me why Roger and Mum told us you were suiciding?'

'I wasn't.'

'I get the feeling you weren't. Or at least that you changed your mind.'

'I got caught in an undertow,' she snapped, and then winced. She sagged back onto her pillows, feeling heavy and tired and very, very stupid. 'I'm sorry. I accept it looks like suicide, but I just went for a swim.'

'After dark, on an unpatrolled beach.'

'It wasn't completely dark. I'd been in a plane for twenty-four hours. The sea looked gorgeous, even if it was dusk. There were people everywhere, having picnics, playing cricket, splashing around in the shallows. It was lovely. I'm a strong swimmer and I swam and swam. It felt great, and I guess I let my thoughts drift. Then I realised the current had changed and I couldn't get back.'

'You must be a strong swimmer,' he said, 'to stay afloat for eight hours.'

'Is that how long I was there?'

'At least. We pulled you up at four-thirty. The sea wasn't exactly calm. I figure you must badly want to live.'

'I do,' she said, and she met his gaze, unflinching. It suddenly seemed incredibly important that his man believe her. 'I want to live more than anything in the world. You see, I don't have to marry Roger.'

Fifteen minutes later Riley headed back to Intensive Care to check on Olive Matchens and he found himself smiling. It was a good story, told with courage and humour.

It seemed Pippa had been engaged for years to her childhood sweetheart. Her fiancé was the son of Daddy's partner, financial whiz, almost part of the family. Only boring, boring, boring. But what could she do? She'd told him she'd marry him when she'd been seventeen. He'd been twenty and gorgeous and she had been smitten to the eyeballs. Then he was lovely and patient while she'd done her own thing. She'd even broken off the engagement for a while, gone out with other guys, but all the time Roger was waiting in the wings, constantly telling her he loved her. He was a nice guy. Daddy and Mummy thought he was wonderful. There was no one else. She'd turned thirty. She'd really like a family. Her voice had faltered a little when she said that, but then she'd gone back to feisty. Why not marry him?

Reason? Two days before the wedding she'd found him in bed with a bridesmaid.

Bomb blast didn't begin to describe the fallout from cancelling the wedding, she'd told him. She'd figured the best thing to do was escape, leave for her honeymoon alone.

She'd arrived in Australia, she'd walked into the luxury honeymoon suite Roger had booked, in one of Australian's most beautiful hotels, she'd looked out at the sea, and she'd thought she had her whole honeymoon ahead of her—and she didn't have to marry Roger.

Riley grinned as he headed for Intensive Care. If there was one thing Riley loved it was a happy ending.

He thought of what would have happened if they hadn't found her. She was alive because of his service. She was a woman who'd been given a second chance because of the skills his team offered.

And she'd use it, he thought, feeling exultant. Right now she was exhausted. She lay in bed, her face wan from strain and shock, her auburn curls matted from the seawater, her body battered and sore, and still he saw pure spirit.

It felt fantastic. Helping people survive, the adrenalin rush of search and rescue, this was *his* happy ending. Solitude and work and the satisfaction of making a difference.

Solitude…

The morning's satisfaction faded a little as the nuances of the word hit home. The fact that his solitude was about to take a hit.

His daughter would be here on Friday. Lucy.

What to do with a daughter he hardly knew? Whose existence had been kept from him because he was deemed inconsequential—not important in the moneyed world Lucy must have been raised in.

There was money in the background of the woman he'd just treated, he thought. He could hear it in Pippa's voice. English class and old money. The combination brought back enough memories to make him shudder.

But the way the woman he'd just left spoke shouldn't make him judge her. And why was he thinking of Pippa? He now needed to focus on Lucy.

His daughter.

She was probably just coming for a fleeting visit, he decided. Her email had been curt to say the least. Flight details—arrival at Sydney airport Friday morning. An almost flippant line at the end—'If it's a bother don't worry, I'll manage.'

If it's a bother… To have a daughter.

Family.

He didn't do family. He never had.

He didn't know how.

But he could give her a place to stay. That had to be a start. He lived in a huge old house right by the hospital. Once upon a time the house had been nurses' quarters, but nurses no longer lived on site. Big and rambling and right by the sea, it was comfortable and close and why would he want to live anywhere else?

Last year the hospital had offered to sell it to him. For a while he'd thought about it—but owning a house… That meant putting down roots and the idea made him nervous. He was fine as he was.

He could see the sea when he woke up. He had a job he loved, surf at his back door, a hospital housekeeper making sure the rest of the house didn't fall apart… He had the perfect life.

His daughter wasn't part of it. She was an eighteen-year-old he'd never met—a kid on an adventure to Australia, meeting a father she didn't know. Had she always known who he was? Why had she searched for him? Had she been defying Mummy?

And at the thought of her mother he felt anger almost overwhelm him. To not tell him that they'd had a child…

Anger was not useful. Put it aside, he told himself. He'd meet Lucy and see if she wanted him to be a part of her life, no matter how tiny.

She'd probably only stay a day or two. That thought made him feel more empty than before he'd known of her existence. It was like a tiny piece of family was being offered, but he already knew it'd be snatched away again.

Story of his life.

He shook his head, managed a mocking smile and shook off his dumb self-pity. Olive Matchens was waiting. Work was waiting.

He'd saved Phillippa Penelope Fotheringham. Pippa.

He did have the perfect, solitary life.

Once Riley left, an efficient little nurse called Jancey swept into Pippa's cubicle to tidy up the edges. Someone was collecting her toiletries from the hotel, she told Pippa, and she bounced off to set up a call to Pippa's mother. 'Dr Chase's instructions. He says if you don't talk to her she'll be on a plane before you know it.'

It was sensible advice. Jancey put the call through and Pippa managed to talk to her. Trying not to cough.

'I'm fine, Mum. I have a bit of water on my chest—that's why I sound breathless—but, honestly, there's nothing wrong with me apart from feeling stupid. The hospital's excellent. I'm only here for observation. I imagine I'll be out of here tomorrow.'

And then the hardest bit.

'No, I was not trying to kill myself. You need to believe that because it's true. I was just stupid. I was distracted and I was tired. I went swimming at dusk because the water looked lovely. I was caught in the undertow and swept out. That's all. I would never…'

Then…

'No, I don't wish to talk to Roger. I understand he's sorry, but there's nothing I can do about that. Tell him it's over, final, there's no way we're getting married. If Roger comes I won't see him. I'm sorry, Mum, but I need to go to sleep now. I'll ring you back tomorrow. You. Not Roger.'

Done. Jancey took back the phone and smiled down at her, sensing she'd just done something momentous. Pippa smiled back at the cheery little nurse and suddenly Jancey offered her a high-five. 'You go, girl,' she said, and grinned.

She managed a wobbly smile, high-fived in return and slipped back onto her pillows feeling...fantastic.

She slept again, and the nightmare of last night was replaced by Jancey's high-five—and by the smile of Dr Riley Chase.

Two lovely people in her bright new world.

Olive seemed stable. Riley was well overdue for a sleep but problems were everywhere.

School holidays. Accidents. Flu. It seemed half the hospital staff was on leave or ill. And now they had a kid in labour. Amy. Sixteen years old. Alone.

She should not be here.

How could they send her away?'

'We need someone to stay with Amy,' Riley decreed. 'She's terrified.'

'I know.' Coral, the hospital's nurse-administrator, was sounding harassed. 'But we can't special her. I have no midwives on duty. Rachel's on leave and I've just sent Maryanne home with a temp of thirty-nine. I know she shouldn't be alone but it was her choice to come here. She knows she should be in Sydney. Meanwhile, I'm doing the best I can. I've put her in with your patient, Pippa.'

Coral sounded as weary as Riley felt. 'That's why I could free up a nurse for Olive,' she said. 'I'm juggling too many balls here, Riley, so cut me some slack. Putting Amy in the labour ward now will scare her and she'll be alone most of the time. Putting her in with mums who already have their babies isn't going to work either. The obs cubicle is close to the nurses' station, and I'm hoping your lady will be nice to her. I've put them both on fifteen-minute obs and that's the best I can do. Meanwhile, we have Troy Haddon in Emergency—he's been playing with those Styrofoam balls you put in beanbags. He and his mate were squirting them out their noses to see who could make them go furthest, and one's gone up instead of out. Can you deal with it?'

'Sure,' Riley said, resigned. So much for sleep.

* * *

Pippa woke and someone was sobbing in the next bed. Really sobbing. Fear, loneliness and hopelessness were wrapped in the one heart-rending sound.

She turned, cautiously, to see. Right now caution seemed the way to go. The world still seemed vaguely dangerous.

When she'd gone to sleep the bed next to her had been empty. Now she had a neighbour.

The girl was young. Very young. Sixteen, maybe? She was so dark her eyes practically disappeared in her face. Her face was swollen; desperate. Terrified.

Last night's drama disappeared. Pippa was out of bed in an instant.

'Hey.' She touched the girl on the hand, and then on the face as she didn't react. 'What's wrong? Can I call the nurse for you?'

The girl turned to her with a look of such despair that Pippa's heart twisted.

'It hurts,' the girl whispered. 'Oh, it hurts. I want to go home.' She sobbed and rolled onto her back.

She was very pregnant.

Very pregnant.

As Pippa watched she saw the girl's belly tighten in a contraction. Instinctively she took the girl's hand and held, hard. The girl moaned, a long, low moan that contained despair as well as pain, and she clutched Pippa's hand like it was a lifeline.

Pippa hit the bell. This kid needed help. A midwife. A support team. She looked more closely at the girl's tear-drenched face and thought she was sixteen, seventeen at most.

She needed her mum.

The nurses' station seemed deserted. Pippa, however, knew the drill.

Hospital bells were designed to only ring once, and light a signal at the nurses' station, so pushing it again would achieve nothing. Unless…

She checked behind the bed, found the master switch, flicked it off and on again—and pushed the bell again.

Another satisfactory peal.

And another.

Three minutes later someone finally appeared. Dr Riley Chase. Looking harassed.

'She needs help,' Pippa said before Riley could get a word in, and Riley looked at the kid in the bed and looked at Pippa. Assessing them both before answering.

'You should be in bed.'

'She needs a midwife,' Pippa snapped. 'A support person. She shouldn't be alone.'

'I know.' He raked long fingers though his already rumpled hair, took a deep breath and focused. He glanced down the corridor as if he was hoping someone else would appear.

No one did.

He stepped into the cubicle.

Once again, as soon as he entered, she had the impression that he had all the time in the world. He'd crossed over from the outside world, and now he was totally in this one—only this time he was focused solely on the girl in labour.

The contraction was over. The girl was burrowed into the pillows, whimpering.

'Hey, Amy, I'm so sorry we've had to leave you alone,' he told her, touching her tear-drenched face with gentle fingers. 'It's hard to do this and it's even harder to do it alone. I did warn you. This is why I wanted you to stay in Sydney. But now you're here, we just have to get through it. And we will.'

Pippa backed away as he took both Amy's hands in his and held. It was like he was imparting strength—and Pippa remembered how he'd felt holding her last night and thought there was no one she'd rather have hold her. The guy exuded strength.

But maybe strength was the wrong word. Trust? More. It was a combination so powerful that she wasn't the least bit surprised that Amy stopped whimpering and met his gaze directly. Amy trusted him, she thought. For a teenager in such trouble…

'I want to go home,' Amy whimpered.

'I know you do. If I were you, I'd be on the first bus out of here,' Riley told her. 'But there's the little problem of your baby. He wants out.'

'It hurts. I want my mum.'

'I wish your mum could be here,' he said.

'Mum thought it was stupid to come.'

'So she did.' Riley's face set a little and Pippa guessed there'd been conflict. 'So now you're doing this on your own. But you can do it, Amy.'

'I can't.'

'Can I check and see how your baby's doing?'

Pippa didn't need prompting to leave them to it. She scooted back to her bed and Riley gave her a smile of thanks as he hauled the dividing curtain closed.

'You've been getting to know your neighbour,' he said to Amy. 'Have you two been introduced?'

Pippa was back in bed with the covers up, a curtain between them.

'No,' Amy whispered.

'Pippa, your neighbour is Amy. Amy, your neighbour is Pippa. Pippa went for a swim after dark last night and came close to being shark meat.'

'Why'd you go for a swim at dark?' Despite her pain, Amy's attention was caught—maybe that's what Riley intended.

'I was getting over guy problems,' Pippa confessed. She was speaking to a closed curtain, and it didn't seem to matter what she admitted now. And she might be able to help, she thought. If admitting stupidity could keep Amy's attention from fear, from loneliness, from pain, then pride was a small price to pay.

'You got guy problems?' Amy's voice was a bit muffled.

'I was about to be married. I caught him sleeping with one of my bridesmaids.'

'Yikes.' Amy was having a reasonable break from contractions now, settling as the pain eased and she wasn't alone any more. 'You clobber him?'

'I should have,' Pippa said. 'Instead I went swimming, got caught in the undertow and got saved by Dr Chase.'

'That's me,' Riley said modestly. 'Saving maidens is what I do. Amy, you're doing really well. You're almost four centimetres dilated, which means the baby's really pushing. I can give you something for the pain if you like...'

'I don't want injections.' It was a terrified gasp.

'Then you need to practise the breathing we taught you. Can you—?'

But he couldn't finish. Jancey's head appeared round the door, looking close to panic.

'Hubert Trotter's just come in,' she said. 'He's almost chopped his big toe off with an axe and he's bleeding like a stuck pig. Riley, you need to come.'

'Give me strength,' Riley said, and rose. 'Can you stay with Amy?'

'Dotty Simond's asthma...' she said.

Riley closed his eyes. The gesture was fleeting, though, and when he opened them again he looked calm and in control and like nothing was bothering him at all.

'Amy, I'll be back as soon as I can,' he said, but Amy was clutching his hand like a lifeline.

'No. Please.'

'Pippa's in the next bed,' he started. 'You're not by yourself.'

But suddenly Pippa wasn't in the next bed. Enough. She was out of bed, pushing the curtains apart and meeting Riley's gaze full on.

'Amy needs a midwife.'

'I know she does,' Riley said. 'We're short-staffed. There isn't one.'

'Then someone else.'

'Believe me, if I could then I'd find someone. I'd stay here myself. I can't.'

She believed him. She thought, fast.

This guy had saved her life. This hospital had been here for her. And more... Amy was a child.

'Then use me,' she said.

'You...'

'I know there's still water on my lungs,' she said. 'And I know I need to stay here until it clears. But my breathing's okay. I'm here for observation more than care, and if you can find me something more respectable than this appalling hospital gown, I'll sit by Amy until she needs to push. Then I'll call you.'

He looked at her like she'd grown two heads. 'There's no need—'

'Yes, there is,' Jancey said, looking panicked. 'Hubert needs help *now*.'

'We can't ask—'

'Then don't ask,' Pippa said. 'And don't worry. You can go back to your toes and asthma. I'll call for help when I need it, either for myself or for Amy. And I do know enough to call. I may be a twit when it comes to night swimming, but in my other life I'm a qualified nurse. Good basic qualifications, plus theatre training, plus intensive care, and guess what? Midwifery. You want to phone my old hospital and check?'

She grabbed the clipboard and pen Jancey was carrying and wrote the name of her hospital and her boss's name. 'Hospitals work round the clock. Checking my references is easy. Ring them fast, or trust me to take care of Amy while you two save the world. Or at least Hubert's toe. Off you go, and Amy and I will get on with delivering Amy's baby. We can do this, Amy. You and me...women are awesome. Together there's nothing we can't do.'

'You want me to ring and check she's who she says she is?' Jancey asked, dubious. He and Jancey needed to head in different directions, fast. Neither of them liked leaving Pippa and Amy together.

'When you've got time.'

'I don't have time,' Jancey said. 'Do we trust her?'

'She's a warm body and she's offered,' Riley said. 'Do we have a choice?'

'Hey!' They were about to head around the bend in the

corridor but Pippa's voice made them turn. She'd stepped out the door to call after them.

She looked…

Amazing, Riley thought, and, stressed or not, he almost smiled. She had brilliant red curls that hadn't seen a hairbrush since her big swim. She was slight—really slight—barely tall enough to reach his chin. Her pale skin had been made more pale by the night's horror. Her green eyes had been made even larger.

From the neck up she was eye-catchingly lovely. But from the neck down…

Her hospital gown was flopping loosely around her. She was clutching it behind. She had nothing else on.

'The deal is clothes,' she said with asperity. 'Bleeding to death takes precedence but next is my dignity. I need at least another gown so I can have one on backwards, one on forwards.'

Riley chuckled. It was the first time for twelve hours he'd felt like laughing and it felt great.

'Can you fix it?' he asked Jancey.

'Mrs Rogers in Surgical left her pink fluffy dressing gown behind when she went home this morning,' Jancey said, smiling herself. 'I don't think she'd mind…'

'Does it have buttons?' Pippa demanded.

'Yes,' Jancey said. 'And a bow at the neck. The bow glitters.'

'That'll cheer us up,' Pippa said. 'And heaven knows Amy and I both need it.'

Assisting at a birth settled her as nothing else could.

Amy needed someone she knew, a partner, a mother, a friend, but there seemed to be no one. Her labour was progressing slowly, and left to herself she would have given in to terror.

What sort of hospital was this that provided no support?

To be fair, though, Pippa decided as the afternoon wore on, most hospitals checked labouring mothers only every fifteen minutes or so, making sure things were progressing smoothly.

The mother's support person was supposed to provide company.

'So where's your family?' she asked. They were listening to music—some of Amy's favourites. Pippa had needed to do some seriously fast organisation there.

'Home,' Amy said unhelpfully. 'They made me come.'

'Who made you come?'

'Doc Riley. There's not a doctor at Dry Gum Creek, and they don't have babies there if Doc Riley can help it. Mostly the mums come here but Doc Riley said I needed…young mum stuff. So they took me to Sydney Central, only it was really scary. And lonely. I stayed a week and I'd had enough. There was no way I could get home but I knew Doc Riley was here so I got the bus. But the pains started just as I reached here. And I'm not going back to Sydney Central.'

That explained why Amy was in a relatively small hospital with seemingly not much obstetric support on hand, Pippa thought, deciding to be a little less judgmental about Amy being on her own.

'Why didn't your mum come with you?'

'Mum says it's stupid to come to hospital, but she didn't tell me it hurt like this. If you hadn't been here…' Another contraction hit and she clung to Pippa with a grip like a vice.

'I'm here,' Pippa told her as Amy rode out the contraction. 'Hold as tight as you need. Yesterday I was staring death in the face. It's kind of nice to be staring at birth.'

Riley was in the final stages of stitching Hubert Trotter's toe when Jancey stuck her head round the partition.

'She's good,' she said.

'Who's good?'

'Our night swimmer. She's been up to the kids' ward in her gorgeous silver and pink dressing gown, and she did the best plea you ever heard. Told them all about Amy having a baby alone. Talk about pathos. She's borrowed Lacey Sutherland's spare MP3 player. She conned one of the mums into going home to get speakers. She's hooked up the internet in the nurses' station and she's downloaded stuff so she has Amy's favourite music playing right now. She also rang the local poster shop. I don't know what she promised them but the guys were here in minutes. Amy's now surrounded by posters of her favourite telly stars. Oh, and one of the mums donated a giraffe, almost as tall as Amy. Pippa has Amy so bemused she's almost forgotten she's in labour.'

'She's a patient herself,' Riley said, stunned.

'Try telling her that. Oh, and I managed to ring the number she gave us in England. I had a minute and I couldn't help myself—she had me fascinated. Her boss says send her back, *now*. Seems your Pippa left to get married two weeks ago and they miss her. Talk about glowing references. Can we keep her?'

'I'm not sure how we can.'

'Just don't give her clothes,' Jancey said, grinning. 'I'm off duty now. We're two nurses short for night shift but I've already stretched my shift to twelve hours. How long have you stretched yours?'

'Don't ask,' Riley said. 'Okay, Hubert, you're done. Pharmacy will give you something for the pain. Keep it dry, come back in tomorrow and I'll dress it again.'

'You'll be in tomorrow?' Hubert asked as Jancey disappeared.

'Maybe.'

'You're supposed to be the flying doc, not the base doc.'

'Yeah,' Riley said. 'Can you ring the union and let them know?'

'Riley?'

He sighed and straightened. 'That'd be me.'

'Amy's moving into second stage.' It was Mary, the night nurse who'd just started her shift. 'Pippa says you need to come straight away.'

She'd been having doubts about the ability of this small hospital to prepare adequately for a teenage birth, but the transition from the cubicle near the nurses' station to the labour ward was seamless.

A nurse and an orderly pushed Amy's bed into a labour room that was homey and comforting, but still had everything Pippa was accustomed to seeing. Riley was already waiting.

He smiled down at Amy, and Pippa was starting to know that smile. It said nothing was interfering with what he was doing right now, and his attention was all on Amy.

He hardly acknowledged her. She'd walked beside Amy's bed simply because Amy had still been clutching her hand. The moment Amy no longer needed her she should back away.

She was in a fully equipped labour ward. A doctor, a nurse, an orderly. She could leave now but Amy was still clinging. Her fear was palpable and at an unobtrusive signal from Riley it was the nurse and the orderly who slipped away.

What was going on?

'Hey, Ames, they tell me your baby's really close.' Riley took Amy's free hand—and Pippa thought if she was Amy she'd feel better right now.

But maybe that wasn't sensible. Maybe that was a dose of hormones caused by Riley's great smile.

'Don't tell me you're an obstetrician, too,' she said, and then she decided her voice sounded a bit sharp. That was uncalled for. She was, however, seriously thrown. Did this guy ever sleep? Hanging from ropes, rescuing stupid tourists in the middle of the night, sewing on toes. Delivering babies. But…

'Amy knows I'm not an obstetrician,' Riley said, still talking to Amy. 'We have an obstetrician on standby. Dr Louise will be here in a heartbeat if we need her, but Amy has asked if I can deliver her baby.' He glanced at Pippa then, and his smile finally encompassed her. 'Amy has need of friends. It seems she's found you as well as me. I know it's unfair but are you okay to stay with us for a bit longer?'

'Of course I can. If I can sit down.'

His smile was a reward all on its own. There was also relief behind his smile, and she thought he'd be feeling the responsibility of being Amy's sole care person. Plus doctor.

'Okay, then, Amy,' he said, taking her hand just as a contraction started. 'You have me, you have Pippa and you have you. Pippa has her chair. We have our crib all ready. All we need now is one baby to make our team complete. So now you push. Pippa's your cheerleader and I'll stand around and catch.'

Then, as the next contraction swelled to its full power, he moved straight back into doctor mode. He was a friend on the surface but underneath he was pure doctor, Pippa thought as she coached Amy with her breathing.

And he was some doctor.

Amy was little more than a child herself. Her pelvis seemed barely mature—if Pippa had to guess she'd have said the girl looked like she'd been badly malnourished. If this was Pippa's hospital back in the UK, Amy could well have been advised to have had her baby by Caesarean section.

'C-section's never been option,' Riley told her in an undertone as Amy gasped between contractions. How had he guessed what she was thinking? 'Neither is it going to be. Not if I can help it.'

'Why?'

'Amy comes from one of the most barren places in the country,' he told her. 'I persuaded her—against her mother's wishes—to come to the city this time. Next time she may well be on her own in the middle of nowhere. You want to add scar tissue to that mix?'

Amy was pushing away the gas and he took her hand again. 'Hey, Amy, you're brilliant, you're getting so much closer. Let Pippa hold the gas so you can try again. Three deep breaths, here we go. Up the hill, up, up, up, push for all you're worth, yes, fantastic, breathe out, down the other side. You've stretched a little more, a little more. Half a dozen more of those and I reckon this baby will be here.'

It wasn't quite half a dozen. Amy sobbed and swore and gripped and pushed and screamed...

Pippa held on, encouraging her any way she could, and so did Riley. Two coaches, two lifelines for this slip of a kid with only them between herself and terror.

But finally she did it. Pippa was already emotional, and when finally Amy's tiny baby girl arrived into the outside world, as Pippa held Amy up so she could see her daughter's first breath, as Riley held her to show Amy she was perfect, Pippa discovered she was weeping.

Riley slipped the baby onto Amy's breast and Amy cradled her as if she was the most miraculous thing she'd ever seen. As, of course, she was.

The baby nuzzled, instinctively searching. Pippa guided her a little, helping just enough but not enough to intrude. The baby found what she was looking for and Amy looked down in incredulous wonder.

'I'm feeding her. I've had a baby.'

'You have a daughter,' Riley said, smiling and smiling, and Pippa glanced up at him and was astonished to see his eyes weren't exactly dry either.

Surely a rough Aussie search and rescue doctor…

Just concentrate on your own eyes, she told herself, and sniffed.

'She's beautiful,' she said, trying to keep her voice steady. She touched the baby's damp little head with wonder. No matter how many births she'd seen, this never stopped being a miracle. 'Have you thought about what you might call her?'

And Amy looked up at her as if she was a bit simple—as indeed she felt. Amy had just performed the most amazing, complex, difficult feat a human could ever perform—and Pippa had simply held her hand.

'I'm calling her Riley, of course,' Amy whispered, and smiled and smiled. 'Boy or girl, I decided it months ago. And I'm keeping her,' she said, a touch defiantly.

Riley smiled. 'Who's arguing? It'd take a team stronger than us to get Baby Riley away from her mum right now.'

'Have you been thinking of adoption?' Pippa said, because if indeed it was on the table it needed to be raised.

'Mum said I had to,' Amy said simply. 'But Doc Riley said it was up to me. He'll support me. Won't you, Doc?'

'It will be hard,' Riley said, gravely now. 'You know that.'

'I know,' Amy said. 'But me and this kid…after this, I can do anything. She's going to have all the stuff I didn't. She'll go to school and everything.' She peeped a smile up at Riley, her courage and strength returning in waves with the adrenalin of post-birth wonder. 'Maybe she'll even be a doc like you.'

'Why not?' Riley said. 'If that's what you both want, we'll make sure there are people who'll help you every step of the way.' He hesitated. 'But, Amy, Riley's best chance of getting that is if you don't have six more babies in the next six years.'

'You don't need to tell me that,' Amy said tartly, and she kissed her baby's head. 'No fear. I had this one because I was stupid. Me and her…we're not going to be stupid, ever again.'

Amy was wheeled away, up to Maternity to be in a ward with two other young mums. 'Because that's where you'll learn the most,' Riley told her. Pippa promised to visit her later, but Amy was too intent on her new little Riley to listen.

Pippa's legs were sagging. She sat, suddenly, and felt extraordinarily relieved the chair was under her. Even her chair felt wobbly.

Riley was beside her in an instant, hitting the buzzer. 'We need a trolley,' he told Mary when she appeared. 'Fast, Mary, or I'll have to pick her up and carry her.'

'In your dreams,' Pippa managed, with a pathetic attempt at dignity. 'No one carries me.'

'I believe I already have.'

'With the help of a helicopter.' She was trying to sound cheeky but she wasn't succeeding. In truth, the room was spinning.

'Warren's the only orderly,' Mary said. 'The trolley will be ten minutes. You want me to fetch a wheelchair?'

'It's okay,' Pippa said. 'I'll be right in a minute.'

'You'll be back in bed in a minute.' And to her astonishment Riley's eyes were gleaming with laughter and with challenge. 'Let's do without Warren or wheelchairs,' he said. 'Fancy inferring I'm inferior to our helicopter.' And before she could realise what he intended, he lifted her high into his arms.

She squeaked.

Mary giggled.

'He does weights,' Mary told Pippa, bemused. 'What you said…that's a red rag to a bull.'

'He's crazy.'

'He is at that,' Mary said, chuckling and holding the door wide to let Riley pass. 'You try getting workers' compensation after this, Doc Riley.'

'Workers' comp is for wimps.' Riley had her secure, solid against his chest, striding briskly along the corridor, past rooms full of patients and visitors, carrying her as if she was a featherweight and not a grown woman in trouble.

Trouble was right. If a doctor did this in her training hospital… To a nurse…

Worse. She was a patient. This was totally unprofessional.

She needed to struggle but she didn't have the energy. Or the will.

Trouble?

She was feeling like she really was in trouble. Like she wasn't exactly sure what was going on. He was making her feel…

'I should never have allowed you to help,' he muttered as he strode, his laughter giving way to concern. Maybe he was feeling just how weak she was.

She wasn't really this weak, she thought. Or maybe she was.

She thought about it, or she sort of thought about it. The feel of his arms holding her…the solid muscles of his chest…the sensation of being held… It was stopping lots of thoughts—and starting others that were entirely inappropriate.

This was why they'd invented trolleys, she thought, to stop nurses…to stop patients…to stop *her* being carried by someone like Riley. It was so inappropriate on so many levels. It made her feel…

'You're exhausted,' he said. 'It was totally unprofessional of me to allow you to help.'

That shook her out of the very inappropriate route her thoughts were taking. Out of her exhaustion. Almost out of her disorientation.

'To allow Amy to have a support person?' she demanded, forcing her voice to be firm. 'What does that have to do with lack of professionalism?'

'You weren't her support person.'

'I was. If you hadn't allowed me to be, I would have discharged myself and come right back. Amy would have said "Yes, please," and it would have been exactly the same except that you wouldn't be carrying me back to bed.'

'In your extraordinary bathrobe,' he finished, and the laughter had returned. It felt good, she decided. To make this man laugh…

And there her thoughts went again, off on a weird and crazy tangent. She was totally disoriented by the feel of his body against hers. He turned into the next corridor, and the turning made her feel a bit dizzy and she clutched.

He swore. 'Of all the stupid…'

'It's not stupid,' she managed, steadying again. 'It's wonderful. Last night you saved my life. This afternoon we've helped Amy have her baby. You've done a fantastic twenty-four hours' work, Dr Chase. Did I tell you I think you're wonderful?'

Mary bobbed up beside them, still chuckling.

'Don't tell him that,' she begged. 'Everyone does. It gives him the biggest head. Riley, really, are you about to hurt your back?'

'Nope,' Riley said. 'Didn't you hear what our patient said? I'm wonderful. Practically Superman. You can't hurt your back if you're Superman.'

'Superman or not, Coral says to tell you that you can't be a doctor in this hospital unless you get some sleep,' Mary retorted. 'Coral said you're to leave and go to bed. Now.'

'Immediately?'

'Put Pippa down first, but leave the tucking in to me,' Mary ordered, as they reached Pippa's bed. 'Off you go, Dr Superman. Sweet dreams.'

'I need to say thank you,' Pippa managed.

'So say thank you,' Mary said, sounding severe. 'Fast.'

Riley set Pippa down. He straightened and she felt a queer jolt of loss. To be held and then released…

She was more exhausted than she'd thought. She wasn't making sense, even to herself.

Riley was smiling down at her, with that amazing, heart-stopping smile. A lifesaver of a smile. 'It's us who should thank you,' he said. 'You were great.'

Her pillows were wonderful. Life was wonderful.

Riley was wonderful.

'You are Superman,' she whispered. 'You've saved my life—in more ways than one.'

'It's what I do,' Riley said. 'Superheroes R Us. Come on, Mary, let's see if we can find some tall buildings to leap.'

'You can leap all the tall buildings you want, as long as you do it off duty,' Mary said tartly.

'Goodnight, then, Pippa,' Riley said. 'We both know what to do.'

Sleep. It sounded good.

She slept, smiling.

She slept, thinking of Riley Chase.

A baby called Riley. A little girl…

Eighteen years ago his daughter had been born and he hadn't known. Marguerite had chosen to have her alone, or with her formidable parents, rather than let him into her life.

He'd thought he'd loved her. He'd thought she'd loved him.

He had no idea what love was. What family was.

He'd watched Pippa with Amy, and felt the strength between

them, the instant bonding of two strong women. That was what he didn't get. Didn't trust. Bonding.

Family.

His daughter was coming. It was doing his head in; delivering Amy's baby, thinking back to how it could have been if he'd been deemed worth being a partner, a father. Family.

Yeah, like that was going to happen. He needed to sleep. Get his head under control.

Or surf. Better. No matter how tired he was, surf helped.

He strode out of the hospital, headed for the beach.

The thought of Pippa stayed with him. Pippa holding a baby girl.

Too much emotion. His head felt like it might implode.

When all else failed, surf.

CHAPTER THREE

SHE slept all night.

She was still right by the nurses' station. It was probably noisy, but there was no noise capable of stirring her.

When she woke, even the hospital breakfast tasted good. She must have been very close to the edge, she decided as she tucked into her leathery egg. She must have been very close indeed, if she was now appreciating hospital food.

Just the concept of food felt great. There'd be lunch in a few hours' time, she thought with a thrill of anticipation. Maybe there'd be a snack in between. Life stretched out before her, resplendent in its possibilities. She lay back on her pillows and thought: This is day two of my honeymoon, what's on today?

At around nine Jancey bounced in, accompanying an intern, and she was aware of a stab of disappointment. The young doctor was efficient, caring, thorough, all the things he needed to be—but he wasn't Riley.

'Dr Chase isn't usually in the wards,' Jancey told her as the intern moved off to sign her discharge papers. Pippa hadn't asked about Riley, but somehow Jancey sensed Pippa wanted to know. 'He's in charge of Search and Rescue, and he does clinics for our remote communities. That's enough to keep any doctor busy.'

'This is the base for Search and Rescue?'

'Yep. We have two crews, two planes and one chopper. There's some coastal work—stuff like rescuing you—but most of our work is clinics and patient retrieval from Outback settlements. It keeps us busy. It keeps Riley very busy.'

'So I won't see him again.'

'Probably not,' Jancey said, giving her a thoughtful glance. 'I know; it seems a shame. He's a bit hot, our Dr Riley.'

'That's not what I meant.'

'Of course it is,' Jancey retorted, grinning. 'I'm a happily married woman but it's still what I think. It's what every hot-blooded woman in this hospital thinks. He walks alone, though, our Dr Chase.'

'Like the Phantom?' Pippa queried, a bit nonplussed.

'In the comics?' Jancey smiled and nodded. 'Yeah, though doesn't Phantom have generations of Dianas, providing generations of little phantoms? As far as we know there's not a Diana in sight. Coral, our nurse-administrator, reckons he was crossed in love. Whoops,' she said as the baby-faced intern harrumphed with irritation from the corridor. 'I know, talking about Dr Chase's love life with patients is totally unprofessional but what's life without a bit of spice? And who's going to sack me with our staff shortage? Okay, I gotta go and minister to the sick, hold the hand of the learning. Will you be okay?'

'Yes.' How else was a woman to respond?

'Are you staying in town for a while?'

'The hotel's paid for until Sunday.'

'Then soak it up,' Jancey said. 'Sleep, spas, maybe a massage. But be careful. Our Dr Chase will be very annoyed if he has to rescue you again.'

'He won't do that,' Pippa assured her. 'It's taken a lot of trouble to finally be on my own. I'm on my lonesome honeymoon and it feels fantastic. I'm not about to need anyone.'

Some wonderful person had fetched her luggage from the hotel. Pippa dressed and said goodbye to the ward staff. Jancey offered to accompany her to the taxi rank, but first Pippa needed to see Amy.

Amy was in a ward with two other young mums, all getting

to know their babies. A lactation consultant was working with her, and there were rumours that Riley Junior was about to have her first bath.

'You were fab,' Amy told her as she hugged her goodbye. 'You and Doc Riley. I wish I could have called her Pippa, too. Hey, maybe I can. Riley Pippa.'

'Don't get too carried away,' Pippa said, grinning. 'You're making friends all over the place. By the time you leave here, this young lady might have twelve names.'

'I won't be here long. I don't like being in hospital,' Amy confessed.

'You're not planning to run away?'

'I won't do that. I've promised Doc Riley I'll be sensible.'

'You and me both,' Pippa said.

It was great that she'd been able to help yesterday, she decided as she left Amy. It had made the terrors of the night before recede. It had made Roger's betrayal fade almost to insignificance.

Birth beat death any day, she decided—and it also beat marriage. Now to have her honeymoon…

Half an hour later the porter ushered her into her hotel suite and finally Pippa was alone.

Her honeymoon hotel was truly, madly scrumptious. It had been years since Pippa had spent any time in her parents' world and she'd almost forgotten what it was like. Or maybe hotels hadn't been this luxurious back then.

The bed was the size of a small swimming pool. How many pillows could a girl use? There must be a dozen, and walking forward she saw a 'pillow menu'. An invitation to add more.

Thick white carpet enveloped her toes. Two settees, gold brocade with feather cushions, looked squishy and fabulous. The television set looked more like a movie screen.

Two sets of French windows opened to a balcony that overlooked the sea. Below the balcony was a horizon pool, stretching to the beach beyond.

It was magnificent—but Pippa wasn't exactly into horizon pools. Or pillow menus.

She gazed around her, and the familiar feeling of distaste surfaced. More than distaste. Loneliness?

That's what these sorts of surroundings said to her.

She was an only child of wealthy parents. She'd been packed off to boarding school when she was six, but during vacations her parents had done 'the right thing'. Sort of.

They'd taken her to exotic locations and stayed in hotels like this. Her parents had booked her a separate room, not close enough to bother them. They had employed hotel babysitters from the time they arrived to the time they left.

As she got older she pleaded to be left at home. There she least she knew the staff—and, of course, there was Roger.

Roger was the only friend who was permitted to visit when her parents weren't around. He was the only kid who wasn't intimidated by her parents' wealth and ostentation. More than that, he'd been…kind. Three years older than she was, she'd thought he was her best friend.

But now…

She gazed at her surroundings—at a hotel room Roger had chosen—and once again she felt tired. Tired to the bone.

The intern had told her to take it easy. 'You've had a shock. Let your body sleep it off.'

Good advice. She looked down at her half-acre of bed and thought she'd come to the right place to sleep.

And to think?

She wandered out to the balcony and stared out to sea. This was why she'd swum so late on Sunday night—from here the beach practically called to her. A lone surfer, far out, was catching waves with skill.

She'd love to do that.

On the far side of the headland she could see the cream brick building of the North Coast Health Services Hospital. A busy, bustling hospital, perpetually understaffed. Perpetually doing good.

She'd love to do that, too.

And with that, the sudden thought—could she?

What was she thinking? Nursing? *Here?*

She was here on her honeymoon, not to find a job. But the thought was suddenly there and it wouldn't go away.

Nursing. Here.

Because of Riley?

No. That was stupid. Really stupid.

'You've been unengaged for less than a week,' she told herself. 'You nearly died. You've had a horrid experience and it's rattled you. Yes, you don't like fancy hotels but get over it. And don't think past tomorrow.'

But…to work in a hospital where she was desperately needed, to be part of a small team rather than one moveable staff member in a big, impersonal city hospital. To make a difference…

Would it be running away?

No. She'd run away to go nursing, deciding it was her career despite her family's appalled objections. Somehow this no longer seemed like running away.

Maybe it'd be finding her own place. Her own home.

'They won't take me till my lungs clear,' she said out loud, and surprised herself by where her thoughts were taking her.

Could she?

She needed to sleep. She needed to gain a bit of perspective. She'd been in the hospital for little more than a day: how could she possibly make a decision yet?

But she already had. Meanwhile… She eyed the ostentatious bed and managed a smile. 'Suffer,' she told herself. 'Unpack one of your gorgeous honeymoon nightgowns and hit that bed.'

Sensible advice. She was a sensible woman.

She did not do things on a whim.

Or not until tomorrow.

She hung a gold-plated 'Do Not Disturb' sign on her door and fell into bed. To her amazement she was asleep before…well, before she'd even had time to feel amazed.

She dreamed. Not nightmares, though.

Sensible or not, she dreamed of Riley.

* * *

He couldn't get her out of his head. Pippa.

Tuesday. Three days till his daughter came.

When he wasn't thinking about Pippa he was thinking about Lucy and the combination was enough to have him wide awake before dawn, staring sightlessly at the ceiling, trying not to think of anything and failing on both counts.

Tuesday. He and Harry had a short run this afternoon, collecting two patients and bringing them back for minor surgery tomorrow. He was due to take a remote clinic on Thursday at the settlement where Amy lived. If she was well enough they might be able to take her home. The rest of the week was quiet—except for emergencies.

He should think of Lucy's arrival. Plan. Plan what? It was enough to drive him crazy.

And on top of that…

Pippa.

He never should have carried her.

It had seemed right. No, he never carried patients unless in dire emergencies—he wasn't stupid—but with Pippa… To wait for a trolley when she was clearly dizzy, when she was wearing that ridiculous bathrobe, when she was clearly in trouble…

How many patients made him feel like Pippa did?

Maybe it was the voice, he thought harshly. Upper-crust English. Maybe that was his Achilles' heel.

Only it wasn't the voice.

He lay back on his pillows, allowing himself a moment's indulgence, letting himself remember the feel of the woman in the fluffy pink bathrobe.

A woman who smiled at Amy, who coached her, who cared. A woman who pushed herself past exhaustion because a sixteen-year-old kid needed her. Her skill had stunned him—she had been totally on Amy's side; she was a midwife any woman would love to have at a birth.

But he also saw her as…a drowning bride at the end of a rope over a dark ocean.

The vision wouldn't go away.

Phillippa Penelope Fotheringham.

Pippa.

Phillippa, he corrected himself harshly. English. Probably wealthy.

She was a nurse. Why would he think she was wealthy?

There was something about her…some intangible thing…the Roger story?

What did it have to do with him? Forget it, he told himself. Forget her. He did not need complications in his life. He already had a big one. Lucy

He glanced out the window. The sun was finally rising, its soft tangerine rays glimmering on the water.

Out at sea he'd have a chance to think. Or not to think.

Surf. And more surf. And medicine.

What was life other than those two things?

On Tuesday evening Riley went to see Amy. She was out on the hospital balcony, cuddling her baby and looking longingly at the sunset over the distant hills.

'Hi,' Riley said from the door, and she beamed a welcome.

'This is lovely,' she said. 'You're my second visitor tonight.'

'Second?'

'Pippa came back to see me, too. Look.' She held up a stuffed rabbit, small and floppy, with a lopsided grin that made Riley smile.

'Cute.'

How long ago had Pippa been in? How much had he missed her by?

These were hardly appropriate questions.

'You missed her by minutes,' Amy said, and he caught himself and turned his attention back to where it should be. To his patient.

'I came to see you.'

'Pippa asked if you'd been in.'

'Did she?' He couldn't help himself. 'Is she still staying at the same hotel?'

'She says her lowlife boyfriend's paid so she'll use it all. She's trying to figure if he has to pay the mini-bar bill. If he does then she's going to turn all those little bottles into a milkshake.'

He grinned. He could see her doing it. The girl had spunk.

More.

Pippa had been his patient. More was not appropriate.

'When can I go home?' Amy asked.

'I'd like you to stay for a week.'

'But you only go to Dry Gum every two weeks. You're due there on Thursday. If I don't go with you then I'm stuck here until next time.'

He hesitated. Four days post-delivery… He'd rather keep her here.

'I hate hospitals,' she said.

She didn't. It was just that she was lonely. And young.

Should he take her home? Medical needs versus emotional needs. It was always a juggling act. There was a medical clinic—of a sort—at Dry Gum. It wasn't perfect but he looked into Amy's anxious face and he thought it would have to do.

'If things are still looking good then we'll take you,' he told her. 'But then I want you to stay with Sister Joyce for a week to make sure you know exactly how to care for your baby.'

'I know most of it,' she said. 'I practically brought Mum's kids up.'

She had, too. This kid had as much spunk as Pippa.

No. More. Pippa had clung to life for a night. Amy had been clinging to life for sixteen years. He'd known her since she was ten, a bossy little kid who ordered her tribe of brothers and sisters around, who herded them into clinic when she felt they needed it, who, he'd heard from others, had even been known to steal to get food for her siblings.

He'd felt sick when he'd learned she was pregnant. He felt like he'd personally failed her. Letting a sixteen-year-old kid get pregnant…

He couldn't protect them all.

He could try.

'There's still stuff you need to learn,' he told her.

'I know there is,' she said, serious in response. 'Sister Joyce'll teach me.'

'You will stay with Sister Joyce for a week?'

'Maybe longer,' she said diffidently. 'I'm not going home to Mum.'

That was a big step. Huge. Riley mentally rearranged his schedule and hauled up a chair. 'So Baby Riley's dad…' he said. As far as he knew this baby was the result of a relationship that had lasted less than a month. 'Jason?'

'He's gotta pull his socks up.'

'Yeah?'

'He wants to live with me,' Amy said. 'I asked Sister Joyce before I came here and she reckons she can get us one of the houses the government's built by the school. Wouldn't that be cool? I asked her if just me and the kid could go into it and she said yes. So I told Jason if he gets a job and sorts himself out he can come, too. Jason's okay.' She smiled then, a smile much wiser than her years. 'He'll be nice if I can keep him straight.'

If anyone could do it, it was Amy, Riley thought, in increased bemusement. Her look was suddenly fierce, determined, focused. 'You know, when you and Pippa were helping me, I thought… That's what I want to do,' she said. 'Be like Pippa. Sister Joyce'll help me. I'm can learn.'

'You're a lot like Pippa already,' Riley said, absurdly touched. 'You both have courage in spades.'

'Yeah, she's good,' Amy said. 'What a waste she has to go back to England.'

She didn't want to go back to England.

She was floating on her back in the sea. Of course she was going back. When you fall off a horse, get right back on. How many riding instructors had told her that?

It was Wednesday. The morning was gorgeous, the sea was glistening, there were flags showing the beach was patrolled and two burly lifesavers were watching her every move.

She wasn't stupid. She didn't go out of her depth. She just floated. Thinking…

What was there to go back to?

Her parents?

No. They wanted her to marry Roger. It had seemed such a neat solution, two sides of business meeting in marriage.

'Marry Roger now,' her father had said. 'You're wasting time messing about nursing. Get the family an heir.'

What sort of feudal system did he live in?

But Roger had been understanding for years, even when she'd said she wanted to break off their engagement and be free while she trained. He'd enjoyed himself then, too, she thought. They'd even discussed their respective boyfriends and girlfriends. Then, when he'd gently resumed pressure to marry, there had seemed no reason not to.

Looking back, she wondered… Had he been relieved to be given free time before he set about doing what he must to cement the family fortune?

It made her feel ill that she'd been so stupid.

'I just wanted him to be my friend,' she said out loud, and heard the neediness of the child within.

But she was no longer a child. She was in Australia. The sun was shining on her face. There were two bronzed surf lifesavers watching over her.

This place was magic, she thought. Whale Cove was two hours' drive north of Sydney. It was a town rather than a city, clustered between mountains and sea, and it had to be one of the most beautiful places in the world.

'But you can't stay in your honeymoon hotel for ever,' she told herself.

'Why not? Roger's paying.' She rolled lazily over in the shallows, thinking about the pros and cons of Roger. She'd made some enquiries before she'd come—enquiries that maybe she would have been wise to have made before she'd got so close to the wedding.

It seemed her bridesmaid hadn't been the only one. He'd gambled on her not finding out.

She had to face it—he'd wanted her money, not her.

Ugh.

Suddenly she found herself thinking of Riley instead, and it was a relief when his image superimposed itself over her ex-fiancé's.

Riley gambled, too, she conceded. She remembered him holding her in that black-as-pitch sea.

You're safe. You don't need to hold on, I have you.

He gambled with his own life to save others.

Melodramatic?

No.

What was he doing now? Off saving more lives?

She rolled onto her back again, watching the lone surfer she'd seen before. He was seriously good.

The waves were forming far out, building and curving and finally breaking, twelve feet high or so at their peak, then falling away to nothing, running themselves out as the water became deep again. There must be a channel between those waves and the beach, because in close the water was calm. Where she was the surf built again to about eight inches. Just enough to float on. Up and down. Watching the surfer. Thinking of nothing.

The surfer caught a huge swell. He was sweeping in on its face then disappearing underneath as the wave curled.

She caught her breath. She'd seen this on videos; being in the green room, they called it, totally enclosed in a tube of water. She watched on, entranced, wondering where he was. Was he still upright?

The wave curled right over, smashing to nothing at the end where he'd entered, collapsing in on itself all the way along, slowly, slowly for its full length.

And out he came at the other end. Still upright.

Riley?

She was suddenly standing chest deep, her hands up to shield her eyes from the sun. Was she imagining things?

Maybe not.

It was time to get out. The sensation that Riley might be sharing her water-space was somehow disturbing. She caught the next tiny wave in, then wandered up to the lifesavers.

She motioned—casually, she hoped—toward the surfer.

'He's good.'

'He is,' the older lifesaver said. 'Bit driven, that one. Surfs no matter what the weather.'

'Who is he?' Though she already knew.

'That's our Doc Riley,' the other guy said. 'Puts himself out there, our doc. Great doc. Great surfer. Not bad with a billiard cue either.'

'Crap at darts, though,' the other guy retorted, happy to chat on a quiet morning. 'The missus says I should let him win because he hauled her brother off his fishing boat when it went down. Doc'd hate that, though. Letting him win.' He gazed out at Riley who'd caught his next wave. 'I sometimes wish he'd come off out there and let someone else save him. Balance things up, like.'

'Like that's going to happen,' the other guy said, and then he turned back to Pippa. 'You're English. Tourist?'

'I'm here for my honeymoon,' she said. It felt absurd to say it. But good. Honeymoons were great if they didn't involve Roger.

'So where's the husband?'

'He never got past fiancé and I left him in England.' The casual conversation was starting to feel like fun. 'Isn't that the best place for fiancés?'

'If you say so.' The younger lifesaver was checking her out from the toes up, and she thought she deserved that. She'd practically thrown him a come-on line. 'Hey, he's coming out. Doc, I mean,' he said, motioning to the surf. 'That's early.'

And Riley was right…there. One minute Riley had been far out at sea, the next he'd surfed across the channel, caught one of the tiddler waves, then reached the beach before she'd figured whether she wanted to see him.

Why wouldn't she want to see him? She tried to think about it while he hauled his surfboard onto dry sand and strolled up to meet them.

The lifeguards greeted him like an old friend. She should greet him as well but she was too busy getting her breath back.

He looked... Awesome.

Weren't surfers supposed to wear wetsuits?

He was only in board shorts. He'd be a lot easier to handle in a wetsuit, she decided.

Handle?

Handle as in come to terms with. Handle as in greet like a casual acquaintance.

Not handle in any other way.

But the look of him... He was every inch a surfer, tall, tanned and ripped. He didn't look like a doctor. He looked like he should be...should be...

Maybe she should just stop thinking. Her silence was starting to be marked.

'Hi,' she managed at last, and he smiled, and that smile.... He had no right to look like that. It threw her right off balance.

'I thought it was you,' he said. 'Have you been looking after her?' he asked the lifeguards. 'This is Pippa, our floater from Sunday night.'

Whoa. How to embarrass a girl. But neither of the lifeguards looked judgmental. Instead they looked impressed.

'You managed to stay out there for eight hours?'

'Not by choice.'

'I'd guess not,' the older lifesaver said. 'And not because of the fiancé left in England?'

'Um...no.'

'I thought you'd stick to the hotel pool,' Riley said, and then a mum yelled from the end of the beach that her kid had his toe stuck between two rocks and the lifeguards left them to go and see.

'More toe trouble?' Pippa said, striving for casual. 'You guys could start a collection.'

'We try to keep them attached,' Riley said. 'There's something a bit offputting about toes in specimen bottles. Even ones painted pink with stars. Are you okay?'

'I… Yes.' What else was a girl to say?

'Nightmares?' he asked, suddenly gentle. In doctor mode. Only he didn't look anything like any doctor she'd ever met. Standing in the sun with water dripping across his eyes, his wet hair sort of flopping, his chest glistening…

Do not go there.

'No,' she managed, and was absurdly pleased that she'd got the word out.

'How's the cough? Mary says you're booked at Outpatients this afternoon for a full check.'

'Cough's settled. I'm all better.'

'I'm pleased to hear it,' he said. 'How's the heart?'

She knew what he meant. Cardiovascular concerns didn't come into this. He was enquiring about Roger. 'Happy,' she said, a trifle defiantly.

'Sure?'

'I'm sure. I'm a bit humiliated but the honeymoon's helping. Especially as Roger's paying.'

'Good ole Roger. Bride living it up at his expense. Is he back at the coal face, paying for it?'

'Don't you dare feel sorry for him,' she snapped, and he grinned.

'I never would. I'm on your side.'

'Guys stick together.'

'Not me. I stick with my patients.'

'I'm not your patient,' she said, and he nodded, thoughtful. 'No. But you were.'

'Meaning you have to be loyal.'

'Meaning I can't ask you out to dinner.'

That was one to take her breath away. She fought for a little composure. It took a while. The way he was making her feel… Maybe it was a good thing she couldn't be asked out to dinner.

'So tell me about Amy,' she said, because he didn't seem to be making any move to leave, to walk away.

'Patient confidentiality.'

'You just told these guys I was the…what did you call me? Sunday night's floater?'

'That was a non-specific impression.'

'So give me a non-specific impression of Amy.'

He hesitated. He shaded his eyes and watched the surf for a bit and she wondered if he'd gone too far already. She was, after all, his patient.

But he didn't leave, and when he spoke his voice was low and lazy and she thought she was exaggerating her importance to him. He was simply settling into his morning on the beach and wouldn't be hurried.

'Amy's amazing,' he said at last. 'She deserves everything we can do for her and more. She's the oldest of ten kids and she cares for them all. She's bossy and smart and tough—she'll fight for what she needs and I've seen her bloodied by it. Only we let her down. We thought of her as a kid. The nursing sister out where she comes from at Dry Gum Creek was gutted when she found out she was pregnant. Her mother would never have told her the facts and Riley junior is the result.'

'So why is she here?'

'We can't deliver babies at Dry Gum—there's no resident doctor. Normally we bring the mums here two weeks before their babies are due but Louise, our obstetrician, was concerned at Amy's age. She thought she'd be better at the teen centre in Sydney. So we took her there but she ran away, here, where she knows me. Sensible or not, she trusts me and she made it here before the baby arrived. We can only be grateful she didn't hitch a ride all the way back to Dry Gum.'

'So now…'

'We'll probably take her home tomorrow.'

'There's no father?'

'That comes within patient confidentiality.'

'Of course.' She hesitated. 'Will you personally take her home?'

'That's what Flight-Aid does—when we're not pulling maidens out of the water after eight-hour swims.'

'I'm sorry,' she muttered.

'Don't mention it. If you know how good it felt to haul you up alive...'

'If you knew how good it felt to be pulled up alive.' She stared out to sea and thought of where she'd be if this man hadn't found her. She shuddered.

Riley's hand was suddenly on her shoulder, warm and strong and infinitely reassuring.

'Don't,' he said. 'Yes, we hauled you up, but you did most of it yourself. In a couple of hours you'd probably have drifted into the next bay and been washed up on the beach. You'd have faced a long hike home but you would have lived happily ever after.'

'We both know...'

'No one knows anything for sure,' he said. 'I could have been hit by lightning right now, while I was surfing. Do I have nightmares because I almost was?'

'There's not a cloud.'

'That's the scariest thing,' he said gravely. 'There's nothing else to pull lightning to except me. I feel all trembly thinking about how close a call I've just had.'

He looked...anything but trembly, she decided.

He also made her heart twist. There was enough gravity behind his laughter to make her think this guy really did care. He really did worry that she might have nightmares.

'There's a psychologist at the hospital,' Riley said gently, and she knew she was right. 'Peter's great with post traumatic stress. Make an appointment to see him. This week.'

She didn't need...

'Do it, Pippa,' he said. 'I should have made the appointment for you but it's...'

'Not your job?'

'I just scrape people off,' he said. 'It's other's work to dust them down. I was only in the ward on Monday because we're permanently short-staffed.'

'So now you're surfing.'

'Who's not on my side now?' he demanded, sounded wounded. 'Our team picked up two car-crash victims north of Dubbo in the wee hours. I'm off duty.'

'I'm sorry.'

'Don't be sorry,' he said, switching back to caring almost immediately. 'It doesn't suit you. You know…' He hesitated. Looked out to sea for a bit. Decided to say what he wanted to say. 'The world's your oyster,' he said at last. 'You're back in the water. You have a honeymoon suite in the most beautiful place in the world. I get the feeling you've been drifting. Maybe you could use this time to figure what you want. What's good for you.'

'Standing here's good.'

'It's a great spot to be,' he said softly. 'And the surf's waiting.'

Then, before she guessed what he intended, he lifted his hand and brushed her cheek with his forefinger. It was a feather touch. It was a touch of caring, or maybe a salute of farewell—and why it had the power to send a shudder through the length of her body she had no idea.

She stepped back, startled, and his smile grew rueful.

'Pippa, I'm not a shark,' he said. 'I'm just me, the guy at the end of the rope. Just me saying goodbye, good luck, God speed.'

And with that he raised his hand in a gesture that seemed almost mocking—and turned and headed back to his surf, back to a life she had no part in.

If he'd stayed on the beach one moment longer he would have kissed her.

He'd wanted, quite desperately, to kiss her. She'd looked lost.

No matter how strong she'd been—walking away from the

appalling Roger, managing not to drown, helping with Amy, all of those things required strength—he still had the impression she was flailing.

She was nothing to do with him. She was a woman he'd pulled out of the water.

Like Marguerite?

He'd met Marguerite on a beach in the South of France. Of course. She had been there as it seemed she was always there, working on her tan. Wealthy, English, idle.

On a scholarship at university in London, he'd been on summer break, the first he'd ever had where he hadn't needed to work to pay for next term's living. His roommate had known someone who wouldn't mind putting them up. The South of France had sounded fantastic to a kid who'd once lived rough on the streets of Sydney.

He'd bumped into Marguerite on the second day in the water, literally bumped when she'd deliberately swum into his surfboard. She'd faked being hurt, and giggled when he'd carried her from the water. She'd watched him surf, admired, flirted, asked him where he came from, asked her to teach her to surf—and suddenly things had seemed serious. On her side as well as his.

The first time he met her parents he knew he was hopelessly out of his class, but he didn't care. For Marguerite didn't care either, openly scorning her parents' disapproval. For five weeks she lay in his arms, she held him and she told him he was her idea of heaven. For a boy who'd never been held the sensation was insidious in its sweetness. She melted against him, and the rest of the world disappeared.

Then reality. The end of summer. He returned to university and the relationship was over. For weeks he phoned her every day, but a maid always took his calls. Marguerite was 'unavailable'.

Finally her mother answered, annoyed his calls were interfering with her maid's work.

'You were my daughter's summer plaything,' she drawled.

'A surfer. Australian. Amusing. She has other things to focus on now.'

He thought she was lying, but when he insisted she finally put Marguerite on. Her mother was right. It was over.

'Oh, Riley, leave it. How boring. You were fun for summer, nothing more. You helped me drive Mummy and Daddy crazy, and it's worked. They still want to send me to finishing school. Can you imagine?' She chuckled then, but there was no warmth in her laughter. There was even a touch of cruelty. 'I do believe they're about to be even more annoyed with me, but they won't know until it's too late, and I'll enjoy that very much. So thank you and goodbye. But don't ring again, there's a lamb. It's over.'

She'd become pregnant to rebel? To prove some crazy point over her parents?

And Pippa?

Pippa was rebelling against her family as well—like Marguerite?

Don't judge a woman by Marguerite.

No, he told himself harshly. Don't judge at all and don't get close. He'd seen enough of his attempts at family, his attempts at love, to know it wasn't for him.

So why did he want to kiss Pippa?

He didn't. A man'd be a fool.

A man needed to surf instead, or find someone else to rescue.

Someone who wasn't Pippa.

She wandered back to the hotel, lay on the sun lounger on the balcony, and gazed out to sea.

Thinking.

'I get the feeling you've been drifting. Maybe you could use this time to figure what you want. What's good for you.'

And…

'We're permanently short-staffed.'

The idea of staying had taken seed and was growing.

To be part of a hospital community doing such good…

'It's romantic nonsense,' she told herself. 'Yes, you should go back to nursing but you know your old hospital will give you your job back.'

But to live here…

She could make herself a permanent home. A home without the ties, the guilt, the associations of a family who disapproved of her, who'd never cease expecting her to be something she wasn't.

She could buy a house. Something small overlooking the sea.

Home. It was a concept so amazing she couldn't believe it had taken her until now to think of it. Maybe she'd never been in a place where the call had been this great until now. Like a siren song. Home.

She could put up wallpaper. Plant tomatoes. Do…whatever people did with homes.

Do it, she told herself. Now, before you change your mind.

And then she forced herself to repeat the question that had been hovering…well, maybe from the time she'd been hauled out of the sea.

Am I doing it because of Riley?

Don't be ridiculous. Her sensible self was ready with all the justification in the world. You're doing it because of you. It's time you settled, got yourself somewhere permanent. And Riley's hardly in the hospital.

He is sometimes.

There was a reason doctor/patient relationships were banned, she thought. Was she suffering a bad case of hero worship?

How could she be friends with Riley? The relationship would be skewed from the start.

'So what?' she muttered. 'I can avoid him. Is hero worship enough to stop me applying for a job, making a home in the best place in the world?'

Yes. Sleep a bit more. Think about it.

I can't drift, she told herself.

Give yourself another day.

Yes, but that's all, she decided. One more day of drifting and then…

Then move forward.

Toward Riley?

No, she told herself harshly. Toward a home. Nothing more.

CHAPTER FOUR

RILEY enjoyed Thursdays. He liked the flights to the Outback settlements. Today he was scheduled for a clinic at Dry Gum Creek and Dry Gum was one of his favourites. It was Amy's home. It was also the home of Sister Joyce, possibly the fiercest senior nurse in the state. He loved her to bits. He pushed open the door to the Flight-Aid office feeling good, and found Harry sitting at his desk, with news.

'No Cordelia,' he said morosely. 'Her head cold's worse and her German shepherd's in labour.'

They stared at each other, knowing each was thinking the same thing. Cordelia was a first-rate flight nurse but she was in her sixties, her health wasn't great and her dogs were growing more important than her work.

'We can go without her,' Harry ventured. Working without a third crew member was fine unless there needed to be an evacuation. There wasn't an evacuation due today—they were simply taking Amy home and doing a routine clinic.

But there was always a chance that a routine clinic would turn into an evacuation. Crews of two were dicey.

They had no choice.

'There's a note for you to go see Coral.' Harry said, shoving himself off the desk. 'Take-off in ten minutes?'

'I'll check what Coral wants first,' Riley said. Their nurse-administrator was good. She usually let them be—that she'd contacted them today meant trouble.

More trouble than a missing crew member?

'Are you sure?' Coral was short and almost as wide as she was tall. She was sitting on the far side of her desk, looking at Pippa's CV like it was gold. 'You really want to work here?'

'I'm not sure if I can get a work visa.'

'I'll have you a work visa in the time it takes my secretary to make you a coffee. You're a midwife?'

'Yes, but…'

'But don't say anything,' Coral begged. 'I'm reading this thinking I'm shutting up about two of your post-grad skills. I could have me a war if this gets out. The surgeons will want you. Intensive Care will want you. I want you. When would you like to start?'

'I need to find somewhere to live. I'd like to find a house but it might take time.'

'We have a house for med staff. Four bedrooms and a view to die for. You can move in this morning.'

'My hotel's paid until Sunday.'

Coral nodded, reflective. 'You are still getting over your ordeal,' she conceded. 'Riley'll say you should rest.'

'I'm rested.'

'Your chest okay?'

'I've been given the all-clear.'

'Hmm.' The middle-aged administrator gazed speculatively at Pippa. 'How about we break you in gently with a training day—give you an overview of what services we offer outside the hospital?'

'I'd love that.' She surely would. Her lone honeymoon wasn't all it was cracked up to be.

'Well,' Coral said, glancing with approval at Pippa's jeans and T-shirt, 'you're even dressed for it.'

'I'm not,' Pippa said, alarmed. 'I came with resort wear. I

bought these jeans yesterday. I'll need to buy serviceable clothes if I'm to nurse here.'

'For where you're going, jeans are great,' Coral said, beaming. 'Just wait until I tell Riley.'

Coral's door was open. She was drinking coffee with someone. That someone had her back to the door but she turned as she heard him approach.

Pippa.

What was there in that to take a man's breath away? Nothing at all. She'd probably come here to thank them. Something formal.

She rose and she was wearing neat jeans and a T-shirt. She looked almost ordinary.

But this woman would never look ordinary. Yesterday on the beach in her bikini she'd looked extraordinary. Now, in jeans, she still looked…

'You two know each other,' Coral said, and he pulled himself together. Coral was intelligent and perceptive, and she was looking at him now with one of her brows hiked—like there were questions happening and she was gathering answers whether he liked it or not.

'I… Of course. You know Pippa's the one we pulled from the water? Who helped with Amy's baby?'

'I do know that,' Coral said, her brow still hiked. 'So you know she's skilled?'

'I know she's skilled.' He felt wary now and he wasn't sure why. Pippa's face wasn't giving anything away. If anything, she looked wary as well.

'I have Pippa's application to work for us on my desk,' Coral said. 'Right here. It looks impressive. You've worked with her. Any reason I shouldn't sign her up on the spot?'

Pippa? Work here? There was a concept to think about. But Coral was giving him no time. Answer, he told himself. Now.

'There's no reason at all,' he said, and was aware of a stab of satisfaction as he heard himself say it. Was that dumb? No, because Pippa was an excellent nurse.

Yes, because the satisfaction he was feeling didn't have a thing to do with her competence. It was everything to do with her looking at him measuringly, those calm green eyes promising a man…

Promising him nothing. Get a grip.

'For how long?' he asked.

'Indefinitely,' Pippa told him. 'I don't want to go back to England.'

'You'll change your mind.'

It was Pippa's turn to hike an eyebrow. She had him disconcerted. Very disconcerted.

But he didn't have the time—or the inclination—to stand around being disconcerted. He remembered work with relief. Harry was waiting. Amy and her baby would be loaded and ready to go.

'This is great,' he said. 'Pippa, welcome to Whale Cove Hospital. But can we talk about it later? I need to leave.'

'I've sent a message to the ward to hold onto Amy for fifteen minutes,' Coral said. 'We have a couple of things to discuss. First, I've told Pippa she can move into the medical house. You have four bedrooms. I assume there's no objection?'

They both stilled at that. He saw Pippa's face go blank and he thought he hadn't been part of that equation.

'You never said I'd be sharing with Riley,' she said.

'It's the hospital's house,' Coral said. 'Riley mostly has it to himself but we occasionally use it for transient staff.'

'I'm not transient,' Pippa said.

'I have a guest coming tomorrow,' Riley said over the top of her.

'You have four bedrooms.' Coral glanced at her watch, clearly impatient. 'If you have one guest, there are still two bedrooms spare. It should suit Pippa for the short term. I'm not going to knock back a great nurse for want of accommodation. Meanwhile, Pippa would like to work immediately but I don't want to put her on the wards until I'm sure she's fully recovered. Cordelia's not coming in. You need another team member. Pippa needs an overview of the service so I'm sending her out with you. Can you fit her up with a Flight-Aid shirt so she looks official? She can tag along while you can talk her through life here. You'll be back by late tonight. Pippa, I'll let you sleep in tomorrow—it'd be a shame to waste that honeymoon suite of yours. You can move into the house at the weekend, you can start here on Monday, and we can all live happily ever after. No objections? Great, let's go.'

It had happened so fast she felt breathless. She had a job.

She was flying over the Australian Outback in an official Flight-Aid plane. Harry was flying it. 'Dual qualifications,' he said smugly when she expressed surprise. 'Triple if you count me riding a Harley. Riley here doctors and surfs. He has two skills to my three. It's just lucky I'm modest.'

Harry made her smile.

The whole set-up made her smile.

The back of the plane was set up almost as an ambulance. Harry and Riley were up front. Pippa was in the back with her patients, Amy and baby Riley.

This was the start of her new life.

She was wearing a Flight-Aid shirt. The Flight-Aid emblem was on her sleeve and there was a badge on her breast. She was about to attend a clinic in one of the most remote settlements in the world.

This time last week she'd been planning her wedding. Four days ago she'd been floating in the dark, expecting to die. Now she was employed as a nurse, heading to an Outback community to help Dr Riley Chase.

The man who'd saved her life.

He was a colleague. She had to remind herself of that, over and over. But in his Flight-Aid uniform he looked…he looked…

'Isn't Doc Riley fabulous?' Amy was headed home with her baby, and things were looking great in her world. She was bubbling with happiness. 'He's made me see so many things. You reckon one day my baby could be a doctor?'

'Why not?'

'I wish I'd gone to school,' Amy said wistfully. 'Mum never made me and there were always kids to look after. Then Doc Riley read the Riot Act and now they all go. My littlie'll go to school from day one.' She glanced at Amy's uniform. 'It'd be so cool to wear that.'

It did feel cool. Wearing this uniform…

Her parents would hate it, Pippa thought. They hated her being a nurse, and for her to be a nurse here…

They still had Roger. They liked Roger.

They didn't like her.

She was getting morose. Luckily little Riley decided life had been quiet long enough and started to wail. That gave her something to do, a reason not to think of the difficulties back home. She changed the baby and settled her on Amy's breast. As she worked she marvelled at how neat everything was in the plane's compact cabin, how easily she could work here—and she also marvelled that she felt fine. She'd had a moment's qualm when she'd seen how small the plane was. If she was to be airsick…

No such problem. She grinned at mother and baby, feeling smug. Somehow she'd found herself a new life. She'd be good at this.

Flight-Aid nurse. Heir to the Fotheringham millions?

Never the twain shall meet.

'So do we use her straight away?'

Riley sighed. He was having trouble coming to terms with their new team player, and the fact that Harry was intent on talking about her wasn't helping.

'She doesn't have accreditation,' he said. 'She's an observer only.'

'But you've left her in the back with Amy.'

'Amy needs company and I'm feeling lousy company.'

'I can see that,' Harry said thoughtfully. 'So is it a problem that we're saddled with a young, attractive, competent nurse rather than our dog-smelling Cordelia?'

'Cordelia's competent,' he snapped.

'And Pippa's not?'

'We don't know that.'

'So you'd rather the devil you know.' Harry nodded. 'I can see that.'

No comment.

Riley was feeling incapable of comment. He sat and glowered and Harry had the sense to leave him alone.

So what was the problem?

The problem was that Riley didn't know what the problem was.

Pippa was a patient. He thought of her as a patient—only he didn't.

She had the same English accent as Marguerite.

He couldn't hold an accent over her.

No, but there were so many conflicting emotions.

Lucy was coming. His daughter. She'd have this accent as well.

His hands were hurting. He glanced down and realised he'd clenched his fingers into his palms, tighter than was wise. He needed to lighten up. Before Lucy arrived?

He hauled out his wallet and glanced at the picture Lucy had sent him when she'd contacted him three months ago. His daughter was beautiful. She was eighteen years old and she was so lovely she took his breath away.

He'd had nothing to do with her life. He'd been a father for a mere three months.

Even then…after that one email, sent from an address that had then been deleted, he'd flown to England and confronted Marguerite. Tracking her down had taken time but he'd found her, married to a financier, living in a mansion just off Sloane Square. She was still beautiful, taking supercilious to a new level, and bored by his anger.

'Yes, she is your daughter but purely by genes. She doesn't

want you or need you in her life. If she contacted you it'll be because she's vaguely interested in past history, nothing more. I imagine that interest has now been sated. Why would she wish to see you? I don't wish to see you—I can't imagine why you've come. No, I'm not telling you where she is. Go away, Riley, you have no place in our lives.'

So tomorrow he was expecting a teenage daughter, coming to stay. And in the back of the plane was a woman called Pippa who was also coming to stay.

Two women. Identical accents.

Trouble.

'It must be bad, to look like that,' Harry said cheerfully, and Riley found his fists clenching again.

'Women,' he said. 'Maybe Cordelia's right. Maybe dogs are the way to go.'

'Women are more fun,' Harry said.

'You have to be kidding.'

For the last half-hour she'd been gazing down at a landscape so unfamiliar she might well be on a different planet. She was gazing at vast tracts of red, dusty desert, stunted trees growing along dry river beds, weird, wonderful rock formations, sunlight so intense it took her breath away, a barren yet beautiful landscape that went on for ever.

Dry Gum Creek was in the middle of…the Outback? There seemed no other way to describe it. Out back of where? Out back of the known world.

The little plane bumped to a halt. Riley hauled open the passenger door and Pippa gazed around her in wonder.

Red dust. Gnarled trees and windswept buildings. Dogs barking at their little plane like it was an intruder that had to be seen off. A few buildings that looked like portable classrooms. A slightly more solid building with a sign saying 'General Store'. A big, old house that looked like it might have once been a stately homestead, but that time was long past. Corrugated-iron huts, scattered far out.

A couple of the rangy dogs came rushing to greet them. Harry fended them off while Riley swung himself up into the back to help Amy with the baby.

'Welcome to Dry Gum Creek,' Harry told Pippa. 'I hope you aren't expecting swimming pools, shopping malls, gourmet eating.'

She smiled, feeling pure excitement. 'I left my credit card at home.'

A couple of little girls were peering out from the hut nearest the plane. They were eleven or twelve years old, with skins as dark as Amy's.

'Did Amy come?' one of them yelled.

'She sure did,' Riley called. 'Come and meet your new niece.'

The girls came flying, all gangly arms and legs, looking as thrilled as if it was Christmas Day.

Riley handed Riley junior down to Pippa. 'Don't let the girls have her unless Amy says so,' he said in an undertone.

Amy was enveloped in hugs, and Pippa thought this was almost the reaction of kids welcoming their mother.

'She could just as well be their mother,' Riley told her, hauling equipment from the plane, and once again she was struck with this man's ability to read her thoughts. It was entirely disconcerting. 'They'd be lost without her.'

'Are you coming home?' one of the kids asked Amy. Amy shook her head. She disentangled herself from them a little and took her baby from Pippa.

'Nope. I gotta stay with Sister Joyce for a week. Then I'm gonna have one of the huts by the school. Me and Baby Riley will live there.'

'Will Jason live with you?'

'Dunno.' Pippa saw Amy's face tense. 'Where is he?'

'He's got a job,' the oldest girl said, sounding awed. 'He's out mustering cattle. He said to tell you.'

'Wow,' Amy breathed. 'Wow.'

'Mum says it's stupid,' the little girl said. 'She says he can live off the pension.'

'It's not stupid.' Amy looked back to Riley for reassurance and Riley was right beside her, his hand under her arm. Amy was sixteen years old. She'd given birth four days ago, and her confidence would be a fragile shell.

'We're taking Amy to Sister Joyce now,' Riley told the little girls. 'She'll stay there until she's strong enough to look after herself.'

'We'll look after her,' the oldest of the little girls said, and squared her shoulders. 'We're good at looking after people. Amy's taught us.'

'And Jason'll help,' Amy told her. 'I know he will. Like Doc Riley.' With Riley supporting her, her confidence came surging back and she peeped an impudent, teasing smile at Pippa. 'My Jason's got a job. How cool's that? My Jason's gorgeous. Even more gorgeous than Doc Riley. Though I bet you don't think so.'

What?

That was a weird statement, Pippa thought. Totally inappropriate.

So why was she trying really hard not to blush?

Pippa had been expecting a hospital but it wasn't a hospital at all. It seemed little more than a big, decrepit house with huge bedrooms. The woman in charge was an elderly, dour Scot with a voice like she was permanently attached to a megaphone. Sister Joyce. She introduced her to some of her residents while Riley started his clinic.

Harry, it seemed, was needed elsewhere. The water pump was playing up. While Harry was here, Joyce decreed, he might as well be useful, and Pippa got the feeling Joyce would be as bossy as she needed to get what she wanted for her residents.

Maybe she needed to be bossy. It seemed Joyce took care of sixteen patients on her own, and even though the place wasn't a hospital, the residents were certainly in need of care.

'We're not defined as a hospital,' Joyce told her. 'We're not even a nursing home because we can't meet the staffing ratio. A lot of our population is nomadic. Every time we try and take a census so I can get funding, everyone seems to go walkabout, so this is a sort of a boarding house with hospital facilities.'

'With you on duty all the time?'

Joyce gave a wintry smile. 'Don't look at me like that, girl. I'm no saint. This place suits me. I can't stand bureaucracy. I train our local girls to help me and I do very well. Amy's been the best. I have hopes she'll come back to work, baby or not. And we have Doc Riley. The man's a godsend. Sensible. Intelligent. He doesn't shove medical platitudes down people's throats. We've had medical professionals come out here with their lectures and charts of the five food groups, holding up pictures of lettuce. Lettuce! Our kids get two apples a day at school, they take home more, but even apples cost a fortune by the time we fly them in. Lettuce!' She snorted her disgust. 'You want to see what Riley's doing?'

'I... Yes, please.' They'd moved out on the veranda where half a dozen old men were sitting in the sun, gazing at the horizon. 'Are these guys patients?'

'Diabetics,' Joyce said. 'You look closely at their feet and you'll see. And half of them are blind. Diabetes is a curse out here. An appalling diet when they were young, a bit of alcohol thrown in for good measure, eye infections untreated, you name it. Most of these guys are in their fifties or sixties but they look much older. Riley's doing his best to see this doesn't happen to the next generation.'

He was. Joyce ushered her into a room at the end of the veranda. Riley was seated beside a desk. A dark, buxom woman who Joyce introduced as the local school teacher was shepherding a queue of kids past him.

'He's doing ear and eye checks,' Joyce told her. 'I do them but I miss things. There's seven steps to go through for each child to make sure they have healthy eyes. He also checks ears. These people are tough and self-sufficient—they have to be—but that causes problems, too. Many of these kids don't even tell their mums when their ears hurt. Infections go unnoticed. In this environment risks are everywhere. So we back each other up. Riley swears he won't let a kid go blind or deaf on his watch.'

'How long's he been doing this?'

'Six years now. He came to do an occasional clinic, then helped me set this place up. There was such a need.'

'How can you operate a hospital without a doctor?'

'We can't,' Joyce said bluntly, while they watched Riley joke with a smart-mouthed small boy. 'But we don't have a choice. We're three hundred miles from the next settlement and most of the older people won't go to the city for treatment even if it's the difference between life and death. I do what I can and Doc Riley is a plane ride away.'

'Always?'

'He's nearly as stupid as me,' Joyce said dryly. 'I need him, he comes. So… You're a qualified nurse. English?'

'Yes.'

'I won't hold that against you. Coral said you're here to watch. Sounds boring. Want to help?'

'Please.'

'You can speed things up,' Joyce said. 'Tell her, Riley,' she said, raising her voice so Riley could hear. He had a little girl on his knee, inspecting her ear. 'I need to settle Amy in and help Harry with the pump. Is it okay with you to let the girl work?'

'Are you up to it?' Riley asked.

'You're not asking me to do brain surgery, right?'

He grinned. 'No brain surgery. We're doing ears and eyes and hair and an overall check. You don't know what you're letting yourself in for. Joyce and I take every inch of help we can get.'

'I'd love to help,' Pippa said simply, and she meant it.

So Riley kept on checking ears, checking eyes, and Pippa took over the rest. She listened to small, sturdy chests. She ran a quick hair check—it seemed lice were endemic but she didn't find any. She did a fast visual check of each child, checking for things that might go unnoticed and blow up into something major.

The kids were good for Riley but they were like a line of spooked calves as they approached Pippa, ready for flight.

'Sam Kemenjarra, if you don't stand still for Nurse Pippa I'll tell her to put the stethoscope in the ice box before she puts it on your back,' Riley growled to one small boy. The little boy giggled and subsided and let himself be inspected.

But the line still fidgeted. Pippa was a stranger. These kids didn't like strangers—she could feel it.

'Nurse Pippa's been sick herself,' Riley said conversationally, to the room in general. He was looking at a small boy's eyes, taking all the time in the world. No matter how long the line was, she had the feeling this man never rushed. He might rush between patients but not with them. Every patient was special.

He was good, she thought. He was really good.

But then… 'She went swimming in the dark and nearly drowned,' Riley said. 'We had to pull her out of the water with a rope hanging from a helicopter.'

There was a collective gasp. Hey, Pippa thought, astonished. What about patient confidentiality?

But Riley wasn't thinking about patient confidentiality. He was intent on telling her story—or making her tell it.

'It was really scary, wasn't it, Pippa?'

'I… Yes,' she conceded. The line of children was suddenly silent, riveted.

'If I hadn't swung down on my rope to save you, what would have happened?'

She sighed. What price pride? Why not just go along with it? 'I would have drowned,' she conceded. So much for floating into the next bay…

'And that would have been terrible,' Riley said, and he wasn't speaking to her; he was speaking to the kids. 'Pippa was all alone in the dark. Floating and floating, all by herself, far, far from the land. There was no one to hear her calling for help. That's what happens when you go swimming in the dark, or even when it's nearly dark. Waterholes and rivers are really dangerous places after sunset.'

She got it. She was being used as a lesson. Her indignation faded. It seemed this was a great opportunity to give these kids a lesson.

It was also settling them.

'I thought something might eat my toes,' she conceded, figuring she might as well add corroborating colour. 'At night you can't see what's under the surface. All sorts of things feed in the water at night.'

'Crocodiles?' one little girl asked, breathless.

'You never know,' Riley told her. 'We don't have crocodiles here,' he told Pippa, 'so it's safe to swim in the waterholes during the day. But at night there's no saying what sneaks into the water looking for juicy little legs to snack on. And I wouldn't be here with my rope. It takes two hours for Harry and I to fly here.'

'But you'd come,' a little boy said, sounding defiant. 'If I went swimming at night you'd come with your rope.'

'It'd take me too long,' Riley said. 'Like Pippa, you'd be floating for a long, long time, getting more and more scared. You were really scared, weren't you, Pippa?'

'I was more scared than I've ever been in my life,' she conceded. 'I was all alone and I thought I was going to die. It was the scariest thing I can imagine. I know now. To swim at night is stupid.'

There was a moment's hesitation—a general hush while everyone thought about it. Then: 'I wouldn't do it,' the little boy declared. 'Only girls would be that stupid.'

'We would not,' the girl next to him declared, and punched him, and the thing was settled. Night swimming was off the agenda.

'And while we're at it, we should warn Nurse Pippa about bunyips,' Riley said, still serious, and there was a moment's pause.

'Ooh, yes,' one little girl ventured, casting a cautious glance at Riley. A glance with just a trace of mischief. 'Bunyips are scary.'

'Bunyips?' Pippa said.

'They're really, really scary,' a little boy added. 'They're humongous. Bigger'n the helicopter.'

'And they have yellow eyes.'

'They sneak around corners.'

'They come up from holes in the ground.'

'They eat people.' It was practically a chorus as the whole line got into the act. 'Their teeth are bigger'n me.'

'You couldn't go night swimming here 'cos you'd get eaten by a bunyip first.'

'Or dragged down a hole for the little bunyips to eat,' the child on Riley's knee said, with ghoulish relish.

'You…you're kidding me,' Pippa said, blanching appropriately.

'Why, yes,' Riley said, grinning. 'Yes, we are.'

The whole room burst out laughing. Pippa got her colour back and giggled with them.

The room settled down to ears and eyes and hair and chests.

Pippa kept chuckling. She worked on beside Riley and it felt fantastic.

She was good. She was seriously good.

Cordelia was dour and taciturn. The kids respected her. They did what she asked but they were a bit frightened of her.

They weren't frightened of Pippa. They were enjoying her, showing off to her, waiting impatiently for Riley to finish with them so they could speed onto their check with Nurse Pippa.

Pippa. They liked the name. He heard the kids whisper it among themselves. Pippa, Pippa, Pippa. Nurse Pippa, who'd almost drowned.

He'd had no right to tell them the story of Pippa's near drowning, but the opportunity had been too great to resist. Drownings in the local waterhole were all too common, and nearly all of them happened after dusk. Kids getting into trouble, bigger kids not being able to see. Pippa's story had made them rethink. He'd told the story to fifteen or so kids, but it'd be spread throughout the community within the hour. Pippa's ordeal might well save lives.

And it had had another, unexpected advantage. Somehow it had made Pippa seem one of them. She'd been given a story.

He'd brought many medics out here—there was genuine interest within the medical community—but mostly the visitors stood apart, watched, or if he asked them to help, the kids would shy away, frightened of strangers. But Pippa was now the nurse who Doc Riley had saved on a rope.

If Pippa was serious about staying…

She wouldn't be. She'd stay until she either made it up with her fiancé or she had her pride together enough to go home. It wasn't worth thinking of her long term.

But even if she was only here for a month or two…she'd make a difference.

He watched her as he worked, as she worked, and he was impressed. She was settled into a routine now, tugging up T-shirts, listening to chests, tickling under arms as she finished so the kids were giggling, and the kids waiting in line were waiting for their turn to giggle. She was running her hand through hair, saying, 'Ooh, I love these curls—you know, if you washed these with shampoo they'd shine and shine. Does Sister Joyce give you shampoo? See how my curls shine? Let's have a competition: next time I come let's see who has the shiniest curls. Every time you wash with shampoo they get shinier. No, Elizabeth, oil does not make curls shinier, it makes them slippery, and the dust sticks to it. Ugh.'

She had the capacity to glance at the child's medical file and take in what was important straight away.

'Can I see your toe? Doc Riley stitched it last month. Did he do a lovely neat job of it?'

Riley didn't have time to check the details Pippa was checking. Cordelia would have decreed it a waste of time. Cordelia followed orders.

Pippa was…great.

The day flew. He was having fun, he decided in some amazement. There was something about Pippa that lightened the room, that made the kids happy and jokey. Harry came in to check on their progress and stayed to watch and help a bit, just because it was a fun place to be.

How could one woman make such a difference?

Finally they were finished. They'd seen every school child, which was a miracle all by itself.

'Half an hour?' Harry said. 'That'll get us back to Whale Cove by dark.'

'I need to do a quick round of Joyce's old guys before I go,' Riley said. 'Plus I need to say goodbye to Amy. You want to come, Pippa?'

'Of course.'

'It's been a long day. I hadn't planned on you working.'

'I've had fun,' she said simply, and smiled, and he thought…

That maybe he needed to concentrate on the job at hand. He did *not* need to think of any woman like he was thinking of Pippa.

Why not?

The question had him unsettled.

Unlike Harry, who fell in love on average four times a year, he steered clear of even transitory commitment, but he did date women; he did enjoy their company. When he'd told Pippa on the beach that he'd like to invite her to dinner, it had been the truth.

But the more he got to know her the more he thought it'd be a mistake.

Why?

She was fascinating. She'd thrown herself into today with enthusiasm and passion. She'd made him laugh—she'd made the kids laugh. She loved what she was doing. She was…amazing.

And there was the problem. He looked at her and knew with Pippa he might be tempted to take things further.

He never had. Not since Marguerite. One appalling relationship when he'd been little more than a kid…

Except it was more than that. A shrink would have a field day with his dysfunctional family. He'd known three 'fathers', none of them his real one. He'd had stepbrothers and stepsisters, they'd always been moving home to escape debts, stupid stuff.

He'd escaped as best he could, physically at first, running away, sleeping rough. Then he got lucky, welfare had moved in and he got some decent foster-parents. There he learned an alternative escape—his brains. The library at school. A scholarship to study medicine, at Melbourne, then England. He'd earned the reputation of a loner and that was the way he liked it.

Only living at university he'd finally discovered the power of friendship. It had sucked him right in—and then he'd met Marguerite.

After Marguerite he'd tried to settle, only how did you learn to have a home? It didn't sit with him; it wasn't his thing.

When he'd come back from England he'd gone to see his foster-parents. They'd been the only real family he knew. They'd written to him while he was away.

They were caring for two new kids who were taking all their energy. They were delighted that his studies were going well. They'd given him tea and listened to his news. His foster-mother had kissed him goodbye, his foster-father had shaken his hand, but they'd been distracted.

He wasn't their child. They'd done the best they could for him—it was time he moved on.

He did move on. His six years in Whale Cove was as long as he'd ever stayed anywhere. He took pleasure in the challenges the job threw at him, but still his restlessness remained.

He had no roots. A surfboard and enough clothes to fit in a bag—what more did a man need?

But as he walked along the veranda with Pippa, he thought, for the first time in years, a man could need something else.

But a man could be stupid for thinking it. Exposing himself yet again.

'Riley?'

Joyce's voice cut across his thoughts. That was good. His thoughts were complicated, and Pippa's body was brushing his. That was complicating them more.

'Yes?' His reply was brusque and Joyce frowned.

'Is there a problem?'

'Not with me there isn't,' he said, pulling himself up. 'I need to see Amy and then we'll go.'

'I'm sorry but I need you to wait,' Joyce told him. 'I've just got a message to say Gerry Onjingi's in trouble. They're bringing him in now. He was climbing the windmill at one of the bores and he fell off. They had pickets stacked up underneath. Gerry fell on one and it's gone right through his leg.'

They weren't going to leave before dark. Bundling Gerry into the plane and taking him back to the coast wasn't an option. Not with half a fence post in his leg.

For the men had brought Gerry in, picket attached. He lay in the back of an ancient truck and groaned, and Pippa looked at the length of rough timber slicing through his calf and thought she'd groan, too. Gerry was elderly, maybe in his seventies, though in this climate she was having trouble telling.

'Crikey!' Riley swung himself up into the tray the instant the truck stopped. 'You believe in making life exciting. This is like a nose bone, only different.'

'Funny, ha-ha,' Gerry muttered, and Riley knelt and put his hand on his shoulder.

'We'll get you out of pain in no time,' he told him. Joyce was already handing up his bag. 'Let's get some pain killers on board before we shift you inside.'

'Will I have to go to Sydney?'

And the way he said it... No matter how much pain he was in, Pippa realised, the thought of the city was worse.

'No promises, mate,' Riley said. 'We need to figure what the damage is. We'll get you out of pain and then we'll talk about it.'

It was amazing how such a diverse group of professionals could instantly make an elite surgical team.

Even Harry took part. By the time the morphine took effect, Harry had organised an electric buzz saw, with an extension cord running from the veranda. 'Electric's better,' he said briefly. 'Less pressure and this fitting's got fine teeth. It'll take seconds rather than minutes by hand.'

The picket had pierced one side of Gerry's calf and come out the other. Pippa helped Joyce cover Gerry with canvas to stop splinters flying. Riley and Pippa supported Gerry's leg while Harry neatly sliced the picket above and below.

'Closest I can get without doing more damage,' Harry muttered, and put the saw down and disappeared fast.

'Turns green, our Harry,' Riley said, grinning at his departing friend. 'Still, if you asked me to pilot a chopper in weather Harry's faced, I'd turn green too.' He was slicing away the remains of Gerry's pants, assessing the wound underneath. It looked less appalling now there was less wood, but it still looked dreadful. 'Pippa, what's your experience in getting bits of wood out of legs?'

'I've done shifts in City Emergency. We coped with a chair leg once.' She made her voice neutral and businesslike, guessing what Gerry needed was reassurance that this was almost normal. Riley's question had been matter-of-fact, like bits of wood in legs were so common they were nothing to worry about.

'You got it out?'

'We did. When he came out of the anaesthetic the publican was there, demanding he pay for the chair.'

'So this little picket…'

'Piece of cake,' she said, smiling down at Gerry. Thinking it wasn't. The wood had splintered. The wound looked messy and how did they know what had been hit and not hit?

'Then let's organise X-rays,' Riley said. 'And an ultrasound.'

'You can do an ultrasound here?'

'Portable kit,' Riley said, sounding smug. 'Eat your heart out, Sydney. Okay, Gerry, let's get you inside. Boys, slide that stretcher in beside him. Pippa, shoulders, Joyce hips, I've got the legs. And picket. Count of three. One, two, three...'

They moved him almost seamlessly and in less than a minute Gerry was in what looked to Pippa to be a perfect miniature theatre.

'I thought this place wasn't a real hospital?' she said, astounded.

'It's not.' Riley was manoeuvring the X-ray equipment into place. 'Dry Gum's too small for much government funding. Joyce is funded for a remote medical clinic, nothing more, but we have lots more. This place is run on the smell of an oily rag. Joyce and I do a lot of begging.'

'And blackmail,' Joyce said. 'Any company who wants to mine out here, who makes money off these people's land, can expect a call from me.'

'Joyce even buys shares,' Riley said in admiration. 'She's been known to get up in shareholder meetings and yell.'

'She's a ripper,' Gerry said faintly. 'Hell, if she had some money...imagine what our Joyce could do.'

'She's doing a fantastic job anyway,' Riley said. 'Okay, Gerry, that leg's positioned, everyone else behind the screen. Let's take some pictures.'

The leg wasn't broken. There was a communal sigh of relief.

The wood had splintered. Surgery would be messy.

The ultrasound came next and Pippa watched in awe. Reading an X-ray was one thing, but operating an ultrasound...

She could pick out a baby. Babies were big. Even then, when the radiographer said look at a close-up she was never sure she was looking at the right appendage.

But that Riley was competent was unquestionable. He was checking for damage that'd mean Gerry had to go to Sydney regardless. He was looking at flow in the main blood vessels—evidence that the artery was obstructed; blockage to blood supply that might turn to disaster when splinters were dislodged.

Despite the trauma Gerry seemed relaxed. As long as he didn't need to go to Sydney, whatever Doc Riley did was fine by him.

'I reckon we can do this,' Riley said at last. He cast a thoughtful look at Pippa. 'How tired are you?'

She was tired but she wasn't missing this for the world. 'Not tired at all,' she lied, and he grinned.

'Right. We have one doctor, two nurses and an orderly. That's Harry. Green or not, he gets to keep the rest of the place running while we work. Pippa, you'll assist me. Joyce, are you happy to anaesthetise?'

'Sure,' Joyce said.

'You can anaesthetise?' Here was something else to astound. A nurse acting as anaesthetist…

'Joyce is a RAN, a remote area nurse,' Riley said. 'RANs are like gold. Sometimes she's forced to do things a doctor would blanch at, because there's no choice. We both do. Like now. I'm not a surgeon and Joyce isn't an anaesthetist but we save lives. If you end up working with us…'

'You'll get to do everything as well,' Joyce said briskly. 'Out here we do what comes next. Okay, Riley, let's not mess around. I have work to do after this, even if you don't.'

She had to ask. This was tricky surgery and to attempt it here… 'I know he's scared,' she ventured. 'But surely it'd be safer to take him to the city.'

'I can do it.' She and Riley were scrubbing fast, while Joyce was booming orders outside.

'Without a trained anaesthetist? To risk…?'

Riley paused then turned to her.

'Think about it,' he said harshly. 'Gerry's seventy years old and he's lived here all his life. No, that's not true. He's lived near here. For him Dry Gum is a big settlement. Even here is a bit scary. If I send him to Sydney I'll be throwing him into an environment that terrifies him. I'll do it if I have to, but it's a risk all by itself. I've had one of my old guys go into cardiac arrest in the plane and I'd swear it was from terror. With three of us… I've weighed the risks and they're far less if he stays here. Accept it or not,' he said grimly. 'We're doing it.'

By the time it was over Pippa had an even greater breadth of understanding of this man's skill. Quite simply, it took her breath away.

He took her breath away.

Joyce was competent but she wasn't trained in anaesthesia. That meant that Riley needed to keep an eye on what she was doing, checking monitors, assessing dosages, at the same time as he was performing a complex piece of surgery that frankly she thought should have been done in Sydney. By surgeons who'd had experience in such trauma, who had skilled back-up…

She was the back-up. She worked with an intensity she'd seldom felt. She was Riley's spare pair of hands and he needed her, clamping, clearing blood, holding flesh back while he eased, eased, eased wood out of the wound. The splinters first of all and then the main shaft….

He had all the patience in the world.

It was a skill that awed her—this ability to block out the world and see only what was important right now.

Few people had it. A psychologist once told her it usually came from backgrounds where the skill was necessary to survive.

What was Riley's background? She didn't have a clue. All she knew was that there was no one she'd rather have in this room, right now, doing what he had to do in order to save Gerry's leg.

They worked on, mostly in silence except for Riley's clipped instructions. That fierce intensity left no room for theatre gossip, and she wouldn't have it any other way.

And finally, finally, Riley was stitching both entry and exit wounds closed. The stockman had been incredibly lucky. To have not severed an artery and bled to death in minutes... To have not even have fractured his leg...

'He'll stay with you for a week, though, Joyce,' Riley said in a seeming follow-on from Pippa's thoughts. 'There's a huge chance of infection. I'll put a brace on and tell him if it comes off in less than a week he'll have permanent nerve damage. It's a lie but it's justified. If he heads off back to camp, we'll have him dead of infection in days.'

'Won't antibiotics...?' Pippa started.

'He won't take them,' Riley said wearily. 'None of the older men will, unless we force-feed them. They see medicine as a sign of weakness. The women accept them now; they see how the kids respond and they believe. We're educating the kids, but Gerry missed out. So he'll wear an immobilising cast for a week. And I'm sorry, Pippa, but we need to stay here tonight until Gerry's fully recovered from the anaesthetic.'

She'd already figured that out. She'd been horrified that he'd attempt such surgery here, but having done it...he couldn't walk away with Gerry recovering from anaesthesia and no doctor on call.

'I can manage,' Joyce said, but Riley shook his head.

'I'll be the one who tells Gerry the rules in the morning. Can you put Pippa up here?'

'It's a full house,' Joyce said.

'Your sitting room?'

'Glenda Anorrjirri's in it,' Joyce said, apologetically. 'Her Luke's asthma's bad and she's frightened. They're staying with me until it's settled.'

'I told you—'

'To keep myself professional? I do,' Joyce said, flaring. 'I keep my bedroom to myself.'

'Which is a miracle all by itself,' Riley growled. 'Joyce has a one-bedroom apartment attached to the hospital,' he explained. 'She has a sitting room and a bedroom, which she's supposed to keep private.'

'I don't mind sharing with Pippa.'

'You're having your bedroom to yourself.' He was dressing Gerry's leg, and Pippa watched as he added a few artistic touches. Scaffolding from toe to thigh. A dressing around the lot.

'He'll think his leg's about to fall off,' Joyce said.

'That's what he's meant to think. You said you have a full house. Do you have room for him?'

'I was counting Gerry. He can have the last bed in Men's Room Two. But you and Pippa and Harry…'

'You know Harry sleeps on the plane. He doesn't trust the kids,' Riley explained to Pippa. 'Neither do I. Would you trust kids with a shiny aeroplane parked in their back yard?'

'You two could use Amy's place,' Joyce said, looking thoughtfully at Pippa. 'I have a little house ready for when she leaves here. There's a bed and a sofa in the living room. I know you have sleeping bags but I don't like the idea of Pippa sleeping rough.'

'I'm not nervous,' Pippa said, feeling nervous. 'I'm happy to sleep anywhere.'

'Pippa swims with sharks,' Riley said, and grinned.

He edged Joyce out of her position at the head of the table and started reversing the anaesthesia. 'Job well done, team. Thank you.'

'Nervous or not, you and Pippa will share Amy's house,' Joyce said.

Riley glanced at Pippa. His grin faded.

'I guess we will,' Riley said.

'Why not?' said Pippa.

CHAPTER FIVE

SLEEPING over was a common occurrence. Riley was used to it.

Harry slept in the plane. 'It's not half-bad,' he told Pippa. 'We have a comfy bed in the back and I always carry some fine emergency literature.' He grinned and hauled a fat paperback out of his back pocket. A buxom woman with tattoos, a dagger and not much else was pouting her lips provocatively on the cover. 'I'm happy as a pig in mud.'

Riley wasn't as happy.

They shared a late dinner with Joyce in the hospital kitchen, then it was time to head over to Amy's little house—with Pippa.

She seemed fine with it. He had the feeling she was even eyeing him askance because she was sensing he was edgy.

Why was he edgy?

Normally he'd roll his sleeping bag out and sleep under the stars. He'd lost count of the number of times he'd gone to sleep listening to Cordelia snoring, or medical students giggling, or sobbing and telling him their latest love life drama—sleeping under the stars did that for some. He didn't mind. He could listen to it all and keep his distance.

So tonight he'd much prefer to sleep under the stars, only that would leave Pippa in Amy's house alone. Or under the stars with him. And something told him…

Pippa wasn't as tough as she made out, he thought as they walked the short distance to the house. Five days ago she'd nearly drowned. He'd learned a lot about trauma in his years in this service—he'd had victims come back and talk to him about their experiences and he'd talked to psychologists. 'There'll be flashbacks,' he'd been told. 'You can't go so close to death without suffering.' And after eight hours in the water believing she'd drown… She'd been close to an appalling edge.

This trip had been meant to break Pippa in slowly, before sending her back to her luxury hotel tonight. To make her sleep outside… Personally he loved it but the sky was immense, and for someone already fragile… Someone who'd just re-entered the world of emergency medicine after being a casualty herself… Even Joyce had seemed to sense it.

It had to be Amy's house.

'I won't jump you,' Pippa said.

He stopped short. 'You won't…'

'I thought I should tell you,' she said. 'Joyce took me aside and told me you were honourable. You're looking worried. Maybe I should reassure you that I am, too. In fact I'm feeling exceedingly chaste. I guess that's what comes from being a jilted bride.'

'You don't sound very jilted,' he said cautiously. He was feeling cautious.

'I'm not,' she said. 'I'm exceedingly pleased to be free, so you needn't walk three yards away from me as if you're afraid I might latch on and not let go.'

'You're pleased to be free?' This conversation had him floundering.

'Yes, I am. I have the rest of my life ahead of me. I've had a very exciting afternoon and a very satisfactory day. I'm starting to make all sorts of plans but men aren't included. And I'm very tired. So show me a bed and then you can do what you want, but you don't need to look after me and you needn't think I'll be needy. I'm independent, Dr Chase, and I'm loving it.'

* * *

Only she wasn't.

He woke at three in the morning and she didn't sound independent at all.

Pippa was sleeping in the double bed in Amy's bedroom. Riley was on the fold-out settee in the living room.

It wasn't sobbing that woke him. It was gasps of fear, then the sounds of panting, breathless terror, muted as if the pillows themselves were drowning her.

If he wasn't a light sleeper he would have missed it, but Riley was a light sleeper at the best of times and he was awake and at her door before he thought about it.

Moonlight was flooding through the window.

Her bedding was everywhere. She was wearing panties and bra but nothing else. She looked like she was writhing in fear. Her curls were spread out on the pillows, and her eyes were wide and staring, as if she was seeing…

Hell?

It was enough to twist the heart.

'Pippa.' He was by her bed, grasping her shoulders, holding her. 'Pippa, wake up, you're having a nightmare. Pippa.'

Her eyes widened. She jerked sideways, as if he was the thing that terrified her.

'Pippa, it's Riley. Dr Chase. The guy in the helicopter. Pippa, it's Riley, the guy you're planning not to jump.'

And somehow the stupidity of that last statement got through. Her body stilled, slumped. Her eyes slowly lost their terror, and the terror was replaced by confusion. She focused. Her gaze found his. Locked.

She shuddered and the shudder ran the length of her body.

She was cold to touch. The temperature in the desert dropped at night to almost freezing. She'd gone to sleep with a pile of quilts, but the quilts were on the floor.

She shuddered again and it was too much. He tugged a quilt from the floor, wrapped it round her and tugged her into his arms. He held her as one might hold a terrified child.

She seemed so shocked she simply let it happen. The

shudders went on, dreadful, born of fear and cold and sheer disorientation.

He should never have agreed to her coming here, he thought, swearing under his breath.

When he'd been a kid, tiny, he'd found a budgerigar—or rather one of the feral cats around the dump they'd been living in had found it. He'd managed to get it free, then brought it inside, warmed it and settled it into a box. A couple of hours later he'd checked and it had looked fine.

Delighted, he'd lifted it out. The little bird had been someone's pet. It was tame, it talked, it clung to his finger, it pecked his ear.

With no adult to advise him, he'd played with it until bedtime. He'd popped it back into its box for the night and the next morning he'd opened the box to discover it was dead.

Years later he'd talked to a mate who was a vet, and he'd told him the sad little story.

'It'll still have been running on adrenalin,' the vet said. 'You weren't to know, but you'll have stressed it more.'

And today… He'd allowed Pippa to come here…

He'll have stressed her more.

He swore and held her close.

'It's okay, Pippa. You're safe. Yes, you're in the middle of the Australian desert with people you don't know, yes, you nearly drowned, yes, your marriage is off, but, hey, the threats are all past. No one and nothing's doing you harm. We'll get you warm, and tomorrow we'll fly you back to the coast. We're intending to fly via Sydney. You could catch a plane home to England from Sydney. How about if we phone your mother? That might make you feel like things are real.'

He was talking for the sake of talking, not waiting for a response, keeping his voice low and gentle, keeping the message simple. You're safe, there's no threat, you're under control.

The shudders were easing. She was curled against his body as if she was taking warmth from him, and maybe she was. He hadn't undressed to sleep—he'd hauled some rugs over himself and relaxed on the settee, knowing he'd be up two or three times in the night to check on Gerry. He was grateful for it now. He was in his Flight-Aid uniform. The shirt was thick, workmanlike cotton. If he'd undressed, as she had…

It'd be skin against skin…

And he could stop his thoughts going there right now.

He did stop his thoughts going there. Discipline. Nineteen years of discipline since…

'I'm…I'm sorry.' She was recovering enough to talk, but not enough to pull away. She was taking every shred of comfort she could find. Huddled against him, spooned against his body, wrapped in quilts, she needed it all. 'I shouldn't… I woke you…'

'Nightmares are the pits,' he said softly, and he smelled her hair and thought…and thought…

And didn't think. It was inappropriate to think.

'I didn't… I mean, I don't know why…'

'You didn't talk to the psychologists back at Whale Cove?'

'I didn't need to.' That was better. There was a touch of asperity in her voice. She had spirit, this woman.

If she didn't have such spirit she'd be dead, he thought, and the idea made him hold her tighter. For some reason…

Well, for a very good reason it was good she wasn't dead. But… Why was it *more* important that it was Pippa?

'I'm okay,' she said, but she didn't move.

'You're freezing. You pushed all the covers off. Stay where you are until you're warm.'

She was silent for a while and he could feel her gathering her thoughts, gathering her senses. Figuring out what had happened. How she'd ended up where she was.

'So I didn't have any blankets on?' she said at last, cautiously, and he grinned. The woman in her was back.

'Nope.'

'Oh, my…'

'Don't worry about it. I've seen worse things come out of cheese.'

She stiffened. She sat up and swivelled. 'Pardon?'

'I'm a doctor,' he said, apologetically. 'I learned anatomy in first year.'

'I am *not* your patient.' That was definite.

'No.'

'I'm your colleague.'

'Yes.' He thought about it. 'Yes, ma'am.'

He felt her smile rather than heard it and it felt good. To make her smile…

But suddenly he was thinking of her back in the water again, and this time it was he who shuddered.

'Hey,' she said.

'Sorry.'

'You're cold.'

'Nope.'

'I'm fine. You can go back to bed.'

'You're still shaking.'

'Not much.'

'I could go across and get some heat pads from Joyce.'

'No,' she said, and suddenly the fear was back in her voice. Born straight out neediness.

It had been some nightmare.

He'd had nightmares himself. As a kid. One of his stepfathers had enjoyed using a horsewhip. The beatings themselves hadn't been so bad. Waking up, though, in the night, when dreams blended reality into something worse…

Okay, he wouldn't leave her.

'The bed's big,' she whispered. 'Sh-share?'

He stiffened. She felt him stiffen, and he felt her immediate reaction. Indignation.

'We're colleagues,' she said, pulling away. Backing against the bedhead. Eying him with something that looked suspiciously like scorn. 'We have one bed. Why does everything have to be about sex?'

'I didn't think it was about sex.'

'It wasn't, until you reacted like that.'

'Like what?'

'Like I'd jumped you. Go back to your sofa.'

'No.' He could cope with her need, he thought. She was a colleague.

No. She was a patient. Think of her as a patient.

The lines were blurring. He wasn't sure how he thought of her. But he knew he couldn't leave her.

'Why not?' she demanded.

'Because one of two things will happen,' he said. 'Either you'll lie and stare at the ceiling for the rest of the night, scared to go back to sleep. Or you'll go back to sleep and the nightmare will be waiting. You're not out from it yet.'

'How do you know?'

He knew. If the shaking hadn't stopped…

'So what's happened to you?' she asked, her voice suddenly gentling, and that caught him so unawares he could have dropped her. Only he no longer had her. She'd slipped back onto the bed and only her feet were still touching him.

He wanted, quite badly, to be holding her again.

The thought jolted him. What was happening here?

He didn't react to women like this, but she'd somehow pierced something he'd hardly known he had. It was like she'd opened some part of him he'd been unaware existed.

It made him feel exposed. He had to get it sealed up again fast, but how could he do that while she was…here?

'Harry says you have a daughter.' Her voice was suddenly prosaic, like they were making polite conversation at a dinner party. She tugged her quilt. He let it go and she pulled it over her. She huddled under it and she tried to hide the next wave of shivers. 'What's her name?'

'Harry talks too much.' He sighed. 'Lucy.'

'You want to tell me about her?' She was eying him over the top of the quilt. 'I'm guessing Lucy isn't one of 2.4 children in a suburban back yard with Mummy in her apron and a casserole warming on the stove.'

'There are no slippers and pipe waiting at my place.' He said it almost self-mockingly and she slid to the far side of the bed and hauled one of her disarranged pillows to the empty side. She patted it.

'You want to tell me about it?'

She was still asking for help. He knew she was. She couldn't camouflage those tremors. This woman was needy.

So what was stopping him lying on the spare pillow, hauling up a quilt and telling her about Lucy?

Pride? Fear? Fear at letting someone as perceptive as she was close?

He wouldn't be letting her close. Or…no closer than she needed to be to get her warm.

She wanted distraction from terror. What harm?

He sighed. He slid onto the pillow and tugged up a quilt. Then, because it was what she needed and he knew it was, he slid an arm around her shoulders and tugged her close. She stiffened for a moment, but then he felt her relax. It was as if she, too, was reminding herself to be sensible.

'Back to front,' he growled. 'I can warm you more that way.'

'Wait,' she said, and sat up, grabbed her shirt and tugged it on.

Two Flight-Aid shirts. Colleagues.

'Needs must,' she said, lying down and turned her back, letting him tug her into him. He felt her force herself to relax. Muscle by muscle.

He was doing the same himself. The smell of her hair, soft and clean and with a scent so faint…if he wasn't this close he could never have smelled it.

'Tell me about Lucy,' she said, with sudden asperity, and he wondered if she realised what he was thinking.

If she had, then a man was wise to stop thinking it. Right now. Tell her about Lucy.

'She's my daughter.'

'I know that much.' She sounded amused.

'She's beautiful. She's dark and tall and slim. Maybe a bit too thin.' According to the one photograph he'd seen. What would he know?

'How often do you see her?'

'Never. I didn't know she existed until three months ago.'

'Wow!' She didn't sound judgmental. She just sounded… interested. It was the right reaction, he thought. She made it sound like not knowing you had a daughter was almost normal. That came from years of medical training, he thought. Nothing shocks.

'Wow's right.'

'Harry says she's coming tomorrow.'

'So it seems,' he said harshly. 'Let's talk of something else.'

'Something else.' She was silent for a while. Absorbing an absent daughter? He wondered if she was drifting into sleep, but apparently not.

'So what about your parents?' she asked.

'What about them?'

'Where are they?'

'My mother's in Perth. Last time I heard, my father was in New Zealand but that was twenty years back.'

'Not a close family, huh?'

'You could say that.' Family wasn't something he chose to talk about but if it stopped the trembling… This was therapy, he decided, and tugged her tighter and thought, Yep, medical necessity.

'You're so warm,' she murmured, and she was relaxing a little, warming a little, tension easing.

'So tell me about your family,' he said, deciding to turn the tables.

'What do you want to know?'

'Why your mother didn't get on that plane and come. She knew how close you'd come to death.'

'Just as long as it didn't hit the papers. That's all she'd care about.'

'Not close either?'

'Too close. They should have had more children. Only one… it's all your eggs in one basket and a girl can't live up to it.'

'Do they like you being a nurse?'

'They hate me being a nurse.' The tension was back again. 'I wanted to do medicine so badly but there was no way they'd support me. I was to go into the family business. That was my grandfather's decree. It's my grandfather who pulls the strings. I've had to work my way through nursing. He fought me every step of the way.'

'But you're doing something you love.'

'I'm not sure,' she whispered. 'Or…I am but I'm not doing enough. When I was trying to stop myself drowning, there was a part of me thinking… If I get out of here, I want to make a difference. Not just…be.'

'I can't imagine you just being,' he said, and she sighed and yawned and snuggled.

'It'd be so easy to sink into my parents' world. Like my hotel room. I have three different types of bath foam.'

'Really?'

'Really.' She snuggled again. His body was reacting. Of course his body was reacting. He'd have to be inhuman for it not to react.

He was wearing heavy-duty pants with a heavy-duty zipper. He was becoming exceedingly grateful that he didn't routinely pack pyjamas.

'I'm so warm,' she murmured. 'I shouldn't let you do this.'

'My pleasure.'

'I'm sure it's not.' Her voice was starting to slur. 'I'm sure it's just that you're a very nice man and a fine doctor. You saved my life and you've rescued me from my nightmare. Now you're making me feel wonderful. I'm so sorry you didn't know about your daughter.'

'I'm seeing her tomorrow. She's the guest I told Coral about.'

'That's great.' She sighed again, a long, sleepy, languorous sigh that made the night feel impossibly sensual. 'That's wonderful.

Tomorrow you'll turn into a father. You're a lifesaver, a doctor, a father, a guy with pecs to die for…and you're holding me. Like three types of bath foam…what more could a girl desire?'

She was making no sense at all. 'Go to sleep.'

'I will.' She smiled—he heard her smile. 'I am. But I first I need to say thank you.'

'It's okay.'

'No, but tomorrow you'll be a father,' she said. 'And a doctor again, and a lifesaver, and I need to say thank you now.'

'Pippa…'

'You saved my life.' She was no longer even trying to make sense, he thought. She was simply saying what came into her head. 'You saved me from Roger. I could have married him.'

'That was hardly me…'

'You were part of it. If you hadn't been there for me… Apart from being dead… if it hadn't been you I might even have been weak enough to let him come. He might have bullied me into believing in him again. Marriage for the sake of family. Ugh.' She shuddered and clung.

'Not now, though. You've shown me how…ordinary it all was. Just ordinary.' Her voice was a husky whisper, part of the dreaming. Filled with pleasure and warmth and something more… 'Today… Not only am I alive, not only do I not have to marry Roger, there's a whole world you're showing me. You're showing me how it is to be alive. New. Wanting…'

'Pippa…'

Was she still dreaming? She wasn't, he knew she wasn't, but still she was in some dreamlike state where normal boundaries didn't apply. Saying exactly what she thought. Feeling what she wanted to feel. Loving the way she was feeling and letting him know that, too.

Her body was heating against his, and he knew…he knew…

That he should leave, now. Put her away from him. Let reality take over again.

But she was holding him, needing him, wanting him, and how strong would he have to be to put her away? She was a mature woman. She was melting against him, sensual, languorous, seductive…

Seductive?

'Thank you,' she murmured again, and before he could realise what she intended she twisted in his arms. She wound her arms around his neck, then pushed herself up, just a little, so she was gazing down at him in the moonlight.

And before he could even think how to stop her, or even if he wanted to stop her—she kissed him.

She surely kissed him.

For this was no kiss of thanks, a polite brushing of lips, fleeting contact and then pulling away.

This was a kiss of a woman wanting a man.

More.

It was the kiss of a woman claiming her man.

Her lips met his and the contact burned.

Maybe his whole body had been heating before this point, and now… It was like the heat suddenly exploded into flame and the point of flame was his mouth, her lips, the melding of the two together.

This woman in his arms.

'Riley.' Had she said his name? She couldn't have, but the sound was between them, a long drawn-out sigh, a sigh of longing, of aching need, of want.

Of need between two people?

This was crazy. Unwise. Cruel even. To kiss her under such circumstances…

He wasn't kissing her—she was kissing him. But maybe the delineation was blurring.

Maybe they were simply kissing. A man and a woman and a need as primeval as time itself.

Pippa.

His defences were disappearing, crumpling at the touch of her loveliness, in the aching need of her sigh, in the heat of their bodies. He was kissing in return, demanding as well as giving, his mouth plundering, searching her sweetness, glorying in her need as well as his own.

Pippa.

She was like no woman he'd ever touched. His body was reacting without control. She was stripping him bare, exposing parts of him he never knew he had, parts hidden behind barriers he'd built up with years of careful self-restraint.

Where was the self-restraint now?

Certainly not with Pippa.

She needed this. He knew it at some basic gut level. She was a mature woman, a woman who knew her way in the world, a woman who fought for what she wanted. Or didn't want.

Right now she didn't want control.

Eight hours in the water had shown her, as his job showed him almost every day, that control was an illusion.

Pippa had cheated death. Her nightmares had brought it back but she was fighting past them.

Tonight was all about life, about affirmation of now. She was taking what she needed to survive.

This woman…

There were so many undercurrents, so many things he should make himself consider, but all he could think was how she felt in his arms. Her kiss, her mouth. Her hands holding him close, demanding he hold her close as well, growing closer…closer…

Her kiss was almost savage in its intensity—fire meeting fire. Sense was disappearing—had disappeared. There was only this woman.

There was only now.

Her fingers were unfastening the buttons of his shirt. He felt the tug, registered it for what it was, somehow made himself react. There was nothing between them but these clothes. If they disappeared…

He hauled back and it hurt, but he made himself put her away, holding her up from him, meeting her gaze in the moonlight.

'Pippa, if we go further…'

'Do you want to go further?' Her voice was steady, as it hadn't been steady until now. The tremors had ceased. She met his gaze squarely, surely, with honesty and with trust.

Trust. The sensation made something inside him wrench open. Barriers… Where were they? Not here. Not now.

'More than life itself,' he said, and knew it was true. 'But it's not wise.'

'I'm not feeling wise.' And before he could realise what she intended, she tugged her shirt off and tossed it aside. Her hands reached behind her back for her bra clip. 'Riley, I'm a mature woman. I've spent the night deep in horror. Yes, I'm using you. I know I am. Can you accept that? Want it even? I want it so much.'

He caught her hands and held. Stopping the bra disappearing.

'No.'

'No?' The tremor was suddenly back.

'Pippa, this is unprotected sex we're talking.'

'I'm supposed to be on my honeymoon. I'm protected.'

'You know as well as I do that—'

'That there's more risks than pregnancy?' Her eyes didn't leave his. 'There is that. I'm safe. Roger's a careful man. Double blind crossover tests, safe from everything except bridesmaids. How about you?'

'You shouldn't believe—'

'Neither should you. But I will believe. Can I be safe with you, Riley Chase?'

'You can be safe,' he said huskily, for the feel of her body over his was making his whole body seem to transmute into something he barely recognised. 'But, Pippa, is this purely to make you forget?'

'Forget?'

'Roger? Near drowning? Hopelessness?'

'No,' she said, surely and strongly. 'It's to make me remember. And before you ask,' she whispered, lowering herself again so her mouth was close to his, 'yes, it's seduction. Yes, I'm using you. I need you to affirm…life.'

She faltered then, suddenly unsure, but he knew it wasn't her actions she was questioning, it was her reasons. 'This night… You… It seems as natural as breathing. I've signed no contract yet at Whale Cove. Tomorrow I can walk away. I well may, because what happens tonight could make working together impossible. But it's not interfering with me wanting you now. And you…do you want me?'

How could she ask?

There was something changing within him. Something he hadn't been aware could be changed. The tenderness…the aching need he had for her…

Pippa.

Was she a fool?

She probably was, but she didn't care. She was in the middle of the Australian desert with a man she didn't know. Or maybe she did know him.

He'd saved her life but this went deeper. Something about Riley Chase resonated with her as no man ever had before.

Someday she'd ask him about his childhood, she thought. If she stayed around that long. If there was a shared tomorrow.

It didn't matter if there wasn't.

Or maybe it did matter, but for now she couldn't allow herself to care, for if she cared she'd allow in caution, rational thought, sense.

She didn't want those things. She only wanted Riley.

She'd told him it was to drive away nightmares. It was, but there was more. More she could hardly admit. More she didn't understand.

She was still resting lightly over him. She let her fingers run the length of his face, feeling the roughness of the stubble on his jaw, tracing the faint indentation of a scar at the side of his mouth, feeling the strength of his features.

She knew this man.

It was a strange sensation, but she believed it. She didn't need to know how he'd got that scar, where the life lines had been formed. Something within this man was stirring a response within her that she couldn't understand but could only believe.

Two halves of a whole? That was fantasy, but there was something. Some basic link.

If he told her now he'd had a happy childhood, a safe, secure existence, she'd never believe him. He was a man who walked alone. As she had, all her life.

As she would again tomorrow?

Maybe, but not tonight, for tonight she was holding Riley, and he was driving away every other thought. Taking away terror, giving her life.

She was exploring his face with her fingers, loving what she was learning. She met his gaze, devouring the look of him.

There was need in his eyes. There was strength and truth and passion.

Another man might have taken what she offered without questions. He was still and silent, making sure…

He could be sure.

'Riley,' she whispered.

'Pippa.' He smiled at her.

And here was a wonder, for the smile said he was loving her. She knew it was just for now, but now was enough.

With his smile, the terrors of the last few days disappeared. As did the betrayal that was Roger, the accusations of her parents, the pressures from home. Even the awfulness of the sea; in the face of Riley's smile it was nothing. For now, for this wondrous moment, the horrors of the past made way. For Riley.

And then control was no longer hers. Impulse was no longer hers. For Riley took her face in his hands, he tugged her down to him, and he kissed her.

He kissed her as she ached to be kissed, a possessive, loving, searching kiss that said for tonight she was his woman and everything else must fade to nothing. This kiss was his seal of commitment. He deepened the kiss, and deepened it still more, and the sensation made her want to cry out with wonder.

He put her away from him once more and she almost cried

a protest. But he was only moving her a little, so once more he could read her eyes.

'This is love-making,' he said softly. 'Pippa, what you're offering…it's a gift without price. I won't take it lightly.'

'I wouldn't expect you to,' she said, struggling to make her voice light in response. 'But I know it's only for tonight. You won't wake up to find yourself with a woman hanging on your sleeve, wanting commitment. I've been engaged to Roger on and off for more than ten years. That's more than enough commitment. I've told my mother where she could put my wedding dress and it wasn't anywhere polite.'

She smiled, finding shared laughter. Somehow she'd kept her voice steady. Somehow she'd made herself sound like she was telling the truth.

She didn't want commitment?

She was under control?

There was an illusion. The truth was that even though she was now independent, since last Sunday night her life had spun totally out of control, and Riley Chase was making it a thousand times worse. Oh, it was no fault of Riley's. She didn't even mind.

In truth, for the first time in her life she was out of control and she was loving it.

'So are you intending to kiss me again?' she teased. 'Because I'm getting a bit uncomfortable. I'm not sure if you've noticed but I'm lying on your chest and it's not quite as comfortable as that nice, soft mattress you're lying on.'

'Then let's fix that,' he growled, and swung her over so they lay side by side. And she was being kissed as she'd never been kissed in her life.

Riley was kissing her, tasting her, exploring her.

Riley was loving her.

And all that must be said had been said. Hesitations were gone.

She closed her eyes, savouring the feel of him, the taste, the touch. His hands were working their magic on her skin, knowing every inch of her, and every tiny movement sent shivers of sensual pleasure through her entire body.

She arched back and he found the clips of her bra. It finally fell away and she loved that it did. His fingers cupped the soft swell of her breasts, tracing her nipples, making her sigh with sheer, unmitigated pleasure.

She wanted closer. She had *his* buttons undone now—how had she done that? She hardly knew but his shirt was gone and she loved that it was gone. The feel of her skin against his…the strength of his body…the sheer maleness of him… It was taking her breath away.

The moonlight washed through the window, and the sight of his body was making her dizzy. His body heat, the touch of his mouth, the feel of his hands…

She was starting to burn.

His breathing was becoming ragged, and she gloried in it, gloried that he was feeling as she was. This was mutual need. Mutual pleasure. This was right, she thought, in some far recess of her mind. This man had given her her life, and this…it felt like giving life in return.

Her hair was tumbled on his face. He tucked her curls behind her ears and then tugged her tight so he could reclaim her mouth.

Oh, his mouth….

It wasn't enough. He was kissing her everywhere, a rain of kisses, her neck, her shoulders, her breasts, and the feeling was so breathtaking she could hardly take in air. Was that what was making her light-headed? She felt like she was floating, and he with her.

She was moving to another place. Moving to another life?

Her breasts were moulding to his chest as his hands tugged at her hips. Her clothing had disappeared entirely. Excellent, but fair was fair. She found the zipper of his jeans and tugged, and then her fingers returned to where the zip had been.

The night was swirling. Her mind was swirling.

Somehow she was shedding a skin, being hauled from her old life into this, the new.

Oh, the feel of him. The joy. He was discovering every secret of her body. She felt herself arch with sheer animal pleasure, abandoning herself to him entirely. He could do anything he wanted with her and she could do the same to him. For this night anything was possible.

The nightmares had faded to nothing. The terror that had lingered was gone, dissolved in Riley's heat, Riley's body, Riley's need.

Her need.

Skin against skin.

She couldn't get close enough.

She was on fire.

'Riley.' She heard herself moan but it wasn't her voice. It was a stranger, a woman Riley was loving. She heard the aching need and wondered at it. 'Riley.'

'My beautiful girl…'

And he was up and over her, his dark eyes gleaming in the moonlight. 'Are you indeed sure?'

Was she sure? For answer she reached and held his hips, she centred him, she tugged…

He was hers.

The night was dissolving around her. Riley…

'Pippa.' His voice was a husky whisper, in her ear. He was taking her slowly, with languorous pleasure, forcing her to wait, forcing himself to wait.

Riley.

This was where she was meant to be. This was her heart, her home, her centre.

This man.

He was a part of her, merged with her, one. Their bodies were riding each other, but there was no physical effort. Her mind was as clear as the stars outside. She came and came again but she didn't lose sight of Riley for one moment.

How could she close her eyes? She marvelled at his body as

he moved within her. His raw strength. His muscles, delineated, beautiful.

Riley. For tonight, her man.

He was deep within her, and her body was taking her rhythm from his. He could take her anywhere he wished. He could love her for ever. This moment…

And the next.

For it went on and on, building, building, and she felt herself weeping with joy. She wept and she held his beautiful body and finally, wondrously, she felt him surge within her—and she knew nothing could ever be the same again. When finally he lay back, spent, when she lay on his chest and felt his heartbeat merged with hers, when she felt his fingers run through her hair with tenderness and wonder and love…

She knew the nightmares wouldn't return.

She knew he'd brought her out from the far side.

She just wasn't exactly sure he'd come out with her.

She slept, cradled in his arms, warm, secure, safe.

Pippa.

What had he done?

He'd slept with her.

He'd made love with her.

He'd never meant to. She'd been his patient. She was his colleague.

She'd woken in mid-nightmare. He'd come to comfort her and he'd taken her.

Or she'd taken him.

It was her need as well as his. What had happened had been the culmination of a need so basic it was almost past comprehension, past his ability to judge on right and wrong.

Because right now, lying in the dark with Pippa's naked body curled against him, it felt right. How could there be anything wrong with something that had felt so inevitable?

It didn't feel like he was holding Pippa. It felt like he was holding a part of himself. If something was to wrench her away right now, it'd hurt like tearing a part of himself away.

He turned his head a little and his face was in her hair. He was smelling the faint clean scent of her. She murmured a little in her sleep, her hand shifted, sought, held. His fingers were entwined in hers.

Pippa.

He was lying in the dark, holding his woman in his arms.

He closed his eyes and a peace he'd never felt before settled over him.

Right or wrong, for now, for this moment, Dr Riley Chase had come home.

CHAPTER SIX

SHE woke and he was gone.

She lay in the filtered dawn light and forced herself to absorb the fact without panic. She was trying to figure where she was, what had happened, what was real and what was dream.

She was naked. The bed smelled of love-making. There was a strong indentation in the pillow crushed beside hers. She rolled over and buried her face in the linen, thinking she could smell him.

She'd made love to Riley Chase.

She'd taken him…

She closed her eyes, letting the sensations of the night before unfold, reveal themselves, sort themselves into some sort of order.

She'd had a nightmare. Riley had come in to comfort her. She'd pulled him to her and she'd made love.

Talk about needy…

She should be mortified to her socks, only she wasn't wearing socks. She was wearing nothing at all.

It felt excellent.

Her body felt new, like she'd done one of those crazy rebirth things she'd heard about. She smiled a little at that, thinking rebirth. Yes, she could have lain in a foetal position and pretended to be pushed, with a birth coach telling her exactly what to do. Or she could have taken Riley to her. She could have allowed him to take her. She could have woken feeling this…

Excellent.

Though maybe a bit sore. They'd woken during the night and made love again. And again.

She stirred and stretched and smiled. The tangerine of the desert sunrise was calling. Life was calling.

She flung off her bedclothes, headed for the shower, and went to find Riley.

Gerry had passed an excellent night. His leg was looking good and he wanted to leave, but the exceedingly large brace fastened from thigh to ankle was stopping him. Riley wasn't about to remove it any time soon. Gerry's wound was large and penetrating, there was access for infection everywhere, and he needed to stay right where he was.

'The nerves were millimetres away from being severed,' he told him. 'And you're not out of the woods yet.' No need to mention the two dangers were unrelated. 'I haven't saved your leg only to have you come back with gangrene or worse. You're staying in this bed for a week and we'll hear no more about it.'

He left the room grinning, and made his way to Amy's room. His grin faded.

Amy was cradling Baby Riley and she was crying.

'She won't feed,' she said. 'My boobs hurt, they're that full, but she won't feed. I fed her at midnight and she hardly drank anything and now she just wants to sleep.'

'Hi.' Pippa was suddenly in the room with them. She was a colleague, Riley told himself, trying hard to greet her as a colleague. But… How could she look so…neat? The last time he'd seen her…

Let's not go there.

'Problem?' Pippa asked, heading for the bed, professional even if he wasn't. Amy was cradling her baby against her breast. 'Hey, Baby Riley, who's a sweetheart?' She looked at Amy's swollen breasts, glanced at Amy's face, and Riley thought she had an instant appreciation of the situation.

'Who's a sleepyhead?' she asked. She stroked the baby's

cheek, the one closest to Amy's breast, and kept on stroking. The baby turned instinctively in the direction of the stroking. Pippa's fingers moved slightly, steering the baby's rosebud mouth. The little lips caught the taste of milk, caught Amy's nipple and started sucking. Though not with gusto.

'Keep stroking her cheek,' Pippa told her. 'No going to sleep, Baby Riley. You have growing to do.'

'She wouldn't...for me,' Amy said, choking back tears.

'I suspect she's a bit jaundiced,' Riley said, watching her suck. 'Not badly, but it's enough to make her sleepy.'

'What's jaundice?'

Pippa crossed to the basin and moistened a facecloth. She washed Amy's face as Riley checked out his namesake. The baby was feeding but not with any energy. He checked her palms, then the soles of her tiny feet. Yesterday they'd been pink. Today there were faint traces of yellow.

Mild jaundice. Early days.

Watch and see, he thought. There wasn't any need for intervention yet.

But watch and see here?

'What's wrong?' Amy asked, breathless with fear, and Riley uncurled the baby's fist and showed her.

'See her palm? The faint yellow tinge is the first sign of jaundice. It's common in babies. As our body's red blood cells outlive their purpose, our liver gets rid of them. If they can't, then we get a build-up of these old cells—the build-up's called bilirubin. Because Baby Riley's liver is so small, it's not doing its job properly. It might take a week or so to adjust.'

'But she'll be okay?'

'She'll definitely be okay. Sunlight helps. We'll pop her by the window with just a nappy on—that's often enough to fix it. The way you're feeding her now is great. It'll take a little more encouraging on your part and we need to make sure she's not getting dehydrated. If she gets any sleepier than she is, we'll pop her under lights like a sunlamp.'

'Sister Joyce will?'

'That's a problem,' Riley said evenly, as Pippa rinsed the face-cloth and bathed her face again. 'Amy, jaundice usually shows up before this. If I'd thought Baby Riley might develop it, I'd have asked you to stay on in Whale Cove.' He met Amy's gaze square on. 'I'm sorry, Amy, but you need to come back with us.'

'To…to the hospital?'

'That would be best.'

'But I don't want to.' It was a wail.

'Then we can organise for you to stay in a hotel near the hospital. Amy, if you were living in Whale Cove I'd be saying keep doing what you're doing, give her a little sunbathe each day, call me if you need me. But I'm a long way away to call.'

Amy's bottom lip trembled. She really was very young, Riley thought. A child herself.

'Jason's out mustering,' she whispered. 'He's due back tomorrow. Can I wait until then?'

'I'm sorry. We need to leave this morning.'

'I don't want to go back to hospital. I hate hospital.' She was crying again, fat tears slipping down her face. She was afraid and alone, Riley thought, and he sent silent invective toward her mother. She hadn't even been in to see her daughter.

'Could one of your sisters come with you?' Pippa asked, diffidently, and he knew Pippa was thinking exactly what he was.

'Mum won't let 'em.'

'Could I talk to your mum?'

She would. He looked at Pippa, in her jeans and her Flight-Aid shirt, her hair bunched back into a loose braid, her face devoid of make-up, and he thought she was just as alone as Amy.

But she had courage in spades. Last night…she'd known what she needed and she'd taken it. She'd taken *him*.

'She'd throw something at you,' Amy was saying, and Pippa blinked.

'Really?'

'Yeah. Or set the dogs on you.'

'Uh-oh,' Pippa said, and Riley smiled at her expression. A dog-setting, missile-throwing mother… Pippa had the sense to back away. 'Okay, that was option one,' she conceded. 'Option two is that you come back to Whale Cove and stay in the house beside the hospital where I'm staying. Where Doc Riley stays. They tell me it's okay to invite guests so I'm inviting you. Do you want to come and stay with me and Riley?'

She was… What the…?

Riley practically gaped.

'Close your mouth, Doctor,' Pippa said kindly. 'After all, it's not like Amy's a patient any more. This baby's called Riley Pippa, and that makes her our family. So will you come and stay with us?'

'But Jason…' Amy seemed bemused. She'd stopped crying.

'We'll leave him a note,' Pippa said grandly. 'If he can get to the coast then he can stay, too.'

'He probably won't want to.'

'That's up to him. Will you come and stay with us?'

'Yes,' Amy said, looking down at her drowsy baby, knowing she had no choice. 'Yes, I will.'

'Are you out of your mind?' Riley barely got the door shut behind them before he exploded. 'What sort of crazy idea is this?'

'What?' Pippa asked, turning to face him. She looked innocent and puzzled, as if she had no idea what he was talking about.

'Inviting Amy to live with me.'

'With us,' she said kindly. 'And not live. Stay.'

'You don't live in that house.'

'I do. Coral says I do. She says I'm to make it my home, so I am.'

'You're not due to move there until Sunday.'

'I'll need to move in straight away,' she said thoughtfully. 'That's a pity. Roger might even get a refund on his honeymoon suite.'

'She's a patient!'

'She's your patient. I met her in hospital when I was in the next bed. She's my friend.'

'You're a nurse.'

'Nurses have friends.'

'It's not ethical.'

'Why isn't it ethical?'

'You don't get involved.'

'*You* don't need to. Coral says you have a big bedroom and you barely use the rest of the house. I know your daughter's coming but Coral says we have four bedrooms. So how does having Amy staying get you involved?'

'You'll need to be involved.'

'I want to be involved.'

'Pippa…'

'Mmm?' She tilted her chin and met his gaze full on. Her eyes were direct and luminous.

He needed to keep building his anger, he thought. He needed to hold to his knowledge that she'd just overstepped professional boundaries, because suddenly all he could think of was how she'd felt last night.

How he'd held her.

How she'd slept, tucked into the curve of his body.

His boundaries were slipping. He felt them shift, and he didn't know what to do about it. Revert to anger?

'She'll have to go to hospital.'

'I've invited her to stay with us. She's stopped crying. You want me to go and tell her you've changed your mind?'

'I haven't changed my mind,' he said explosively. 'It's you…'

'Maybe you could stay in the honeymoon suite,' she said, thoughtfully. 'Though I'm not sure how I'd explain that to Roger. And then there's Lucy…'

'Of all the…'

'You don't want a honeymoon?'

'No! Neither do I want people staying in my house.'

'Coral said it's the hospital's house. And you already have Lucy.' She sighed, suddenly repentant. 'I'm sorry. I know I should have talked to you before I offered, but I couldn't bear it. She's so alone. I know what it's like to be alone, Riley, and I suspect you do, too, but I've never been as alone as Amy is right now. I can fix that. I'll take care of her.'

'You'll be working.'

'I will be,' she said, her tone suddenly severe as his objections grew weaker. 'You think Amy wants me there twenty-four seven? She'll take what I can give, but that's a whole lot more than she has now. So...are we heading back to Whale Cove or not?'

'Pippa...'

'Yes?' Her eyes were now expressionless. She was waiting for more anger, he thought. She was expecting more anger.

He didn't have it in him. Not when he looked at her.

'Last night...' he said.

'Was wonderful,' she said, quickly, before he could go any further. 'But you needn't worry. Yes, I used you to escape from my nightmares and, yes, it was fabulous, but I'm not about to step over the boundaries there either.'

'That's not what I was about to say.'

'Then what were you about to say?'

'That I thought it was wonderful, too,' he said, and her face lit in response, softening, her eyes lighting with laughter. She hadn't expected him to say it. She loved it that he had, he thought, and that felt...excellent.

'Snap,' she said, and she stood on tiptoe and kissed him, on the lips but lightly, fleetingly. 'It was indeed wonderful,' she said. 'But it doesn't mean I'm pushing past your boundaries. I needed you last night and you were there. I'll always be grateful. And now I intend to be there for Amy. See, we're both soft touches in our own way.'

'I didn't... Last night was more...'

'I know it was,' she said, firmly and surely. 'Like I said, it was fabulous. I'll remember it for ever. But we both know it was for one night only. We both know we need to love that it happened, and now we need to move on.'

They couldn't move on, not for a couple of hours. Joyce was waiting for them and cornered them before they reached the veranda.

'Ear infection,' she said. 'Coming in within half an hour. I'll make you breakfast. And while you're waiting, I'm concerned about John Thalderson's feet. He's cracked his heel,' she explained to Pippa. 'He's diabetic—lousy circulation. I'm dressing it every day but he came in ten minutes ago… Have a look, Riley, while I cook you breakfast.'

They both looked. John Thalderson's feet were truly appalling. He should be headed for Sydney, Pippa thought, or Whale Cove at the very least, but once again neither he nor Riley seemed to think it was an option.

Riley injected local so he could do a thorough debridement, cleaning up the messy edges. He dressed the wound with care, while Pippa assisted.

'You'll stay on the veranda for the week,' Riley told him. 'No argument. Look after Gerry for me.'

'Sure thing, Doc,' John said, and limped out, leaning heavily on his stick.

'Why not Whale Cove?' Pippa asked. 'He's not about to go into cardiac arrest and surely he needs intensive, long-term treatment.'

'I told you,' Riley growled. 'I can't risk it. He'll lie in a clean white hospital bed, he won't eat the food, he'll turn his face to the wall and he'll get worse, not better. Yes, here his feet may well not heal. He may even face amputation, but even if he does we'll take him down to Whale Cove, we'll get it done as fast as we can and we'll get him back on this veranda. He'll certainly die faster than he would if he had optimum treatment but that's his choice.'

'So what Joyce is doing…'

'She's saving lives,' Riley said. 'By running this place and by turning her back on government regulations, she's keeping these guys alive, and I'm doing all in my power to help her. And now… she's even cooking bacon and eggs for us, so we're not keeping her waiting.'

Breakfast was massive.

Pippa ate and thought. Ate and watched. Then watched and

listened, while hunger grew for something that had nothing to do with food.

Harry and Riley and Joyce chatted like the old friends they obviously were. They were doing such good, she thought. The three of them.

She wanted to be a part of it. Fiercely. More fiercely every moment.

Had she messed with that by sleeping with Riley?

Maybe she had. He was terse with her this morning, like he wasn't quite sure how to react. That was fair. She wasn't sure how to react to him either. And she'd foisted Amy onto him.

He was laughing at a story Joyce was telling him. The dour nurse thought the world of him. She could see it in the way Joyce smiled at him, the way she ladled more and more bacon onto his plate.

A team…

She wanted to be a part of it so much it hurt. She set down her knife and fork and pushed her plate away. Joyce looked at her in concern. 'Had enough?'

'I'm feeling disoriented,' she confessed. 'Like it's taking some time for my head to catch up with my body.'

'You're doing too much,' Riley said. 'We'll get you back to Whale Cove and you and Amy can lie on the veranda and let your heads catch up all they want.' He glanced at his watch. 'We should all be moving. One ear infection and then home.'

'Sydney,' Harry said. He demolished the last of his bacon and stood up. 'In case you'd forgotten, your daughter's due to arrive at lunchtime. And the plane's due for a service. Yesterday's plan was to return to Whale Beach, then take the plane to Sydney this morning. We've run out of time. Today's plan is therefore straight to Sydney.'

'We'll have Amy and the baby,' Pippa said blankly.

'Riley'll have to hire a car to take you all home,' Harry said cheerfully. 'I'm having a weekend off. Staying in Sydney until the plane's done. Home Monday.'

'Hell,' Riley said.

'Yeah, I thought you'd forgotten the time,' Harry said, and grinned. 'Now, what can you have been thinking of to make you forget you have a daughter arriving?'

Riley said nothing.

That was pretty much the last Riley spoke for the morning. He retreated into some place no one was allowed to enter. Pippa and Joyce helped Amy and her sleepy baby back onto the plane. Once again Pippa sat in the back with Amy.

Amy was subdued. Pippa tried to keep up happy chat but she didn't succeed.

Even with the headsets turned off, she knew that Riley was deep in silence, too.

There were so many emotions swirling around she couldn't make sense of any of them.

Inviting Amy to stay had problems. It meant she'd have to stay in Riley's house—in the hospital house, she corrected herself—as well, and she was starting to think her wisest path was for her to retreat to her honeymoon hotel and close the door.

Or retreat back to England?

That wasn't going to happen. Not! For she'd fallen head over heels in love with this job. With what Riley was doing. With what Joyce was doing. She wanted to help with a hunger that was deeper than anything she'd ever known.

As a child, on television in some long-forgotten luxury hotel, watched over by some anonymous hotel sitter, she'd seen a documentary. A doctor in South America, treating children's eyes. She'd watched in fascination as bandages were removed and sight was restored, and something had resonated with her at a level she hardly understood. She wanted to work like that, and the desire had never left her.

Nursing in England had been great. She loved her work, and there was always need. But the last twenty-four hours was causing the emotions she'd felt after the documentary to come crowding back.

She *had* to be allowed to be a part of it.

She might have messed with that, she conceded, by allowing last night to happen. And by pushing Amy onto Riley?

Riley was stuck with her and with Amy and her baby as he went to meet his daughter for the first time. This for a man who walked alone? It was a wonder his head wasn't exploding.

What had she been thinking, making love to him last night?

She knew what she'd been thinking. She'd watched Joyce smile at him this morning and she'd thought, Yes, that's how he should be smiled at.

Like he was loved.

And her heart twisted. Love…

Wouldn't it be stupid if it caught her now? Engaged—on and off—for years. Almost married.

What was she thinking? Her engagement had been broken off a little more than a week ago, and here she was thinking of the possibility of falling for another man?

Not just another man.

Riley.

'What's wrong?' Amy asked, and the girl put her hand out and caught Pippa's. 'You look like it's the end of the world.'

She caught herself and managed a smile. The boundaries of friendship and professionalism were certainly blurring. She was a Flight-Aid nurse and she was supposed to be caring for Amy.

'Nothing. Just…dumb thoughts.'

'You didn't really want to drown yourself last week?'

'I… No!'

'I didn't think you did. But you're missing your boyfriend?'

'No,' she said. 'No, I'm not.'

'You're missing someone,' Amy said wisely. 'I can tell.'

CHAPTER SEVEN

FLIGHT-AID had arrangements in place in Sydney so transferring patients, with any delays that involved, could be achieved in privacy and comfort. Collecting patients who'd needed complex medical care and taking them home—back to Whale Cove but more usually back to their Outback homes—was part of Flight-Aid's charter. When they reached Sydney, therefore, Riley was able to take Amy and baby—and Pippa—into a reserved medical lounge and leave them there.

Harry was busy with the plane. Pippa was happy to take care of Amy.

Riley was about to meet his daughter and he was feeling like his head didn't belong to his body.

Pippa. Lucy.

A week ago he didn't have a complication in the world. He wanted, quite badly, to turn back the clock. To head back to Whale Cove, grab his surfboard and ride some waves.

He'd gone to bed last night planning a dawn start. They'd get back to Whale Cove, drop Pippa off and keep going to Sydney. He'd figure what to say on the way down. How to meet your daughter for the first time?

But he'd figure it. He'd collect Lucy, put her in a hire car and drive her back to Whale Cove. He'd be calm, collected, a guy in charge of his world. A man worthy of being a father?

He'd woken this morning, diagnosed jaundice, knew the early getaway wasn't possible. Then Pippa was suddenly filling his house with people. Acting as if what she'd offered was reasonable.

Pippa.

She was messing with his head. More than it was already messed.

Pippa.

He didn't do relationships. He'd learned it as a kid, maybe even earlier. Keep yourself to yourself and you don't get hurt. For one crazy summer he'd forgotten, and the knife had twisted so hard he'd thought he'd go crazy.

Relationships were for other people. They caused pain.

They'd caused…a daughter.

His eighteen-year-old daughter was about to walk through the arrivals gate.

Three months back, when first contact had been made, he'd written saying he wanted to meet her. If there was any way she wanted him in her life, if there was anything she ever needed, she just had to ask. No reply. That email seemed to have gone through but his next had bounced— the email address had seemingly been cancelled. He'd gone to England to find her, only to be told she'd gone away, she didn't want anything to do with him. He was her father in name only.

Relationships caused pain.

He couldn't avoid this one.

She was a tourist, he told himself. Curious about a father she'd never met. Checking out Australia and her unknown biological father as an aside.

The huge metal gates were opening and closing as each passenger cleared customs. Reunions were happening everywhere. Families were clinging, sobbing, laughing.

There was a couple beside him. They were in their seventies, and their anticipation was palpable.

The doors opened and a family emerged, mum and dad and three littlies. The elderly lady gasped and clutched her husband's hand. The little family reached them and was immersed in joy.

He did not do this.

When Lucy emerged… She'd be a kid on an adventure, nothing more, he told himself as he'd told himself over and over. Though why her grandparents weren't funding her to luxury…

Like Pippa was funded to luxury?

Pippa.

It was the sight of the elderly couple holding hands. It made him think he wanted…

He didn't want. He'd spent his life ensuring he didn't want.

The doors slid open.

Lucy.

He recognised her. Of course he did. How many times had he looked at the photograph she'd sent him in her first email? She was thin, tall and pretty, but not like her mother. She looked… like him?

She stood behind her luggage trolley—searching?—and he saw his eyes, his dark hair. And fear.

There was a boy beside her, seemingly arguing that he should push the trolley. He was long and lanky, a kid of about twenty. Worried. He had dark hair curling wildly and olive skin. Then he pushed the trolley sideways and Lucy stepped out from behind.

She was pregnant.

Very pregnant.

She saw him. His picture was on Flight-Aid's website—that's how she'd originally contacted him. He was in his Flight-Aid uniform now so there was no need for red carnations in buttonholes. But there was no wide smile and ecstatic wave like he'd seen from most of the reuniting families. There was a tiny, fleeting smile of recognition. A smile backed with fear.

He thought suddenly of Amy. Same age. Same terror.

The thought settled his nerves. Put things in perspective. This wasn't about him. The boy took over trolley duty. Lucy walked out from the barricade then stopped a few feet from him. 'D-Dad?'

'Lucy.' Despite his wish to stay calm, neutral, all the worry in the world was in the way he said her name, all the things he felt about this frail slip of a kid. And she must have heard it because suddenly she sobbed and stepped forward. Somehow he had her in his arms. She was sobbing on his chest, sobbing her heart out, while the kid beside her looked on with worry.

Lucy. His daughter.

He held her close, waiting for the sobs to subside, wondering what a man was to do. Then he glanced over her head—and suddenly Pippa was there, in the background. She caught his gaze and smiled, fleetingly.

Problem? No. She gave a silent shake of her head, waved slightly, backed away.

And it settled him. For some reason it made him feel that he wasn't alone, with a pregnant daughter and who knew what other issues? Pippa would help.

He didn't need help.

He might, he conceded. *His daughter was pregnant.*

Lucy was drawing back now, sniffing, and the boy beside her was handing her tissues. He looked like he was accustomed to doing it. There'd been lots of crying?

'It's great to meet you,' he said softly, looking down into the face of this half-recognised daughter. A part of him? 'You don't know how much.'

'Really?'

'Really.'

'But I'm…I'm pregnant,' Lucy said, half scared, half defiant.

'I noticed that.' He managed a smile. 'How pregnant?'

'Eight and a half months.'

What the…? He gazed at his daughter in stupefaction. She didn't look so far gone, he thought, but, then, some women didn't show as much as others. 'You can't fly at eight and a half months.'

'Mum paid a doctor to say I'm only seven and a half months. I have a medical certificate.'

'Your mother bribed…'

'She wants to get rid of me,' Lucy whispered. 'Because of

Adam. This…this is Adam.' She clutched the hand of the boy beside her.

'H-Hi,' the boy said.

'Good to meet you,' Riley said, and held out his hand.

The kid was Eurasian, he thought. And with that, he had it figured.

He thought of the way Lucy's grandparents had reacted to him, an illegitimate scholarship kid from Australia. White trash. Marguerite's father had called him that to his face. And now… for Lucy to bring Adam home, as the father of her baby…

'I'm starting to see,' he said.

'They tried to break us up,' Lucy whispered. 'They even bribed someone at Adam's university to kick him out. They accused him of cheating. They rang Immigration; said he was illegal. We can't fight them over there. Mum says if I keep the baby she washes her hands of me. Grandpa says he's raised one kid he didn't want, and he's not helping with another. So we thought…maybe we could start again here. We were hoping… I was hoping that you'll help us. You said in your email…'

He glanced behind his daughter again, and discovered he was searching for Pippa in the crowd. She'd gone.

He was alone with his unknown daughter. And her boyfriend. And their baby?

Their baby. *His grandchild?*

'Of course I will,' he said manfully, and he took his daughter's trolley and summoned the most reassuring smile he was capable of. Which didn't feel to him like it was all that reassuring. 'We need to find a car—or maybe a small bus—and head back to Whale Cove. That's where I live. But first there's someone I'd like you to meet. I have a feeling you're going to like her.' He paused and thought about it. 'I have a feeling we're all going to need her.'

Pippa had headed out to the airport pharmacy to replenish her nappy supply. She needed to get her head around supplying an air ambulance; this was an oversight unworthy of a trained midwife but two days' worth of nappies had slipped from her radar. Maybe she'd been thinking of other things.

Like Riley.

So she'd slipped out to buy nappies, she'd passed the arrivals hall and she'd seen Riley meet his daughter. His pregnant daughter.

He looked like he was drowning.

Riley was a man who walked alone—she knew that. You couldn't be near the man without sensing his reserve. And now... he'd been thrown in at the deep end.

He'd be a grandfather.

She almost chuckled, but she didn't.

She bought what she needed, then hesitated before returning to Amy, taking a moment to try and get her thoughts in order.

Riley.

Last night she'd needed him. She'd clung and he'd held. He'd made love to her and she'd lost herself in his body. He'd lifted her out of her nightmare, and in doing so he'd settled her world. She'd woken this morning feeling that all was right with her world, that she was on a path for life.

With Riley?

No. That was dumb. One night of love-making could never make a permanent relationship. But he'd made her feel wonderful, alive, young, free.

All the things he no longer was. His face just then... He had a pregnant daughter and her heart twisted for him.

She'd seen him holding a daughter he'd never met before. A teenager, bearing his grandchild.

He wouldn't walk away. She knew that about him, truly and surely. He was a man of honour, Riley Chase.

And with that...another twist.

He was so different from Roger. So different from any man she'd ever met. She felt...she felt...

She wasn't allowed to feel. Riley had so many complications, the last thing he needed was her throwing her heart into the ring.

She couldn't. She didn't.

Nappies.

She headed back to Amy, her arms full of nappies, her head full of resolutions. Keep cool and professional. Never be needy again. Support him from the sidelines.

So why was the look on his face as he'd held his daughter etched onto her heart?

Why did her heart still twist?

He hired a family wagon. A seven-seater. Three rows of seats.

The luggage filled the trunk to overflowing. Lucy and Adam didn't travel light. Neither did Amy—babies needed stuff.

Amy was in the back seat, with Baby Riley strapped in beside her.

Adam and Lucy were in the middle seat, holding each other like they were glued.

Pippa was in the front passenger seat next to Riley.

Mum and Dad in the front seat, kids in the back.

Riley was looking…cornered.

She thought back to the evening before, to this same man calmly attempting surgery that was complex and risky. He'd worked through challenges single-mindedly. There was no one she'd rather have around her in a crisis than Riley Chase and that wasn't just because he'd hauled her out of the water. It wasn't just that he'd saved her life.

She'd slept with him last night. It had shifted their relationship to a different level. It could never return again.

Forget last night. She told herself that harshly, but she knew she never could. Somehow she had to move past it, though, to immediate need.

From living on his own, Riley was now faced with living with her, with Amy and her baby, and with his daughter and boyfriend. She thought of his lovely quiet existence and tried to think how she'd feel landed with what he'd been landed with.

Hey. She actually had been landed with it. She, too, was a loner. An only child. A kid who'd learned to like her own company. A woman who'd been independent, whose engagement to Roger had probably lasted as long as it had because she was so independent.

She, too, would be in Riley's house. She was part of Riley's problem—but he was part of hers.

He'd have a bedroom close by hers. That might be a problem all by itself. She needed to put a lid on her hormones.

So what to do?

She was stuck in Riley's house. She'd promised Amy she'd be there.

Riley was stuck as well. Amy needed him to be there.

Riley needed space.

Maybe…

She swivelled. Lucy and Adam could scarcely be any closer. They truly were scared kids.

They had a whole lot facing them, she thought. A baby within weeks. A new country. A future to work out.

A relationship to forge with Riley.

They all needed space.

'Is the house set up for Lucy and Adam?' she asked, loud enough to talk to the car in general.

'Sorry?' Riley seemed a hundred miles away.

'The house,' she said patiently. 'The housekeeper's expecting me on Sunday. She's expecting Lucy today but as far as I can figure, she's expecting a lone Lucy. And she's not expecting Amy. So apart from your room, do we have three more bedrooms—with a single bed apiece?'

'Yes,' Riley said cautiously, not sure where she was going. 'But we can move in a stretcher bed for Adam.'

'A stretcher,' she said disparagingly. 'Lucy, Adam, you guys look really tired.'

'We didn't sleep on the plane,' Lucy admitted.

'So all you want to do is sleep, right?'

'Yes.'

'Then I have a suggestion,' Pippa told her. 'For reasons too complicated to go into right now, we also have one luxurious honeymoon suite in a swish hotel ten minutes' walk away from our house. The suite's paid for until Sunday. Would it make sense if you, Lucy and Adam, had the honeymoon suite until we can set the house up with more beds?'

Silence.

She'd interfered in something that was none of her business, she thought, but this could give Riley space to come to terms with what was happening. And it obviously had its attractions for the scared kids.

'A honeymoon suite,' Lucy breathed.

'King-sized bed. Room service. A bath so big you can swim in it.'

'Compared to a single bed?'

'Hey, it's a pink single bed,' Riley said, sounding affronted.

There was a moment's stunned silence—and then everyone laughed.

It was a good moment. The tension dissipated. Riley's hands unclenched on the steering-wheel and the thing was settled.

Lucy and Adam were to have the honeymoon suite. Riley only had Amy and baby Riley to contend with.

And Pippa.

CHAPTER EIGHT

THEY dropped Lucy and Adam at the hotel with promises to check on them later, then took Amy to the house. They settled Baby Riley in her carry cocoon by the window, showed her the view.

Baby Riley didn't seem impressed by the view but she seemed to soak up the late afternoon rays. 'They'll help cure her,' Riley said. He turned on the heater so the baby could stay in a nappy only, and he tucked the nappy right down so almost all her body was exposed. 'Mother Nature's cure—no medicine needed.'

'It's awesome,' Amy said, gazing around the house in wonder. But Amy was used to living in a corrugated-iron lean-to. Pippa was less impressed.

'How long have you lived here?' she demanded as Amy disappeared for a sleep.

'Six years.'

'Not a picture on the wall?'

'There's a view.'

There was. A veranda ran all around the house but she didn't have to go outside to see the view. The sea was practically in the house. But still…

'No blinds. Bare boards. And this furniture…it's hospital stuff,' she said. 'Even the beds…. Single, cast-iron, a couple of them are even rusty. How can you live like this?'

'It does me,' he said stiffly, and Pippa shook her head in disbelief.

'If I'm to live here, we need rugs. Curtains. Pictures.'

'You're not living here.'

She stilled. 'I thought I was.'

'I don't think that's wise. After last night.'

'I can hardly go back to the hotel,' she retorted. 'I've promised Amy.'

'Amy's only staying until the jaundice settles.'

'Then you want me out?'

'I'm not saying that,' he said wearily, raking his hair in a gesture she was starting to know. 'Pippa, this whole situation… Lucy and Adam…'

'You think they'll want to stay here?'

'No!' The word was an explosion.

'No?'

'They'll want a place of their own.'

'They won't be able to organise that any time soon. They're your family, Riley.'

'I don't do family.'

'You don't have a choice.' She might as well say it, she thought. It was the simple truth. 'Your daughter's eighteen and she's about to deliver your grandchild. Adam seems even more terrified than she is. They need you, Riley.'

'They wanted to go to your hotel.'

'Of course they did. A nice, impersonal hotel where they can cling to each other without the world intruding—or a single bed and a stretcher with a guy they hardly know.'

'That's what I mean. They don't know me.'

'They don't know you but they need you. They're terrified kids. What was Lucy's mother thinking, to let them go?'

'She'll have orchestrated the whole thing,' he said, anger rising. He dug his hands deep in his pockets and she saw his hands clench within the denim. 'She and her parents. Lucy said she wanted her to get rid of it. When that didn't happen, faced with a granddaughter, a child of Eurasian descent… She'll have shipped her off to me. Of all the…'

His face was etched with pain, and she felt ill. For all of them.

'You must have been a baby yourself when Lucy was born,' she whispered, half-scared to probe.

'Nineteen.' He wasn't seeing her now, she thought. He was staring out at the sea, at the past, at nothing. 'A raw kid. I knew nothing.'

'Enough to conceive a child,' she said, and he gave a raw, half-laugh.

'Yeah. Med student. I couldn't even stop that.'

'It takes two to make a baby.'

For a while she thought he wasn't going to answer. But finally… 'It does,' he said at last. 'I had a…well, dysfunctional family doesn't begin to cut it. Home was never home as anyone else knew it. My mother went from one low-life boyfriend to another, but she liked the sea and there was always a school library at every place we went to, so study and surfing were constants. Finally I got lucky, found some decent foster-parents, got some help. I got into medicine at sixteen. Child prodigy, they said, but obsessive study produces the same effect. Then a scholarship to London. Off I went, delighted to be shot of the mess that family wasn't.'

'Oh, Riley…'

He didn't hear. He was talking to the sea, to something out there that had no connection to anything.

'Marguerite was beautiful, loving, warm, and it blew me away that she wanted me. It was only later that I figured it out. I was straight from the surf. I was big and bronzed and I was Australian. Her friends thought I was cool and her parents thought I was appalling. It was the combination she wanted. I did know she was in full rebellion mode, but I didn't figure it. That I was simply part of that rebellion. Maybe she sabotaged the condoms, I don't know. All I knew was that at the end of summer she wanted nothing more to do with me. She'll have got pregnant for her own reasons. She never told me.' He closed his eyes. 'To have had a daughter for eighteen years and not know…'

'Oh, Riley…'

'Dumb,' he said. 'I even thought I was in love.' He turned

to face her then, and his face was as bleak as death. 'Last night…'

'I'm on the Pill. And I'm not Marguerite.'

'I don't do family,' he said. 'I never have.'

'You don't or you haven't? It seems to me that family's found you. Your daughter…'

'She's my daughter in name only.'

'No, in need. It's not Lucy's fault,' she said, striving to keep her voice even. 'How she was conceived.'

'You think I don't know that?'

'So you found out…'

'Three months ago. An email, nothing more.'

'Then you must have responded magnificently,' she said, quietly but firmly, 'for her to come. You must have told her you care. Three months ago she'll have been five, six months pregnant and terrified. She'll have contacted you looking for options and you've responded with concern. That's what she needs right now. Caring. Family.'

'I'm not family.'

'You are,' she said, and she took his hands in hers and tugged until she had his full attention.

This was important, she thought, for her, suddenly, as well as for him. Her parents had been cold and distant. Riley's had hardly been parents at all. For Riley to be a dad seemed huge. Bigger than both of them.

It was so important she had to fight for it.

'Riley, both our parents messed things up for us,' she said, and she knew she was going where she had no right, but she had no choice. There was something about this big, solitary man that touched a chord.

He'd travelled a harder road than she had, she thought, and he'd come out more scarred. Scars couldn't disappear completely but he could move beyond them. He must.

Riley. She was holding his hands. Strong hands, capable, skilled, loving. Hands that had made her feel…

Don't go there. He didn't want her. Last night was all she could have of him.

Deep breath. He'd been there for her. He'd saved her life.

She was halfway to falling in love with him, she thought. Stupid, stupid, stupid.

He didn't want her, but he was alone. The thought was suddenly unbearable. And with that…

If all that was left for him was his daughter, she'd fight for Lucy. She'd give him a family whether he wanted it or not.

'Lucy is your family,' she said. 'You just have to let her see you care.'

'I don't have a choice. You've landed me with everyone!' It was an explosion of vented frustration and anger. It caught them both on the raw.

Silence.

She could respond with anger. With hurt.

This was too important for either.

'Riley, let's get things in perspective,' she said, somehow keeping her voice even. 'You're not stuck with us. Not for ever. Last night was what I needed to let me move on. It's made things hard between us but not impossible. I don't have a money problem. I need to stay here until Amy goes but that's the extent of it. I would like to stay working in Whale Cove—with you, if that's possible, as part of your team, but that doesn't mean I'm part of your life. I'll get my own apartment. Amy will go back to Dry Gum. I suspect Lucy and Adam will want their own place as well. This is temporary and I haven't stuck you with anything.'

'Pippa, I didn't mean…' He tugged away and raked his hair again. 'Last night…'

'No,' she said evenly. 'You did mean. But we're mature adults. We don't need to let one night mess with our working relationship. And you don't need to see me as the bad guy in what's happened.'

'I don't. Of course I don't. But… You seriously think we can work together?'

And this was the other non-negotiable. He had a daughter. She wanted to work in Whale Cove. 'I want to be a Flight-Aid nurse,' she said, flatly and definitely. 'I'll do whatever that takes, Riley Chase, including never again thinking about what happened last night. Agreed?'

'There's no choice.'

'Of course there's a choice,' she said, and she managed to smile. 'You can walk out that door right now. Pick up your minimal baggage and your surfboard and walk away.' She glanced around the bare walls with distaste. 'It'll be just as it was before you arrived—you'll have left no trace. But I'm staying in this town. For now I'm here to take care of Amy, and if you go then I'll look after Lucy and Adam, too. Because...'

She squared her shoulders and she made herself sound a lot stronger than she felt. 'Because, do you know, I want those ties,' she said. 'I want pictures on my walls. I want mess, baggage, a sense of belonging. Being a Flight-Aid nurse...it's what I've been wanting for a long time and I won't let it go. It feels like home.'

'It's a job.'

'It's home,' she said stubbornly. 'So now... I can see some flowers growing on the cliff face. I have no idea what they are but I'm heading out to pick a bunch. Then I intend to try and make a chocolate cake. I'm the world's worst cook but it feels like the right thing to do. I may only be in this house for a couple of weeks but from this moment on...as long as I'm working for Flight-Aid then I'm home.'

He was called out that night and it was almost a relief.

He wasn't supposed to be on duty. Jake and Sue-Ellen and Mardi were on call over the weekend, but at four in the morning Jake rang.

'Fisherman off the rocks at Devil's Teeth,' he said. 'Wife's only just contacted the police. He was due home at dusk. What was she thinking, waiting this long? Cops have found his gear washed up on the rocks—looks like he was hit by a wave, swept straight in. Sue-Ellen says she can't hack it. Going down ropes, getting bodies... She's hit a wall. She'll do it if you can't, but she's asking...'

It was almost a relief. He'd been lying in bed staring at the ceiling, trying not to think how close Pippa was. Yes, there was a bedroom between them, but that was two thin walls away. If he lay still he could imagine her breathing.

He wouldn't mind betting she was staring at the ceiling as well, and when he dressed and headed out, he found it was a variation of a theme. She was on the veranda, staring out at the ocean.

She heard his footsteps, boots on bare boards. He was in full uniform. It was a bit hard to disguise where he was headed.

'Problem?' She turned and she was wearing a negligee so tiny it took his breath away. Or…maybe it wasn't exactly tiny. It reached her knees. But it clung. The moon was almost full and he could see her body silhouetted beneath the soft silk.

He had work to do. Dreadful work. He couldn't afford to be distracted by a woman in a silk nightdress.

'You want me to come?' she said.

'No need.' He sounded brusque and tried to soften it. 'I'm filling in for Sue-Ellen with the other crew.'

He had a couple of moments to explain. It took Mardi five minutes to get from her home to the helicopter pad. It took him two. He told her and saw her flinch.

'So go,' she said, and he knew she was reliving her time in the water.

'It won't count so much tonight,' he said grimly. 'He went off the rocks at Devil's Teeth, not a calm beach like you did. For him to survive in that water for more than half an hour would be almost impossible and it's been at least eight. There's not a lot to be done but pick up the pieces. Go back to bed.'

'Oh, Riley…'

'Go back to bed.'

How could she go back to bed? She made tea, let it get cold and she didn't notice. Things were happening inside her that she hardly understood, that she had no idea how to deal with.

Riley had stood in the living room in his Flight-Aid uniform, shrugging on his sou'wester, readying himself for what lay ahead. He needed a shave. He didn't look as if he'd slept. He looked big and bad and dangerous…only he was on the side of good.

He was off to haul a body from the sea. It was what he did.

He'd seemed more alone than anyone she'd ever met.

Things were settling inside her. Things she didn't necessarily want.

She was falling in love.

Was that just neediness speaking? The neediness that had seen her reluctant to leave the hospital she'd trained in because that was where her friends were, and friends were the only family she'd ever truly known? The neediness that had finally had her agreeing to marry Roger, because he was her friend, she could have children, she could be part of…something?

The something she'd found here. Riley's team. This hospital. The Outback clinic. Something that called her.

Like Riley called her. Like Riley made her feel.

She was falling…

She'd fallen.

When?

Back in hospital, when she'd woken and seen him at the end of the bed, smiling at her, reassuring her that she was solidly grounded, she was safe, the nightmare was over?

When she'd watched him tease the children at his Outback clinic, making injections a source of fun, a test of bravery that all could face?

When she'd watched him hug Joyce goodbye, his deep affection for the elderly nurse obvious to all of them?

When he'd held her in his arms and blown the terrors away with the heat of his body? When he'd made love to her with tenderness, passion, wonder?

Or when she'd watched him with his daughter, not knowing where to start but wanting so much? Needing so much.

He was on the outside looking in, she thought. For Pippa, who'd been a loner herself, it was an identity she knew too well, and maybe that was what was making her heart twist.

But it wasn't just the one thing making her heart twist, she thought. It was all of him. The complete package. Doctor, lifesaver, father, lover.

Riley.

She thought of his face as he'd left tonight. He knew what he was facing and she knew it hurt something deep within.

Never send to know for whom the bell tolls, it tolls for thee...

Where had that come from? She thought about it, remembering the whole quote. Donne. *No man is an island.*

Riley would like to think he was an island, she decided. He *did* think he was an island. But if you cared as much as he did...

He couldn't stay solitary—it was hurting too much—and if he had to be connected... Could she find a link?

He didn't want a link. Last night shouldn't have happened.

She hugged herself in the chill of the night and gazed out to sea a while longer. She should go back to bed.

Riley was out there, facing a nightmare.

She'd wait here until he got home.

Stupid or not...she'd wait for however long it took.

Like a lovesick teenager...

Or a woman who was starting to see exactly where her home was. Who could heal, and heal herself in the process.

Jake was already in the chopper, and Mardi arrived thirty seconds later. Ten minutes later they were hovering over Devil's Teeth.

One look at the sea told them there was no hope for a happy outcome. Searchlights were already playing over the base of the cliff. Police were searching the rocks—cautiously as the sea was huge—but the outcome was inevitable

Two hours later, just on dawn, they found what they were looking for and it gave them no joy at all. There was no use for Riley's medical skills. He retrieved the body, then he and Mardi worked to disguise the worst of the damage before they landed on the clifftop.

The family was waiting. The family was always waiting, Riley thought grimly, as he watched the tragedy play out. Ambulances, police cars, desolation, all the accoutrements of heartbreak.

The chopper landed but there was no surge forward. No one wanted to take the first step, to be first to acknowledge death.

And in the end Riley's medical skills were needed. The man's mother-in-law, an elderly Greek lady, collapsed with shock. Riley was about to board the Squirrel but the paramedics called him back. Two minutes later she arrested.

They got her back but only just.

One ambulance left with the elderly woman inside. The second ambulance drove off more slowly, carrying its sad cargo. Finally the Squirrel could leave. Mardi and Jake sat up front. Riley sat in the back and gave in to grey.

Family, he thought.

One death and the ripple effects stretched outward. He'd just watched a wife become a widow. He'd watched a mother-in-law nearly lose her life. He'd watched children and family and friends, all gutted.

He'd watched paramedics and emergency service personnel take on this load of tragedy and carry it with them. Every one of them had a family. Every one of them was exposed to the same kind of grief they'd seen tonight, the type of grief he saw over and over.

Joyce had it right, he thought. Joyce cared for the community as a whole. She put her life into working for the people she cared about, but she'd never let herself be part of that other scary thing, the thing that ripped everyone apart.

Family.

He had a daughter. A pregnant daughter. In a while he'd have a grandchild.

He was thirty-eight years old. The concept of being a grandfather was ridiculous.

It didn't matter how old he was. The concept of being a grandparent was still ridiculous. Terrifying.

And then there was Pippa.

Pippa of the warm body, of the huge smile, of the heart that gave and gave. Pippa who'd given herself to him—was it only last night?

She was back at his house. His home?

Waiting for him?

No one ever waited for him. No one ever would—not if he could help it. His was a solitary world and he liked it like that.

But he had a daughter.

And Pippa was…not waiting?

His solitary world was starting to seem besieged.

CHAPTER NINE

AT DAWN Pippa helped Amy feed a still sleepy Baby Riley. Amy and baby went back to sleep. Exhausted, Pippa abandoned her sentry duty and crawled into bed. When she woke it was ten and Baby Riley was squawking for her next feed.

The jaundice might well recede without the need for phototherapy, she thought, but mostly she thought…had Riley come home?

She padded down the passage and just happened to glance into Riley's bedroom on the way.

No Riley.

Were they still searching, or was he needed at the hospital?

She flicked on the radio to the local news and listened to the account of last night's tragedy.

A drowning followed by a heart attack. In an understaffed hospital that could be enough to keep him busy for hours. Or was he was staying out because of her?

Was she making herself more important than she was?

Keep busy, she told herself. Don't think about him.

Easier said than done.

She helped Amy bathe Riley Junior, encouraged her to feed again then settled them both to sleep in a patch of sunshine.

Lucy and Adam arrived. They'd walked round from their hotel. Lucy's legs were swollen. To fly for almost twenty four hours at full term… There were reasons for regulations.

She settled Lucy on the settee, raised her legs, massaged her swollen feet, working on getting circulation happening.

Sent Adam out for supplies. Made sandwiches.

Riley still didn't return.

The place was like home without its hearth. Maybe that was a dumb thing to think but there it was. He should be there.

'I can't believe Dad lives here,' Lucy said, relaxing a little. 'This place is like a barn. Has he only just moved in?'

'He's lived her for six years,' Pippa said. 'But he's a guy.'

'I resent that,' Adam retorted. He was also relaxing—maybe because Pippa was obviously caring for Lucy, and being twenty and the only one to care for a very pregnant girlfriend was truly scary.

'Your dad needs posters,' Amy said, hopping into her third sandwich. 'Pippa rang up this really cool poster shop when I was in labour and next thing we had posters everywhere. The nurses said the poster shop's huge.'

'But I don't have any money,' Lucy said sadly. 'Mum's cut me off without a penny. Adam's broke, too. But it'd be great to decorate this place.'

And Pippa couldn't help herself. She'd run out of things to do. She couldn't just sit still and wait for Riley.

'I'd love some posters,' she said. 'If you order them, I'll pay.'

'Really?' Lucy demanded, astounded.

'I kind of think this house is boring as well. What about surfing posters? That's your dad's thing.'

'My dad surfs?' Lucy demanded. 'Awesome.'

Had Marguerite told Lucy nothing about Riley? Her heart wrenched for both of them, and her resolution built. Family. That meant shared interests. Surfing.

'Let's see what the shop has,' she said.

'Maybe we could intersperse surfing with skiing—it's the same sort of theme,' Lucy said. 'Dad looks like the kind of guy who'd ski.'

He did, Pippa thought. An outdoor adventurer. Living life on the edge. Alone.

He was the kind of guy who'd hang out of a helicopter, who'd risk his life to save hers.

He was also the kind of guy who'd make love to her to take her out of her terror. And mean nothing by it?

She'd told him it meant nothing.

Something was happening inside her she hadn't meant to happen.

It no longer meant nothing.

He spent the morning deep in the paperwork a death by misadventure always entailed. Then, inevitably, he was at the hospital when a car crash came in, and how could he not assist? Finally he was free. He walked back to the house, entering from the veranda the way he always did. Entering his house.

It was no longer *his* house.

For a start it was full of people.

Amy was in an armchair, holding her baby. Lucy was on the settee and Adam was beside her. Lucy had her feet propped up on Adam's knees. She looked even more pregnant today, he thought. The baby seemed to have dropped, settling low.

Uh-oh.

And, of course, Pippa was there. She was seated at the dining table behind a sewing machine, surrounded by fabric. She looked…worried?

His gaze met hers and held. The look she gave him was one of defiance, but her worry stayed. Like…I'm not sure I should have done this.

This?

This would have to be the house.

His breath drew in and wasn't replaced. Breathing seemed extraneous.

He'd left at four that morning. It was now mid-afternoon and it was a different house.

The sea had come inside.

There were huge montages of surf and sky and beach and sun, and smaller montages of skiing, snow and sun.

He saw a series of ten posters of dolphins riding the waves, taken as stills one after the other, from the moment the pod entered the back of the wave to when they twisted triumphantly out as the wave crashed out onto the shore.

And there weren't just posters.

There were cushions. Throws. And curtains! He stared around in amazement. Every window had curtains, great folds of blue and gold, draped from rods with huge wooden rings.

How the...?

'Pippa bought a sewing machine.' Amy seemed the only one not nervous; she was breathless with excitement. 'The fabric shop delivered rolls and rolls of fabric and rings and rods. Adam put up the rods. Pippa's sewed and sewed, while me and Lucy stuck up posters. Adam told us where to put them—Lucy says he wants to be an artist. And Pippa's taught me how to sew curtains. They're easy. She says I can have the sewing machine for a baby present and the leftover material for curtains when I get home. Do you like it?'

They were all looking at him.

It felt...

He wasn't sure how it felt.

There was a part of him that loved it. His house was being converted into a home. More, this was a home designed specifically for him. The views from outside were echoed, but softly, the sunlight diffused, the harsh yellows turned to soft gold. Here a man could take sanctuary. He wouldn't have to head to the surf—the surf had come to him.

He looked at the people surrounding him, Lucy and Adam, tremulous with hope that they'd done something good, Amy, beaming with pride and excitement.

Pippa, looking...wary.

She'd organised it, he thought.

She'd given him a home.

And that was the problem. Did he want a home? Had he ever? He lived out of a duffel bag. He'd never put down roots.

As a kid, his mother had always been dragging him from one place to the next, from one substitute father to the next, from one disaster to the next. Now he made sure his escape route was always open. He'd been here for six years but every moment of that time he'd known he could walk away.

How could he walk away now? He couldn't. Amy was depending on him. Lucy and Adam were depending on him.

Pippa was still looking wary. She looked…as if she expected to be hurt.

Was she depending on him?

'It's fantastic,' he said, as sincerely as he could, and everyone beamed except Pippa.

'It's so cool,' Lucy said. 'It's even better than the hotel. I thought…if we buy a cheap mattress and put it in the spare room on the floor…could Adam and I stay here, too? The hotel was fine last night but here's better. Pippa's been so nice.'

She had been nice, Riley conceded. She'd invited Amy into his house. Her niceness was drawing Lucy in, too.

Nice.

But she was so much more…

'I'm not staying here long,' Pippa said, still wary.

'You'll be here until I have to go,' Amy said, panicked. Pippa cast another sidelong—wary—glance at Riley, and nodded.

'Yes.'

'I want you to be here when our baby's born,' Lucy breathed. 'Amy says you helped with her baby. She says you were lovely. You and Dad both. You know, if you two were here, why do I have to go to hospital? I could lie on the veranda and watch the sea when I'm in labour and I wouldn't have to do any of that scary hospital stuff. And…' Her happiness faded. She gave her father a scared glance. 'It might be better. I… I don't have insurance.'

'You don't have…' Riley was speechless.

'We couldn't get any insurance company to cover me,' she said. 'Not here.'

'Of all the…' He turned and stared at Pippa—who was looking at a half-made curtain. Studiously not looking at him.

His life had been under control until this woman arrived. Since then… 'This is you,' he said.

'Me?'

'It's down to you.'

'How exactly am I responsible for Lucy not having insurance?'

'You're responsible for telling her she can have her baby here.'

'She hasn't,' Lucy said, astounded that he was attacking Pippa. 'It's just… I've heard of lots of people having home births. I thought maybe I could, too. I knew you were a doctor. I knew… I hoped you'd help me. But if you won't…' She sniffed and clutched Adam's hand. 'Adam will.'

Adam swallowed. Manfully. 'I…I expect you will need to go to hospital,' he said, sounding terrified. 'We can figure out how to pay later.'

'But the debt…'

'There's lots of stuff we have to figure out,' Adam said, squaring his puny shoulders. 'Baby first. You first. Let's take care of you. Nothing else matters.'

And Riley looked at his daughter's terrified face, at Adam's terrified response—and he knew his anger at Pippa was totally unjustified.

Lucy was eighteen years old. This was her first baby. She was alone except for Adam, and Adam was scarcely older than she was.

'Will you help us, Pippa?' Adam asked, while Riley fought to make a recovery.

'Of course I will,' Pippa told him, turning stiffly away from Riley. 'Lucy, Adam's right. There's no need to worry. All you need to concentrate on is welcoming your baby into the world. Do you have any good books? There's lots of stuff to read about what to expect, and it might be fun for you and Adam to read them together. I can borrow them from the hospital.'

'And you should learn breathing,' Amy said wisely. 'I bet Pippa could teach you.'

He was being excluded, Riley thought. Maybe justifiably. What the hell was he doing, putting his needs before Lucy's?

'We'll do this together,' he growled, and he spoke to Adam rather than Lucy because now that Lucy had Pippa and Amy behind her, it was suddenly Adam who was looking the most worried. 'The hospital might be best. I can help you…'

'We can decide that close to the time,' Pippa said, and her tone was suddenly resolute, almost daring him to defy her.

'I hope I'm still here to help,' Amy said. 'Having a baby is awesome.'

'It doesn't hurt at all,' Pippa teased, and Amy giggled.

'It does hurt a bit,' she conceded. 'But then you get this baby at the end of it and it's fabulous. I'm not going to have any more until I'm about thirty but I loved it. Can I help Pippa teach you to breathe?'

'I can breathe already,' Lucy said, and peeped a glance at her father. Who was glaring at Pippa. 'I'm sure I can. Why are you looking at Pippa like that?'

'She's organising my life.'

'I'm not,' Pippa said. 'If Lucy and Adam are staying here, maybe I should go back to my hotel.'

'No,' Amy said, suddenly panicked. 'You promised.'

'I need you here,' Lucy said, sounding even more panicked.

Maybe *he* should go to the hotel, Riley thought, absorbing the fact that he was in a house that had been transformed suddenly into a home—his home—and it was full of people who were depending on Pippa.

'It's like having family,' Lucy said.

And he thought, Exactly.

It was exactly why he wanted to walk away right now.

Another bombshell was about to land.

Amy retired to have a nap. Pippa went back to curtain sewing and Adam put up more rods. Lucy took her father on a tour of the posters.

'I'll pay you for these,' he said, trying to make up for his less than enthusiastic initial response. 'They must have cost a fortune. Plus the sewing machine and the fabric...'

'I didn't pay for them.' Lucy said. 'I don't have any money. Mum said if I stay with Adam then she'd cut me off with nothing. And Adam's an art student.'

'You've come to Australia with nothing?'

'Adam sold his motorbike. That just got us here.'

That made him feel...dreadful. The money itself didn't worry him. He had twenty years of savings, he earned an excellent wage and the overtime in the work he was doing now was truly astounding. But to have Lucy so helpless... And who'd paid for the posters?

'So Pippa paid?'

'It doesn't matter to her. She says she's not your girlfriend, but, Dad, if I were you I'd make a move. She's funny, and she's kind, and she's loaded.'

'Loaded?'

'You didn't know?'

'What are you talking about?'

'I didn't recognise her but Adam did, as soon as he heard her full name. We got the posters delivered. She paid for them over the phone by credit card. She's Phillippa Penelope Fotheringham.'

'It that supposed to mean anything to me?'

'Yeah. It is. I sort of knew about her. She's an heiress. And we know even more, 'cos Adam read a story about her last month while I was getting tests at the hospital. Adam read the glossies while he waited. There was a piece on Pippa. He says her grandfather made millions with some food company. Her parents are socialites—worse than Mum. Even I've heard of them; they're always in the news. But Pippa's not social. The story said Pippa went nursing when she was seventeen. Her family hated it but she did anyway. She's been quiet ever since. The article was about her grandpa saying she's the best of his relations and he's left the company to her. Oh, and she was going to marry the company's chief accountant—that was what the piece was about. You know, heiress finds true love, that sort of thing. I don't know what happened, but what I do know is that she's seriously, seriously rich.'

Dinner was steak and salad, cooked on the barbecue. With Riley thinking Pippa had paid for the steak.

Amy and Baby Riley were asleep before the washing-up was complete. Adam and Lucy headed back to their hotel with baby books. They couldn't get a mattress until Monday but they looked wistful as they left the house.

Riley headed out to the veranda, and Pippa followed.

She stood and watched him for a while. He watched the sea and said nothing.

'You can take the posters down after everyone's gone,' she said at last.

'Why would I want to do that?'

'Because you like bare walls?'

'I don't actually like walls at all. How rich are you?'

'Very rich.' There was no sense in denying it.

'So what the hell are you doing here?'

'I'm not accepting free board and lodging,' she said warily, because there was nothing in his voice to suggest any warmth. 'I'm staying here because of Amy but I'm paying rent to the hospital. The same as you.'

'That's not what I meant. You took the job with Flight-Aid under false pretences.'

'Under what pretences?' she demanded, starting to feel angry. 'Are you saying I had no right to apply? Because there's money in my background?'

'You can apply for what you like.'

'Because I'm rich?' Anger was coming to her aid now, pure and simple. 'I didn't pay for Coral to employ me at Flight-Aid. I was employed on the basis of my experience and my qualifications.'

'It's a plaything.'

'Excuse me?'

'You'll do it and leave.'

'I might,' she said, astounded. 'So might you. I did, however, work in the same hospital in Britain for over ten years. Match that, Dr Riley.'

'What are you doing here?' It was like an explosion. He turned to face her and his eyes were dark with anger. 'What are you playing at?'

'I'm not playing.'

'Filling my house with...what's the quote? A monstrous regiment of women.'

'Like three,' she said, gobsmacked. 'Three!'

'Four. Even Baby Riley howled when—'

'When you gave her her blood test. I'd howl too if someone pricked my heel. Whatever. You're putting her in your conspiracy theory, too? Riley Chase, his life hijacked by women. What about Adam?'

'He'll figure it out,' Riley said harshly. 'Lucy's grandparents... her mother...they're angry with her now but they'll want her back. They'll haul her back into their lives and Adam will be left on the outside.'

'Are we talking of Adam, or are we talking about you?'

'It's none of your business.'

'And neither is my money any of your business. What earthly difference does it make?'

'Why are you working?'

'Because I want to.' She was almost yelling. Almost but not quite. 'I left my job to marry Roger. The deal was that we'd have a long honeymoon, then we'd go back to London and, guess what, I'd find another job. Nursing. I love what I do. Believe it or not, I love it a lot more than I ever loved Roger. And guess what? I've fallen in love again, only this time I've fallen in love with Flight-Aid. With the whole package. With Whale Cove Hospital, with Jancey, with Coral, with nurses who care so much they don't even see the end of their shifts coming. Who see the place as an extension of their lives; their community.'

'That's not—'

'Shut up and let me finish,' she said. 'Because I need to say it. Because I love what you do, too, and I'm not intending to walk away from it. I love the search and rescue component of the job—all the worthwhile things. I sneaked into the hospital when I went for a walk this morning and I talked to Jancey. I know what you did for that family last night. You got his body back so they could grieve, but more. You stayed with them. You talked them through their grief. You made George's body presentable so by the time they saw him he didn't look like he'd died in terror. And then you cared for Maria, you reassured her, you were just there. Jancey says sometimes you doubt that a doctor should be on these search and rescue missions, but everyone here thinks exactly that.'

'This is nothing to do with—'

'Me? Yes, it is, because I'm a Flight-Aid nurse. I've signed Coral's contract. And there's more. Joyce's clinic. Her house-cum-hospital. It took my breath away. I want to be a part of that so much it's like a part of me I didn't know was missing. And I will be a part of it. Jancey says there's two complete crews, two medical teams who cover inland settlements. She says if you and I can't get along then we'll swap teams. Mardi can come to you and I'll go on Jake's team.'

'You talked to Jancey? About me?'

'Everyone talks about you,' she said wearily. 'Everyone worries abut you. They love you, Riley Chase, only you don't get it. You do this loner thing and no one can get near. Jancey says you had the pits of a childhood. Alcoholic mother. No parenting to speak of. One of the older nurses knew your mother and she said—'

'I don't have to listen to this.'

'No, you don't,' she said. 'Like I don't have to listen to you saying my medicine is a plaything. I've come from money and neglect; you've come from poverty and neglect. Either way, we've ended up here. The only difference is that I intend to make here my home. I'll buy an apartment here and you know what? I won't need Adam and Lucy and Amy to make it a home for me because I'll do it myself. Oh, and by the way, while you're busy getting your knickers in a twist, here's something else to get on your high horse about. I'm about to throw more money about. I'm about to set up a trust for Joyce's House. I'll use whatever I need to set it up as an accredited hospital. I'll do it anonymously but I'd imagine you'll find out, so you might as well despise me now. Not for the act. For having the capacity to do it. For what I was born into rather than what I am.'

He didn't speak. He stood staring at her in the moonlight like she was someone he didn't know—and didn't want to know.

'I know how Lucy's mother and grandparents treated you,' she said, her anger finally fading at little as she remembered the bald outline Lucy had told her. She had every right to be angry, but money had messed with so much of her life that in a way she understood his confusion. His emotion. If she could come to this man on his terms…

But there was no way she could. Her money was there, like it or not. She would help Joyce, and she would help other communities, even if it meant Riley looked at her the way he was looking at her now.

'I'm not my money, Riley,' she said softly. 'That's not me. I'm who you pulled out of the water, a woman at the end of her life, a woman with nothing. But one thing this week has taught me is that I only have one chance at life. And Flight-Aid is what I want. But you know what? There's a part of me that wants more. There's a part of me that wants…'

She faltered. She couldn't say it. He was a stranger, standing aloof against the balcony rail, a shadow against the moonlight and the fluorescence of the sea.

He didn't want anything. He didn't want the posters and curtains and the accoutrements of home.

He didn't want her.

What was she doing, being angry with him? She had no right. He'd made love to her only because she'd been needy.

She had to move on.

'I'll stay here for as long as Amy needs me,' she said, making her voice even, almost calm. 'You're stuck with me until then and I'm sorry. I invited Amy here and that was a mistake. I should have got an apartment for her and for me. But moving now…I don't think that's possible without heartbreak. So I'll stay here and we'll lead separate lives. On Monday I'll talk to Coral about being rostered onto a different crew from you. We'll work apart. That's the best I can do, Riley, but I won't do more than that. I can't walk away completely.'

She closed her eyes and bit her lip. This was so hard.

Just say it.

No.

Yes. Why not?

Why not be honest?

'I can't walk away because I've fallen in love,' she said softly now, but with her dignity intact. 'With Flight Aid, with Jancey, with Amy, with Whale Cove.'

Deep breath. Just say it.

'And I'm very close to falling in love with you,' she whispered. 'Because…there's this connection. I don't get it, I can't figure out why I'm feeling it, but I am. Like we're linked. Our backgrounds. Something. I'm sorry but there it is. Honesty on all fronts. But I'm a big girl. I've walked alone all my life and I'm good at it. I know you don't want whatever I'm feeling, and that's more of a reason for me to get myself as apart from you as I can without leaving Whale Cove. So for now…you need to put up with posters, put up with sharing your home, put up with people in your life for another week or so. And then… I'm not sure what you'll do with Lucy, but that's up to you and Lucy. For the rest of it I'll respect your right to be alone.'

'Pippa…'

'There's nothing else to say,' she said, and then before she could stop herself she stepped forward, took his hands in hers and stood on tiptoe.

She kissed him and it was a kiss of farewell. She wasn't leaving but she was moving away.

He didn't respond. He didn't touch her.

There was nothing else to be said. She released his hands. She walked inside and she closed the door behind her.

CHAPTER TEN

THEY didn't swap crews. There was no need. Riley simply held himself distant.

Pippa was introduced to full crew membership and she loved it. She loved the work, she loved the remote clinics, and after a couple of days she figured she and Riley could handle a professional, working relationship.

They were both good at holding themselves contained. Practice.

On Tuesday they did a retrieval upcountry—a truck had rolled with three kids in the back. It took all their medical skills to get a good outcome—three kids recovering in Sydney Central—and it felt fantastic.

She could do this.

The house was trickier.

Amy's Jason arrived late on Wednesday night, dusty and worn from hitchhiking for six hundred miles.

'I couldn't wait any longer to see my kid,' he said simply. 'I'll sleep on the beach; I don't need a bed.'

His boss had told him he could take time off to settle Amy and the baby. Amy was so proud she looked like she might burst, so there was now another mattress on the floor. The pair sat and watched their baby slowly work her way through her jaundice. They waited every night for Riley to tell them she was doing well.

Lucy and Adam sat on the veranda, read their birthing books and practised the breathing Amy proudly taught them—and waited every night for Riley to tell them they were doing well.

They depended on him.

Except…they didn't. None of them depended on him. Not really, Riley thought as the week wore on. Because there was Pippa.

She was like the sun with planets spinning around her. She was the life of the house.

She was embracing life like she'd never realised she was alive until this moment, soaking up every moment of this new, wonderful world she found herself in. Her joy was impossible not to share.

Except he didn't share it. Not if he could help it, because it seemed like a void. It seemed a sweet, sensual lure, a vortex that if he entered he'd end up as he'd ended up twenty years before when he'd met Marguerite.

Maybe he wouldn't.

Maybe he wasn't brave enough to find out.

Thursday night. He was on the beach, looking back to the house. Pippa's curtains were left undrawn. The lights were on and he could see them all. They were squashed on the divans, watching television. Pippa had been making popcorn when he'd left. He could see them passing bowls. Laughing.

He'd go back soon. He was necessary in the house. He had to sort Lucy's life. He had to check Amy's baby.

He was useful.

He was…loved?

No. Love was an illusion. Something that happened to others, not to him.

He didn't need it.

He had everything he needed—his medicine, his surf, his independence. He'd set Lucy and Adam up in their own place. Next Thursday Amy would go back to Dry Gum. Pippa would move out.

The ripples in his calm existence would roll to the edges and disappear.

He glanced again at the lit windows and thought he could be in there.

Pippa. Child of money. A siren song.

Stay outside, for as long as it takes.

She knew he was out there but there wasn't anything she could do. He didn't want to be a part of this house.

If it wasn't for Riley, she'd be loving it.

Pippa had gone from general nursing training to Surgical, and then to Intensive Care. Then a case one night had touched her more deeply than she cared to admit. A woman had come in to have her fifth child. During second stage her uterus had ruptured.

Emergency Caesarean. They'd lost the baby and the mother had come so close to death it didn't bear thinking about. Pippa had cared for her in Intensive Care. She'd watched the little family's terror, and their grief for the little life lost.

Five children and each one the most precious thing in the world.

The following day she'd put in her application for Midwifery, she loved it and here was the perfect midwife job. She was caring for Amy with her newborn baby, and at the same time she was preparing Lucy for birth.

Lucy was like a sponge, listening to everything Pippa told her, reading, reading, reading about childbirth, and Adam was almost as eager. But what was more wonderful was that Amy was teaching Lucy. In Amy Lucy had a teenaged ally who'd gone through birth only a week before, who scorned her fears as garbage.

'It's like a teenage antenatal clinic,' Pippa told Riley six days after Lucy arrived, and then winced as Riley grunted a sharp response and went on to do what he had to do.

He was doing exactly that—what he had to do. He was organising life for Lucy and Adam. He was watching Baby Riley's progress. He was making sure Lucy had all her checks; that everything was done that had to be done.

There were enough practical tasks necessary for Riley to deflect emotion.

He'd get his life back soon enough, Pippa thought as the end of the first week neared. In one more week they'd take Amy home and Pippa would have no reason to stay. Then all Riley had to do was sort out a relationship with his daughter, and that had nothing to do with her.

His solitary life suited him.

She had to respect that.

So she'd move out and she'd be more professional than… than… Who did she know who was strictly professional? Who did she know who had no emotional attachment at all?

Riley?

Not Riley. Or not the Riley she knew.

But the Riley he almost certainly wanted to be.

Saturday afternoon. Riley was in the Flight-Aid headquarters, not because he needed to be but because three women and two men and one baby were sun-baking on his veranda. There was no way he was joining them. It wasn't a trap but it felt like it.

They'd be talking babies, he told himself, quashing guilt. There was no need for him to be there.

But there was no need for him to be here either—he could be on call at home—so when a call came he grabbed the radio with relief.

'All stops.' Harry sounded frightened, which, for Harry, was amazing. 'Kid stuck in a crevice off the rocks south of McCarthy's Sound. Tide's coming in, water's rising and he's at risk of drowning. I'm calling Pippa. Take off in two minutes whether you're on board or not.'

They had six minutes in the chopper to take in the information being relayed to them. Harry had met them looking as grim as death and he had reason.

'The kid slipped off a ledge while his dad was fishing. The cliff's not sheer but it's crumbling sandstone, so he slid and bumped, which is why he wasn't killed outright. Just before water level there's a bunch of rocks. He's gone straight down a crevice. He can't get up. In breaks between waves they've heard him screaming. His dad tried to get down and fell—probable broken ankle. He only just managed to get up himself. The local abseiling club's trying to get their members there but no one's available and the tide's coming in. The report was hysterical—seems he's below the high-tide mark.'

It was enough to make them all shut up.

Pippa and Riley sat in the back—this was where they'd operate from if they needed to lower someone to the scene.

Pippa felt ill. Was she ready?

With Cordelia remaining off work she'd been catapulted into the team with little training, but even with the emotional undercurrents, Riley had worked at getting her professional. It had been a quiet week, which was just as well.

She'd learned to operate the winch as Riley was lowered. She'd been lowered herself. She knew the right way to make physical contact with a patient for retrieval. She knew how to operate harnesses. She knew, in theory, all she needed to make her a viable member of the rescue outfit.

But for a call such as this…

They should have called Mardi, she thought, or another of the members of the second crew. But there'd been no time. Mardi was five minutes away. In the doctor's house, she was right there.

'We're almost there,' Riley said, watching her face, knowing what she was thinking. 'You can do this, Pippa.'

Of course she could. There was no choice—but what was before them took her breath away.

People were clustered on the cliff top. A police car. An ambulance. Half a dozen people.

Even from here she could pick out the father. Someone was holding him back from the edge. He was kneeling, screaming, sobbing.

Another car was pulling up. A woman. Kids.

She couldn't hear the screaming, but she felt it. She watched the woman run to the cliff edge, the policeman hold her back. She watched her crumple.

A part of the cliff seemed to have fallen away, making a rough ledge of rocks at the base, huge boulders scattered randomly. There'd been strong winds for the last two days and the sea was stirred up crazily. The wind had eased now, but the sea was still vicious. It was crashing into the boulders at the foot of the cliff.

Somewhere amongst those boulders was a child.

'He's eight years old,' Harry said over the radio. 'Name's Mickey.'

'If I go down, can we get directions to exactly where he is?' Riley demanded. 'Get the father on the radio. Have someone hold him while he watches but if he saw his kid go he'll be the only person who can pinpoint exactly where he is. Pippa, you're in charge up here. Total control. You know you can do it.'

Did she know? Of course she did. She gulped.

How long did normal paramedics have to train? Not six days.

''Course she can,' Harry said, injecting forced lightness into his voice. 'Or you can come up front and pilot the chopper while I do it. Piece of cake. Just hover and don't hit anything.'

'I think maybe I ought to hold Riley's winch,' Pippa said faintly. 'I'm not all that good at hovering.'

'You never know what you can do until you try,' Riley said, and he caught her gaze and held. 'We accepted you into this crew because you're good, Pippa. Now's the time to prove it.'

It was the longest five minutes of her life.

She operated the winch while Riley was lowered carefully down to the rocks. Despite what Harry said about 'just hover and don't hit anything', she knew it took huge skill to hold the chopper steady. They were so close to the cliff. The people on the cliff top were forced to move back as Harry took the chopper almost to ground level to give Riley minimum swing as he lowered himself down.

The father's voice crackled over the radio, thick with sobs.

'The big rock to the north of where he is. A couple more yards. Yeah, down there, between that one and the flat one to its side. Oh, God, there's a wave...'

Riley had reached ground level. He was on the flat rock, no longer swinging from the harness. He was on his stomach, peering down. Waves were breaking over the rocks, not much, intermittently, but Pippa thought, How far had the child slipped? How far was the water going in?

'Mickey.' They heard Riley through his headset. He was bracing himself against the wash, trying to see. He'd taken his flashlight down with him and Pippa could imagine him peering down into the void.

'H-help.' It was a child's whisper, choking off, and through the radio system they heard it clearly.

Dear God...

'Can you catch a rope, mate, if I throw it down to you? It's a harness. You can loop it under your arms.'

'My hands... I can't... One of them's behind me. It won't... I can't get it out. The other doesn't... I can't...' There was a muffled sob and then a gasp.

Riley was pushing himself down into the chasm, reaching as far as he could. Swearing. 'Hold on, mate. Hold on.'

Another wave. A scream cut short.

'Dear God...'

He had no choice. He was as far into the chasm as he could reach. The water was swirling round his face, sucking back out of the chasm. There'd be more waves coming.

He couldn't reach.

He couldn't reach!

He was wasting time. There was no way he could haul the child free. If he pushed himself any further, they'd both drown.

There was one choice and one choice only.

It nearly killed him. To ask her…

He had no choice.

'Pippa?' It was Riley, using a voice she didn't recognise. She'd seen the sea wash over him. She'd thought… She'd thought…

'I'm here.' Of course she was. Every sense was tuned to the drama below. She felt like retching.

This was no time for retching.

'He's more than a metre out of reach,' Riley said, and she could feel his anguish. But still his words were clipped and decisive.

'I can't get in—the chasm's too narrow and my chest's too wide. The sea's rising—that last wave went over his head and I damn near stuck. There's only one way we can do this. I'm unfastening the harness. Harry, get onto the cliff and pick up one of the cops—they'll know how to operate the winch. Then, Pippa, I need you to get down here. You're half my size across the shoulders. Do you have the courage to be lowered feet first to grab him? We wait five minutes and we lose him. Even now… Can you do this?'

'Yes.' No hesitation.

'Of course she can,' Harry said. 'Get that harness off, Chase, so we can get it onto Pippa. We're moving.'

To ask her to do this…

He had no choice. Not if the child was to live.

But to ask it of Pippa… To ask it of anyone…

Watch the sea.

'We're coming,' he called to the child below, not knowing if he was still capable of hearing. 'Hold on, mate. Pippa's coming.'

Riley was on the ledge with no harness. A wave could wash in at any time. Below him was a child, trapped where the sea washed in and out.

Pippa's fear for them both didn't leave room for any fear for herself.

Besides, there were things to do. Fear was for later. She had the winch up and was wearing the harness by the time they landed on the cliff top. A burly sergeant ran forward, was in the chopper, was demanding instructions as the chopper lifted off. Harry had forewarned him.

'I know the basics,' he said. 'Quick run-through?'

See one, do one, teach one? Pippa had to choke back a hysterical laugh. Surely this was the mantra at its most dangerous. Harry and Riley had spent a couple of hours teaching her about winching. They'd intended to do more with her but that initial teaching was all she had.

So she'd seen one. She was about to do one. Her life, and Riley's and Mickey's, depended on her teaching one as well.

But needs must and it all flooded back to her, the mantra Riley had drilled in. Steadiness, keeping control at all times, watching the wind, being ready to re-winch at any moment, watching for sway, safety, safety, safety.

The sergeant was good, calm and unflappable, or maybe he was as good at hiding panic as she was. By the time Harry had the chopper centred again over Riley and the child below, he was behind the winch, putting his hand on her shoulder as if it was she who was the trainee.

Maybe she wasn't as good at hiding panic as she'd thought.

'You can do it, girl,' the big policeman said, calmly and steadily. 'We know you can. Pom, aren't you? Never mind, even if you guys are hopeless at cricket, I reckon you can do this. You can sing "Rule Britannia" all the way down.'

She almost laughed.

But then she was slipping out of the chopper, her feet were no longer touching anything and she was heading down to Riley. She was no longer even close to laughing.

The last time she'd hung above the sea her life was being saved. Now…

Concentrate. Do not sway. Hold yourself firm, steady; Harry and the sergeant can only do so much, you have to do the rest. Head straight down.

Riley was below her.

Down, down—and he caught her. A wave washed over the rock as she landed and she gasped with the shock of the cold water—but Riley had her, holding her, steadying her.

'It's okay. You're safe, Pippa. But Mickey's not and we need to work fast.' He shone the flashlight down and she could see a shock of red hair, a child crumpled into an impossibly narrow crevice.

'Mickey,' Riley called, and there was no response.

'I can't get down to him and he's drowning,' Riley said, and she heard the desperation in his voice. The water from the last wave was being sucked out of the crevice now. How far had it come up?

'I'm watching the sea. At the next break you go down head first with me holding your feet,' Riley said. 'You'll still wear the harness. If the crevice is too tight or another wave comes then I pull you straight out—this isn't about losing you as well. You get the harness under his shoulders or you grab him any way you can and then you get out of there. Old surf mantra—every seventh wave is a biggie, and it seems to be working. Straight after the next biggie and you're down.'

They were working as he spoke, adjusting her harness. He was looping ropes around her waist and shoulders, tying them so he had a rope on either side of her.

'Wait,' he said as she stooped, and it nearly killed her to wait—and it nearly killed him as well.

Then, as the next big wave struck, he held her tight, hard against him, so the wave couldn't move them. His body gave her courage. He gave her courage.

The wave rocked them, filled the crevice, and she thought, Mickey, Mickey…

The wave sucked out again. Deep breath. And then… Riley gave her a hard, swift kiss as the water cleared from around their legs. The kiss was a blessing.

Then she was on her knees, stooping, leaning in…

Letting go.

Riley held her. Her hands touched the side of the crevice, feeling her way straight down. Hauling herself in. She couldn't worry about the waves—that was Riley's lookout.

She trusted him.

It was so tight—she had to hunch her shoulders as hard as she could to squeeze down.

She had no room to work with a torch and her body blocked the light.

Her hands touched Mickey's hair. She pushed herself further down, fighting to get a hold on his shoulders. He was crammed in hard. Maybe he'd wriggled to get out, wedging himself in further.

'Mickey…'

No response. He'd have been under water, over and over.

His shoulders were hunched forward like hers. In front of his clavicle…a tiny amount of wriggle room.

She got her hands down under, gripping like death.

She couldn't fasten a rope. No room. She grabbed handfuls of his windcheater and tugged. He didn't move. She firmed her hold.

'Pull,' she yelled at Riley, and he pulled and the child shifted. If she could hold him…

She couldn't, he was too heavy, the grip of the rocks too great. But he was up far enough now for her to get a harness around him. Sort of.

She was holding and tying, keeping the deadweight steady, and if anyone asked her afterwards how she'd done it, she could never tell them. She didn't know.

All she knew was that she wasn't letting go. If the water came in now she was still holding on for dear life.

The water did come in, but not enough to reach her, not enough either to cover Mickey's head, not now she'd tugged him a little higher. Oh, but he was so limp.

She couldn't think that. She could only think harness.

She had him. She was fastened to Riley. Mickey was fastened to her. They were going to have to rise as one. If Mickey came out without support…if his head fell sideways and caught…if another wave twisted him…

There was no winch on top. Only Riley. Would he have the strength?

Like her, he had no choice.

'Pull,' she yelled, and she felt her harness tighten. She held to Mickey for dear life. His harness held…

And she felt the rocks release them.

She came free just as another wave hit. She hauled Mickey up and they were out. Riley was holding her, holding Mickey, they were falling backwards against the rocks, simply holding until the sucking power of the wave eased.

And the moment it did Riley was working on Mickey.

There was no room for the niceties of a mask. 'Breathe for him,' he snapped as he set Mickey down on the highest piece of rock so they could work on him. 'I'm on chest and wave watching.'

He still had to watch the sea. If another wave hit, they'd have to stop to hold on. There was no point in getting Mickey breathing again if they were all to be washed back into the waves.

So Riley watched the sea but still he worked, compressing his chest as steadily as if he was in the emergency department of her training hospital. All his focus was on the little boy's chest.

She checked Mickey's airway again—she'd done a fast check and given him a quick first breath as they'd come out of the crevice but now she had time to be careful. She breathed.

If Riley could be steady, so could she. If Riley wasn't panicking, neither would she.

She had her fingers on the boy's carotid artery. Feeling desperate.

A pulse?

It was barely there but she was sure she'd felt it.

'Pulse. Don't even think about stopping,' she told Riley, but he barely acknowledged her. He kept working. When the next big wave hit they worked as one, lifting the child, holding him high, bracing themselves against the rock. Pippa kept on breathing as much as she could. Riley's chest compressions were more hugs during the worst of the wave. As the wave receded Mickey was down on the ledge again and they kept right on.

And then…the little boy stirred. His chest heaved.

He took a gasping, searing gulp of air, and Riley had him on his side in an instant.

He was horribly, wonderfully sick.

And then, amazingly, he started to cry.

Pippa was beside him, on the rock, her face almost touching his. She held him tight as the water washed over the rock's surface. She was making sure his airway wasn't blocked. This time the wave wasn't high enough to be threatening.

How could anything threaten them now?

'You're safe, Mickey,' she said, holding him close as his retching eased. 'Doc Riley's come in his helicopter and we've rescued you. Your mum and dad are on the top of the cliff. The helicopter's lowering a stretcher right now so we can pull you up. How cool to tell the kids at school you were rescued with a helicopter? You just stay still and let me hold you until we get you back to your mum.'

She was amazing.

Pippa…

Riley stood back as Mickey was embraced by his family. He'd done what needed to be done. Mickey's airway was clear, he had oxygen flowing—he was conscious and lucid so there appeared to be no long-term threat from his near drowning. He had a fractured arm and maybe further fractures to his pelvis and ribs but nothing life-threatening. The painkillers were taking effect. He was almost managing to smile.

His mother was holding his good hand and she didn't look like she'd let go any time soon.

His father was hugging Pippa. He didn't look like he was letting go any time soon either. He was sobbing and Pippa was holding him tight, cradling him like she'd cradled Mickey down on the ledge. Soon Riley needed to work on him—he was sure the guy's ankle was fractured—but the man wasn't worried about his own pain. He was only worried about his son.

'It's okay. He's safe,' Pippa told him.

'If not for you… I don't know how we can thank you.'

'Hey, Doc Riley held my legs and watched the waves. It's Riley who's the hero. Plus my gym back in England. How cool that I lost a little weight for my wedding?' She set him back a little, smiling. 'Happy endings. I love 'em. By the way, did you guys catch any fish?'

'I… Yes.' The paramedics were loading Mickey into the ambulance. Riley was helping, but Pippa's conversation had him distracted.

'How many?' Pippa demanded, and Riley blinked. He was thinking of giving the guy some morphine; Pippa was thinking about fish?

'We caught three,' the man managed.

'What sort?'

'Whiting.'

'Oh, yum, are these them?' She seized a fishing basket and peered inside.

'Yes, they are,' the man said, and Riley realised what Pippa was doing. She was dragging him back from the nightmare into a fragment of reality.

Mickey's mother was holding Mickey. The paramedics were making sure he was immobilised for the journey. Riley had his pain under control; there was a moment for normality to resurface and Pippa was making the most of it.

'I guess you guys won't be eating fish for tea tonight,' she said, sounding suddenly wistful. And a little bit cheeky. 'What with having to sit around hospitals waiting for Mickey to get a cast. And you might need one on your foot. That'll take ages. I guess you'll have to eat dinner at the hospital cafeteria.'

The man took a deep breath. He looked at his wife and son. He looked at his other kids—three littlies being held by someone who might be an aunt. He looked back at Pippa.

He looked at his fish and Riley saw the instant when nightmare moved to thought. Pippa had found her reality.

'Would you like a fish?' the man asked.

'I thought you'd never ask,' she said, and she chuckled.

She was incorrigible, Riley thought. She was soaking wet—how she wasn't shivering was a wonder. There was an ugly graze on the side of her face where she'd thumped against the rock on the way up or down. Her knuckles had lost skin.

Her hair was dripping wetly down her back. She looked about ten years old.

But her smile was enough to make anyone smile. To make anyone's nightmares recede.

He'd been comparing her to Marguerite? He was out of his mind.

'You can have all three,' the fisherman said, handing over his basket. 'They're great fish.'

'Really?'

'Really.'

'Oh, and I have a huge family I can feed them to,' Pippa said, beaming, gathering them to her like gold. 'Thank you so much.'

'You saved my son.'

'And you gave me fish.' She kissed the guy, lightly on the cheek. 'It looks like Mickey's ready to go. Let Doc Riley check your foot and then into the ambulance with you. Oh, and do your fishing a hundred feet from the edge from now on.'

'I'm buying my fish from the fish and chip shop,' he growled—but the man was smiling. Everyone was smiling. Everyone had heard the interchange. Even Mickey…

'So can we buy shop chips?' the little boy ventured, and his mother burst into tears. But she was smiling through her tears.

'Happy endings,' Pippa said in satisfaction, heading back to the chopper with her haul of fish. 'I love 'em.'

And when the ambulance moved away, as their chopper rose, she made Riley leave the slide open. She kept her harness on. They rose and she leaned out as far as Riley permitted.

She had a fish in each hand and she waved goodbye with fish.

Cheering.

Then she settled back into the chopper with her basket of fish on her knee. And beamed.

And Riley…

The armour he'd surrounded himself with for years, the protective barriers which let him want no one, need no one, were gone.

Pippa.

She could have drowned.

He was totally exposed.

She was taking her fish home to her family, Riley thought, dazed. *Her family.*

That would be Amy and Jason and Baby Riley. And Lucy and Adam.

And him?

Yeah. Tonight it would be him.

There was no way he was not being part of those fish.

Mickey was being taken by road to Sydney. He'd need specialist orthopaedic care so there was no medical need for either Riley or Pippa to stay involved. Harry started his routine check of the chopper. Riley and Pippa walked back to the house. They needed a shower. They needed a change of clothes. They also needed to talk, Riley thought, but he didn't know where to start.

What had just happened?

He'd lowered a slip of a girl into a chasm and he hadn't known if they could all survive. As simple as that. If the sea had turned on them…

There'd been no choice. The alternative had been impossible to contemplate—to leave Mickey to drown. But he'd had to ask Pippa to risk her life and she'd come up laughing.

She'd come up talking of fish and of family.

He was feeling like he'd shed something he'd barely known he had. He felt light and free and…bewildered.

He was carrying her fish. He was caught up in his thoughts, so it was Pippa who saw Amy first. She paused and looked across as Amy yelled wildly from the veranda.

'Will you two hurry up? We're having a baby.'

CHAPTER ELEVEN

THEY were indeed having a baby. Lucy was crouched like an animal in pain on the living-room settee. She moaned as they arrived, a deep, primeval moan that told Pippa they were deep into first stage.

'How far apart?' she asked Amy. There was no use asking Lucy anything for the moment.

'Two minutes,' Amy said. 'And she won't go to hospital. She's scared. She just wants you guys. Gee, I'm pleased to see you.'

'But Amy's fantastic.' Adam looked terrified but he gave Amy a sheepish smile as Lucy's moan trailed away. 'She's real bossy.'

'Yeah, well, I know what to do,' Amy said.

See one, do one, teach one. Pippa almost grinned. Then she glanced at Riley and her grin died. He looked like she never wanted a support person to look. Fear was infectious. What was he doing, with a face as grim as death?

'We need to get you to hospital,' he told his daughter as the contraction eased and her body slumped. 'No argument. I'll phone Louise and take you now.'

'Hey, how about, "Hi, Lucy, great to see you, we brought you some fish?"' Pippa demanded, astonished. The last thing Lucy needed was an implication of fear from her doctor.

But, then, she thought, Riley wasn't Lucy's doctor. Riley was Lucy's dad. Maybe terror was understandable.

So maybe someone else had to take charge.

The contraction was easing. Lucy looked up from the settee and gave them a wavering smile. 'Fish?' she managed.

'Three beauties,' Pippa said, deciding normal was the way to go. Who needed panic? 'Your dad and I caught them from the helicopter. Sort of. While you've been having fun here. But now we're here… Okay, fish aside, it looks like baby's next.'

She gave Riley a sideways glance, trying to figure what to do for the best. He looked under such strain… He'd want Louise, but most obstetricians only worked in hospitals. To have Louise take on her care, that's where they had to go.

'Lucy, love, why don't you want to go to hospital? It's two minutes away.'

'I'm not going to hospital,' Lucy said, in a voice where the fear came through. 'Please. I don't want to. This feels like family. You guys can deliver babies. I don't want my legs in stirrups.'

Where had she learned about stirrups? The internet, Pippa thought, or old documentaries, pictures of labour wards where obstetricians put their patients in stirrups in second stage as a matter of course.

'Why can't I stay here?' Lucy wailed, and grabbed Adam's hand and held it like she was drowning. 'I don't want to do this. I'm so scared. I want to go home.'

'To England?' Adam sounded terrified. 'We can't.'

'I won't go to hospital. Dad'll help.'

'Lucy, I'm your father. I can't be your doctor.'

'Lucy's not asking you to be her doctor,' Pippa said, figuring she had no choice but to intervene. Riley sounded strained to the limit.

He was right. He was Lucy's father. That had to be his role. Nothing more. But Lucy also needed a professional.

That would be her.

'You all know I'm a trained midwife,' she said, speaking more confidently than she felt. 'The checks Lucy did with Louise on Wednesday showed no problems. Everything's beautifully normal. Lucy, you're delivering a week early but that's fine. I suggest we let Louise know what's happening in case we need back-up. Then we settle down here, with all of us supporting you every step of the way. But if you get exhausted, or if there are signs that your baby's exhausted, then we take you to the hospital straight away and Louise takes over. That has to be the deal. Do you agree?'

'Yes,' Lucy managed, but it was a strangled gasp.

'Cool,' Amy said. 'Do you want us all to stay?'

'Yes,' Lucy yelled, gripping Adam's hand so tight that Pippa saw him wince in pain. 'I want you all.' Then… 'I want my family.'

Family…

Was she still talking about wanting to go back to England?

Somehow Pippa didn't think so.

But she had no time to think about it. Riley was grabbing her wrist as Lucy rode her contraction. 'I'll talk to you outside,' he said through gritted teeth.

'It'd better be quick,' she told him. 'That's a minute and a half between contractions. I need a quick shower to get rid of fish before I can turn into a midwife.'

He wasn't interested in showers. He hauled her through the door then tugged her along the veranda until they were out of earshot.

And let fly.

'What the hell do you think you're doing?' he demanded, practically apoplectic. 'She's going to hospital.'

'Why is she going to hospital?' His face was dark with anger. She tried to stay calm, but her very calmness seemed to infuriate him.

'It's safer. We need incubators, resuscitation equipment, oxygen, a fully trained obstetrician. Louise is a specialist. Lucy needs the best.'

'You delivered Amy,' Pippa said, striving to keep her voice even. 'Amy didn't deserve the best?'

'Amy was frightened. She didn't know anyone.'

'And Lucy?'

'She has Adam. She has all of us.'

'In a labour ward in hospital? Louise can't work with five of us. Amy and Jason would have to stay here, and Amy's giving Lucy courage. Look at her.' She glanced in through the window—the contraction was past and Amy was making some sort of a joke—making them all smile. 'This is like gold.'

'She could have Amy with her.'

'And Adam?'

'Yes.'

'And you?'

'I don't…'

'She needs you. In the background yes, but she does need you. You're her dad. She wants family.'

'Her family's in England.'

'I don't think so,' Pippa said. 'What mother would pack her eighteen-year-old to Australia to have her baby? Didn't you hear her? Her family's here.'

'You can't make a family in a week.'

'You can if you're desperate. Lucy's desperate.'

'You have no right—'

'To tell her she can have her baby here?' Pippa hauled her wrist away and stepped back, anger coming to her aid. 'Actually, I do. This isn't your house. You've never bought it. You've never thought of it as home. But I'm working for Flight-Aid and I'm renting part of this house. Contrary to you, I've put up decorations. I've bought rugs and made curtains. So this is my home, Riley Chase, and I have every right to ask Lucy to stay. And you know what?'

She tilted her chin, knowing she had no right to say what she was about to say but she was saying it anyway.

'Lucy wants family,' she said, and she couldn't quite stop a wobble entering her voice. 'If you know how much that means… It's the reason I finally said yes to Roger. It's the reason I almost married. I've never had family—not a proper, loving family—and I want it more than anything in the world. I know it's the last thing you want, but that's your problem. For now Lucy and Amy need me. When Amy's gone I'll somehow figure how to get a family of my own, even if it means dogs or parrots, but right now the only semblance of a family I have is here. Lucy needs my help to deliver her baby. So if you'll excuse me, Dr Chase, I have a baby to prepare for. Your grandchild. Family, whether you like it or not. And by the way, you stink of fish, too. Do you want to take a shower and join us, or do you want to go surfing? Alone? While your family operates without you? Your choice. Your choice alone.'

So Lucy didn't go to hospital.

Riley and Jason were consigned to the background.

He and Jason paced. Talked. Lit the barbecue, made a big fire, stoked it. Watched logs crackle and burn and turn to embers.

They'd cook the fish in the embers, Riley decided, when the baby was born.

'Did Amy go through this?' Jason asked, awed, as another moan rocked the house.

'She did.'

'I shoulda been here,' the kid said. 'Only she said she didn't want me. Not if I was just going to hang around. Then she went to Sydney and I missed her and I thought…okay, I'll get a job. If that's what it takes. So she went through this by herself. And look at her now. She says she wants to be a nurse. You reckon she could?'

'She'll need to do part of her training in the city,' Riley said, watching through the open windows. Adam holding Lucy's hand. Or rather being clutched by Lucy. Amy was designated coach, talking Lucy through every step of the way.

'Luce, this is brilliant. Pippa says six centimetres, and you remember the book? Every time it hurts you're opening up a bit more. Every time it hurts it means your baby's closer. That contraction was awesome. You're awesome.'

It was amazing for both of them, Riley thought. For all of them. For Lucy had a team second to none.

She had Adam, whose love for her was transparent. She had Amy, who was even younger than Lucy but wise for her years and whose assistance now could, Riley sensed, validate and direct Amy's existence for the rest of her life. And she had Pippa, preparing warmed towels, organising the sterilised equipment she'd sent him over to the hospital to fetch, overseeing her little team…

Pippa looked happy.

She was a woman he hardly knew. A woman of independent wealth, British, straight from the English class system he'd thought he loathed.

He'd made love to her out of need. Her need.

But…

As he watched through the window, as he saw her smile, chuckle, give steady encouragement, he knew things had changed. She was wearing jeans and T-shirt. Her feet were bare. Her hair was wet from her shower…

She was beautiful.

He thought of her down the crevice and he felt himself shudder.

'Hey, it's okay.' Jason put his hand on his shoulder, searching to comfort. 'She'll be great. She's got my Amy and your Pippa helping her through. You gotta trust women, mate. Amy says if I toe the line we can get married. How awesome's that? To have your own woman… And Amy…' He glanced in at his Amy. 'I mean…not that Pippa's not great. She is. But it's one woman for every guy, right? Look at Adam. He's in a blue funk now 'cos of Lucy. Look at me. I've even got a job. I'll even come to the city to help her if she wants to train as a nurse. And you…what would you give up for Pippa?'

He and Pippa weren't a couple. He should explain. But there was no time for explanation. Lucy hit full roar in mid-contraction. There wasn't space for a reply and it was just as well.

But the question stayed.

What would he give up for Pippa?

What would he gain?

'You're so close.' The labour had moved fast—five hours from the first contraction and now she was fully into second stage.

Youth, Pippa thought. Emotionally, young mums had it hard, but physically they had so much going for them. Lucy was practically shooting this baby out.

'I can see the head,' she told her. 'Adam, do you want to help deliver your baby? Amy, can you support Lucy's shoulders so she can see?'

'Awesome,' Amy breathed. 'Lucy, you're fabulous. Do you want your dad to see?' She hesitated. 'And… Jason didn't see my Riley born. Lucy, would you mind…?'

'You can bring in the whole bloody army as long as they stay up my end of the bed,' Lucy moaned. 'Oooooohhhh…'

'Nearly there,' Pippa said. 'One more push.'

'Get my dad,' Lucy yelled, suddenly desperate. 'I need my Adam and I need my dad. Ooooooowwwwwww…'

So after eighteen years of not being permitted to do a thing for her, he was there beside his daughter as she gave birth. Riley knelt at the head of the settee, supporting Lucy's shoulders as she saw her baby born, and he didn't feel like a doctor at all.

One more push and the head slipped into view. Pippa was there, with warmed towels, warming the tiny head even before the shoulder came out.

'Stay underneath with the towels,' she told Adam as a last massive contraction ripped through.

And so, as Amy and Riley held Lucy up to see, Riley's grandchild slipped into the world, to be caught by Adam, who looked like the sky had opened to reveal the secret of the heavens.

'What…? What…?' Lucy gasped as Adam gazed down in awe and Pippa did a fast check of the baby's airway, making sure that everything was in working order. 'What is it?'

'Look for yourself,' Riley growled, and felt a bit…a bit like Adam looked.

'I have a boy. Oh, I have a boy!' Lucy burst into tears. And then… 'Ohhh…'

For Pippa was quietly directing Adam, showing him what to do, and Adam was settling his tiny son onto Lucy's breast.

The tiny baby hadn't made a sound, but his eyes were wide open, wondering, and now…

He stirred and wriggled, skin against skin against his mother's breast. Without prompting, Adam carefully guided the little mouth to where it needed to be.

He found what he was looking for. His tiny mouth centred—and Riley's grandson found his home.

And Riley's world shifted once more. He glanced up and saw Pippa's eyes filled with unshed tears—and maybe his were the same.

His grandson had arrived into his family.

His family.

It was almost midnight before they ate their fish, and for all of them it was a truly memorable meal.

Jason and Amy cooked the fish. Pippa produced a salad. Riley found some chocolate biscuits.

You could spend thousands on a meal and not get better, Riley decided. They were all out on the veranda. The boys had lifted Lucy's settee, Lucy and all, out where she could see the luminescence of moonlight off the ocean. She ate her fish and her chocolate biscuits—she was starving. She had a little name discussion with Adam, then she snuggled down to sleep, her baby beside her.

Adam watched their baby as if it was only he who stood between his son and all the threats of a dangerous outside world.

Adam had grown ten years in this afternoon, Riley thought. He'd make a good partner for his daughter.

He'd be a son-in-law to be proud of.

Part of a family to be proud of?

Until the meal was ended there were things to do, but now… Amy and Jason were snoozing on the sun loungers. Soon they'd roll into bed. Both babies were asleep.

'I'm going to the beach,' Pippa said abruptly. She'd been carrying stuff into the kitchen. Now she came out and walked straight down the steps to the garden. 'See you later.'

He let her go. He was feeling…discombobulated.

His grandson was right beside him. He was thirty-eight years old and he felt a hundred.

He was watching Pippa in the moonlight.

She was wealthy. English. Good family.

He was a guy from the wrong side of the tracks. He was a guy who'd had a kid at nineteen, who was a grandpa at thirty-eight.

Pippa reached the gate leading down to the beach and he realised with a shock that she was no longer wearing jeans. She was wearing a sarong.

He'd seen it before. She wore it over swimmers.

'You're not going swimming?'

'I won't go out of my depth.'

'What about night-feeders?'

'I've painted my nails with Anti-Chew. Precautions R Us. You going to sit on the veranda for the rest of the night… Grandpa?'

Grandpa… The word still had him stunned.

She chuckled, she tossed her towel over her shoulder and she headed down the cliff path.

Grandpa.

Family.

Pippa.

CHAPTER TWELVE

CONTRARY to what she'd told Riley, Pippa had no faith at all in Anti-Chew. She consequently had no intention at all to bathe in the ocean.

There was, however, a rock pool at the edge of the cove. It was a naturally formed ring of rocks. At high tide the waves washed over it, meaning it was full of clear seawater. At low tide—now—there was an almost eighteen-inch rim of rock. The pool was five feet deep at the most. There was no way night feeders could get in. It was safe and she needed to swim.

It had been one incredible day. First Mickey. Then Lucy's baby. And watching Riley…

His face had been changing all day. It was like he was fighting some desperate internal war, and he wasn't winning.

She'd fallen in love with him.

How had she ever thought she could marry Roger? Oh, if she had…

She shuddered and dived into the rock pool. The water was cooler than she'd thought it would be, fresh from the sea, and she shuddered again.

She decided to swim and stop thinking.

The thoughts wouldn't stop.

Riley.

Could she stay on at Whale Cove if he didn't want her love?

He'd made it plain that he didn't. Lucy was hauling him into family whether he liked it or not, but to have a needy, besotted nurse at his side as well…

'It's not going to happen,' she told herself, and then she thought of how she'd felt that morning, on the rock, clinging to Mickey, clinging to Riley.

Feeling like…if she died now at least she'd known Riley. At least she'd had one night.

'I want more nights,' she said out loud, and started doing laps, up and down the length of the rock pool. She was tired to the bone, but she also knew she wouldn't sleep. She might as well exhaust herself properly.

What would she do?

She wanted to stay here. She wanted to be part of this community, this job, but how much was the job and how much was Riley?

Tonight had been magic. Friends, family, kids, babies, barbecues at midnight, no clear delineation between work and home, saving Mickey, waving her fish from the helicopter, loving Riley…

She almost sobbed, only it was hard to sob when she had her head down, swimming hard. She closed her eyes and let the darkness envelop her.

Something touched her foot.

She pretty near had a palsy stroke. A night feeder…

She whirled in the water to face whatever it was, expecting teeth—and two hands landed on her shoulders, holding her up. Riley's voice growled into the night.

'I thought you'd have learned your lesson about night swimming.'

She'd whirled too fast. She had a mouthful of water. She spluttered and choked and it took a couple of moments before she could breathe properly, let alone reply. But finally…

'If I'd died of fright,' she said, with as much dignity as she could muster—which actually wasn't very dignified when she was still spluttering and when his nose was only inches from hers—'it would have been your fault.'

'No deaths today,' he said gently, in a voice she didn't recognise. 'Only life. First Mickey. Then Lucy's baby.'

How to answer that? She fought for something innocuous. Something safe.

'Did...did they decide what to call it?' She was practically gibbering.

'It seems they thought of calling him Riley,' Riley told her, gravely. 'Only there's a bit of a run on the name. They're moving to William instead.

'I like William,' she said, and then managed a tentative smile. 'Do you? Papa?'

'Papa,' he said blankly.

'Papa. Or Grandpa? Grandfather? Sir? Hmm.'

'You want to get ducked?'

'Gotta be one,' she said, recovering courage. 'There's no getting away from the fact that you're a grandpa.'

'I don't think I want to get away,' he said, and there was enough in that to give her pause.

'You don't do family.'

'I haven't done family.'

'You don't want—'

'I haven't wanted. Until now.'

She paused. She was suddenly acutely aware that Riley was holding her up. They were in the deepest part of the pool. He could stand up. She couldn't.

She was at a disadvantage. She needed to put her feet somewhere solid, but Riley was holding her and not letting her go.

'I thought you might die,' he said, almost conversationally, and instead of moving to shallow water where a girl could set her legs down, he swung her up into his arms. 'Today with Mickey... You risked your life and, more than that, it was me who asked you to. You just...did it. And then tonight you delivered Lucy's son. You've made Amy happy. You've made Lucy happy. You saved Mickey. Wherever you go, life follows. And you know what? I've been sweating on an accent and on money and on past history, and they haven't let me see what's before my eyes.'

'Golly,' Pippa said, which ridiculous but she couldn't think of anything more sensible to say. 'I don't think I'm that good.'

'And you're practical, too,' Riley said, ignoring her interruption, and she heard his smile. From where she was she couldn't see his face.

She could feel, though. She was enjoying feeling. She was starting to enjoy feeling very much indeed.

'Even at the cliff this afternoon,' he said, almost conversationally, 'I was worrying about Mickey. I was worrying about practicalities, transport, shock, you, even about dry clothes—and suddenly you were organising fish. You had your priorities. Free fish. That's a woman in a million, I thought. And then you know what else I thought? I thought I really want to kiss you.'

'Really?' she said, cautiously. Something inside her was starting to feel…good.

'Really.' He tugged her higher then, and he kissed her. He was shoulder deep in water. He was holding her hard and he was kissing her as she wanted to be kissed. As she ought to be kissed.

A girl had a right to be kissed like this.

'So…so what…?' she ventured when she could finally get a word in. 'What made you think…you might want to kiss me?'

'Adam,' he said. 'And Jason.'

That didn't make sense. She waited, hoping for an explanation, and finally it came. After the next kiss.

'They're sitting on my veranda like two smug old men—fathers!' he told her. 'And they're looking at me like they're sorry for me. And you know what? They're right. I'm sorry for me.'

'You don't sound very sorry.'

'That's because I'm planning,' he said. 'I have a plan.'

'A plan.'

'I'm not exactly sure how I feel about you being rich.'

'You're not exactly poor.'

'Shut up, my love,' he said. 'I need to tell it like it is.'

'Okay,' she said—happily now, for how could she stop

the wave of happiness engulfing her? She had no intention of trying.

'I love our house,' he said, and she blinked. Our house. This wasn't the sort of declaration she'd been expecting.

'It's a great house,' she managed.

'It's a magnificent house. And now you've decorated it...'

'I can do better, given time.'

'That's just it. I'm worried. The hospital offered to sell it to me last year and they gave me a figure. If the valuer sees it now, with its curtains and its posters, it'll double in price. I'm parsimonious. Just think of the extra fish and chips we can have if I buy the house now.'

'You want to buy the house?'

'I do,' he said. 'Because I've been thinking... If I buy us a house...no, if I buy us a *home*...then anything else is icing on the cake. No matter what either of us earn, no matter what you decide to do with your fortune, my pride is catered for. Oh, and I might want to start an Amy nursing-training scholarship fund as well, but I've been thinking I might invite you to join me. My pride could take that.' He smiled. 'My pride might even enjoy it.'

'Your pride?' She was still being cautious. He was circling the issue, she thought. She thought she knew where he was heading, but a girl had to make sure. 'You're saying you want us to fund Amy—and you want us to stay being housemates?'

'No.'

'No?'

'Well, only so much as... Are you housemates when you're married?'

'Married.' The word took her breath away.

'If you want to be,' he said. 'I want to marry you more than anything else in the world—but it's your call.'

'But...why?'

'Because I love you,' he said simply, and he did set her down then, moving so they were waist deep in water and he could take her hands and gaze down at her in the moonlight. 'Pippa, this morning… If I'd lost you, I couldn't bear it. I won't ever ask you to risk your life again.'

'Of course you will,' she retorted, diverted. 'We both will. It's what we do. We rescue people.'

'How about ourselves?'

'You mean…' She tried to think it through. She was feeling so happy she felt like she was floating, but she needed to make her fuzzy mind focus. 'You rescue me and I rescue you right back?'

'That's the plan,' he said, softly and surely in the moonlight. That's the dream. 'For as long as we both shall live.'

'That sounds extraordinary,' she whispered.

'Is that a yes?'

She made herself pause. She made herself consider.

Once upon a time she'd agreed to marry Roger. That had taken her years to decide and she'd still made a mistake.

But Riley…

She looked up into his lovely anxious face and all the answers, all the years to come were written in his gaze.

He loved her. From this day forth…

Her Riley.

But…er…

A thought had occurred. Something important.

'You're a grandpa,' she said, suddenly astringent. 'If you're a grandfather and I marry you…I will not be Granny.'

'I've thought about that, too,' he said, sounding suddenly smug. 'Just now. When you called me Papa.'

'You have?'

'I'll be Poppa,' he said. 'I like it. I know I'm young but the word has a certain cachet. And you're Pippa. Poppa and Pippa. A matching pair. How about that for a plan?'

'Oh, Riley.'

'Is that a yes?'

'I believe it is,' she said.

'I believe I love you—Pippa,' he said.

'And I love you—Poppa,' she murmured, and he laughed and hugged her hard—and then she wasn't able to say anything at all for a very long time.

And almost twelve months to the day, to Pippa and to Riley, one baby. Any minute now…

On the veranda of the house overlooking Whale Cove Pippa crouched on a settee and moaned. A lot.

She had the right.

Jason and Adam were in the back yard, firing up the barbecue. Organising fish. Since saving Mickey there always seemed to be fish arriving at this house. The fishing community was big and the locals remembered. '*For our Doc and our Pippa.*'

Our Pippa.

But Riley wasn't noticing fish now.

Lucy and Amy were taking turns to coach.

Jancey was in the background. A woman had to have a professional there.

Pippa's fingers were clinging so hard to Riley's that he might end up scarred.

But Riley wasn't noticing his fingers either.

'It's coming,' Amy said. Six months into nursing training, she was already an expert. 'Pippa, you're nearly there.'

'We can see the head,' Lucy breathed. 'Hold her up, Dad, so she can see for herself. Pippa, one more push.'

'You can do it,' Jancey said.

A monstrous regiment of women.

Riley remembered the quote. He almost grinned. Jancey and Amy and Lucy—and at the centre his own wonderful Pippa. How had he ever thought…?

But then…

'Push,' Jancey ordered. 'Biggest one yet. Keep going. Again. Go, girl. You rock. Lucy, Amy, hold Pippa so Riley can catch his baby.'

He couldn't sit around thinking all day. He had work to do.

He had to disengage those fingers.

'Push,' he told his beloved. He kissed her hard and fast and then he put her into the care of Lucy and Amy. Her family. His family.

And he moved to where he needed to be.

The head... It was certainly coming. 'Push.'

'Don't tell me what to do,' Pippa yelled. 'I'm pushing.'

'Push harder.'

'I'm... Ooooohhhhhh.'

And there she was, sliding into the outside world. Caught by her father. Held like she was the most precious creature in the world.

His daughter.

'What...? What...?' Amy and Lucy were supporting Pippa so she could to see her baby. Jancey stood back with a smile wide enough to split her face. With this family, what need for a midwife?

'We have a daughter,' Pippa murmured, awed. 'Oh, Riley.'

'I have a sister,' Lucy sniffed, jubilant. 'Oh, wait, that means William has an aunt. Our family's getting bigger and bigger.'

'As it should,' Riley managed, so choked he could scarcely speak. 'It's perfect. She's perfect.'

And he moved, carrying his brand-new daughter so that he could kiss his wife. His Pippa. His love.

And as Pippa cradled her newborn, as he gathered her into his arms, as he held her close, and as they felt this new little life between them, he accepted what he knew for sure.

'We have the perfect family.'

'It might get bigger,' Pippa whispered, dazed.

He kissed her again and he smiled and looked up at the people around them.

'A bigger family sounds great to me,' he told her. 'Just as long as you stay at its heart. My Pippa. My love. My wife.'